THE QUANTUM COP

Books by Lesley L. Smith

Temporal Dreams
Kat Cubed
Reality Alternatives

The Quantum Cop Series:
Book 1: *The Quantum Cop*
Book 2: *Quantum Murder*

The Quantum Cop

By Lesley L. Smith

Quarky Media

Boulder Colorado

The Quantum Cop
Published by Quarky Media, PO Box 3332, Boulder, CO 80307
www.quarkymedia.com

ISBN: 978-0-9861350-3-3 (ebook)
ISBN: 978-0-9861350-2-6 (print)

This is a work of fiction. Names, characters, places, and incidents are either the product of the author's imagination or are used fictitiously, and any resemblance to actual persons, living or dead, business establishments, events, or locales is entirely coincidental.

THE QUANTUM COP

Chapter One

If I'd known my morning was going to split into two possibilities, I would have bought two cinnamon rolls–one for me, and one for the other me.

"What time did you get into town last night?" my cousin Ryan Martin asked me.

"About one a.m. Thanks for leaving the door unlocked and thanks for letting me stay with you guys." We stood on the corner across from campus, waiting for the light to change. We were on our way to work and had just stopped at Boulder Brews for coffee and cinnamon rolls. Ryan was the chief of the university police and I was a new physics professor.

"I'll be out of your hair as soon as I can." Shifting my book bag on my shoulder, I took a big bite of my roll. It was still warm with gooey cream-cheese icing. Mmm. My other hand was starting to cramp as it held the almost too-hot paper cup of coffee.

"No hurry, Madison," he said. "But if you're still staying with us when the baby's born you'll have to help out."

"My pleasure." I squinted up at him. The sun was as blinding as a laser. Colorado definitely seemed sunnier than Missouri. I wished I'd worn sunglasses. I wished I owned sunglasses. "I volunteer to help no matter where I'm living." Who wouldn't want to help with an adorable little baby?

"Thanks." He smiled at me from his six-foot-plus height. "So, are you excited about your new job?"

As I stood there, it was taking all my self-control not to break into a happy dance right there on the sidewalk. "Does a supernova spew heavy elements?"

He raised his eyebrows at me.

I grinned. "That's a yes. I'm excited. I've been working towards this for the last decade. It's a dream come true."

"What did Ted say about it?" Ryan asked, staring at me. "Did you guys break up?"

My boyfriend Ted was still back in St. Louis. Debating what to say, I took a sip of coffee. "We didn't break up, but it wasn't pretty."

"Tell me what happened," he said. "You owe me. I confided in you when I was getting ready to propose to Sydney. And look how good that turned out. Five years of bliss."

"True." I pointed at him with my coffee cup. "And now a little one on the way. How many more days until she's due?"

"Nice try, but you don't get to change the subject that easily. What happened with Ted?"

"At first he seemed supportive," I said. "He said congratulations and everything."

"And then?" He prompted.

"He asked me if I took the job–as if there was some question about it." My voice started rising. "Obviously I took it, anybody would take it, which is what I told him. Then he got all whiny, asking what it meant for him and me. He actually brought up that we had talked about talking about getting married." Some coffee slopped out of my cup as I gestured with it.

"Talked about talking?" He laughed. "So, he didn't ask you marry him or even talk about getting married? I never liked the guy."

"I know." The crowd waiting to cross the street was getting quite large. There must have been twenty or thirty people on the sidewalk. "Geez, this is a long light."

"Don't change the subject," he said.

"I knew Ted was just upset because he loves me and he thought I was leaving him, but I started getting a little torqued. So..."

"So, let me guess, you blew up at him?" Ryan asked.

"Yeah, there was some yelling then." I grinned. "But later we made up, and let me tell you, the make-up sex was great."

He frowned. "Too much information."

I laughed. "You're such a guy, Ryan."

I took another sip of coffee and thought about Ted. It was wonderful being with a guy like Ted who actually understood what I did for a living. Mentioning elementary particles like quarks and neutrinos to most folks made their eyes glaze over.

I was still thinking about him when the walk sign finally lit up and I absentmindedly stepped off the curb into the crosswalk.

Something slammed into me. My coffee and cinnamon roll flew out of my hands in slow-mo and my book bag thumped against my back before taking its own trajectory. My left leg and hip crumpled as I hit the pavement with a splat. As my fingertips dug into the gravel and asphalt, I struggled to lift my head up off the ground. What was going on and why didn't it hurt?

"Oh, my God. Madison," Ryan screamed as he dropped his coffee and kneeled over me. "Madison, say something. Are you all right?"

I knew I should answer him, but I felt like I was separated from him, separated from everything, by layers of cotton batting.

Curiously, I had also hesitated before stepping into the crosswalk and a car had whizzed by against the light. I felt odd, disconnected.

Ryan screamed and lurched forward into the street. He knelt over a woman lying in a heap in the crosswalk. "Madison, say something. Are you all right?" Who was he talking to? It couldn't be me. I was right here on the sidewalk.

"Did you see that?" a bystander said. "She just flew into the air."

Students in a variety of leggings, jeans and t-shirts crowded around to get a look at the woman who had apparently been hit by a car.

I craned my neck to get a look. She was in her late twenties, of average height and weight, had long blonde hair, and was wearing a killer suit. Actually, her suit looked just like mine. Come to think of it, the rest of her looked just like me, too. I stared. Was she blurry?

One thing was clear: Ryan looked really worried.

As I lay in the street, to my left, a car's tires squealed as it backed up and swerved around me and the other people in the crosswalk.

My fingers on the asphalt looked blurry and insubstantial.

A couple of the bystanders yelled. "Hey, watch it."

"Hey, you can't leave."

"Come back here."

Ryan stuck his face right in my face. "Madison, please answer me. Blink or something."

This fuzzy, floaty feeling couldn't be good. I concentrated on lowering my eyelids.

He nodded. "Good. Can you talk?"

The entire world had shrunk to Ryan's freckly face, and his eyes bored into mine through his wire-rimmed glasses.

I should be able to talk. I used to be able to talk, didn't I? This whole scene was just wrong. It was all wrong. I should still be on the corner.

I looked at the corner and there I was, still standing on the sidewalk. That was much better.

On the corner, the guy standing next to me said, pointing, "Is that your twin?"

I didn't have a twin. Was that me in the crosswalk? I looked down at my panty-hose-clad legs and the sidewalk under my shoes. I was still standing on the corner. I could feel my bookbag weighing down my right shoulder and my big toe chafing against my fancy shoe. I looked kind of blurry.

The woman in the street looked kind of blurry, too.

"I'm calling 911," one of the bystanders yelled.

I was getting a nagging sense of déjà vu. Had I been blurry before? Had I been in two places at once before?

Standing on the corner felt better, more right. I focused on that. The morning rush hour traffic on highway 36 a half-block away sounded like ocean waves breaking on a beach. My heavy bag, filled with books and papers, kept banging against my hip as I shifted my weight slightly. Both my hands were full, one with a very hot paper cup of coffee, and one with a cooling pastry. It was really too much to carry at once. Geez, that cup was hot. My toe hurt as it pressed up against the inside of my fancy shoe.

How could I be standing on the sidewalk and lying in the street at the same time? How could I be in two places at once?

My odd feeling of déjà vu solidified into memory...

I tripped headlong into frigid water. I gasped and couldn't breathe. An icy liquid vice crushed my chest. I didn't even have enough air to scream for help.

And at the exact same time, I felt warm sun and a light breeze on my face as I crouched on the deck of a boat. I'd been in two places at once back then, too.

Now, apparently, I was standing on the corner and I was lying in the street at the exact same time.

In the street, I thought, a car must have hit me. Excruciating pain started to seep into my awareness.

I struggled to calm down. Focus, Madison. You can get out of this if you focus like you did when you fell off the boat. Back then, I focused on the situation I wanted and the other one disappeared, leaving only memories.

I knew which circumstance I preferred now–the one where I still had the cinnamon roll and wasn't crumpled in the crosswalk. I picked that possibility.

Purposefully, on the sidewalk, I opened my mouth wide and took a bite of roll. I tasted sugary-sweetness on my tongue. Bite. Chew. Cinnamon was real.

The woman lying on the ground surrounded by crouching people was dimming. I did my best to ignore her. She was not real. Not real. Not. Real. I was real, not her.

On the corner, I jostled my coffee and a few scalding drops fell on my foot. Ouch.

The other woman faded away.

I did it.

The people trying to help injured other-Madison stood up in confusion.

"Where'd she go?"

From the distance, a siren approached.

"Madison, is that you?" Ryan asked. "What just happened?"

He stepped back onto the curb, his face ashen. "I could have sworn I saw you get hit by a car. But here you are." He shook his head. "Madison, answer me." Ryan's face beaded with sweat beneath his sandy brown hair and steam grazed the bottom of his glasses where they touched his face. "What the hell's going on? Are you okay?"

Not sure I could talk, I nodded. That was a close one. Too close.

We were jostled as more people came up from behind and joined the crowd.

"C'mon, let's go," someone in the crowd said.

"You've got the walk signal."

"Go for Christ's sake."

Students flowed around us into the crosswalk.

Glancing up at the red decreasing numbers in the walk signal, my hands started shaking violently. Coffee slopped out of the cup, splashing onto the sidewalk. I dropped my partially eaten cinnamon roll. I looked down at the splattered curb, reluctant to step into the crosswalk. I couldn't move.

The ambulance pulled up and the EMTs jumped out.

"Who got hit?"

Everyone who hadn't crossed the street yet pointed at me.

"Her."

"That lady, there."

I tried to take a sip of coffee to calm down, but my shaking hands just spilled more on the curb.

The EMTs came up to me.

"Miss, are you all right?" the balding one asked. "You shouldn't have moved."

"We need to assess your injuries," the other said.

I shook my head. "Near miss." I attempted a smile. "Wasn't hurt." Thank, God.

"Glad to hear it," one of the EMTs said.

"No," Ryan said, shaking his head. "I saw her lying in the street."

"You don't look so good," an EMT said. "You better let us check you out."

"I'm fine. Need to get to class. Right, Ryan?" I looked at him for support.

"Madison, you should let them check you out," he said uncooperatively.

They led me over to the back of the ambulance.

"I wasn't hit by the car," I said repeatedly. I was starting to get a huge headache, though. "I have to get to class. I'm a professor. It's my first day. I can't be late on my first day." I needed to put this bizarre incident behind me ASAP.

I jerked away from the ambulance and started speedwalking to campus. When I reached the safety of the other curb, I sighed in relief.

Were that tall good-looking kid and the chubby Asian kid next to him staring at me? I was careful not to make eye contact as I walked past them.

"Madison, come back here," Ryan yelled after me. "I need to know what the hell just happened."

But I couldn't explain it to him. I didn't understand it myself.

Yet.

Chapter Two

"It was bizarre, man."

"Yeah. She was, like, in two places at once. I've never seen anything like it."

I walked into my basement classroom to find the students clustered together engrossed in conversation. They were oblivious to me. It wasn't the most auspicious beginning to my professorial career.

I put my stuff down on the battered wooden table at the front of the classroom and slowly got out my notes. I took a deep calming breath and then cleared my throat. "Sorry I'm late." I forced a grin. "First day and all. It won't happen again." Hopefully nothing freaky like that would ever happen again.

The students glanced at me, scowling, and went to their desks. Were they disappointed I interrupted their gab session? If so, too bad. They appeared to be a typical twenty-ish assortment of male nerds in various colors and sizes.

As the crowd dispersed, the two young men in the center of the group looked familiar: a tall kid with Italian features and an overweight Asian kid. As they looked at me, their eyes lit up with recognition. Ugh. They were the young men that had been staring at me on the street corner. How'd they get here before me? And how much had they seen?

The chubby one pointed. "That's her. That's the woman that was hit by the car and wasn't."

"Huh?"

"Say what?"

"That's crazy."

The tall, good-looking one raised his hand. He flashed me a perfect white smile. "Professor what? What's your name?"

Yikes. I hadn't even introduced myself. "I'm Professor Madison Martin."

He smiled again. "Madison. We could have sworn..." He stopped to point at himself and his friend.

I interrupted. "That's Professor Martin, please." I glanced down at the class roster. "And please give me your name."

His smile lost some of its wattage. "I'm Luke Bacalli. Anyway, what just happened? It was like we, Griffin and me, could see two contradictory things happening at once. We rushed over to you and tried to help when you, ah, got run over."

I sipped the dregs of my coffee to stall for time, but that only took so long. I put the cup down. "That's a good question." I paused, considering what to tell them. The truth seemed reasonable. "Actually, I don't know."

Luke crossed his arms.

I reached into my bag for the syllabus. "But we have lots of stuff to do today and not a lot of time to do it. Let's get to work. Here's the syllabus." I gave the stack to one of the guys in the front row. "Please pass these back." I stepped in front of the white board and picked up a marker. "This semester we are going to learn about quantum mechanics−the most bizarre theory known to man or woman." I grinned. "I like to tell students if quantum mechanics makes sense to you, you don't really understand it."

I began the lecture by asking, "Does anyone know what light is?"

The students looked at one another like it was a trick question.

Griffin said, "Like light from the sun?"

I nodded. "Yes, the very same."

"What do you mean? It's light," Griffin said, squirming in his seat.

"True," I said. "But I was looking for a little bit more than that."

"I know what she's getting at," Luke said. "Light is electromagnetic radiation."

"Yes," I said. "That's what I was looking for. Light is a wave of electromagnetic radiation or energy. You can see this when a prism splits white light into a rainbow of colors."

The natives were getting restless, muttering and shifting in their seats.

"Yes? Did someone have a question? Feel free to just shout out questions, by the way. The only dumb question is an unasked question, I like to say."

A guy in the front row raised his hand.

"Yes," I said. "What's your name and what's your question?"

"I am Pankaj," he said. "I am sorry, but what does this have to do with quantum mechanics?"

"I'm glad you asked," I said. "It turns out that quantum mechanics basically started when a fellow named Albert Einstein−maybe you've heard of him−said light is both a wave and a particle." I turned back to the white board. "This brings us to the quantum mechanical idea of wave-particle duality. It turns out all particles are also waves."

As I continued the class, my brain started to tingle. There was something important here and I was on the verge of remembering it. Waves meant wave properties including wavelengths and wavefunctions. Hmm.

After class I climbed up to the ground-floor physics department office to do my paperwork and find out where my office was. I should have done it before class, but what with my mishap, I didn't have time. Oh, well, it couldn't be helped.

The department office consisted of a large room, split in half by a long wooden counter. It contained an assortment of desks and chairs, only one of which was occupied. Several doors led off from the room, and along one wall there was also a matrix of wooden mail cubbyholes. The whole place looked ancient.

"Can I help you, honey?" the Chicana sitting back by the windows said. She did not look ancient at all. She looked young and lively. "Are you selling books or something?"

"Hi, I'm Madison Martin. I'm the new physics professor. I think we met on my interview trip?" Of course, I couldn't remember her name.

She jumped up from her desk, causing her brunette curls to bounce. "Oh, sure. Hi. I'm Nancy, the department's administrative assistant. We've been wondering where you were." She glanced at the clock and frowned. "I don't mean to alarm you, but your class was at nine o'clock."

"I taught the class."

"Phew. That's a relief." She smiled. "I'd hate to see you get in trouble on your first day."

"I meant to stop in beforehand, but something came up." I didn't know what else to say. I was hit by a car, but got over it?

"Oh, dear. Nothing serious, I hope?"

I grinned. "Apparently not. So, anyway, do you guys have papers for me to sign? Is Professor Chen around?" He was the physics department Chair I'd met on my interview trip.

She leaned over the counter. "Yes, but he's meeting with a grad student, Alyssa, the poor dear," she whispered. "Her advisor dumped her because she broke some equipment or something. I'm sure it was an accident. Alyssa's a little clumsy. Scientists can be so mean."

Surely she knew I was a scientist? I just looked at her.

She blanched. "No offense."

I forced myself to smile. "So, paperwork?"

"Right this way." She pointed to her desk, ruffled through the papers lying on it and handed some to me.

They included the typical forms, a bunch of memos, and also a piece of paper with ten names and email addresses. "What's with this list of names?" I asked. One of them looked familiar: Luke Bacalli.

She glanced at the paper. "Oh, those are your undergrad advisees. You pretty much just sign off on their class schedules. That type of stuff. All the faculty have to advise some undergrads."

"Since classes have already started, what do I need to do?" I asked.

"Just send them an email telling them you're their new advisor." Nancy cached some curls behind her ear. "I doubt you'll hear anything from them unless they're adding or dropping a class."

A young woman burst out of Professor Chen's office into the main office.

He followed her, all six-feet-plus of him.

"It's not fair!" She seemed to be on the verge of tears. "It wasn't my fault." As she put her partially unzipped backpack on her back, one of her notebooks fell out. "Dammit." A couple of tears made their escape as she bent to pick it up.

Poor kid. She reminded me a little of myself at that age, in that she was a woman in a man's field and having a tough time.

"I'm sorry, Alyssa," Professor Chen said. "I can't force a faculty member to be your advisor." Chen was very tall and slender, with a mop of straight grayish-white chin-length hair.

I stepped up. "Hi, Professor Chen. What seems to be the problem here?"

He glanced at me. "Professor Martin, nice of you to show up. Just a minute."

"I couldn't help overhearing," I said. "I could be an advisor, if she needs someone." I always promised myself I would mentor female physics students if I ever had the opportunity.

Alyssa quit sniffling and looked at me through the auburn hair that had fallen in front of her eyes. "Who are you? Would you really be my advisor? What's your area? I was in experimental high energy physics."

I smiled. "I'm Professor Madison Martin, at your service." I held out my hand. "I'd be happy to be your advisor, if you'd like. My area is elementary particles, basically the theories behind high energy physics. Does that interest you at all? We could focus on phenomenology."

She smiled tentatively and her eyes lit up as she reached for my hand. "I'm Alyssa Long."

Chen stepped toward us. "This might work. You might do better in theoretical physics, Alyssa." He turned to face me. "But are you sure you're up for it, Madison? Usually we give new faculty members a grace period before they start supervising grad students."

I nodded firmly. "Piece of cake. I have a feeling Alyssa and I will work great together."

That rated a full-fledged smile from her.

Alyssa and I made plans to meet later.

I finished my paperwork and got my keys. Nancy told me my office was in the Gamow Tower, so I headed east to the elevators.

THE QUANTUM COP

The four-foot by four-foot by seven-foot elevator crept up the physics tower at the speed of snail. When it finally got to my floor, the doors didn't open, and I started to panic. I was about to scream when they finally clunked apart. Look at me, frazzled after only one class. Some professor I was. The thrill from my first lecture as a tenure-track professor was wearing off quickly.

Of course, the near traffic accident might have had something to do with my nerves.

I shuffled around the corner to my new office, passing two closed offices. The hall was in the shape of a square, twenty-feet long on a side, and the hallway itself was only about three feet wide. There were no windows and all the closed office doors made it dark. Where was everyone on this tiny floor? It was like a diminutive ghost town.

As I unlocked my new office door, a head popped out from the next door down. "*Hola*."

I glanced over at the thirty-something Chicano man standing there. He was as fine as controlled nuclear fusion. "*Hola*."

He came over to my door and smiled. "Are you my new neighbor?"

I shrugged. "If that's your office there, I guess so."

"I'm Andro Rivas." He held out his hand. "Nice to meet you." He wore black dress pants and a dramatic cerulean-blue dress shirt.

I took his proffered hand. "Nice to meet you. I'm, uh, Madison Martin." I almost forgot my name there for a second, lost in his beautiful blue eyes. They were striking with his dark hair and skin.

"I can't help noticing you have no wedding ring." He held my hand a little longer than necessary.

Ted. Think of Ted. We had made up after our big fight. He was the love of my life. Probably. Maybe. "Right. I'm not married, but I have a serious boyfriend. Did I tell you my name? I'm Professor Martin."

He chuckled as he withdrew his hand. "In that case, you can call me Professor Rivas."

I blushed and looked away. "Oh, right. Sorry. Call me Madison." I pushed open my office door, and he followed me inside.

My small office was crammed with a battered desk, an ancient couch, one wooden bookshelf, a mini-fridge, and three old chairs. It definitely needed some books and posters to spruce it up. Right now, the only positive thing my office had going for it was its little window framing the campus and the Rocky Mountain foothills. And maybe Professor Rivas. Through the window, I could see the dramatic red-tiled rooftops set off by the iron-shaped rock formations to our west. I'd have to be careful not to get distracted by the view, or the man, when I was supposed to be working.

I plunked my bag on the desk and sank down in a chair.

He leaned against the wall, arms crossed, with an amused grin. "Tough day already?"

I tried not to look directly at him. "You have no idea." I shook my head.

I sighed and pointed at one of my guest chairs. "Have a seat."

He sat down carefully on the rickety wooden chair. "So, what's your area of expertise? I'm in APS."

I turned to him. "I'm in theoretical elementary particle physics. I've been studying neutrinos a lot lately. APS, huh? I'm sorry I'm not up on all the acronyms around here."

Andro grinned. "Yeah, there are a lot of them. Don't worry about it. APS stands for Astrophysical and Planetary Sciences. Personally, I do model work on stellar evolution."

"That sounds interesting. When you say model work, you mean what?"

He leaned forward. "I work on big computer programs trying to simulate the lives of stars."

I grinned. "So, let me get this straight. You use giant, complicated Fortran programs?"

He nodded. "*Sí*."

"What do you know? I guess we have more in common than one might think. Me, too."

"I bet we have even more in common." He leaned back. "What are you teaching this semester? I've been here a few years now so, I might be able to give you some advice."

"I don't want to bore you with my whining." Truth be told, I didn't want to scare off my first new potential scientist friend.

"Whine away. Then, I can whine to you sometime. We

scientists have to stick together. Let's hear it."

Considering we'd just met, he was really very sweet to listen to me. "For one thing, you would not believe how much my quantum mechanics class complained about their homework assignment."

A powerful bass laugh erupted out of him. "You assigned homework on the first day of class?"

I sat up straight. "We have a lot of material to get through. Plus, they're upper-classmen. What did they expect?"

Andro was smiling and shaking his head. "This is a party school, didn't you know that?"

"I've heard the stories, but there are Nobel Laureates and MacArthur Fellows on the faculty. How big a party school could it be? Besides those so-called surveys aren't statistically significant."

He chuckled. "You are a scientist, aren't you?"

"Anyway, I was easy on them. All we covered today was early quantum mechanics and the most basic wave mechanics. Plus, they're all physics majors, right?"

He leaned forward. "Maybe, maybe not. Let's see your roster."

I pawed through my bag and extracted the rumpled sheet. I traced one column with my finger. "It's mostly physics majors with a few electrical engineering and computer science majors thrown in for good measure." One of my undergrad advisees was also one of my students. Was that a conflict of interest? "Do you have undergrad students you advise?"

He nodded. "Sure. Everyone does."

"Have you ever been an advisor for one of your students? I mean someone who's enrolled in your class?" I asked. "Is that okay?"

"It shouldn't be a problem. What student?" He scooted his chair toward me and looked over the names.

He smelled good, like Polo aftershave.

"Here." I pointed at Luke's name on the roster as our heads bent together over the piece of paper.

"Luke Bacalli," he said. "He's a bit of a pain. So is his trusty sidekick Griffin Jin. They're troublemakers, smart, but lazy. They'll try everything to get out of working."

Those were the kids who saw my street mishap. That

reminded me. "How much quantum mechanics do you know?"

"I had two semesters of quantum in grad school, so bring it on." He smiled.

The smile was dazzling. Wow, ignore that smile, Madison. "This morning in class I introduced particle-wave duality. Eventually this will lead to wavefunctions, which will lead to probabilities. Which will in turn lead to all kinds of weirdness."

"Yeah." He leaned forward.

"Like that Schrödinger's Cat experiment." I had forgotten about that this morning. My scalp crawled. I must be getting closer to the truth.

He nodded. "I know how the Schrödinger's Cat experiment works: there's a cat in a chamber with a subatomic device that can kill the cat. Since it's a subatomic mechanism it has to obey quantum mechanics and be described by a superposition of all the possible states. Thus, according to quantum mechanics, inside the chamber all the possibilities are true including the cat is both dead and alive."

That had to be it. I was in a superposition of states this morning. Different possibilities existed at once: one in which I was dead or at least severely injured and one in which I was okay.

I pointed at Andro. "And until we open the chamber and look, we don't know if the cat is dead or alive." That was it. Looking collapsed the wavefunction and picked out only one possibility. I understood what happened this morning.

"I guess Schrödinger didn't like cats." He chuckled. "I always wondered how it could be both dead and alive. It just goes to show that the superposition of states in quantum mechanics only works on the subatomic level."

"What if that's not true? What if we could have a superposition of macroscopic objects?" I leaned toward him. "You're not going to believe this, but I was hit by a car this morning and I wasn't."

"What?" He squinted.

"I was hurrying to class and had to cross that road south of campus. I got the walk signal and stepped into the crosswalk and, bam, something slammed into my side and I flew in the air. At the same time I stood on the sidewalk and watched a car zoom through the crosswalk against the light. It must have been a superposition of states. And then I collapsed the wavefunction and picked the one where I wasn't hurt."

The small room filled with the sound of silence.

After a moment, Andro said, "Are you joking?"

I shook my head.

"A car driving through the light wouldn't surprise me. Cars are trying to sneak through those lights all the time. I'm surprised more folks don't get hit." He paused. "But as for your macroscopic superposition of states, are there any witnesses to this miracle?"

Was he implying I imagined it, or made it up? "As a matter of fact there were a bunch of people there. But I'm not sure what they saw."

"What did you see?" He leaned back in his chair, crossing his arms.

I noticed he still hadn't said he believed me, but I couldn't blame him. I wouldn't have believed it myself it I hadn't been there. I wasn't entirely sure I believed it even now.

"I think I saw and felt two different states in the superposition of all possible states. I was hit by a car and severely injured. People crowded around me trying to help, and I stood on the corner and safely watched the car go by. And then I picked the state where I wasn't hurt."

He scowled and shook his head, his shiny brown hair flopping back and forth. "That's pretty incredible."

"A common interpretation of quantum mechanics, the von Neumann-Wigner Interpretation, says a conscious mind is necessary to collapse the wavefunction and pick out one state from all the possible states. The Copenhagen Interpretation also says the act of observation collapses the wavefunction." I wasn't at all defensive. No, not me.

He rubbed his chin. "But that's why the Schrödinger Cat thing is a paradox. It's not supposed to work for macroscopic stuff. Although now that I think about it, I could have sworn I heard of some experiments here at JILA and down the street at NIST where they created some funky superposition states."

I raised my hands. "JILA? NIST? Help me out here."

"Sorry. They're the Joint Institute for Laboratory Astrophysics and the National Institute of Standards and Technology, I think, give or take a preposition or two anyway."

I nodded. "Oh, right." I should have known that. I guess I was still rattled. Or maybe gorgeous Andro made me nervous.

He stood up abruptly. "I must admit it has been interesting meeting you. But I should probably get back to work." He walked toward the door.

I stood up, too. "You don't believe me, do you?"

He turned back to face me. "No. I can't say that I do." He took a step toward me. "Can you prove it? Can you produce witnesses? Can you show me this phenomenon?"

I thrust my chin out. "Maybe. A lot of people saw it."

"I look forward to the evidence, then." He turned and gave me a curt nod. "Good day, Professor Martin."

"Good day, Professor Rivas."

He left.

Well, that could have gone better.

As soon as I had a second to myself, I realized I had to call Ted and tell him what happened this morning. If anyone could help me make sense of it, he could. As I dialed his cell my hands were shaking I wanted to talk to him so badly.

"Ted's phone," a female voice said.

I disconnected.

Why was a woman answering his phone?

Chapter Three

While I waited in my office to meet with Alyssa I managed to restrain myself from going next door and pestering Andro into believing my quantum adventure.

To while away the time, I dashed off emails to the undergrads on my advisee list informing them that I was their new advisor. No doubt they'd be thrilled and would rush right in to meet me. Ha.

A few minutes after the scheduled Alyssa meeting time the elevator pinged.

Shortly thereafter I heard a thump and a crash.

"Shi-oot," a woman said in the hall. It had to be Alyssa.

I popped into the hall to see what the thump-crash was about.

Sure enough, Alyssa was sitting on the floor, papers fanned out around her and her unzipped book bag next to her.

Andro leaned over her. "Are you all right, Miss?"

She froze as if she was at absolute zero as she gazed into his eyes.

He frowned and stood up straight. "I said, are you all right? Should I call for help?"

I strode down the hall. "Alyssa. There you are." I turned to face him. "This is my new grad student, Alyssa."

He gulped. "Alyssa Long?"

"Yes." I nodded. "Why did you say it like that?"

"You've heard of me?" She slowly started gathering her belongings.

"Yes." He took a step back. "Just that you are a grad student, here, in school." He took another step toward his office. "It appears you aren't injured. I'll see you ladies later." He hurried back to his office and shut the door. Gee, that wasn't suspicious at all. What was up with him?

I helped her pick the rest of her papers up off the floor. "I'm glad you didn't hurt yourself. What exactly happened here?"

"Oh, I tripped. Sometimes I do that. Who was that man? Is he a physics professor?" She smiled briefly. "I can't believe he's heard of me." She glanced at me. "Did you tell him about me?"

"That was Professor Rivas and I didn't mention you."

She gazed dreamily at his closed office door. "He's hot. I wonder if he'd agree to be my advisor?"

Good grief, kids were moony these days. I'd never get mesmerized by Andro's gorgeous blue eyes like that.

"Anyway," I said loudly. "We had a meeting scheduled. Come on."

Alyssa and I successfully rounded up her stuff and made it into my office, where she promptly knocked over the lamp on my desk. "Sorry."

I righted the World-War-I-vintage desk lamp. "No worries." I flipped it on. "It still works."

She sighed. "Thank goodness. Sometimes they don't."

Once we got settled I said, "Please tell me where you are with your degree. Have you finished your classes yet?"

She fidgeted with her papers and a few fell on the floor. "I'm done with classes and I passed Comps Two. That's why I got into the high energy group."

"That sounds good. What exactly happened with them, if you don't mind me asking?"

"We were working on some new hardware for the latest iteration of the Booster Neutrino Experiment at Fermilab and I shorted out some pieces, which caused a fire–very small, mind you. And then some other equipment sort-of got crushed–it's not important how. Anyway, to make a long story short, we had to go back to the drawing board. Professor Zhang said several months of work was ruined and he fired me. He was so unfair. It wasn't my fault–at least not totally."

"I see." But I didn't really. How could so much go awry? "Maybe it's for the best if you get out of the lab as Professor Chen suggested. You could still study neutrinos. How would you like that?"

She nodded energetically. "That sounds great. Where should we start?"

"Let's start with a literature review. Have you ever used the Web of Science?"

She shook her head. "But I've heard about it."

"Come over here to the computer and I'll show you something really neat. Practically every science paper ever published is in this database."

Alyssa and I looked up a bunch of neutrino papers and copied them to her tablet for her to read.

Once she was gone, Andro poked his head in my office. "Got a minute?" He smiled hesitantly.

He must have gotten over his bad mood from earlier. I automatically smiled back at him. He was hard to resist. "Sure. For you, any time." Down, girl.

He glanced down the hall and closed the door as he came in.

"Oh, this is a closed-door talk," I joked. Maybe he was going to ask me out. "I should tell you I have a serious boyfriend."

"What? No. This is about Alyssa." He stepped near my desk. "I'd think twice about taking her on as a student. Things tend to go wrong when she's around."

"So, you're saying she's bad luck?"

He nodded.

"Oh, come on. I don't believe in bad luck, and I can't believe you do either. There's no such thing as luck. It's not scientific. At best, it's some kind of self-fulfilling psychological effect."

"Sure. You're probably right." He walked toward the door, and then turned around. "What was that about a boyfriend? You already told me you had a boyfriend. What did you think I was going to say?" He grinned.

"Uh, that thing about Alyssa. What you said."

He was downright chipper as he went out the door. "Yeah. Right."

I groaned and pushed away from the table which was still laden with chicken, baked potatoes and triple-chocolate cake. Ryan and his perky, petite very-pregnant wife had kindly cooked me dinner since I was new in town.

"I ate too much," I said. "Sydney, you outdid yourself. This was great."

Sydney beamed at me in her Tuscany-inspired kitchen. "It was a big day. You only have a first-day-as-a-professor once, right?" The rosy glow in her cheeks matched the rosy walls. The walls were no doubt the result of some fancy painting technique I couldn't master.

"It was excellent, honey," Ryan said. "I'm glad to see you still remember how to cook something besides tofu."

She poked him playfully. "Yeah, well, don't get used to it. Tomorrow we're back to healthy eating."

"Can I clean up?" I asked. "After I digest a little of course."

Sydney looked shocked. She pushed a perfect brunette curl behind her ear. "No. It's your special dinner. Ryan will clean up, right dear?"

He was smiling, with his hands resting on his stomach. "After a dinner like that, anything you say, dear. But I need to digest a bit, too."

Sydney stood up. "In that case, does anyone want coffee?"

I perked up. "Coffee?"

She gave a little laugh. "It's decaf. Any takers?"

I nodded. "Sydney, there's something you should know about me: I never turn down coffee."

Ryan pounded his fist loudly on the table. "Coffee. Definitely. Bring it on, woman."

She gave him an amused smirk as she turned to get it.

He leaned over the table toward me. "You still owe me an explanation about what happened this morning, Madison. I've been patient all day. I could have sworn you went all fuzzy and see-through and split in two. It was the weirdest thing I'd ever seen."

I tried to laugh it off. "See-through? Split in two? Oh, come on. Are you sure you weren't just on a sugar high?"

Sydney came back with the coffee. "Sugar high? Oh dear, I didn't give you guys too much sugar tonight, did I?"

I shook my head. "No. Dinner was awesome. I was talking about this morn–"

Ryan was shaking his head vigorously and waving his hands at me. He cleared his throat loudly.

"Oh, this morning." Sydney turned to face him. "If you think for a minute, mister, that I don't know where you go on your way to work, you're mistaken." Ooh. Busted.

She filled up our mugs. "What happened this morning, Madison?"

I sighed. There didn't appear to be an escape.

Ryan said, "We were about to cross Baseline Road, when Madison fuzzed-out and became kind of transparent and then there was another fuzzy Madison who got hit by a car."

Sydney grabbed her chair. "Ryan, are you feeling all right?" She peered at her husband, tiny wrinkles creasing around her eyes.

"Yes," he said. "I'm fine."

I waved my hand. "He's okay. It's true. I think I did something similar once before." How was I going to explain this to them when I didn't fully understand it myself?

Sydney crossed her arms, frowning. "This better be good."

"You've heard of quantum mechanics, right?"

She wrinkled her nose. "Is that one of those Einstein theories?"

I nodded. "Sort of. It's the theory of really small things like elementary particles."

They gave me a blank stare.

"An example of elementary particles would be electrons, you know, they're part of atoms. Quantum mechanics is the theory about how these tiny particles act. It turns out they don't act the way we might think. For example they don't behave like basketballs and footballs. Subatomic particles are fuzzy. They only have probabilities that they will be in a certain place with a certain energy. You can't predict exactly where they will be."

Ryan nodded. "I think you told me about that."

"Yes, I have. But the weird thing about quantum mechanics is it says every possible thing does happen, and it takes a conscious mind to collapse the wavefunction and pick which one of the possibilities lasts."

Sydney quirked her eyebrows. "Really? That's the actual theory?"

I nodded. "Basically."

"But it sounds like science fiction," she said.

"Yes, it does," I said. "That's why it's so neat."

Ryan pointed at me. "So, you're saying this morning there were two possible Madisons, and you picked out a certain Madison and made her real, made her permanent?"

I kept forgetting my cousin was much smarter than he looked. "Yes. That's what I'm saying. I think that's what happened."

Sydney said, "That's incredible."

"I don't get it." He shook his head. "If that's true, why don't you do it all the time? Why don't you pick whatever you want to happen? Or, if it's possible, why doesn't everyone do it?"

"I guess everyone doesn't do it because they don't know about it," I said. "Maybe I was able to do it this morning because I know about it and also because it was a matter of life and death. I perceived a possibility in which I was hit by a car and severely injured. I think my subconscious didn't want to accept that so it picked another possibility."

"Can you do it whenever you want? Can you do it now?" Sydney asked.

"Uh." For a split-second, I tried to pick a possibility in which there was a brand new, uneaten triple-chocolate cake sitting in front of me among the dirty dishes on the table. Nothing happened.

I shook my head. "I don't think I can control it." I wished I could.

"But you did it before?" Ryan asked.

"I think so," I said. "Do you remember that vacation our families took to Lake Michigan? All the cousins went? We were in middle school?"

He smiled weakly and nodded, glancing at Sydney. "Yeah. Back then we were little hellions always running around chasing each other and screaming. I don't know how our parents put up with us all."

Sydney patted his hand as if to say their child wouldn't be like that.

"Do you remember when we went sailing?" I suppressed a shudder, remembering the ice cold water.

"What does that have to do with this morning?" Sydney asked.

"One day Ryan and his brothers and I went sailing and I fell in. Remember?" I remembered gasping and being unable to breathe as an icy vice crushed my chest. I couldn't even scream for help.

"No. I don't remember that," he said.

"And I didn't fall in." I felt warm sun and a light breeze on my face as I crouched on the deck of a boat. "There was a huge splash and you guys couldn't figure out how I made it because I was totally dry. Remember?"

He looked puzzled. "Vaguely. I remember something about liar-liar-pants-on-fire."

Ugh. That was coming back to me, too. "That time I focused on the possibility in which I didn't fall in and willed the drowning me out of existence. But I don't think I really understood what happened."

"Wow," Sydney said.

"That summer I announced I was going to be a physicist when I grew up. Do you at least remember that?"

"I remember you were a huge nerd back then and your folks had to pry you away from your books to go outside even when we were on vacation." He grinned. "Come to think of it you haven't changed a bit."

I gave him a rude look. "On that trip I discovered quantum mechanics. I read that a conscious mind is required to collapse the quantum wavefunction and pick a possibility. And I actually believed it."

Ryan's cop persona had been aroused. "Can other physicists use their minds to do this kind of thing? Pick possibilities and bend reality to their will?"

I shook my head slowly. "I've never heard of anyone else doing it. You have to understand only physicists know about collapsing the wavefunction and they're taught it only applies to tiny particles. I first heard about it when I was an impressionable teenager, and I didn't know it wasn't supposed to work on macroscopic things. And, like I said, even though I believe in it, I don't think I can control it."

I paused. "I know it's pretty incredible." It was like saying everyone had a potential superpower they didn't know about. "The scientist in the office next to me, Andro, didn't believe me when I told him about it today."

"Can you blame him?" Sydney asked.

"No." It still sounded crazy to me. "I guess I'll have to figure out a way to prove it to him." And everyone else.

Ryan finished off his coffee and put his cup down. "I hope to hell other scientists don't start doing it."

I nodded. "Me too. I'd hate to see what would happen to reality if everyone tried to change it at once."

For my second day as an official university professor, I dressed in jeans and a t-shirt with a picture of Einstein on it. It was really neat: Einstein's head was made entirely out of tiny equations.

I stepped into Sydney's kitchen before work. She was sitting at the table with Ryan. "What are you wearing now? You've gone from one extreme to the other. Yesterday you were dressed like a CEO and now you look like a student."

"Today, I thought I'd dress for comfort." I shook one of my sandal-clad feet at her. "Look, I'm blending in."

She grinned. "I'll say. Hey, you better ease into this blending thing, or next thing you know, I'll find you wearing a unitard, in the scorpion position."

The what? "Thanks for sharing, but I really don't want to hear about your sex life, Sydney."

She giggled. "Well, I guess you're not in any danger yet."

"Are you ready to go?" Ryan asked. "If we're walking to campus, we should leave now. Are you up for it, Madison?" It was sweet he was concerned about me.

I nodded. "I think so." I could face down the infamous corner, couldn't I?

Sydney, still wearing her gingko-leaved pajamas, stood up. "Can I get you some chicory in a travel mug on your way out?"

Chicory? What was that? "Uh." I caught Ryan's eye.

His back to his wife, he grimaced and shook his head almost imperceptibly, and then turned back to her. "We need to get going." He leaned way down and gave Sydney a peck on the cheek. "Bye, dear."

Sydney, who even very pregnant was about half the size of her husband, followed us to the front door. "Bye. Have a nice day. Better than yesterday, anyway."

"Thanks." That shouldn't be too hard to do. It was unlikely I would get hit by a car and not get hit by a car again today.

Ryan's pace down the sidewalk was too quick as usual.

"Slow down, please," I said.

He glanced back at me. "Sorry." He slowed down some. "I'm starving. I need some sugar and real coffee ASAP."

"I thought you just ate breakfast." I still had to hustle to keep up with his long stride and I couldn't enjoy the scenery. We were speedwalking through a 1950s-era neighborhood of brick ranch houses and I wanted to check out their front gardens.

"Ugh." He shook his head. "That soy, fake-egg, veggie, chicory crap wasn't any kind of breakfast. Since Sydney's gotten pregnant she's been on a health kick." He turned to face me. "Whatever you do, don't eat the breakfast she makes. It's horribly healthy." He shook his head.

I couldn't help smiling. Ever since I'd known Ryan, which had been all his life, he'd been a quintessential meat-and-potatoes man. "You poor thing. That sounds like torture."

He nodded and looked at me sorrowfully. "Yeah. But I have to support her while she's pregnant, right?"

I nodded. "Yes. Good for you." I glanced down the street. "Are we going to that coffee shop from yesterday?" We'd stopped there just before my incident.

"Yeah. That's okay, isn't it? I mean, I don't want to remind you of what happened yesterday. But it is the only coffee place between our house and campus."

"You talked me into it." I gave up trying to look at the scenery and sped toward the shop at the end of the block.

As we stepped into Boulder Brews, I breathed in the aromas of roasted coffee beans and cinnamon. This must be what heaven smelled like. The scent alone was almost enough to wake me up.

Ryan's face lit up as the odors registered. He rubbed his hands together. "Now, that's more like it."

Unfortunately, we were not fated for immediate gratification. There was an inconvenient line of teens and twenty-somethings in front of us. Bummer.

I impatiently glanced around the room and spied huge metal cylinders along the south wall. Surely, they didn't roast coffee beans here? I poked Ryan. "What are those?" I pointed at the cryptic containers.

He glanced over. "Brewery stuff. They brew beer here." He grinned. "Actually, I like to stop here on my way home from work too."

I eyed him, thinking perhaps his bulky physique did make sense despite Sydney's purported health kick.

The tall kid in front of Ryan snorted. "Brewery stuff? Obviously, you aren't much of a zymurgist." He pointed. "That's the tun, that's the spargetank, that's the brew kettle. Those are fermenting and aging tanks." He had a sexy, slightly cocky smile. "Oh, hey, Mad–, er, Professor Martin." His chocolate-brown eyes twinkled.

Apparently, I knew him. He certainly knew me, anyway. I tried to wake up my brain and finally recognized him. It was that kid, Luke, from my class. "Hi, Luke. How's that homework coming?"

He scowled.

Could it be that some college kids didn't start their homework immediately after it was assigned?

"Professor Martin, did you figure out what happened to you yesterday morning?" he asked.

"Next." The woman behind the counter motioned crossly at him. "What do you want?"

"Sort of," I said. "Let's talk later, Luke."

He turned his attention to the woman behind the counter.

"Who was that?" Ryan asked, pushing his glasses up the bridge of his nose.

"Just a student," I said.

"So," Ryan said, "what does Ted think about your collapsing the wavefunction adventure?"

That was a good question. "I don't know what Ted thinks. I haven't been able to get a hold of him, yet."

"Isn't he in elementary particles, like you?" he said. "I bet he could help you figure this all out."

I nodded. "I bet you're right. Hopefully he'll call me back soon." I took out my cell phone to check that it was on. It was.

The grumpy employee barked at us, "What do you want?"

We approached the counter with the focus of a proton beam caught in an accelerator.

Ryan got out his wallet. "I'll have a gigante Rinca Dragon with caramel and whipped cream."

The employee asked him, "Do you want chocolate sprinkles on that?"

He nodded. "Yes. Oh, and two cinnamon rolls." He turned to me. "Your turn."

I felt a little queasy thinking about a gooey sugar-covered dragon. I got up to the counter and scrutinized the menu. "How about just a plain coffee? Do you have that?"

"No." The woman popped her gum. "What do you mean, like, the coffee of the day?"

"Yes. I'll have the coffee of the day."

She sighed. "What size?"

"Big?" I asked.

"We don't have big," she said. "We have medio, gigante, and enorme."

"Just get the gigante," Ryan said under his breath.

"Gigante."

"What do you want in it?"

"Nothing. No whipped cream, no chocolate, just the coffee. And a cinnamon roll."

She shrugged. "Suit yourself."

Ryan paid.

"Thanks," I said. "I'll get it next time."

He nodded.

Two giant paper cups and two brown paper bags appeared as if by magic. I guess they were used to the morning rush. I took a sip of coffee. Blech. It was so horrible I almost spit it out. "What the hell is this?"

Ryan glanced at the specials board and roared with laughter. "Oh, no, Madison, the coffee of the day is chicory."

I glared at my gigante cup. I really wanted some coffee. I needed coffee, real coffee. But when I looked at the queue snaking across the room, there was no way I was going to get back in that line. Maybe it wasn't as bad as I thought.

I thought about yummy delicious fresh-brewed coffee. I took another sip. It tasted different. It tasted like coffee. "I was wrong. It's not so bad." Had my tastes changed, or had the coffee changed?

Outside the coffee shop at the infamous corner my knees were knocking. I managed to cross the street when the walk signal came on, after looking both ways about fifty times.

When I got to my office, the floor was as deserted as the library on Saturday night. I resolved to try to call Ted again although my expectations were low. I couldn't believe he hadn't called me back yet.

He picked up on the second ring. "Hello?"

Yay. "Oh, Ted. It's so good to hear your voice."

"Madison? How's it going?"

"Good," I said. "How's it going with you?" Apparently we were not scintillating conversationalists.

"Fine. You don't sound so good. Are you sure you're okay?" he asked.

"I, uh, just miss you." I cleared my throat. "Why didn't you call me back?"

"Did you call me? I didn't get any messages," he said.

Damn. He was right. A woman answered and I didn't leave a message. And here I'd been waiting and waiting for him to call me back.

"Madison?"

"I'm fine. Ryan and his wife have been great. My class is going well so far. Boulder is kind of weird. They have stuff here like unitards and tofu and chicory."

"Chicory? What's that?"

"I'm not entirely sure." I mustered up a smile. "So, do you have time to chat? I want to tell you about something."

He hesitated. "Not a ton of time. The group meeting's in a little while. Remember those? But I have a little time. So go ahead, shoot. Tell me what's on your mind. But not if it's that you met someone else." He laughed weakly. "That's not it, is it?"

I took the phone away from my ear and stared at it for a second. He didn't seem to grasp the concept of long-distance relationship. "Ha, ha. No. Yesterday morning I was hit by a car and–"

He interrupted me. "Hit by a car! Shit, Madison. Are you okay?"

"Yes, I'm fine."

"Thank God," he said. "In the future, you might want to think about leading with the most important thing."

I pictured him shaking his head like he was wont to do.

"So, anyway," I said. "I was hit by a car, but I collapsed the wavefunction and picked out a possibility in which I wasn't hit by a car. Hence the fine part."

"What was that about a wavefunction? You don't sound fine. Did you see a doctor after you were hit by the car?"

I sighed and my gaze drifted out the window to the red-tile roofs and the mountains beyond. "I'm really fine. Thank you for your concern." I was glad he cared, but this wasn't getting me anywhere. "Forget the car accident. New subject. How could a person prove an Interpretation of quantum mechanics?"

"You can't prove it," he said. "It's not empirical. It's an interpretation, like the Many Worlds Interpretation."

"I know that." Let's come at this another way. "What's an easy way to prove quantum mechanics then?"

He was quiet for a moment and then said, "I guess you could try the electron double-slit experiment."

"Of course." Why didn't I think of that?

There was a beep on the other end of the line.

I smiled. Ted and his beeping alarm. How many times had I heard that? I had a sad thought: how many more times would I hear it?

"Oops. Sorry, Mad. I hope you're really all right, but I have to go get ready for the group meeting. For some reason I have more work than ever."

I knew the reason. Me. Since I'd left, he had his work and my work, too. "Sure, hon. Go get ready for the meeting. I understand. I love you."

"Yeah. Love ya'." He hung up.

Talking to Ted hadn't made me feel better, after all. Why had he sounded so insincere when he said he loved me?

Chapter Four

As soon as Andro got in, I dropped by his office solely to ask him where they kept the experimental equipment. That was the only reason, I swear. "*Hola*, Professor Rivas." Today, he wore a dramatic burgundy silk shirt.

He looked up from the papers on his desk. "*Hola*, Professor Martin." His expression was carefully neutral. "How go things with Alyssa?"

"Fine. No troubles." I smiled in what I hoped was a convincing fashion.

"Is there something I can help you with?" His direct glance almost knocked me over he was so handsome. Those might've been the longest eyelashes I'd ever seen on a man.

Focus, Madison. There was a reason I'd come over here. "Yes. You know that discussion we had yesterday? I thought of an experiment that should prove my point about collapsing the wavefunction. Actually, my boyfriend Ted thought of it. Can you tell me where the physics department keeps the equipment for demonstrations and labs and stuff?"

My eye was drawn to a framed portrait featuring Andro, a beautiful twenty-something Chicana and two cute little girls. "I thought you said you weren't married." My voice may have risen a bit, but I definitely didn't shriek.

"Why would you care?" He smiled. "I thought you had a boyfriend? You certainly mention him enough, maybe too much?"

He sobered, pointing at the picture. "That's my sister Yasmin and her daughters Maria and Theresa. They live with me. I'm very sorry to say Yasmin is a widow." He shook his head, grimacing.

He took care of his widowed sister and nieces? My conception of him underwent a paradigm shift. I could almost hear it creak as it rearranged itself. “A widow? That’s horrible. Poor Yasmin and those poor little girls. That’s awful. What happened, if you don’t mind me asking?”

He rubbed his forehead with his palm. “Yasmin’s husband, Armando, was in construction. He had just been promoted to foreman and his crew was driving to a job on highway 36 when some equipment fell off their truck. They pulled off to the side of the road and Armando got out and was hit by an SUV.” His mouth tightened. “The *diablo* didn’t even stop. Armando was pronounced dead at the scene. They said he died instantly. It happened over a year ago and Yasmin’s still a wreck.”

“That’s just horrible. I’m so sorry.” I didn’t know what to say. Words were inadequate. “Did they ever catch the guy that hit him?”

“No.” He shook his head.

“Do they have any leads?”

“No. And I don’t think the cops are trying too hard.” His face had taken on a fierce stillness.

“I’m sorry.” I’d have to ask Ryan if he had any cop buddies he could ask about it. “I’d be happy to babysit some time, for free, if you and Yasmin need any help.” My heart went out to those poor little girls.

“That’s kind of you.” Some of the life came back into his eyes. “I’ll ask Yasmin. Anyway, what were you asking me?”

“I just wondered if you could tell me where the department equipment is. But I can go ask Dr. Chen if you’re too busy.”

He smiled a smile that didn’t quite reach his eyes. “I can see you are going to be a difficult neighbor. It’s always something with you, isn’t it?”

“I apologize if I’ve been bothering you,” I said quickly.

“I’m kidding.” He gave me a real smile. “You’re the first person in the physics department to ask me about Armando.” He stood up and pushed his chair under his desk. “Come on, I’ll show you.”

It turned out the physics department had all the equipment I needed to do the experiment. I decided to set it up on carts in the deserted hall outside my office since there was no room inside my office. After all, no one seemed to be using that floor except Andro and me and I didn't think he'd mind.

Of course, if he did, that'd give me a perfect excuse to talk to him again.

I lined up the electron gun with the condenser lens, aperture, objective lens, another aperture, intermediate lens, electron biprism, and the two-dimensional detection apparatus. I also pointed a digital video camera at the detection apparatus. I turned everything on and waited.

Slowly a series of lines appeared on the detection screen due to the electron waves interfering with each other. The screen refreshed and I concentrated on removing the interference so that only two blobs, indicating particles, appeared. For a few moments both patterns were superimposed on the screen, resulting in much fuzziness and then the two blobs won out. Awesome. The theory said we should get a series of lines. Blobs were definitely not predicted. I turned off the gun, very curious to see what the camera had recorded. As I was checking it, someone came up behind me.

"Hey, Professor Martin. What's all this equipment doing here in the hall?" Alyssa asked. She was wearing a t-shirt that said *Physicists do it at the speed of light.*

I jumped into the air like steam erupting from Old Faithful. "Wow, you startled me, Alyssa. And call me Madison, by the way. I like your t-shirt." Although I wasn't sure doing it at the speed of light was something to brag about.

"Thanks, Madison," she said a little hesitantly.

"I'm doing a quantum mechanics experiment," I said. "Would you like to try it?"

"Really? You'd let me do an experiment? You're not afraid I'll break something?" Why'd she ask that?

"Nope," I said. "Do you want to try it?"

"Sure." She examined the experimental setup as I reviewed the data on the video camera. "This looks fun," she said. "What's it do?"

The camera had recorded both of my previous efforts, including the unexpected blobs. I moved away from the equipment to give her room to work. "Why don't you turn on the electron gun and see what happens?"

She narrowed her eyes at me. "Is it safe?"

I smiled. "Yes, no worries. It's safe."

She looked it over carefully and then turned it on. As soon as she did, sparks started shooting out of the power source. "Oh, no."

I quickly reached over and unplugged the source from the wall. "That was a close one. But no harm done."

"I thought you said it was safe."

"I thought it was. Don't worry about it, Alyssa. Obviously this power source is defective. I'll just go get another one and we'll be in business." I did so and soon we were ready to roll.

As I turned the new power source on, I chuckled. "I must admit those sparks did get my blood pumping."

Alyssa nodded. "Me, too."

Two tiny dots appeared on the detection screen, gradually forming two bigger blobs.

"Is that what's supposed to happen? It's not very impressive." She turned around to face me.

"Just wait. More electrons have to get through the apparatus." I pointed. "Watch the detection screen."

I concentrated and again two different patterns were superimposed but gradually the two dots became part of a series of lines.

Alyssa's eyes crinkled up. She seemed puzzled. "What did you do? How come the first time we got two blobs and then we got a bunch of lines? And why do they get fuzzy? And then why does the fuzziness go away?" She got closer to the apparatus and leaned over, inspecting it. "Is it some kind of trick?"

The detection screen refreshed.

I stepped back and leaned against the doorjamb of my office. "No trick."

She straightened up. "Then, make it change into two lines."

I concentrated and this time the row of lines coalesced back into two lines after some intermediate fuzziness.

"That's neat." She nodded. "But what does it mean?"

This explanation might call for sitting down so I turned off the apparatus. "Grab a chair."

We pulled chairs from my office and sat down in the hall.

I cleared my throat. "If the electrons are particles, we should see two blobs on the screen, corresponding to the two different paths the electrons take as they go through the biprism. If they are waves, which quantum mechanics advocates, we should see an interference pattern, namely a row of many lines, on the screen."

She touched her palms and fingertips together, thoughtfully. "Right. I studied this. As I recall, they're supposed to be both particles and waves. But doesn't quantum mechanics mean they should show the series of lines, the interference pattern? What would make the pattern change like that?"

"Me." Apparently collapsing the wavefunction really did work.

Alyssa's mouth hung open for a second, her hair dangerously close to falling into it. "So you're saying you have some kind of psychic powers?"

"No. Quantum mechanics is a theory of possibilities, remember? Infinite possibilities, really. I'm saying the path of the electron comes into existence only when a consciousness observes, or in this case, picks it and collapses the wavefunction." Geez, collapsing the wavefunction was a mouthful.

"That does sound familiar. What about my consciousness?"

I smiled. "What about it? Your consciousness can collapse the wavefunction, too. Try it." She should be able to do it if my idea was correct. And I really wanted it to be correct.

"I don't know." She rubbed her cheek nervously.

"No. Really." I pointed at the equipment. "Please try it. If I can do it, you can do it. Or do you believe I have psychic powers?"

She grinned. "Well, if you're going to put it that way, I don't see how I can refuse."

She approached the equipment and leaned over it, turning it on.

The screen refreshed but the dots made the expected line interference pattern.

"It's not working. I can't do it." She pursed her lips.

I approached. "So, you do think I have psychic powers? Or do you disbelieve what you saw with your own eyes? You saw two blobs earlier."

Alyssa shook her head. "I don't know what to believe any

more. You do it again and maybe I'll believe you."

I focused on making blobs after the screen refreshed again. They didn't seem to want to move into that pattern. Ugh. Now I couldn't do it. What was going on?

I focused more intently on the blobs. Nothing. I looked at Alyssa. "Are you standing there thinking I can't do it?"

"Yes." She looked startled. "How'd you know?"

"It seems harder now than it was earlier. Move away from the equipment and try to clear your mind." She had to be affecting it somehow.

She backed away from the experiment.

I approached the apparatus and concentrated again as the detection screen refreshed. Slowly, it got blurry, and then two blobs appeared. "Ha." I grinned and looked back at her.

Approaching the apparatus, she narrowed her eyes and stared at the screen as it refreshed.

I turned back to the screen as one line of dots slowly coalesced out of fuzz. That was unexpected and very neat.

"One line. You did it Alyssa. Awesome." Secretly, I was relieved to see someone else could do it and it wasn't due to some bizarro psychic powers.

She beamed at me as she walked closer. "Madison, this is amazing."

"You go, girl," I said. "But why one line? That's kind of weird."

"Why not?" she asked. "You said I'm picking among all the possibilities. I just picked one of them."

I followed her words to their logical conclusion and had an epiphany. She was more right than she knew. I focused on the screen. After the screen refreshed, it became blurry and then slowly a first blob formed an *H* and a second blob formed an *o*, and then an *l,* and finally an *a*. Oh, my God, it worked.

Alyssa gasped.

I groped for a chair and sank down. I was shaking like we were in the middle of a magnitude nine earthquake.

"But, but that's just weird. How?" She plopped down on the chair next to me.

"You said it. We're picking from among all the infinite possibilities." I focused on the screen again. Slowly, the word *Comprende* formed. It was getting easier to control.

Alyssa paled and then concentrated on the screen. The letters *Yes* formed. "I think I am getting better at this."

"Yes, it does seem to be getting easier. I'm not sure why."

"Maybe our brains are getting used to the idea."

I shrugged as I got up and turned off the apparatus. "Paradigm shift? That's as good an explanation as any."

"Madison..."

I raised my eyebrows and looked at her as I sat back down.

"How far does this go? I mean if we can pick out unlikely patterns with this apparatus, what's stopping us from picking out unlikely patterns in the real world?"

Indeed. "I don't think anything is stopping us, except maybe our own expectations. Macroscopic objects are made up of particles like these electrons, so if it works for them, it should work for groups of them." I dipped my head. "In fact, I think I picked out an unlikely possibility Monday to avoid getting smashed by a car."

"What?" She opened her eyes wide.

Alyssa was a bright graduate student. I was interested in hearing her reaction to my adventure. "I was on my way to work Monday morning. I stepped into the crosswalk on Baseline Road south of campus and a car slammed right into me."

She gasped.

"And I didn't," I said.

"Huh?"

"It was like I split in two. I could feel myself lying in the road *and* standing on the sidewalk."

"That's crazy," she said.

"I'm telling you, that's what happened."

"So how did you get out of it? How did you join back together?" she asked.

"I'm not entirely sure," I said, slowly. "But I think the conscious observer, me, selected the reality in which I was okay."

"So, you were the cat in the Schrödinger experiment?" she asked.

A burst of laughter erupted out of me. "I hadn't thought of it that way, but basically yes."

She just looked at me for a few moments.

"But that would mean we can control reality." She paused,

seemingly overcome by the possibilities.

"Yes," I whispered.

"But that's crazy," she whispered.

We sat in silence for a couple minutes.

"I see you got the experiment set up," Andro said from down the hall near the stairwell. "How's it going? Did you get it to work?"

Alyssa jumped up, knocking the biprism out of alignment. "Oops. Sorry." She hurried to straighten it.

I stood. "Yes, we did get it to work. Unusually well, in fact. Would you like to give it a try?"

He shrugged. "Sure. I haven't done this experiment in years, but I think I know how it's supposed to go. Fire it up."

We realigned the biprism, fired it up, and waited for him to be blown away like we'd been.

And we detected a series of lines. That was it, nothing but the conventional interference pattern.

Alyssa looked at me, stricken. "I'm sorry. Did I break something?"

I shook my head. "I doubt it." Secretly I concentrated on making the series of lines into one line. Did it get blurry there for a minute? I hated to admit it, but nothing unusual seemed to be happening.

Andro nodded. "And we proved quantum mechanics. This is a nice experiment. Good job."

"I don't get it," Alyssa said to me quietly.

"Keep up the good work, ladies." He sauntered into his office.

"I'm not sure I get it, either. Let me think about it some. Check in with me later this afternoon, okay?"

"Okay." She glanced at her phone. "It's almost lunch time anyway. See you later."

I was very confused. In my office, I reviewed the digital recording we'd made. Everything was there including *Comprende*. There was also something else in part of one of the frames. It almost looked like a hand, but it was too blurry.

I called Ted but got his voice mail again. This long-distance thing was going to be more difficult than I thought. I was used to seeing Ted in our lab all day and now I couldn't even get him on the phone. I missed him.

While I was watching the tape a second time, Andro stopped by. “Do you want to get some lunch?”

I turned off the camera and nodded. “Sure. What do you have in mind?”

“Have you been to Burritos and Beers on The Hill?”

“No. I can’t say that I have. But it sounds like my kind of place. *Si, senor.*” I grinned.

The décor of Burritos and Beers was sparse, consisting of random graffiti-covered tables and mismatched chairs. Once I tasted the Poblano Pesto Mole Burrito and Lemon Hefeweisen beer, however, I sighed in contentment. “We should come here every day.”

Andro patted his stomach. “I don’t think I could afford it.” He took a bite of burrito. “Nice job with that experiment earlier.”

“Thanks. Although, I have to say Alyssa and I didn’t quite get the same results you did.” I told him what happened when we did it.

“Are you joking with me, Madison?” He frowned. “That doesn’t make any sense. I don’t believe it.”

“Ah ha,” I said. “Maybe that’s why it didn’t work for you. It worked for me and Alyssa. We collapsed the wavefunction to pick out unlikely possibilities. I have it recorded. I’ll show it to you.”

In the face of my adamant assurance he seemed hesitant. “Okay. I’d like to see that.” He took a swig of his Negra Modelo. “So, you said your boyfriend came up with the idea for you to do the experiment?”

While taking a bite of burrito, I nodded. “Yep. Ted. He’s an elementary particle physicist, too.”

“How come I haven’t met him?”

“He doesn’t live here. He’s back in St. Louis.”

“Is he moving out here?”

I shook my head. “No. Not right now, anyway.”

“Still, he must be a good guy if he believes your collapsing the wavefunction stories.”

I wasn’t sure what he’d make of the experiment this morning. I forced a smile. “Yeah. He’s a good guy. We help each other with our research and other things.”

I flashed back to the last time I'd seen him, in our bed, when I was supposed to be on the road to Boulder already. The tender kisses, the caresses, and the way our bodies fit together so well. I caught Andro in my peripheral vision. I wondered how our bodies would fit together?

"Earth to Madison," he said. "Hey."

"Sorry. I guess my mind wandered there for a minute."

"You're flushed," he said. "Was it too spicy for you?" He gestured at the burrito.

I grinned. "Just spicy enough."

After lunch as we strolled back to the Gamow Tower, I mulled over the concept of changing reality. At the stop light at Broadway, I concentrated on changing the red light to green with my newly discovered powers. When it actually turned green, I flinched. "I did it. I made the light turn green."

I fervently checked right and left for oncoming traffic though as we stepped into the crosswalk.

Andro raised his eyebrows. "Let me get this straight. We stood at the corner for about five minutes and then *you* made the light change? That must be some experiment you did this morning." He chuckled and shook his head.

As we walked down the sidewalk, a young man approached us on his bike. I tried to make him stop by thinking: stop the bike. He rode on by without even slowing down. A girl sat on a bench, talking on her cell phone. I concentrated on getting her to hang up as we walked past her.

"Like, totally. I know what you mean." She seemed oblivious to my efforts.

A group of boys were playing catch with a Frisbee in the Norlin quad. Drop the Frisbee. One of the boys did drop the Frisbee.

"Hey, Andro. Look." I pointed. "I made that guy drop his Frisbee."

He sighed. "Yeah, right."

We got to the crosswalk at Eighteenth Street. There was no traffic light and no cars to be seen, just a steady flow of students streamed across the street. We joined in the flow. Quickly we were at the physics building.

He opened the west door. "I suppose you made me do that?"

"Uh." I had just been thinking: open door.

"You're *loco*." He guffawed. "Influencing a couple of electrons is a far cry from making people do what you want."

Had I changed reality? I thought I did Monday morning in the crosswalk. And what about the chicory? And what was the blurry thing in that one frame of tape?

When we got back to our offices in the Gamow Tower I handed Andro the video camera and he smirked as he queued up the experiment.

As he watched the recording, he nodded, and then he squinted and shot me a look. Then he frowned and his mouth fell open. Finally he said, "*Mi Dios.*"

He shook his head as he handed me the camera. "I can't believe it. I know we don't know each other very well, but be honest with me. This isn't some kind of trick, is it?"

I grinned. "Nope."

"Can you show me this in person?" He pointed back into the hall where the experiment was still set up.

I stood. "I can try."

We decamped into the hall and turned on the equipment.

Unfortunately, we only got the standard interference pattern although it was pretty blurry for the most part. I couldn't understand this. Why couldn't we collapse the wavefunction now to get anything unusual?

After a while, he said, "This has definitely been interesting. You've succeeded in thoroughly confusing me, Madison." He flashed me a grin. "But I have to go now. I have a class." He stopped in his office to get some papers and then went to teach.

I was a little bit relieved and tromped down to the department office to get some coffee.

Alyssa arrived at my office as soon as I got back.

I showed her the recordings Andro and I'd just made.

She was as mystified as I. "It's weird how sometimes it works and sometimes it doesn't," she said. "Like when I first tried to do it by myself and then when you tried to show me and it didn't work. But then it always worked with the two of us at the end."

I nodded and sipped. She was on to something. "Right. Initially, I couldn't get the pattern to change because you thought I couldn't." I jumped out of my chair. "Let's go try it again." I had a hypothesis I wanted to test: the wavefunction collapsers had to truly believe they could modify the patterns.

She took some kind of thermos out of her bag and in the process of taking a drink, dropped it on the ground. It made a shattering noise. We both jumped.

"It's metal," I said, pointing. "What broke?"

She shrugged. "It must've been the liner or something. It's not the first time something like this has happened."

We turned our attention back to the experiment. When we turned it on, the image on the detection screen was very blurry.

"That's weird." Alyssa said. "Why is it just blurry like that?"

"I'm not sure. Maybe if we both focus on the standard interference pattern."

As soon as the words were out of my mouth, the screen cleared to show a series of lines.

"Now try two lines."

After a second of blurriness, two lines appeared.

"Good grief, how come this didn't work when Andro was here?" I stepped away, irritated. It could only be that he didn't really believe me.

"Andro." She sighed. "How about making a heart shape?"

The image on the screen got very blurry and then gradually a heart appeared.

"Nice job, Alyssa." I glanced at her. She looked strange, sort of blurry around the edges. I rubbed my eyes and stepped closer to her. There was no change. Alarmed, I said, "Do you feel all right?"

"Sure. Why?"

"Look at yourself."

She held up her hands, which still appeared slightly fuzzy. "Oh, no. What's wrong with me?"

Quickly I pulled the plugs out of the electrical outlet.

Alyssa's slight blurriness went away. Thank goodness.

"I'm so sorry," I said. "How do you feel? Would you like me to take you to the health center?"

"What would we say? I suffered from fuzziness?" She forced a laugh. "I think I'm okay. I feel totally normal. That was weird though."

"I'll say. You're sure you're okay?" I felt awful. I couldn't believe I'd put her in danger. I was a horrific advisor.

She reassured me at length that she was fine, but I still sent her home to rest.

And then I took the experiment apart as fast as humanly possible.

When Andro came back from his class, he popped his head in my office. "I see you took the experiment down. Too bad. I wanted to try it again."

I shook my head. "No, you didn't." I told him what happened with Alyssa and showed him the new digital recording we'd made.

He shook his head, pointing at the heart. "This is just amazing. You're almost starting to convince me."

"That's when Alyssa started to go fuzzy," I said. "Who knows what would've have happened if we'd continued?" I shuddered.

"It's too bad you didn't get a recording of her," he said. "When you try it again, you should record the experimenters too."

"I'm not planning on trying it again. I'm going to focus on my class and my research and help Alyssa with her research. That's it. No more weirdness. That's totally over." Totally.

He smiled gently. "Who are you trying to convince?"

Chapter Five

In class Wednesday I said, "Recall, last time we said one of the main ideas of quantum mechanics was particle-wave duality. That means we can describe particles with wave properties like wavelengths."

Pankaj held up his hand. "Can you give an example?"

"Actually, light, also known as electromagnetic radiation, is a good example," I said. "Light is part of the electromagnetic spectrum with certain wavelengths. There's also ultra-violet light and infrared light and others that have different wavelengths. But electromagnetic radiation is also little particles called photons. It's both things. Does that make sense?"

Pankaj nodded.

"Good. In quantum mechanics we use wavefunctions to represent waves," I said. "Here, let me show you." I started writing on the board.

Luke came up to me after class. "Hey, I got your email." His voice took on a cocky tone. "I guess you're my new advisor, huh?"

"Yes. That's right," I said. "Do you need some kind of help with your schedule?"

He crossed his arms and leaned against the front table. "Yeah." He smiled lazily. "I'm dropping a class."

"Do you need me to sign something, then?"

"Oh." He dropped his arms. "I guess I forgot the form."

That was a little odd. "Okay," I said. "Stop by my office some time with the form."

He smiled broadly. "I look forward to it, Madison."

"You mean Professor Martin, right?" I said.

He just smiled his cocky smile.

If I didn't know better, I'd think he was flirting with me.

Wednesday night I was all too happy to join Ryan and Sydney for dinner right up until Sydney started dishing it out. It had started out looking like meatloaf with a mushroom sauce but as Sydney passed out the servings, I discerned it was definitely not meatloaf. "This looks interesting, Sydney," I said.

Ryan took his plate with a forced smile. "I warned you," he said under his breath as she walked to the refrigerator to get the soymilk.

She came back to the table, holding up the carton. "Madison? Soy milk?"

How do you milk a soy? What was soy, anyway? "Do you have any regular milk, like from a cow?" I asked.

She shook her head, seemingly amused.

I shrugged. "Sure, I'll try the soy."

As she poured, I asked, "So, what do we have here?" I pointed at my plate. "I'm guessing it's some kind of extra special, uh, loaf?" The soymilk was interesting. It did taste a little bit like milk.

"Yes. It's tofu-loaf, a new recipe," Sydney said. "Ryan loves it, don't you honey?"

He took a bite. "It beats the other–"

She shot him a look.

"Er, yes. It's yummy." He had an expression that would seem to contradict his statement.

"It's got garlic and onion, carrot and parsley as well as tofu, and look how nice it slices up." Sydney settled into her chair and placed her napkin in her lap. "Sometimes tofu-loaf can be a bit dicey to slice."

"You don't say." I looked at my forkful of mystery-substance. It didn't even qualify as mystery-meat. I tasted it and it was definitely interesting. The garlic tasted good. "Please pass the rice and the salad," I said. "Thank you for this nice dinner, Sydney." I knew my manners.

Conversation lagged as we dug in.

After I'd eaten all the healthy stuff I could stand, I said, "Ryan do you have any cop friends?"

"As a matter of fact, I do." He grinned. "Don't tell me, you're finally throwing over that guy Ted and you want me to fix you up." He puffed out his chest. "Us law-enforcement guys are quite a catch."

Sydney made a noise that started out sounding like a laugh and ended up sounding like a cough. "Something must have gone down the wrong way. Sorry. You were saying Madison?"

"No. Not a fix-up." Why would he say that? "One of my new friends from work told me about a hit-and-run fatality on highway 36 about a year ago." I gulped as my own near hit-and-run a few days ago tried to surface in my memory. I forced it down. "This friend, he's still pretty broken up about it, and he implied the cops weren't trying too hard to solve the case."

"Why would he think that?" Sydney asked.

"The victim was Chicano," I said.

"Well, maybe–" Sydney said.

"Impossible." Ryan pounded his fist on the table. "I'm sure the officers are doing their best. It must be a tough case is all. Give me all the information and I'll check with my man Ben."

Thursday, Luke stopped by my office hours. "Hey, Teach. I brought my form." He handed it over.

As I scanned and signed it, he said, "Are you ever going to explain what happened to you on Monday morning on Baseline Road?"

The last thing I needed was another blurry student. My plan had been to avoid the topic and hope he forgot all about it. Apparently that plan wasn't working too well.

I handed the form back to him.

"I thought you said you welcomed questions and there were no dumb ones." He grinned uncertainly.

Could he be nervous about talking to the big professor? I should be nice. He was trying to learn, after all. "That's true. I did say that. I have made some progress in understanding what happened. But to understand it, you have to know quantum mechanics, so I didn't think you guys were ready for it. And frankly, now I think it's dangerous. You're better off not knowing."

"Dangerous? Come on, Teach. What could be dangerous about an old physics theory? Give me a hint." He leaned over my desk conspiratorially.

What could it hurt? He was totally ignorant about quantum mechanics except for two measly lectures. "I do admire your enthusiasm for physics, Luke. Okay, here's a hint: Copenhagen Interpretation."

He put his finger on his chin. "Copenhagen Interpretation. Interesting. Thanks. See ya' Teach." He strolled out.

As soon as he left, I called Ted. I felt the urge to hear his voice.

We mostly chatted about how our research was going, but Ted seemed distracted.

Finally I said, "I really miss you."

This was met by silence.

"Do you miss me?" I asked.

"Sure," he said. "It's been nice catching up, but I have to go now."

"So soon?" It had been less than five minutes.

"Yep." He hung up.

Screw this long-distance thing.

Friday morning before I could start class I got a question.

Luke said, "You said last time that wavefunctions had something to do with possibilities. Could you go over that again?"

"I'm glad you asked," I said. "In quantum mechanics, we can never predict where something will be as a function of time. We can only talk about possibilities of motion from one position to another, for example. The wavefunctions describe these possibilities."

"That's whacked," Luke's buddy said.

"So, you're saying everything is just possibilities?" Luke said. "I disagree. There's a hundred percent probability that I'm sitting here in this class. I'd say that's a certainty."

I grinned. "I'm saying everything is just possibilities in quantum mechanics until it becomes a certainty." A shiver passed over my scalp and crawled down my back. This stuff had to explain what happened the other morning.

"So how does it become a certainty?" Luke asked.

A human mind has to collapse the wavefunction. But these students weren't ready for that yet. "That is a very good question. Stay tuned and you'll learn how later in the semester." I beamed as I turned back to the white board. That would hook them for sure.

Alyssa checked in with me after lunch and we discussed what her dissertation project would be. She also assured me there was no lingering blurriness or other ill effects from our experiment. We dodged a bullet there.

And then I actually got to focus on my own neutrino research the rest of Friday afternoon. Wonder of wonders.

Ryan and I had made plans to stop at Boulder Brews on the way home for a refreshing beverage. On my way out, I invited Andro along. Ted wouldn't mind, right? Ryan was there to chaperone, after all.

So, five-thirty Friday found the three of us sitting there, toasting the end of the work week.

"Check her out," Ryan said, pointing at a young woman who entered. "Wash your hair, honey. White girls aren't supposed to have dreads."

Andro guffawed into his mug of beer. "Maybe she doesn't know she's white."

"Maybe she's not white," I said. "We don't know. Anyway, dreads are neat." I took another sip of my Back-to-School Bock, one of the seasonal brews. It was strong. I smacked my lips.

"And look at that weird patchwork skirt made out of jeans," Ryan added. "Wash it much?"

"She's not as bad as the boys with their saggy pants." Andro pointed at the young men a couple tables over.

Ryan chuckled. "I love the baggy pants. Our criminal apprehension rate has gone way up on campus because the kids keep tripping on their pants when they run away."

Andro laughed. "That is hilarious. I love it." I wasn't sure I liked how Ryan and Andro acted together sitting there making fun of people.

I would not let myself laugh. "You guys sound like old fogeys."

"You should see them running away," Ryan said. "Their pants

fall down around their ankles and they fall right on their face. Splat."

Andro guffawed. "This guy is great," he said pointing at Ryan.

"Thanks," Ryan said. "Hey, you should come to our barbecue tomorrow night." Were Andro and Ryan becoming friends?

"Barbecue? What barbecue?" I asked.

"Oh, didn't I mention it?" Ryan asked.

"No," I said. Was this barbeque at their, aka my, house? That seemed like something I should know about.

"Sydney and I host an annual beginning-of-the-school-year barbecue for the campus police department," Ryan said. "You're invited."

"Gee, thanks," I said. Nice notice.

"Can you come, Andro?" Ryan asked.

"Can I bring my family?" he asked.

"Totally," Ryan said. "It's a family thing. A lot of the guys will bring their families. And a dish. You're supposed to bring something to eat."

"That sounds great," Andro said, staring at me intently. "I know just what to bring."

For some reason, condoms popped into my head.

I slept in on Saturday and was awakened by the clanging of pots and pans in the kitchen. According to my alarm clock, which I'd batted across the room hours ago, morning was almost gone. I put on my robe and shuffled into the kitchen. Ryan sat at the breakfast bar bleary-eyed, sipping something, and Sydney was mixing up some batter.

"Morning." I grunted. "Is that coffee? Real coffee?"

Ryan nodded.

"Yes, honey." Sydney got a cup out of the cupboard and poured me a cup. "Here you go."

"You are a lifesaver." I plunked down on the other stool and took a big gulp." Ah. "You guys look as tired as I feel. Any particular reason?"

Sydney frowned. "Yeah. Sorry about the commotion last night."

"There was a commotion?" I asked. Now that they mentioned it, I vaguely recalled being awakened by doors slamming and the car starting up.

"It was nothing." Ryan mustered up a smile. "Sydney thought she was going into labor, so we had a practice run to the hospital. That's all."

"Are you all right, Sydney?" I asked. "Is the baby all right?"

"Everything's fine. The baby's fine and the doctor even said I should make it to my due date." That was a relief.

"Good." I pointed with my elbow at the heating griddle on the stove. "So what's all this?" Ted and I used to go out for brunch on Saturday mornings. I sighed. I missed Ted and I really missed brunch.

"Martin family tradition: we always have special breakfasts on the weekend." She smiled. "I'm making pancakes with organic blueberries. They're loaded with antioxidants. Would you like some?"

Organic blueberries? When in Rome, do the Romans. Wait, that's not right. I needed more coffee. I nodded and took another sip. "For sure. Thanks. Uh, wait. You must be tired. Would you like me to help?"

She shook her head. "Thanks, but not right now." Sydney ladled some batter onto the griddle and it sizzled nicely. "We do have a lot to do today before the barbecue though."

"Oh, yeah," Ryan said to Sydney. "I invited another family, friends of Madison."

Sydney raised her eyebrows as she flipped a pancake. "The more the merrier, I guess." She turned over more toasty circles of gold.

My mouth started watering. "Ryan invited one of the other physics professors, Andro. I guess he's going to bring his widowed sister and his nieces."

"A widow? That's sad." Sydney scooped the first pancakes onto a plate and offered them to me. "Madison?"

I pointed at Ryan. "I think sleepyhead here deserves them more than me."

Sydney gave them to him and ladled more batter out.

Ryan doused his pancakes in syrup and attacked them with gusto.

"Actually, Ryan, that reminds me. I wanted to ask you if you found out anything about Armando's death."

"I asked my buddy, Ben, who's with the Boulder PD about it. He looked up the case and there's hardly any information on it."

Sydney tsk-tsked as she lifted a pancake on the griddle to check the underside.

"Really?" I asked. "Any chance we could get a copy of the reports?"

Ryan snorted. "You really don't know how law enforcement works, do you?"

I guess not. "Okay. Thanks, anyway." I continued sipping coffee and eventually some of the stimulant reached my brain. "Thank you for making breakfast, Sydney. I owe you."

Sydney flipped the second batch of cakes. "Madison, can you make it tonight? Ryan was supposed to invite you several days ago, but I'm guessing he forgot."

"Actually, he did invite me last night. It sounds fun." I nodded. "I'll be there."

"Good." Sydney shot a look at Ryan who was finishing off his pancakes. She scooped up her latest batch and handed a plate to me.

"Thanks," I said. "So, what can I do to help with the barbeque? I'd be happy to do whatever."

Sydney beamed and patted her stomach. "Thank you. That would be nice. I'm a little slower than usual." She distributed more batter.

If this was Sydney in slow-mo I'd hate to see her revved up. "Whatever you need."

I took a bite of pancake. Mmm. They were really good, crispy on the outside, fluffy on the inside, and the blueberries were like hot little fruit explosions. "Sydney, these pancakes are great."

"Thanks." She shot another look at Ryan.

He took the hint. "That's my Sydney. Everything she does is perfect."

"Thanks." She turned the latest batch. "So, Ryan, you're on meat detail. You need to put the meat in the marinade, and of course you'll be the grill-master during the party."

I sopped up the last of my syrup. After I shoved in the last bite, I thought: I ate too much.

"Ry, I'd like you to clean off the patio this afternoon and put out the extra tables and chairs. Oh, dear." She put her hand over her mouth. "You need to mow the lawn too."

I raised my hand. "I can mow the lawn."

"Sounds good. I guess Ryan's off the hook for that." Sydney put the latest pancakes on a plate.

I jumped off my stool. "Here. Sydney take my seat. I'm done eating. I can watch the next batch." I glanced at Ryan. "I'm guessing there'll be another batch."

He nodded.

Sydney took my stool and I manned the griddle as we delegated the rest of the barbeque tasks.

Later that afternoon, after I finished my chores, I checked my email. There was nothing there from Ted, so I decided to call him.

"You've reached the voicemail of Dr. Theodore..."

"Dammit." I took a breath and spoke carefully after the beep. "Hey, Ted. How's it going? It's me. I was thinking about coming to visit. How does next weekend sound to you? Call me back when you get this." I was used to talking to him several times a day. Why was he so hard to get a hold of? Long-distance relationships sucked like vacuum through a breached airlock.

The weather for the barbeque was perfect. Ryan fired up the grill as the first guests arrived, a group of young single men from campus police.

I went over and introduced myself. They didn't really seem to want to talk to me. I think they may have been only being polite because I was related to their boss. I guessed I couldn't blame them.

"I hope I'm not interrupting anything, Madison," a man behind me said.

I twirled and accidentally fell into Andro's eyes. "Uh, hi Andro. I'm glad you could come. You brought your family, didn't you?" He looked delicious in jeans and a black t-shirt.

Andro held a casserole dish, and a woman and two little girls stood right next to him. "This is my sister, Yasmin, and her little girls, Maria and Theresa." He pointed at each in turn. The three of them were wearing similar festive black cotton dresses with colorful embroidery.

Yasmin's broad smile lit up her brown eyes. "Thank you so

much for inviting us." She glanced at Andro. "We don't get many invitations from university folks."

"Your dresses are so pretty." I clasped her outstretched hand with both of mine. "That's about to change. It's very nice to meet you, Yasmin." I crouched down in front of two adorable miniature versions of Yasmin. "And it's very nice to meet you girls too, Maria and Theresa."

They beamed.

The younger one, Maria, fussed with the hem of her dress and twisted back and forth.

Theresa, sporting a red ribbon in her hair said, "I'm Theresa." She pointed at her little sister. "She's Maria."

"Thank you for that information, Theresa." I straightened up. "Come on Rivas family, I'd like to introduce you to my cousins Ryan and Sydney."

"Good. I made tamales." Yasmin said.

"Tamales?" I asked. "What are those?"

Andro chuckled. "Heaven. You'll see."

We went off to find Ryan and Sydney, who were talking with another family.

As we approached, Ryan said, "This is the Gonzales family. Roberto is my right-hand man."

"Nice to meet you. I'm Madison. Is this your family?"

"*Si*. This is my wife Garymar and my daughters Pauline and Dorothy and my son Roberto junior." Garymar seemed happy to be chatting with the hosts, but her kids were poised to run around.

I smiled. "It's nice to meet everyone. I wanted to introduce the Rivas family." I waved toward them. "This is Andro, Yasmin, Theresa and Maria. I work with Andro in the physics department."

Theresa, twirling her ribbon, said, "I'm Theresa, she's Maria."

Yasmin giggled. "Yes, dear, that's right." The group laughed.

Theresa looked proud enough to burst.

"It's very nice to meet you," Sydney said. "I'm so glad some of Madison's friends could come." She pointed at the pan in Andro's hands. "Did you bring something for us?"

Yasmin nodded and started to reply but Theresa interrupted her. "Tamales! And I helped."

Sydney grinned and took the casserole from Andro. "Then,

they are extra special. Here, let me take them into the kitchen with the rest of the food."

Yasmin said, "Can I help you, Sydney?"

"Yes. I would be happy to help as well," Garymar said. "We put our dish of enchiladas on the counter."

"Thank you. I'll take all the help I can get," Sydney said, laughing.

As they went inside Yasmin said, "Sydney, is this your first child? When are you due?"

"Two more weeks..." floated back to us on the evening air.

Pauline, who appeared to be about eleven, took control of the smaller kids. "I see a hammock over there," she said.

They all went off to investigate.

That left Ryan, Roberto, Andro and me standing near the grill.

Flames erupted as sizzling fat from the meat hit the coals. The cooking meat smelled delicious, making my mouth water. I was not a very good tofu girl.

"Does anyone want a beer?" I asked.

"Got one." Ryan pointed at his bottle with condensation beading it.

"I'll take one," Andro said.

"Me, too," Roberto said. "But you stay put, Madison, I'll go."

Ryan pointed toward the house. "They're in the coolers there near the door."

"Thanks, Roberto." I said.

As he left on his beer quest, Andro said, "So, did Madison tell you the latest development with her blurry adventure?"

Ryan took a swig of beer. "No. Madison?"

"I'd rather not get into it right now," I said. "Let's talk about it later."

An awkward silence ensued. I pointed at the grill. "The meat smells good."

Ryan nodded. "Thanks. It's my special marinade." He had a special marinade? Nice.

Roberto came back with beers.

Andro nodded as he took the drink. "*Gracias, Senor* Gonzales."

"Yes. Thanks," I said.

"So, we were thinking of hiking a fourteener," Roberto said.

"Have you guys done any?"

I interrupted. "What's a fourteener?"

Ryan grinned at me. "A fourteener is a mountain over fourteen thousand feet. Coloradans make a quest out of hiking as many of them as they can."

Yikes. That sounded even less fun than being Schrödinger's Cat. The guys chatted for a while about hiking while I listened.

Sydney approached. "How's it going over here?" She indicated Yasmin and Garymar. "Thanks to these ladies, things are ship-shape in the kitchen."

"The meat is coming along." Ryan prodded a chicken breast with his spatula.

I piped up. "It smells really good."

"We can eat as soon as the meat's ready." Sydney took me aside. "Madison, can you check on the kids and see what they want to drink?" she said softly.

I checked out the yard and it was as if the kids had each reproduced via fission because there seemed to be twice as many of them. I gulped. "Uh. Sure."

"I better come too," Andro said. "Sometimes Maria gets confused with English."

We turned and walked to the lion's den. Most of the girls were fooling around with the hammock so we went over there first. When we arrived on the scene, the older girls swung Maria high into the air in the hammock. She squealed and it was not in delight. "Stop that," I said as I approached. "You're scaring her."

One of the girls, Theresa, I think, jerked the rope and Maria fell out, headed straight for the metal support beam.

I saw a blur, and then somehow, a blurry Andro appeared under Maria and caught her.

Maria's expression of sheer terror turned into a smile of relief as she looked up at him.

"Good catch," Pauline said.

It was an awesome catch. Impossible, in fact.

"How'd you get here so fast?" one of the other girls asked him.

"That's a very good question," he said.

I knew the answer: quantum mechanics. Andro finally believed.

Andro looked shaky. He set Maria down carefully and glanced at me. “No more playing with the hammock now. We’re getting ready to eat. What do you girls want to drink?”

Much later, after everyone had eaten barbeque and most had gone home for the evening, Ryan, Sydney, the Rivas family and I sat on the patio. Earlier in the afternoon Ryan had strung white twinkly Christmas lights over the patio, and they framed the stars. Theresa and Maria snoozed on the chaise lounge as the grownups chatted. A light wind rustled the leaves of the stately old oak next to us.

Sydney sighed in contentment as the breeze ruffled her hair. “I think that went well.” She rubbed her belly.

Yasmin nodded. “It was lovely. Thanks again for inviting us.”

“Andro, how do you feel after your adventure?” I sipped my beer. “You look normal.”

“I think I’m okay,” Andro said, “considering I may have altered reality.”

Yasmin put her hand up. “Whoa. Altered reality? You better explain that.”

I said, “It all started on Monday when I got hit by a car and didn’t.”

Andro interrupted. “I’ve told her all about that.”

“We’ve all heard about that,” Sydney said, sighing. Or maybe it was the wind?

“Okay,” I said. “The other day my grad student and I did an experiment where we were supposed to get electrons to make a series of lines on a screen, but instead we got them to spell out words and stuff,” I said.

“Yeah, that was really something.” Andro shook his head. “If I hadn’t seen it on the recording for myself...”

“So, I’m guessing you believe it now,” I said, not at all smugly.

Andro glanced at the drowsing Maria. “Apparently.”

“Somebody just tell us what the adventure was,” Sydney said.

“I used quantum mechanics to save Maria,” Andro said quietly, wonder in his voice.

Ryan jerked in his chair. “Does that mean this stuff is spreading?”

Chapter Six

In class Monday morning I started with, "We've been talking about wave-particle duality. Now we're going to discuss some ways of representing waves using math."

Luke had his hand up. "Professor Martin?"

At least he got my name right. "Yes, Luke?"

"I was reading ahead and I wanted to ask you a question." Reading ahead was a new one.

The other students mumbled amongst themselves, and I thought I heard one say suck-up.

"Yes? Go ahead," I said.

"Could you explain the Copenhagen Interpretation?" He grinned widely.

"That's an excellent question. We'll study it in detail later in the semester. For now, as a preview of coming attractions, I'll say quantum mechanics involves possibilities and the Copenhagen Interpretation says a measurement picks one reality out of many possibilities."

Luke's brow wrinkled and he looked like he was trying to understand what I was saying.

Everyone else looked bored.

"I'm sorry if that doesn't make sense right now, but it will in a few weeks," I said.

"Now let's try to represent some quantum mechanical waves using math." I turned to the white board and was soon carried away by equations.

After class, Luke came up to me while I was gathering my papers together. “Hey, Teach.” He smiled cockily.

What was that smile about? “Hi, Luke. Is there something I can help you with?”

He nodded. “I’ve been reading up on quantum mechanics, this Copenhagen Interpretation. It’s fascinating.”

“It is fascinating.” I nodded. “But strictly speaking, the interpretations aren’t part of quantum theory. It’s an interpretation, not a scientific law. There’s some leeway.”

“Was there some leeway when you collapsed the wavefunction and saved yourself from that car Monday morning?” he asked.

I didn’t have an answer for that but was starting to regret the whole conversation. What could a smart troublemaker do with this information?

I was grading homework after class when Andro stuck his head in my office.

“Nice party. Yasmin wanted me to thank you again. So, thanks.” He stepped into the doorway wearing a plum-colored dress shirt and gray slacks. He looked elegant. But then again, I guessed he always looked good. I knew from the barbeque he looked gorgeous in jeans and a t-shirt, for example. I bet he’d even look even better in just jeans, or even nothing at all. Yikes. Don’t go there, Mad.

“You dress so nice for a guy,” I said. After that first day, I had reverted to slacks and blouses for class days and jeans and t-shirts on non-class days. No more panty hose. Or high-heels. Or splitting in two, for that matter.

“Thanks. And thanks for teaching me about collapsing the wavefunction. I hate to think what might have happened to Maria if I hadn’t been there to catch her.” He walked into my office.

“So, no lasting ill-effects from Saturday?” I asked. I really hoped not.

“Nope,” he said. “Why? Did you think there would be?”

We hadn’t seen any lasting effects, but this whole thing hadn’t been going on long enough to know for sure. “I guess not. But there’s no way to tell without further experimentation.”

"Which you're against," he said.

"Right."

My phone rang. I hoped it was Ted.

"Just a sec, Andro." I picked up the phone and only heard breathing.

"Hoo hoo hoo."

"What?" What that supposed to be heavy breathing? It sounded more like Santa Clause's *Ho ho ho*. This had to be some kind of joke. "Hello?"

The person on the other end of the line didn't answer.

"If this is supposed to be a dirty phone call you should slow down that heavy breathing, buddy. You might faint."

"Hee hee hee. No. It's Sydney. My water broke. I can't reach Ryan. He's got all his phones on voicemail. I'm at the hospital. Can you go get him and bring him here?"

"Your water broke!" I jumped out of my chair. "Oh, my God. You're not due for another two weeks."

"Hoo hoo hoo. Hee hee hee. Just find Ryan. I need him. I'm scared. And I don't want him to miss the birth of our first child."

"I promise I'll find Ryan and get him to the hospital ASAP."

"Thanks." She hung up abruptly.

Andro approached my desk. "What's going on?"

"Sydney's in labor and she can't find Ryan. He's not answering his phones."

"I hope she's okay. The first one's the toughest. Can I help with anything?"

My mind raced. The campus police department office was across the street at the stadium. "Can you call us a cab and tell it to meet us at campus police? I'll run over there and try to find him."

"No problem. Good luck. And let me know what happens with the baby." He rushed back to his office.

I grabbed my bag and ran down the stairs, out the door, down the sidewalk and across the street. I pushed open the door of the campus police and tried to talk but I couldn't breathe. "Ryan. I. Need. Ryan. Emergency." I gasped in air. Evidently, I should have trained for emergencies involving running across campus. Well, live and learn.

The officer behind the desk stood up in alarm. He was lanky, with shiny black hair and brown skin. He looked a little familiar. I wondered if I'd met him at the barbeque. "Are you having some kind of attack?" he asked. "Should I call an ambulance?"

"No." Pant, pant. "Emergency."

"What is it? Fire? Murder? Assault? Car accident?" He grabbed his radio. "This is Base."

I shook my head, and tried to catch my breath. "No. Baby. Emergency."

"It is a baby emergency. I repeat, a baby emergency." He put down the radio. "Oh, how awful. A baby was abducted? Lost? In a car accident?"

What was with this guy? "Ugh. No. Ryan's wife is having a baby now. I have to find him right away and get him to the hospital.

The officer smiled. "Aw."

His radio squawked. "Repeat, Base. Did you say baby emergency? What is a baby emergency?"

The officer answered. "All officers in range locate Officer Martin. His wife is having the baby now. He needs to proceed to the hospital ASAP. Officer Martin, do you copy?"

Someone on the radio answered. "Officer Thomas here. Dude, Officer Martin is in the President's office, and said not to disturb him."

"I think that's on the other side of campus." I glanced out the window and could see the taxi was here already. Andro must have lit a fire under them. I turned back to the man at the desk. "I'll take the taxi over to the west side of campus. In the meantime you try to get him out of the meeting."

Me and the taxi driver drove across campus, narrowly avoiding multiple students. When the cab got to the Administration Offices, Ryan was waiting outside impatiently with a younger officer, scanning the street. Before the taxi'd even stopped he grabbed the door handle.

"Let's go," he said as soon as he got in.

Soon, we pulled up to the hospital and Ryan ran in as I paid the driver.

By the time I got inside, there was no sign of him, so I went up to the admissions desk. "Excuse me. Do you have a Sydney Martin here in labor?"

The middle-aged nurse looked at me over her spectacles. "Yes, dear. And you are?"

"Madison Martin."

"Can I see some ID, please?"

I fished out my wallet and showed her my driver's license. "It's not a very good picture."

She chuckled. "I'll say. You look like a convicted felon."

I was anxious to find out how Sydney and the baby were. "Can we move this along?" I put my ID back.

She sighed. "It's a first child, right?"

"Yeah. How'd you know?"

"The new dads and aunts and uncles and grandparents are always so impatient. You know, it'll probably be hours before she delivers."

My face fell. "I think she said she'd been in labor for a while already. Please, can you just tell me which way?"

She gave me directions and I jogged over to the Maternity Ward where I found Ryan standing in the hall.

He was bouncing on the balls of his feet nervously. "I only got to pop my head in and say hi. She's in some special delivery suite she picked out. Now, she's busy with nurses and one of them went to get me a gown." He looked at me, stricken. "Her mother isn't coming for two weeks. She's really upset. We thought her mom would be with us in the delivery room."

Poor Ryan. "Do you want me to go call her mom?" I asked.

"Yes, that's a good idea. And call my mom, too." He touched my arm. "Madison, I don't know if I can handle the delivery on my own. Can you come in?"

"Take a breath, Ryan. Calm down. Childbirth is a perfectly natural process. She's surrounded by trained professionals." I smiled. "I can come in if you guys want me to. You better check with Sydney, though."

Ryan grabbed me in a big bear hug. "Okay, that would be great." Then he held me out at arm's length. "Between you and me," he said softly, "I'm terrified. What if something goes wrong?"

"If something goes wrong all the great doctors here will deal with it. All new dads are terrified," I said. "It goes with the territory."

A bunch of scrubs-wearing folks came out of Sydney's

room as a nurse arrived from down the hall with a pile of green material. “Here, Mr. Martin. Please put these on and you can go in.” She turned to me. “And who do we have here?”

“Hi, I’m Madison. I might go into the delivery room, too.” I hoped I could. I’d helped one of my friends deliver a couple years ago and it was amazing being present when a new person entered the world.

Ryan had taken the green bundle and was looking around. “Where...?”

The nurse sighed. She had short gray hair and her scrubs were rumpled. “Just put them on over your clothes. I wish someone would have told me so I didn’t have to make two trips.”

A balding doctor came up to us as she left. His neatly pressed dress pants peeked out from under his lab coat and his black leather loafers looked very shiny and expensive. “Are you Mr. Martin?”

Ryan nodded, eyes wide, holding his breath.

“Sydney’s okay, right?” I asked. “I’m her cousin, Madison.”

The doctor nodded. “Sure. She’s doing great so far.”

Ryan took a breath.

“Even though she’s not due for two weeks?” I asked.

“Yeah,” he said. “This situation’s pretty common. The due date was just an estimate.”

“I know, but...” Ryan said.

The doctor put his hand on Ryan’s back. “Calm down, son. Sydney’s already eight centimeters dilated. She’s going to need you to be strong for her.”

Ryan nodded. “Yes. I better go change.”

“You do that,” the doctor said. “I’ll see you folks in there.” He turned and looked down the hall. “I need to go check on some other patients. I’ll be back in a bit.”

I stepped away to call the two grandmothers. They were both very excited and wanted updates as soon as possible.

As soon as I went back to Sydney’s room and had thrown on a set of scrubs, Ryan gestured me in.

Sydney’s room was beautiful. The floor and walls were hardwood. The hospital bed was flanked by wood cabinets containing medical equipment. Behind me were a rocking chair and a sofa. Music played softly in the background. Two nurses were fiddling with equipment. My mouth was hanging open. I hadn't even known such pretty hospital rooms existed.

"Madison," Ryan said.

Sydney looked like she was focused on breathing. "Hee hee hee."

"Hi, Sydney," I said. "How are you doing? Are you sure we're in the right place? This doesn't look like a hospital room." This was way fancier than my friend's room.

Ryan nodded. "Yep. Welcome to the Family Birth Center."

"How do you think I'm doing?" Sydney said. "Hoo hoo hoo. Hee hee hee." Her face was red and her hair was in disarray–very unlike her.

"I think you're doing great," I said.

"Did you call our parents?" Ryan asked.

"Yes," I said. "I got a hold of your folks. Sydney, your mom said she'd be on the next plane out here."

Sydney sighed. "Ooh. That was a strong one. I can't wait to see my mom. Madison, you don't have any experience with childbirth, do you?"

I smiled. "As a matter of fact, I do."

"I mean, I know you don't have kids, but..." she said.

I nodded. "One of my best friends in grad school had a baby. I was with her when she delivered."

Sydney looked a little relieved. "Good. It could be any time now. Women in my family have quick deliveries. Ooh. Hoo hoo hoo. Hee hee hee."

"You seem to be doing fabulous, Sydney," I said. "Keep it up." I wasn't about to tell her my friend's labor was over twenty-five hours.

Ryan's watch-clad wrist flew in front of his eyes. "Those contractions are coming close together. Where's that doctor?"

The nurses seemed busy and didn't answer him.

"I can go check." I stepped into the hall and spied the doc way down at the end. I jogged to him. "Doc, her contractions are very strong and close together. You better come check on her."

He looked at his watch. "I doubt she's ready yet."

"She says the women in her family have quick deliveries. Come on." I resisted the urge to grab his arm and drag him down to Sydney's room.

"All right." He sauntered down the hall after me.

When we got inside her room, he lifted up her gown. "Let's take a look here. Hmm. She is fully dilated." He popped his head up.

Sydney's only reply was, "Hoo hoo hoo. Hee hee hee."

One of the nurses, a curvaceous redhead, walked up to the doctor and they discussed something very softly. She led him over to one of the monitors, where the other nurse, a skinny blonde, pointed emphatically at the machine.

"I don't mean to alarm you, but according to the monitors, the baby isn't doing as well as I'd like," the doctor said finally.

Sydney's face turned white and Ryan grabbed her hand.

The blonde nurse frowned. "The baby seems to be in distress."

The doctor studied the baby's vital signs on the monitor and grimaced.

Ryan saw his grimace and glanced at me.

"What's happening?" Sydney demanded. "Can I push? I need to push."

The doctor held up his hand. "No. Do not push."

Sydney closed her eyes.

Ryan rubbed her shoulder gently. "It'll be all right, honey. What's happening, doctor?" he asked.

The doc shook his head. I've seen symptoms like this before. I think the umbilical cord is wrapped around the baby's neck."

Ryan's eyes filled.

"Sydney, we need to do a Caesarean section," the doctor said. "Ryan? Okay? Do you give permission? Nurse, call the O.R."

The nurse stepped to the phone.

Sydney's eyes remained closed. "Oh no," she whispered.

"Yes, of course doctor," Ryan said. "We give permission." He gently stroked his wife's face. "Sydney? Sydney? Are you okay? Answer me." Tears pooled in the corners of his eyes.

She didn't answer.

If there was ever a time to modify reality this was it. No babies were getting hurt on my watch! I closed my eyes pictured a different scenario with the umbilical cord not wrapped around the baby's neck. Everything was totally normal. The baby was safe and healthy. The cord was not around her neck. I focused on the new image willing it to happen. It. Was. Happening. Now.

"Dammit," the doctor said. "This machine's going out. Everything's all blurry."

Sydney opened her eyes and looked at Ryan.

"Sydney?" he said.

She nodded slightly.

"Doctor? The vitals look better," the redheaded nurse said.

The doctor checked out the monitor. "That's odd. Things do seem better all of a sudden."

"It looks good," the blonde nurse said.

"The cord isn't around her neck," the doctor said. "Sydney. It's time to push. Push! Push for all you're worth."

Sydney scrunched up her face.

"I love you, babe," Ryan said. "You can do it."

She pushed, grunting.

The doc leaned down. "The baby is crowning. Here comes the head. Keep pushing. Here come the shoulders. I've got her. She's a beautiful baby girl." He grasped the baby. "Stop pushing."

Sydney collapsed back on the bed. "Is she okay?"

"She looks good," the doctor said.

"Good job, Sydney." Ryan rubbed her shoulders. "You did it."

It was a tiny, goopy, perfect person. "Congratulations, Sydney and Ryan!" The baby was beautiful. She looked so little and helpless and red. She made me want to scoop her in my arms and take care of her. My eyes threatened to overflow. "Oh, Sydney. She's beautiful," I whispered.

It was amazing to behold a brand new person.

"Yes," the doctor said. "I'm guessing the Apgar will be high."

Sydney smiled as tears streamed out of the corners of her eyes and ran down the sides of her face. "Thank God."

The doctor lifted up the baby. "Dad, do you want to cut the cord?"

Ryan nodded as he took a step toward the doctor and child.

He blinked back tears as he carefully cut the cord. "Hello there, Daughter." Ryan's voice was hoarse. "Welcome, little Emily. We promise to love you and take care of you forever."

The baby started crying as she was handed to the redheaded

nurse.

"Is she all right?" Ryan asked the nurse, wiping his eyes.

The baby nurse said, "She's perfect. Just wait a moment and you can hold her for mom."

The doc studied Sydney. "You're doing great. Almost done. You just need to birth the placenta."

Sydney nodded.

Ryan's mouth fell. "My wife's going to be okay, isn't she?"

"Yes, she'll be fine," the doctor said. "We're almost done."

"The doctor said she was fine, Ryan," I said. "Don't worry. And you have a new daughter. How wonderful." Maybe I should start thinking about getting my own bundle of joy.

Ryan smiled limply and inhaled. "That was weird how the baby was in distress and then she wasn't." He turned to look at me for a second. "Don't you think?"

"Uh." I was kind of proud of myself, but wasn't about to say anything. Had I collapsed the wavefunction to save little Emily? Maybe. Maybe not. I decided all that was important was that Emily was all right.

The baby nurse approached us, cradling beautiful little Emily. "Ryan, do you want to hold your daughter?" she asked.

"Definitely," Ryan said. He gingerly took Emily in his arms, and put his face right in front of hers. "Hi, honey."

Sydney and the doctor finished up.

The doctor straightened and said, "Okay, we're done. Great job, Sydney." He motioned to Ryan. "Why don't you bring Emily to her mom?"

Sydney sat up with help from one of the nurses. "Come here, Emily honey." She held out her arms. "Come to Mama."

Ryan placed Emily gently in Sydney's embrace. "Emily this is your mommy, the best mommy in the world." His voice was hoarse again. "The best woman in the world." Ryan put his arm around Sydney as she cradled Emily. They both bent over Emily, studying her, entranced.

I felt myself tearing up again. "I'm going to leave you guys alone for a little while. I'll call the grandmas." I also had to call Ted and share this amazing experience with him.

They barely noticed as I stepped out of the room, which was as it should be.

I went down the hall to the waiting room, plunked down on a couch, got out my cell and called the grandmas. They both answered immediately and seemed overjoyed.

Then, I called Ted.

He answered the phone. Yay.

"Hi, Ted. It's me," I said. "Guess what? Sydney had her baby already." I was so excited, I was practically shouting.

"Madison?" he asked.

"Yes. Isn't that great? And the baby is perfect. You should see her adorable little fingers and toes and nose. You should come out to visit. What about next weekend?" I was dying to see him. And who wouldn't want to meet such an adorable baby?

"Next weekend isn't good for me." He paused. "But congratulate your cousins for me."

"Okay." I nodded. "What about I come out there for a visit?"

"I have work to do," he said. "I don't think it's a good idea."

How could he say that? "But, I love you. I really miss you, Ted." My voice broke. "Don't you miss me?"

"Sure. Of course." He sounded impatient, and not at all like he missed me.

"You don't sound very sincere," I said.

"Give me a break, Madison. I'm at work. I'm busy. I don't have time to chit-chat."

"Chit-chat." My voice rose like the space shuttle taking off.

"What are you getting so emotional for?" he asked. "It's not like you."

"Excuse me for being emotional after I've just witnessed a miracle."

"Whatever. I have to go." He hung up.

I stared in disbelief at my phone. What was his problem? How could he not be more excited about the baby? I took a deep breath. Whatever it was, it was his problem. I wasn't going to let it ruin the wonder of Emily's birth. I forced Ted out of my mind.

My fourth call was to Andro.

He answered on the first ring. "Hello? Madison? Is that you? What's happening with the baby?" He stopped to take a breath.

"They had a girl," I said. "It was amazing. Her name is Emily and she's adorable."

"That's awesome!" He was yelling into the phone.

Now that was an appropriate response to a new baby. Why couldn't Ted be more like Andro?

Chapter Seven

Tuesday morning I was happy to see Andro in his office. After the experience with Emily, my resolved moratorium on wavefunction collapse experiments was wavering and I needed to talk. Ted hadn't given me a chance yesterday, and I wasn't about to intrude on Sydney and Ryan's new-baby glow.

I rushed right into his office without an invitation. "*Hola*." It was nice to see a friendly face.

He looked up from the papers he was grading and smiled. "*Hola*, yourself. Being a first cousin once removed seems to agree with you." Was that what I was?

I beamed. "I'm just thinking of myself as Emily's cousin. She's wonderful."

He graciously waved at his plush guest chair. "Have a seat. How's everyone doing?"

I sat. "Very well. I'll tell them you asked about them." I leaned forward. "Andro, I told you about Emily's birth yesterday, but what I didn't tell you is I think I moved her umbilical cord from around her neck by collapsing the wavefunction."

He put down his red pen. "If that's true, that's awesome. But what happened to your rule against collapsing the wavefunction?"

"I couldn't just let a defenseless baby die." I took a breath to calm down. "Let's just say, recent events have caused me to revisit the issue."

"Now you sound like a politician." He smiled. "What's that supposed to mean?"

"It means maybe I was too hasty. Maybe some good can come of it. Maybe we should do some experiments."

He nodded. "Maybe." Was he thinking about his niece Maria?

"How many times did we successfully collapse the wavefunction?" I asked. That really was a mouthful. Maybe we needed to come up with a shorter term for the phenomenon?

"I saved Maria," he said.

"Yes. That was excellent." I wracked my brain, trying to recall any other instances of wavefunction collapse. "Alyssa and I did it with the double-slit experiment. It might have worked with the traffic light and Frisbee players at lunchtime the other day."

He frowned. "You mean when we went out to Burritos and Beers? I don't recall anything out of the ordinary."

"Okay, those last ones were probably wishful thinking. It definitely didn't work with the girl on the phone when we were walking back from lunch or with the boy on the bike."

"Well, we agree on something," Andro said with a small smile.

"But I really think I saved Emily yesterday," I said. "And you saved Maria at the barbeque. Maybe it's too important to let it go. If we can save people's lives, we need to learn more about it."

He nodded. "You may be right. Don't forget you saved yourself from that car Monday, too."

I shuddered. "Don't remind me. I still have trouble crossing that street."

"We do need to learn more, if it can be used to help people," he said.

"But, studying collapsing the wavefunction might be dangerous," I said. "Are you ready for that? In light of your family responsibilities," I pointed at his family portrait, "maybe you shouldn't do it."

"Dangerous?" he asked. "Do you really think so?"

"You got blurry when you saved Maria. And Alyssa got a little fuzzy when she did the electron double-slit experiment. I don't know what blurriness means, but I don't think it's good." Actually, it was pretty scary.

He stared at Yasmin's beautiful face smiling at him from the photo. "Maybe I could assist you when you do experiments? That shouldn't be too dangerous, should it?"

"I don't know." I shook my head. "That's the problem. We don't know much of anything. Hence the need for studying."

We were lost in thought for a few moments. Was it

dangerous? Had I ever gotten blurry? Finally, I said, “We need to set up a series of organized experiments so we can test when a person can collapse the wavefunction and when they can’t and what the effects are.”

He nodded. “That sounds like a good idea. We should try to be methodical and quantitative if possible.”

“But if we investigate collapsing the wavefunction, you have to promise me you won’t tell Alyssa, okay? I can’t put a student in danger.” That sparked a memory. Oh, no. I forgot about a meeting with Alyssa yesterday. Shoot.

“If we do this?” A ghost of a grin flitted across Andro’s face. “Are you still on the fence?”

I shrugged. “I guess not.”

“Then I guess I won’t tell Alyssa,” he said.

“Can you help me experiment tomorrow afternoon?” I asked.

He glanced at his calendar and nodded. “That should work.”

“Maybe we should come up with another term for it, too,” I said. “Collapsing the wavefunction is too long.”

“You’re not wrong,” he said. “Do you have any ideas?”

“Quantum...” My imagination petered out.

“Quantum collapse,” he said.

“Not bad,” I said. “What about q-collapse? Or, q-lapse? It’s short and catchy.”

He nodded and glanced at his phone. “Sorry, Madison. I have to go to class.” He stood up. “So?”

“So, what?”

“So go to your own office.” He shooed me out. “And good job with the new name. Q-lapse sounds great. Simple.”

Back in my office, I called Alyssa to apologize for missing the meeting yesterday, but it went straight to voicemail.

Then, I chewed on the end of a pencil as I considered calling Ted. But, after his comments yesterday, I thought he should be calling me to apologize, so I decided against it.

I pulled out a pad of paper and started jotting notes for q-lapsing experiments. We should start by duplicating the electron double-slit results we got earlier, but with two cameras: one on the detection screen and one on the experimenter. It would be a good idea to set up some kind of instantaneous power cutoff in case things got dicey.

"I said, there you are, Professor Martin," a woman said from the hall.

I jumped into the exosphere, managing to knock a bunch of papers from my desk onto the floor.

It was Alyssa and she didn't look happy.

"Hi, Alyssa. I'm sorry I missed our appointment yesterday," I said right away.

The corners of her mouth continued to point toward the earth's molten core.

"I left you a voicemail. Just a sec." I leaned over to pick up the papers which were all from my *Things To Do* pile. It was a very large pile. I piled them back on the desk. "I have a good excuse. My cousins Ryan and Sydney had their baby. It was two weeks early and there was some excitement, but it all turned out well."

"Ooh, a baby?" she cooed. "That is a good excuse. That's awesome. Do you have any pictures?" Smiling, she pulled a chair up to my desk.

I glanced at my phone. Darn. I should have taken some pictures. "Not yet. I haven't had a chance to take any. But her name's Emily and she's adorable." I realized I didn't know anything about Alyssa's personal life. "Do you have kids?"

She pulled her chair closer to my desk. "No I don't have any kids yet. But I definitely want to have some. Do you have any?"

"No." I shook my head, debating if I should tell her my developing theory based on recent events with Ted: being a physicist interfered with being a mom. I decided against it. Why discourage her?

"I'm between boyfriends right now." She giggled. "But yesterday I met the cutest guy. He's tall, dark and handsome. He has the most charming smile, and he's really smart. We had the best discussion about the Copenhagen Interpretation, even though he's only an undergrad."

An undergrad interested in the Copenhagen Interpretation? Uh oh. I had a feeling I knew exactly who she met yesterday. But, I said, "That sounds nice. Where did you meet this guy?"

"I met him here, outside your office."

Yep. It had to be Luke. "You didn't by chance tell him about the quantum experiments we've been doing, did you?" Please, not.

She nodded. "I couldn't help myself. He seemed so interested in what I had to say, and when he smiled at me I just melted." She grinned.

"I think it would be better if you didn't discuss this stuff any more, okay?"

"But it's so neat." She pursed her lips.

"But remember, you got blurry." I pointed at her. "I don't think it's safe."

She sighed. "Oh, all right."

"Let's talk about those physics papers you read."

Wednesday morning I got to my quantum mechanics class early. I was impatient to start, but the students trickled in slowly, seemingly oblivious to my wishes.

They sported jeans or shorts, flip-flops or tennis shoes, and t-shirts. Except Pankaj, who had on pressed khakis and oxford shirt, buttoned all the way, and leather dress shoes. Griffin had on his *Byte Me* t-shirt again which I think he wore all last week. I really hoped he washed it. Luke sported a shirt that said *Geekfest 2014*, whatever that was. He gave me a cocky, challenging, grin.

I didn't take the bait and just smiled politely back.

It was one minute after nine o'clock, time to start class. "Now we're going to get into some more ways of representing waves using math," I said. "First, the Schrödinger Equation."

"Is that Schrödinger thing related to Schrödinger's Dog?" Pankaj asked.

I nodded. "Yes, if you mean Schrödinger's Cat. Same guy." I looked out at their sea of faces. They seemed interested. Excellent. "What the heck, let's talk about Schrödinger's Cat."

They smiled.

"It's actually related to the Copenhagen Interpretation which I briefly touched on last time. Schrödinger's Cat is a thought experiment. The idea is there's a cat in a big box with a device. If a subatomic particle in the device decays, the cat dies. If the particle doesn't decay, the cat lives."

The students were still smiling. They'd probably all heard this before or were just glad I'd strayed from the syllabus.

"Since the device has a subatomic mechanism it has to obey

quantum mechanics and be described by a combination of all the possibilities. Thus, according to quantum mechanics, all the possibilities exist and the cat is both dead and alive."

A couple of the kids snorted.

"It isn't until we open the chamber and look that we essentially pick one possibility and know if the cat is dead or alive." I smiled. "We collapse the wavefunction." I resisted the urge to tell them about my new word: q-lapse.

The students fidgeted like they thought the thought experiment was unbelievable.

"Speaking of dead or alive, that reminds me, I have your homework." I got their graded homework from last week out of my bag and started passing it out.

At noon-ish on Wednesday, Andro saw me working in the hall on the electron double-slit equipment and asked me if I wanted to go get a bite with him. That sounded heavenly. I really wanted to, but realized that wouldn't be fair to Ted, so I said no.

He seemed disappointed, but went to lunch on his own.

My strong reaction to his lunch proposition had finally clued me in to the fact that I was attracted to him. A lot. So, I was a little slow when it comes to interpersonal relations. It's balanced out by the fact that I'm super fast when it comes to physics. Right? That was my story, anyway, and I was sticking to it.

I'd set up the equipment the way we had it last week: electron gun with the condenser lens, aperture, objective lens, another aperture, intermediate lens, electron biprism, and the two-dimensional detection apparatus. I also set up a digital video camera to capture the detection screen, and a second camera to capture the person standing near the detection screen.

By one o'clock I was raring to work on the experiment when Andro came back. Professionally, I was glad to see him, but personally, I was not excited to see him. Yeah, right.

"*Hola*, Madison," he said with a big grin, his blue eyes practically twinkling.

"*Hola*, Andro." I suppressed an answering grin. Mad, think of Ted. Be professional. "So, I thought maybe you could man this camera here that's recording the experimenter? And if anything weird happens, you could pull this power cord, okay?"

He nodded. "I can handle that. Are you ready?"

"Yep. Let's roll." I turned on the equipment as he stepped over to the camera and examined its tiny screen.

Some out-of-focus dots appeared on the detector screen.

He straightened up. "This is riveting."

I grinned. "Patience."

Some more blurry dots appeared on the screen.

"So far, no weirdness detected over here. You look normal." He glanced at me over the top of the camera. "Those jeans are flattering, by the way."

I turned away so he wouldn't see me blush. "Thanks." What was wrong with me? I had a boyfriend and it wasn't Andro. "I have to concentrate. So maybe it'd be better if we didn't chat."

"Yes, ma'am." In my peripheral vision, I saw him grin and salute.

A fuzzy series of lines was developing on the detection screen. "Good. That's the standard result. That's what I was going for." I reset the detection screen. "Now let's try something else."

I stared at the screen, concentrating on Q-lapsing to make two blobs.

Instead, I got a series of very hazy lines−the interference pattern again. "Frip!"

Andro looked over the top of the camera. "What, may I ask, is a frip?"

I smiled weakly at him. "You know what a frip is. Or at least you can guess. It's not good." Why wasn't it working? "What are you thinking?"

"Uh." He gave me a look that said he was thinking about my jeans again.

I was getting flustered. "I mean, are you thinking I can't change the pattern?"

"I guess I wasn't thinking you could change the pattern."

"The experiment isn't working, is it?" I waved my hand around.

"I guess we're not getting the results you wanted." He took a step away from the camera.

He was totally distracting me. I said, "Maybe you should take a break and I'll try it on my own for a while. When I get results I'll come get you before I do anything really weird, okay?"

He shrugged. "Okay." He walked over to his office.

"Please shut your office door," I said, totally not checking out his fine derrière.

I tried the experiment again but it was no good. I couldn't concentrate. I kept thinking about that jeans-look he gave me. What might have happened if I wasn't involved with Ted? I felt very confused. I went in my office, closed the door, and sat down at my desk.

After a few minutes, I heard Andro's office door open and his footsteps as he walked over to my office and knocked.

What did he want now? "Come in," I said.

He opened the door. "Are you giving up already?"

I forced a smile. "Just taking a break." I pointed at my large to-do pile. "Maybe you could help me with the experiment tomorrow morning?"

Still gripping the doorknob, he said, "I didn't mess it up, did I? I was sort of distracted."

"No. You were great, er, I mean helpful and professional. I appreciate your help. How about tomorrow?"

"Sure." He glanced at the floor. "Madison."

"Yes?" I asked.

He looked like he wanted to ask me something. He opened his mouth and then closed it. "Nothing. I'll see you in the morning." He left, closing the door behind him.

After he'd gone, I exhaled. Get a frippin' grip, Madison. Did I have some kind of hormone imbalance? I stared at the wall, imagining Andro on the other side, sitting at his desk. Was he imagining me sitting at my desk? If only there was some way we could be together.

As I stared at the wall, it began to get fuzzy. I slowly got out of my chair and walked over to it. Up close, it definitely appeared hazy, not at all like cinderblock. It resembled a wall of fog. Although, where fog would come from inside the physics building, I did not know.

"Madison? Are you seeing what I'm seeing?" he asked through the fuzz.

I nodded and reached my fingertips out to touch the former wall. "Yeah." As I did so, I realized my fingers were blurry and out-of-focus. I'd just glanced down at the rest of me, when I distinctly heard "*Mi Dios*" coming from right in front of me.

When I looked up again, there was Andro, framed by a brand-new door-sized hole in the wall.

Chapter Eight

"What happened to the wall?" I stared at Andro through the new doorway between our offices. "Did we q-lapse? At least you don't look blurry." Glancing down at myself, I didn't appear to be blurry anymore, either. I did have a huge headache, however. Ugh.

"That's all you have to say?" he said at a rather loud volume.

"Don't yell at me. I guess we q-lapsed. How do you feel? Are you okay?" I gingerly touched an edge of the opening. It was spongy, totally unlike cinder block. My fingertip pressed against the substance and bounced back.

"I don't appreciate being experimented on." He seemed agitated.

"I didn't do anything to you. And I don't think I could do this," I pointed at the hole, "without your help. What were you just thinking?"

"None of your business!"

I was trying to be understanding. He was probably just freaked out, but enough was enough. "I said, quit yelling at me!"

"What am I supposed to do about this huge hole in my office?"

"I guess you can just q-lapse and fix it." I turned and stormed out to get some coffee. Maybe it would help with my headache.

When I got back, Andro had pushed a humongous bookshelf in front of the hole. That was just as well. I didn't want to deal with him when he was in such a snit.

Truth be told, I was pretty confused about what was going on with Andro and me. There was a palpable spark between us earlier. What did that mean for Ted and me? And I really needed to discuss this q-lapsing stuff with an expert. So I decided to call Ted.

"You've reached the voicemail of Dr. Theodore..."

"Dammit. Fripping Frip!" After a second, I decided I was going to pay hard-to-get-ahold-of Theodore a visit this weekend. I started looking on the Internet for low airfares.

The next morning I got into the office bright and early armed with an enorme coffee. I'd gotten virtually no sleep the night before because Sydney, Ryan and Emily had come home from the hospital. Emily was adorable, but she had quite a set of lungs on her, and the transition from the hospital was traumatic if her crying was any indication. On the bright side, we'd gotten lots of photos.

At work, I'd planned to do a series of experiments with the double-slit apparatus and the two digital cameras. And I was determined to do them with or without Andro. He did not appear to be around. So, I tried to set up the second camera to point at me. This involved a lot of running back and forth to check the image in the second camera and guessing where I'd been standing.

About then Alyssa showed up.

"Did we have an appointment?" I asked. I hadn't forgotten another one, had I?

"No. I just thought I'd take a chance and see if you were in." She pointed at the equipment. "I thought you took this down because it was too dangerous."

"Yes." She'd caught me red-handed, or maybe it was fuzzy-handed. I didn't know what to say.

"So?" she said. "Why did you set it up again?"

"That is a good question," I finally said. "There have been some developments which seem to indicate this area of inquiry might be too important to ignore."

She grinned eagerly. "That sounds interesting. What developments?"

I really didn't want to put her in danger. She was my responsibility. "I'd rather not get into it right now. I don't have enough information."

"Hence the experiments?"

I nodded. "Right. Hence the experiments."

"So can I help?" She paused to smile winningly. "Please. I

promise I won't break anything."

"Uh." I took a gulp of coffee to stall for time. Surely, she wouldn't be in danger if she just manned the second camera? And were we absolutely sure blurriness connoted danger? Not absolutely.

"Professor Martin, I'm starting to get the idea that you're treating me like a kid. I'm not a kid." She frowned. "I'm twenty-four years old." Her vocal volume was increasing linearly, or maybe exponentially. What was it about someone yelling at you, or even almost yelling, that made a person want to yell back?

Be calm, Mad. "I know you're not a kid. I apologize." I paused. "It would help me out a lot if you could use this camera to record me as I do the experiment." I had a brainstorm. "Actually, why don't you take it way down to the end of the hall and use the zoom? That should be safe."

She agreed and carried the camera and tripod to the end of the hall, only dropping it once. "I don't think it broke."

"Focus in on me," I yelled down to her.

She nodded. "I got you. Go ahead," she yelled back.

I ran the experiment and got the standard interference pattern. As far as I could tell, I wasn't blurry at all.

I turned off the equipment for a moment and moseyed down to Alyssa. "So how does it look?"

"Those jeans are kind of tight for a professor," she said. They were the same jeans I'd worn yesterday.

I suppressed a sigh of exasperation. "I meant did I get blurry?"

She shook her head. "Not that I noticed."

"Okay. Now I'll try to make one big blob. Try to keep focused on my hands and face." I walked back down to the apparatus and flipped it on. I concentrated on q-lapsing and making the stream of electrons hit the screen in the same place. It had to work. If it didn't that would mean I didn't understand what was going on. Or, maybe I was just crazy. My stomach roiled with nerves.

It worked. Unfortunately, I was so busy concentrating on the electrons, I forgot to observe if I was getting blurry.

I rushed back down to her. "So? Anything weird happen this time?"

She stared at the tiny screen. "I can't tell. Your fingertips might be a teeny bit blurry, here."

"Shoot." Squinting at the miniscule image was starting to give me a headache. "I guess you're going to have to move closer. Come on."

We tried it again, with Alyssa much closer and the camera pointing at my hands. Now I had the added worry that I was putting her in danger. I was even more of a nervous wreck.

Eventually I got the unusual pattern and my hands did seem to be slightly blurry. But what did it mean?

"Let me try the first pattern again," I said. "And then I'll do something weird on screen like *Hola*."

With the standard interference pattern she said, "Normal. You look normal."

The screen refreshed and I q-lapsed to form the word *Hola* on the screen. It had to work.

She drew in a breath. "I think I might see something unusual."

Quickly I looked down at my hands. For a split-second I thought I saw something weird. When I looked back at the detection screen however, *Hola* was gone. The screen had refreshed.

She was rewinding. "I think we got something on the camera."

Again, we squinted into the tiny screen. I could barely make it out. "This is ridiculous. Come on in my office and let's try to upload the movie onto my computer so we have a decent-sized image to work with." I grabbed the camera off the tripod.

When she followed me into my office, she gasped. "What happened here?" She pointed at the back of Andro's bookcase, visible through the large gaping hole.

"Oh, that." In the excitement of the experiment I had totally forgotten about the huge hole in my wall. "I'd rather not say."

"Is this one of the interesting developments?" She walked over to the wall and carefully touched the edge of the hole. "Did you do this by collapsing the wavefunction?"

"Uh." I reached for my coffee, but the cup was empty.

She added, "I bet you did. Will you show me how?"

"No. Not now. I'm getting a headache, Alyssa. Can we just focus on the recording of the experiment right now?"

She turned around to face me, putting her hands on her hips.

"Are you treating me like a kid again?"

I could tell she was very upset, but I didn't know what to do about it. "I apologize for whatever you want. Actually, I'm not feeling very well right now. Can we continue this discussion later?" What was with all my headaches lately?

"Whatever." She turned on her heel and stomped out.

"What a crappy week," I said to the empty office as I lay down on my old but comfy couch. A little get-away this weekend would be the perfect pick-me-up.

On Friday promptly at nine o'clock I said, "Today we're going to continue to discuss quantum mechanical waves and review chapters one and two."

My students grumbled.

"Because of particle-wave duality, quantum mechanics says we represent things as waves," I said. "This means they have wavelengths and a mathematical representation called a wavefunction."

The students mumbled amongst themselves. Hopefully it was because this all sounded familiar to them.

"These wavefunctions describe possibilities," I said. "Recall, everything is just possibilities in quantum mechanics until it becomes a certainty."

The students fidgeted.

"Yes? Does anyone have a question? A comment?" I glanced at Luke, but he was playing it cool. He just flashed me a cocky grin.

"I am thinking I understand. But this quantum mechanics is definitely freaky," Pankaj said.

I nodded. "I totally agree." And he only knew the tip of the iceberg.

By dinnertime Friday evening, I'd flown over eight hundred miles and my arms weren't tired at all. As the taxi pulled up in front of my former St. Louis driveway I was practically giddy with excitement. Ted was going to be so surprised and excited to see me. I was excited to see him. This was going to be fun. How could I have been confused about my feelings for him?

I carefully unlocked our front door. I could hear the television on in the family room. Perfect. I left my stuff near the door and crept down the tile hallway toward the sounds, passing the hole in the drywall Ted accidentally made with the corner of his giant fish tank when we moved in. As I stepped into the family room, the first thing I noticed was the back of the couch and a car commercial on his huge TV.

As I walked toward the TV, the second thing I noticed was a bottle of red wine on the wooden coffee table and two wine glasses. That was weird. Since when did Ted and his buddies drink wine? For that matter, since when did we have wine glasses?

The third thing I noticed was Ted lying on top of someone on our chenille sectional sofa.

Kissing.

"Ted," I squeaked. What are you doing?"

He lifted up his head and leaned away from his conquest.

It was Jessica, the grad student from our lab. Her blouse was open, showing off her lacy black bra with Ted's hand beneath it.

The blood drained from my head. This couldn't be happening.

"Madison!" Ted pulled his hand away from Jessica's breast and quickly stood up. "What the hell are you doing here?"

Jessica's face turned bright red and she feverishly tried to button her blouse. "Dr. Martin, I didn't know you were coming over. I'm so sorry."

I felt like I was going to faint and reached out to hold on to the couch. "I said I might come out for a visit."

"And I said that wasn't a good idea," Ted said.

Jessica succeeded in buttoning her blouse and she jumped up from the couch just as I sank down onto it.

"You told me you broke up," she said to Ted.

I couldn't believe it. The second my back was turned he hooked up with someone else. I bet Andro would never do that. But then again, he was a guy. Maybe he would.

"I better let you guys talk," Jessica stammered. "Bye." She ran for the front door.

Ted sat down on the matching chenille chair. "I told you not to come."

I did not appreciate being told what to do. And Ted knew that. "Excuse me?" I said, my voice as hard as industrial diamond.

I slowly stood up and stepped over to him. “What the hell was going on here?” I jabbed my finger at his chest. “We were together three years. This is bullshit. I don’t deserve to be cheated on.”

He leaned away from me. “I figured we were broken up.”

“Did we say we were broken up?” I didn’t think I’d ever been so mad at someone.

“No,” he said. “But you moved away. You left me.”

I stomped my feet on the beige carpeting. The resulting noise was disappointingly muffled. “You asshole. We went over this. I didn’t leave you.” I clenched my fists. “At least not then. But I’m leaving you now!”

I shook with rage. I’d never been so angry. All I could think was I wanted to get away from him as quickly as possible.

For some reason, then the room seemed to fill with mist.

And then the room was gone.

Chapter Nine

Where the hell was I? I had no idea. I had been yelling at Ted in my former family room, but I definitely wasn't there now. I couldn't feel the floor beneath my feet. Shit, I couldn't even feel my feet. My anger was replaced by fear.

It looked like I was in some kind of nondescript fog, but couldn't feel it on my skin. Apparently I had no skin. That couldn't be good.

Come to think of it, I couldn't smell or hear anything either. I must've had a head though because I had a universe-sized headache. Was I dying? I almost hoped it was true, so I'd be released from the pain.

I tried to focus on something, anything, but it was no good. Eventually, I was exhausted from trying, and I think I passed out.

When I came to, it seemed like a lot of time had passed. I still couldn't see anything but white fuzzy blurriness. Was something wrong with my eyes?

On the bright side, my headache was slightly less hellacious.

At some point, I passed out again.

I had no way of knowing how long I was in that fuzzy limbo, but my head felt a little better every time I came to.

And then I was lying on my office couch. It was night, but which night? Friday night? Saturday night? Some night in the year 2100? 1900? For a second I considered that I'd dreamt the whole trip to visit Ted. But the memories were too vivid and it was all too horrible, so sadly I had to reject that hypothesis as wishful thinking. I got up and flipped on my office light. I checked the time and date on my computer to discover I'd been in no-man's-land about fifty-one hours.

Thank God I'd made it back from wherever it was. Glancing down, I also thanked God I appeared to be in one non-blurry piece. Shaky, I sank down into my desk chair.

Where had I been? And how did I get back here? If I hadn't already had so many bizarre experiences, I might think I was losing my mind. But I wasn't losing my mind. It had to be quantum mechanics that was responsible for this latest misadventure. Definitely. I took a deep breath and leaned back in my chair.

I noticed Andro had moved his bookcase away from the gaping hole in the wall. I wondered why.

Looking over my messy desk, I realized I was also relieved I hadn't missed any class, and so wouldn't lose my new job. This stuff would be even harder to figure out from the unemployment line.

Shoot. My phone and purse must still be at Ted's. I picked up the landline to call home, and Ryan answered on the first ring.

"Martin residence, this is Ryan," he said with a hopeful lilt to his voice.

I could just picture him pushing his glasses up the bridge of his nose. "Hi, Ryan. It's Madison. I need a favor. Can you pick me up at–"

"Madison? Where have you been?" he demanded.

What was he all worked up about? "I told you I was going to Ted's for the weekend."

"Ted called Friday night and said you got all fuzzy and then disappeared right in front of his eyes. He was totally freaked out."

"Good. It serves him right." The jerk. I forced the image of him lying on Jessica out of my mind.

"If he'd been talking about anyone but you, I'd say he was crazy," he continued. "But since it was you, we were worried. We've been looking all over for you."

"Take a breath, Ry," I said. "I'm sorry I worried you guys. Can you come pick me up at the south side of the physics building?"

"The physics building? What are you doing there?"

"Please, just come. I feel like crap and I want to go to bed."

"Okay. I'm leaving now," he said.

I emailed Ted a terse note asking him to ship my stuff to the physics department office ASAP.

Downstairs on the street, I jumped in Ryan's Prius as soon as he showed up. "Thanks." I didn't think I'd ever been so glad to see someone in my life. Whatever had just happened to me was well and truly over. I hugged him. I felt so much safer and more real with him by my side. I may have teared up a bit.

"Are you okay?" He frowned in concern.

I nodded half-heartedly. "I think so."

"Where have you been?"

"I'm not really sure. It was like a misty limbo. I think I collapsed the wavefunction to get away from Ted, but then I didn't end up anywhere else. I just now woke up on my office couch." We were already at the entrance to our neighborhood. I sighed. "He was cheating on me with our grad student."

"The jerk. I never liked him," Ryan said.

I did.

"Wait. What was that about limbo?" he asked. "Maybe I should take you to the hospital?" He glanced at me.

"No. I don't think that would be a good idea." I looked at him. "What would they say? Don't you think they'd think I had a mental problem?"

"Yeah." He nodded. "If you told them about some weird misty limbo, they would." He was quiet for a moment. "Well, crap. I don't know what to make of all this."

"Me neither."

"You have to call Ted and let him know you weren't blown up or something."

I had another flashback of Ted lying on Jessica, and shuddered. "I can't. But I emailed him to send me my stuff so he knows I'm alive."

He looked at me. "You know, you are my most difficult cousin."

I mustered up a smile for that one. "I'm practically your only cousin. And you are my favorite cousin."

He nodded. "Now, that's what I want to hear. You are one smart lady." He grinned. "And I'm telling my bros you said that."

He pulled the car into the driveway. "How about Andro?"

I startled. "What about him? He's not my favorite cousin. Or, are you telling him you're my favorite cousin?"

"I called him when we were looking for you," he said.

"Why would you think I was with Andro?" Did Ryan know I was attracted to Andro?

"We called everyone we could think of. He let me into your office through that huge hole in the wall. We're going to have a discussion about destroying university property at some point, by the way." We got out of the car.

I still wasn't a hundred percent. "What was the question?" I asked.

"How about Andro? Can you call him and tell him you're okay?"

"Yeah." I didn't have the energy to nod.

"Home sweet home," he said, unlocking the front door. "Please be quiet. I think everyone's asleep."

"Even Emily?" I whispered.

He dipped his head. "Yep," he whispered.

"Awesome."

My conversation with Andro was short and to the point.

"Rivas residence," he said.

"Hi, Andro. It's Madison. I'm back safe and sound."

"Good," he said. "See you tomorrow."

"Is that it?" I asked.

"I was asleep," he said. "It's, like, midnight on Sunday night."

"It's ten-thirty," I said.

He didn't say anything in response.

"I'm sorry I woke you," I said.

"I'm glad you're safe and sound," he said with a smile in his voice.

"Thanks," I said. "See you tomorrow."

Monday morning Ryan and Sydney were too engrossed in Emily to grill me about my weekend. It was just as well. I had time to get an enorme coffee on my way to class. So, I was a caffeine addict–it wasn't a problem.

When I got into my classroom, most of the students were already there.

Luke came up to me. "So, Alyssa Long." He crossed his arms and leaned against the front table, grinning.

I raised my eyebrows at him.

"She's your student, huh?" he said.

"Yes." I had no idea where this conversation was going, but I had a bed feeling.

"She's been teaching me a lot of interesting stuff." His smile was as wide as the Rockies. "Among other things, she told me about that hole in your office wall. Can I come see it?"

I wanted to tell him he'd better not break Alyssa's heart, and it wasn't right to use someone to get information. But it wasn't my business who he, or Alyssa, for that matter, dated. And he was basically a kid who I had to give the benefit of the doubt, right? My instincts were telling me otherwise however. "I'm glad you're so interested in physics, Luke. You're free to come to my office hours, if you like. But, please take your seat now. It's time for class to start."

He went back to his desk.

I cleared my throat. "Today, we're going to look at some equations with wavefunctions."

I kept my eye on Luke the rest of the class, but he didn't act up at all. Maybe my instincts were off base.

Or maybe not.

After class I got to work taking down the double-slit experiment and putting the equipment back in the storeroom. After my limbo adventure I'd decided the q-lapsing stuff was way too dangerous to mess around with again. I didn't want Andro or Alyssa to end up in some weird limbo.

I came back from the storeroom and Andro's office door was open so I stopped by to say hi.

When he saw me, he jumped up from his chair and came over and gave me a hug.

"Wow, Andro. It's nice to see you, too." He smelled like Polo and his silk shirt was smooth and warm against my cheek.

He stepped back. "Sorry I was so short with you last night. I was half asleep. I was worried about you after Ryan called. And he was really worried about you. I guess that boyfriend of yours was freaked out."

"Ex-boyfriend." I grimaced.

He raised his eyebrows. "Oh?"

"He was cheating on me. Like a man."

"I'm sorry." He expelled a burst of air through his mouth. "You know, not all men cheat. I would never cheat."

I forced a smile. "Is that relevant?"

"Well, now that you're a free agent, maybe you'd like to go out some time?" he said slowly.

"No." I crossed my arms. "I'm swearing off men for a while. I'm taking a man-cation."

He leaned back against his desk. "Do you need a travel agent for that trip?" He grinned.

"Yes, the Sisters of Perpetual Loneliness." I grinned back at him.

He held his arms out at his sides. "Well, if they're missing out on all this, more like the Sisters of Perpetual Sorrow."

A chuckle escaped from me. "I can't believe you said that. Aren't you Catholic? Was that disrespectful? Nuns are married to Jesus, aren't they?"

"I'm not such a good Catholic any more." He frowned. "As my family will tell you."

"Oh?" I imitated his raised eyebrow thing.

"It was Armando. I can't seem to wrap my head around God letting such a cruel and senseless thing happen."

I bobbed my head up and down. "I can understand how you might feel that way."

"He was my brother-in-law for almost ten years and a real *hermano* to me. I miss him everyday." His face froze, as if he had to suppress what he was feeling. "And Yasmin and those poor little girls."

At his obvious distress, I started to tear up.

"But, whatever." Andro shook his head a little. "I can't believe I told you all that."

I wiped the corner of my eye, surreptitiously. "I didn't mind." I liked learning more about him. But even I knew it didn't bode well for my man-cation.

"What do you say we go get some coffee and you can tell me about your adventure?" he asked.

My enorme was long gone. "Coffee? You know me too well, Professor Rivas," I said.

"After you, Professor Martin." He pointed at the doorway.

We got some coffee from the machine in the physics department main office and returned to Andro's office. He sat at his desk and I sat in the cushy guest chair. It was way more comfortable than any of the chairs in my office.

"So, what happened?" he asked. "Apparently this Ted character said you turned into smoke and disappeared?"

I took a big sip of coffee. It was not good, not unlike my Ted story. "First of all, I walked in on Ted making out with our grad student on the couch I picked out and we bought together."

He grimaced. "Ouch."

"She ran out, and Ted and I had a huge fight and broke up." I stared at my coffee. "I was super angry. I was so angry I was shaking, and all I could think was I had to get away from him." I looked up at him. "And then I was."

"Where'd you go?" he asked.

"I have no idea." I pressed my lips together for a moment. "It was like I went nowhere. It was a blurry, foggy nowhere. And I had a huge headache. I actually thought I might die. Or be dead already."

Andro put down his mug. "That does not sound good."

"No." I shook my head. "It was not good. I'm just glad I finally came out of it. I materialized in my office last night."

"I'm glad you came out of it, too." He paused. "So, you q-lapsed to instantiate a reality in which you were not at Ted's house. Then you did it again to end up in your office?"

"I guess." I nodded. "Yeah. That's my theory."

He exhaled. "This q-lapsing is risky. There's no telling where a person might end up."

"Yeah. That's my theory, too." I finished off my coffee. Already. Darn it. "That's why I took down the equipment again."

"Did you make any progress on understanding when it works and when it doesn't?" he asked.

"You mean so I can avoid doing it by accident again?" I frowned. "Not really. But there has to be some pattern to it. Let's try to figure it out."

He pulled out a pen and pad of paper. "Okay. I did it at the barbeque to save Maria from serious injury." He jotted notes on the pad. "You did it the first day of the semester to avoid dying in a car accident. Did it work any other times?" He looked up at me.

I was getting déjà vu. "I saved Emily in the hospital. Did we already have this conversation? And I think I did it as a kid to save myself from drowning. I told you about that, didn't I?"

"No. And that doesn't make sense. You didn't know quantum mechanics then."

I held up a finger. "Ah, but I did. I had read a bunch of quantum mechanics books already."

"How old were you?" he asked.

"I was about thirteen."

He smiled. "What a nerd."

I ignored his impertinence. "And don't forget to write down that giant hole in the wall behind you, and my misadventure over the weekend."

"What about the double-slit experiment?" he asked.

"Yes," I said. "That worked. But only twice, and only when I was working with Alyssa."

"Hmm." Andro tapped his pen on the pad. "There were four times when it worked to save someone's life, or least save them from serious injury. There were two double-slit experiments and two weird times it worked. I don't see a pattern."

"I was involved in all of them," I said.

"Except when I saved Maria."

"Oh, right." I frowned. "I don't see a pattern either." I paused. "I was really mad Friday night. Could emotions have something to do with it?"

"I was terrified when I saw Maria in danger. And that fits with your life-saving events. But what about the double-slit experiments? And the wall?"

I was experiencing a strong emotion right before the wall thing. Lust. But I wasn't about to admit that. "I was rather agitated before the wall thing. I was, uh, upset that the experiment wasn't working."

"Hmm. I was rather agitated, too." He glanced at me. "Let's say for now that it fits the strong emotion profile. But the double-slits don't."

"Of course, the modification to reality we saw with the double-slit experiment wasn't nearly as dramatic and weird as those other cases," I said.

He nodded.

"Maybe the stronger the emotions, the weirder the result of q-lapsing can be," I said. That sort of made sense. Finally something about this business was starting to make some sense.

"And the more dangerous," he said. "But what do you really mean by emotions?"

That was a good question. Against my will, my mind was drawn back to Friday night. That was definitely a fight or flight situation. "What about adrenaline?"

"That's a good hypothesis. But that means the double-slit experiments really don't fit with the other cases. You didn't have adrenaline in your system then."

Bummer. We were so close to figuring this stuff out.

Monday afternoon I had a meeting scheduled with Alyssa regarding her Ph.D. project. Namely, picking one. She showed up right on time. However, her auburn hair was a mess and she was wearing a *Geekfest 2014* t-shirt. I'd seen that shirt before. On Luke. Yikes.

"Hi, Alyssa. How was your weekend? I'm guessing good."

She giggled. "I'll say. I–"

I held up my hand. "I don't really want to hear any details, unless they're about physics. Are they?"

She shook her head.

"Okay, then," I said. "Ph.D. project. What have you decided?"

"I want to do it on collapsing the wavefunction," she said.

"Absolutely not," I said. "I won't agree to that."

"But why not?" she asked. "It's so cool."

"For many reasons."

"One of them better not be that it's too dangerous for me," she said.

It was, but I could tell she wouldn't go for that. "One." I held up one finger. "Collapsing the wavefunction is an interpretation of quantum mechanics. And interpretations of quantum mechanics would be a philosophy of science study. Do you want to transfer to the philosophy department?"

She scowled. "No."

"Two." I held up a second finger. "Studying quantum mechanics itself would have been cutting-edge research in 1900. As your advisor, part of my job is steering you toward a thesis that will get you a job. 1900-era research will not do that."

I continued. "Three." Third finger. "It's weird. You probably won't even be able to get your results published in a scientific journal. Let's try to keep all this quiet for now. Four." Fourth finger. "It is dangerous."

"But we got it to work. I successfully participated in an experiment. Me." She pointed at herself. "Sure, there was that tiny fire in the hall the first time."

Andro appeared in the middle of the hole in the wall. "Fire? What was that about a fire? Here in the physics building?"

Alyssa continued. "And I know you were aggravated with me that second time because I said your jeans were too tight. Is that what this is? Are you trying to get back at me?" She paused. "Hi, Professor Rivas."

He looked at me. "How emotional were you during those two experiments? Did you have adrenaline in your system?"

I didn't remember being nervous. "Uh..."

"You said the first time that the fire made your blood really pump," she said. "And I know you were nervous the second time because you kept muttering to yourself *this has to work*. And I broke my thermos, remember?"

"No. I don't really remember." I looked at Andro.

He looked back at me.

"I know what you're going to say," I said. "This means all the cases that worked involved adrenaline."

"Ya, baby." He smiled.

I couldn't help smiling back.

Chapter Ten

Later Monday afternoon I was summoned by my boss−never a good sign. When I got down there Chen was waiting for me in the main physics department office. “Madison what's going on with Alyssa Long? She just gave me an earful. You won't let her do the thesis project she wants to do?”

I sighed. “Did she tell you what the project was?”

“Something about quantum field theory?” he asked.

I shook my head. “No. Try quantum mechanics.”

“Quantum mechanics?” He squinted. “That hasn't been an active field of research since the early 1900s.”

I shrugged. “I know. I told her that.”

“She said you were carrying out experiments? In the hall outside your office?” He frowned. “That doesn't sound right. You're a theorist.”

Think fast, Mad. “I was just duplicating a famous historical quantum mechanics experiment as a possible demonstration or activity for my class, and I didn't have enough room in my office.”

“Oh.” Chen leaned against the front counter. “What's wrong with that girl?”

“There's nothing wrong with her. She just got excited about quantum mechanics. It's sort of neat really.” I forced a smile.

“There was nothing neat about how she was in here yelling. She's been a problem student in the past, you know. Her previous advisor basically fired her. We had to scramble to find her a teaching assistantship this semester.”

“I know,” I said. “And I appreciate everything you've done for her. I'm sure she does too.”

“I hate to say it, but if she doesn't shape up we aren't going to be able to give her any funding next semester.”

Ugh. That was tantamount to expelling her. "Please don't do that. She just needs to cool off. She's not a problem."

"Perhaps I was hasty in giving you a grad student your first semester." He peered down at me from his six-foot-three height.

Geez, that wasn't intimidating at all. "No, sir. You weren't hasty. You didn't make a mistake. I'm sure it will all work out."

"It better." He paused. "In another matter, I had a bizarre report from the housekeeping staff. Something about a hole in your office wall?" At least Alyssa didn't tell him.

"Yeah, there's a little hole," I said. "I'll deal with it." Hopefully q-lapsing worked to fix things as well as break them.

Chen gave me one last judgmental glance before sauntering back into his office.

I grabbed the landline and tried to call Alyssa. It went straight to voice mail. I glared at the phone.

"If you're trying to reach Alyssa she's teaching her recitation right now," the woman behind the counter said.

I'd met her my first day and passed her often since then on my way to the coffee pot, but I could not remember her name. "Thanks, uh..."

She squinted at me. "Don't tell me you don't know who I am."

I knew she was an administrative assistant. "I'm just really bad with names."

"Good quality for a teacher," she said drily. "I'm Nancy."

"Thanks, Nancy. Can you tell me what room Alyssa's recitation is in?"

"For her sake I will." She muttered something else I didn't catch as she looked up the room on the computer. "It's G2B47."

"Where's that?"

"Downstairs, in the basement."

I started walking for the door.

"But she doesn't get out until almost three o'clock."

"Oh." I turned around. "Thanks, uh..."

"Nancy!"

I quickly ducked out of the room.

Back in my office, Andro poked his head through the giant hole in the wall. "You just missed that Luke kid. He seemed a little torqued that you weren't here."

I sighed. "I'm sorry I missed him, but it wasn't my office hours.

Maybe he just came to see the hole," I pointed, "for himself. I assume he saw it."

He nodded. "Oh, yeah. He saw it all right. And I think you're right. He was very interested in it." He took a breath. "Should we be worried about this hole?"

"Actually, Chen already found out about it," I admitted. "I told him it was a little hole and I'd take care of it."

He stared. "And how are you going to do that?"

"How do you think?" I asked, smiling. "Do you want to help?"

"What about adrenaline?" he asked.

"Good question," I said. "I guess this will be a good test of our adrenaline hypothesis. Go back to your side and let's try to q-lapse to fix it." I shooed him back to his office and squinted at the hole as I concentrated. The. Wall. Is. Back.

Nothing happened. I kept trying.

After a couple minutes, Andro poked his head back through. "It doesn't appear to be working."

I nodded. "You're right. We'll have to get some adrenaline and try again later."

He agreed.

Of course I wasn't sure exactly how to procure adrenaline, but that was a minor detail.

At two-forty-five I went down to the basement to find Alyssa, but I missed her.

I went back to grading papers. One of them had an URL scrawled in the margin, www.controlreality.info. That sounded intriguing and I was getting sick of grading, so I clicked it out.

Imagine my surprise when I discovered a webpage giving instructions on how to control reality, complete with a picture of the hole in my office wall. I proceeded to run right through said hole into Andro's office. "Did Luke have a camera with him?"

He appeared to be grading papers too. "No."

"There's a picture on the web of our wall, or lack thereof. You didn't take a picture of it, did you?"

He shook his head. "No, but Luke had his cell phone out."

"Damn." So much for keeping a lid on all this. "Sorry to bother you. Go back to whatever you were doing." I slunk back to my office.

This day just kept getting worse. I needed to get that

webpage taken down. But whose was it? It had to be Luke's, right? Unfortunately, when I investigated the control-reality site, I found out it was owned by John Smith on Main Street. Yeah, right. That was a dead end.

I forced myself to leave the webpage mystery and go back to work. I spent the rest of the afternoon grading papers and working on my notes for Wednesday's class. At about five p.m., I debated going back to the calculations I'd started for my research, but deduced I was too tired to make any mistake-free progress. It was time to call it a day.

Ryan, Sydney, and Cathy, Sydney's mom, seemed surprised to see me when I got home. Sydney was feeding Emily as Cathy looked on with a rapt smile. Cathy looked almost exactly like Sydney, a petite, perky, brunette. You had to get up close to see Cathy's crow's feet and the hint of gray at her root line. I'd heard rumors that Cathy had arrived, but hadn't had a chance to talk to her yet, being in limbo and all.

"Hi, Cathy," I said. "It's nice to see you again. It's awfully nice of you to come help out."

"Oh, hi," she said. She didn't even glance my way. Her undivided attention was on the baby.

"Madison? Is that you?" Sitting on the couch, Ryan pushed his glasses up his nose. "Or is it some pod-person who's impersonating Madison? If so, pod-Madison, I have to tell you she usually doesn't come home until late." Truth be told, I had been trying to avoid Sydney's tofu dinners.

I forced a smile. "Ha ha. Everyone's a comedian. I'm just a bit tired." I dropped my bag on the couch next to Ryan. "So, what's for dinner?"

"Oh, dear," Sydney said. "We're getting a bit low on groceries. Ryan, honey, could you make a trip to the grocery store?"

He sighed. "Another trip to another store?"

I raised my hand. "I volunteer to order pizza."

"Okay, but get lots of veggies," Sydney said.

"Forget that, get lots of meat," Ryan said.

"I can handle it," I said. I compromised with lots of veggies and lots of meat and it arrived in thirty minutes or less.

After we ate, we attempted to watch *Scenes of Law Crime Orders and Investigations* or something like that on TV.

Right away, I dozed off. Unfortunately my nap was not fated to last long because soon Emily started crying. Looking around the room, I judged I wasn't the only one to have fallen asleep and been rudely awakened.

Ryan pushed himself up off the couch. "Here, Syd, let me take her."

Sydney slowly nodded and handed off Emily. "I don't know how much more of this I can take."

"It's only been a few days, honey," Cathy said. "You'll get used to it. Why don't you let me draw you a bath?" They departed for the bathroom.

"Are you as tired as me?" I asked Ryan over his daughter's cries.

"I'm pretty tired." He held Emily in his arms and rocked her back and forth. "What's wrong, little girl? You just ate." He sniffed her. "You don't need a new diaper."

She continued to cry.

"I don't know how you parents do it," I said.

Ryan smiled, despite the racket. "I love her so much, I don't mind all the crying and the diaper changes and the rest. I didn't know I could love someone so much."

"That's awesome." I stood up. "I think I'm going to bed." I gently patted squalling Emily on the head. "'Night, sweetie."

"'Night honey-pie." Ryan grinned. "Aren't you going to say goodnight to Emily?"

A chortle escaped my mouth. "Goodnight Ryan. Bid the rest of the family goodnight for me."

"Can do."

In my room, in bed, I could still hear Emily loud and clear, so I figured there was no chance I'd be able to get to sleep even though my weekend had been bizarre and exhausting.

Some time later I was jarred awake by the jingle of the telephone. Soon after that Emily started crying again. I checked the time and it was after one a.m. Uh, oh. Nothing good ever came of a one a.m. phone call. I threw on my robe and went out into the living room.

Ryan was nodding and talking on his cell. His expression was grim. "I'll be right there."

"Nobody died, I hope?" I asked over Emily's wailing.

"No. Just a break-in at the UMC. I have to go over to campus."

"UMC? Remind me?"

He grunted. "How long have you been here, now? It's the University Memorial Center."

I must have looked blank.

"You know, the student union, where they have the cafeteria and the ballroom and the bowling alley and all that."

There was a bowling alley on campus? "Oh, right. I knew that." I paused. "Would you like me to come help out?" It wasn't like I'd be able to get back to sleep with the continuous crying. Poor Emily.

Ryan gave me a look that said, *What, are you crazy*? "No."

I went back to bed, but at about one-thirty, the phone rang again. This time it was my cell. It was Ryan. "Can you come over here?"

"Sure, but I thought..."

"Just get over here," he said. "I'll meet you at the main south doors, off that big patio."

When I got there, Ryan was waiting impatiently. "It's about time."

"I think it took me all of seven minutes," I said. "What's this about?"

"Just, come on." Ryan speedwalked and I followed.

We found ourselves in some kind of office area I hadn't been to before. "What's going on?" I asked.

Ryan continued marching ahead until we found the campus police guys I'd met at the barbeque milling about in the hallway.

I heard bits of conversations.

"Why'd they take the debris with them?"

"If you're going to break something down, why not the door?"

"Doesn't make any sense."

"What are you guys doing?" Ryan asked. "I told you to collect evidence. Get out of the way." He pushed through them to the wall and pointed. "Does this look familiar?"

A huge portion of the wall was gone.

I exhaled. "Wow. Can I touch it?" I wondered if the edges had the same weird spongy consistency as the hole in my office. They did look the same.

"No," he said. "Fingerprints."

"Give me some gloves, then," I said.

"Did you do this?" He handed over some gloves. "Andro showed me that hole in your office wall."

"What?" I said. "Of course not."

"I should talk to Andro. He didn't do this, did he?"

I touched the edges of the hole. Spongy. Check. "No. He wouldn't do something like this."

Ryan glared at me.

"Well, not on purpose," I added. "Anyway, what's the big deal? So they have to fix the wall."

"This isn't just a prank," Ryan said. "One of my officers talked to the student in charge of the club in this office. Several thousand dollars were stolen."

"Oh. That is bad." I felt sorry for the kids who lost their money and I felt doubly sorry that quantum mechanics might have something to do with it. Okay, quantum mechanics probably did have something to do with it.

"Yes, it is." He stopped glaring at me, and shook his head. "I'm glad you guys weren't involved. I like Andro."

Andro? "Gee, thanks," I said.

Ryan sighed. "Obviously, I like you too, Madison."

He turned back to his men. "Please continue taking evidence, photos, trace evidence, the works. And when you're done with that you can go home. We'll start the next step in the investigation first thing in the morning."

Ryan and I started walking to the exit.

"Ryan, I have to tell you something," I said. "Two of my students, Alyssa Long and Luke Bacalli, know a little about this collapsing the wavefunction stuff."

He stopped cold.

"And there may be a webpage about it," I said.

"Come on," he said impatiently. "You better show me this webpage." He held out his phone.

I fired up the webpage that explained how to collapse the wavefunction and instantiate reality.

As Ryan took it in he said, "Shit. This just made my job a whole lot more difficult." He shook his head. "Anybody could've seen this." He almost looked like he was going to cry.

"Is there anything I can do?" I asked.

"Not unless you can get rid of this webpage."

"That's tough since we don't know who the domain-owner is. I looked it up, but it just says John Smith, which is of course, fake." A light bulb went off in my head. "I could try to use my powers." I didn't mention my lack of adrenaline and the unsuccessful attempt to q-lapse earlier in the day.

"I couldn't ask you to do that," he said. "Isn't it dangerous to use those powers?"

That was true, but things seemed to be going downhill and it was probably my fault. "You're not asking. I'm offering. Here it goes." I concentrated on the screen, willing the wavefunction to collapse and remove the webpage. The only thing that happened was I yawned.

"Wow, that's amazing," Ryan said. "You made yourself yawn."

"Sorry. I'm tired." I was definitely going to have to get a stash of adrenaline and soon.

"Aren't we all?" he said. "I'm too tired to think straight. Let's attack this in the morning. I'll stop by your office. Hopefully this crime's an isolated incident."

Hopefully.

Chapter Eleven

I didn't drag my butt into work until ten-thirty Tuesday morning.

Andro stepped into my office through the hole in the wall, his crisp blue shirt matching his eyes perfectly, took one look at me and said, "Late night?"

"Yeah," I grunted, grabbing my cup of coffee.

"Why? I know it couldn't be a man, what with your man-cation." He grinned.

He was entirely too chipper in the morning. "For your information, I was up until two-thirty helping Ryan with an investigation. Which, on Andro-time, would be what? Like five in the morning?" Now, it was my turn to grin. "So I've got a good excuse for being tired. Man-cation or not." It was fun sharing an office with him. I enjoyed our verbal jousts. Maybe we didn't need to fix that hole in the wall.

"Really?" he said. "Ryan asked for your help with an investigation? Why would he do that?"

I proceeded to tell him about the robbery at the UMC, ending with, "The hole in the wall looked like this hole in the wall." I pointed at the breach he had so recently strolled through. "The edges were spongy, like here." I resisted the urge to touch those edges. I'd been doing it every time I entered or exited the office. "And there was no rubble or anything, just like here."

He rubbed his chin thoughtfully. "Yeah, I can see why Ryan wanted your help. I'm surprised he didn't want to talk to me, too."

My world tilted for a second. "You didn't have anything to do with this, did you?"

"No." He squinted at me. "I meant because of this." He directed his hand at the unnatural opening. "We should really fix it if we can."

"He does want to talk to you. Didn't I mention that?" I took another gulp of coffee. It didn't seem to be doing its job today.

"No," he said.

"Yeah. Ryan said he'd be stopping by our office today."

Andro frowned. "Did he say what time?"

"Nope."

My stomach had just started growling when Ryan showed up.

"Lunch, anyone?" he asked.

"Sure," I said.

He smiled. "What a shock. Madison hungry." He poked his head through the hole in the wall. "Andro?"

I couldn't hear Andro's response too well but Ryan said, "No. Of course you're not a suspect. I'm just trying to understand this stuff." He touched the edge of the opening, absentmindedly.

I heard Andro say, "mumble, mumble, mumble."

Then Ryan glanced at me and said, "Yeah. She is trouble. But it's a good kind of trouble."

I jumped up from my desk. "What'd he say?"

Ryan ignored me. "Don't worry, I'm buying." He stepped back into my office, and gestured toward the door. "Well, come on, then."

I had just taken a huge bite of a cinnamon roll at Boulder Brews, when Ryan asked me, "You said you had two students who might know how to do this freaky wavefunction collapsing stuff? I don't get how students do it. If they can do it, why can't everyone do it?"

I chewed furiously.

Andro said, "As far as we've been able to determine there are three required components: knowledge of quantum mechanics, belief that you can do it, and adrenaline. Few people possess all of these, or at least all at the same time."

"Adrenaline?" Ryan said. "I haven't heard anything about that." He bit into his flame-broiled, all-the-fixings burger.

I swallowed. "Yeah, we just figured out the adrenaline thing yesterday. And I'm sorry to say my grad student, Alyssa, does know about that. She was there when we were discussing it." I peered over my pricey coffee drink at Andro. "But I don't think she'd be involved in a robbery."

"Oh? What do you know about her?" Ryan asked.

"I know she's smart. She's finished all her Ph.D. classes. I know she has kind of a reputation as a klutz. An undeserved reputation."

"Maybe it's deserved," Andro said. "Didn't you say something about a fire when you were doing the double-slit experiment?"

Ryan blanched. "Fire? On campus?"

I conveniently didn't hear him. I took a smaller bite of the roll. "I'm pretty sure she's dating one of my undergrad students, Luke. There's a chance she told him about the adrenaline thing."

"Is that all you know about her?" Ryan asked. "That's not much."

"I know she's a good person," I said forcefully. "And she should be a physicist."

"And what about this Luke kid?" Ryan asked.

Andro snorted as he cut into his enchilada with his fork.

"He's an undergrad physics major." I took another bite. "His roommate, Griffin, is in my class, too. Luke's smart. He's sort of cocky." I wasn't about to tell these two I thought Luke was handsome. They didn't need any more reasons to make fun of me. "I'd have to say this Luke's got a way with women. Alyssa seems to find him hard to resist, but then she may be a bit naïve."

"Takes one to know one," Ryan muttered.

Andro laughed.

"Hey." I narrowed my eyes. "Anyway, I'd like to think Luke wouldn't do anything really wrong, but I'm not so sure."

"And then there's the whole issue of the webpage," Ryan said.

"Oh yeah. You mentioned that earlier." Andro perked up. "What webpage?"

"Www.controlreality.info", I said. "It has all the gory details."

"It's too bad you couldn't get rid of it last night," Ryan said. "But now that I know about the need for adrenaline, I understand. Have you thought of trying to get some adrenaline so you can experiment?"

"Yeah. But where would we get it? As for why everyone

doesn't q-lapse," I said, "frankly, it's too dangerous. You run the risk of being caught in some foggy quantum limbo."

"Wait. What'd you say? Q-lapse" Ryan asked.

I nodded.

"Yeah," Andro said. "We got tired of saying collapse the wavefunction. But regarding the limbo, data seems to indicate the danger increases with the weirdness of the reality created."

"Really?" Ryan asked, moving his burger away from his mouth.

I thought about the various experiments we'd done from the double-slit to transporting myself eight hundred miles and then nodded. "Yes. I agree with that."

Back at the office, Andro asked me to show him the webpage. I brought it up on my computer. Very unfortunately, it had been updated since yesterday with the adrenaline information. "That's not good. I wish I could help Ryan out by getting rid of this."

Andro shook his head as he peered at the computer screen. "It actually spells out how to control reality. It could definitely cause trouble." He regarded me with raised eyebrows. "I think we should get rid of it."

"I agree, but it's a moot point," I said. "How do we get rid of it? Do you happen to have some adrenaline lying around? Or maybe a friend that works over at the medical center?"

Andro stepped close to me. Too close. "I've been thinking about that. I bet I know a way to get your blood flowing." He gazed deep into my eyes. "It'd be for science."

My temperature rose like a global-warming-detection device. I took a step away from him. "I'm sure I don't know what you're talking about."

He took a step toward me. "Yes, you do." He leaned down.

I was caught in his blue eyes and couldn't escape. "If it's for science..."

He pressed his lips against mine, and the laws of physics were suspended as I pressed back. I'd never had a kiss like that before.

Then, he straightened up and said, "Quick. Focus on q-lapsing to get rid of the webpage."

It took me a second to get my bearings, but eventually I caught up and joined him in squinting at the computer screen.

The webpage got blurry, the words and pictures running together, and then it morphed into a blank gray page.

"Yes." Andro threw his fist in the air in triumph.

"We did it." I grabbed him for a hug. "All right!"

Feeling his warm chest against my breasts brought me to my senses. I pushed him away and crossed my arms. "I can't believe you kissed me."

He grinned wickedly. "It was purely for science. And your cousin Ryan. And to foil nefarious criminals." He took a step closer to me. "Do you want to kiss again? We could try to fix the wall if you need an excuse."

I wanted to do it again so much it scared me. "Absolutely not. I told you I was taking a break from that stuff for a while."

"Right," he said. "Your man-cation. You were serious about that? How's that going for you?" The corners of his delicious lips turned up.

I tried not to look directly at him. "Great. Fabulous." In reality, my man-cation was in serious jeopardy. I sat down at my desk. "Now, go away, I have to get ready for my class tomorrow."

Andro looked me up and down. "Or you could do some more q-lapsing before your blood pressure goes down." He gave me one last parting grin before stepping into his office.

"Put that big bookshelf back," I yelled after him.

And then I really, really tried to think about something besides Andro, muscles rippling, as he pushed the bookshelf back between us.

I called Ryan and let him know the good news about the webpage.

He had mixed feelings about it. "I guess that's good news, but it might make it more difficult to track down the owner."

"I wouldn't know about that. That's regular detective work." I paused. That reminded me of something. "Hey, speaking of detective work, did you ask your Boulder PD buddy again what the story was on Andro's brother-in-law?"

"Yes," he said. "They don't have any leads. In fact, I saw the file, and the witness statements are not helpful."

"What do you mean?"

"They're short and vague. Like, *he got hit*."

"Oh. That's a bummer."

"Yeah. See you later at home." We hung up.

This news was sufficiently disheartening that I did manage to calm down. So, I returned to working on lecture notes for my quantum mechanics class. I had successfully moved on to grading papers when Alyssa showed up.

"I can not believe you sicced the campus cops on me. That was low." Her hands were on her hips and her eyes flashed in anger. "They showed up and practically dragooned me and Luke, making us come with them to the campus police office for questioning."

I stood up. "I'm sorry you're upset," I said evenly. "Please calm down. I did not sic anyone on you. I had an obligation to tell Ryan who might have the ability to use quantum mechanics to control reality. I also told him you did not do it."

"I think Luke blames me for them bringing us in. He got really mad at me. This is all your fault! I thought we were friends," she said. Loudly.

"I respect you and think you're a good student. And I think you will be a good physicist. However, I am not your friend. I'm your advisor. And I'd advise you not to yell at me." Despite my best intentions, I was starting to get mad.

Alyssa sputtered. "But, well, I..."

"As your advisor, I'm also saying you don't have an infinite number of opportunities here at the university. You need to get your priorities straight. Right now your priority should be finishing your degree. If that means breaking up with some boy, then maybe that's what you need to do."

"Don't you tell me what to do," she said. "My personal life is my business."

"I agree, until it interferes with your degree, which it clearly has."

"No, it hasn't. And quit treating me like a little kid."

"Then, quit acting like a little kid."

"I can't believe you said that."

I sighed. At this rate she was going to get kicked out of school. I truly didn't want that to happen. "Alyssa, please, get your act together. I'm on your side, here."

"I don't think you are. I think you're jealous of me, because I have a boyfriend and you don't."

Now that was just rude. “My personal life is totally irrelevant.”

“So is mine. You are so fired as my advisor.” She stomped out of my office and all the way down the hall.

Well, that was fun. Not.

Despite her hissy fit, I did want Alyssa to succeed with school. Right now it didn’t look good for her. I’d just have to wait and see if she came to her senses.

Chapter Twelve

I was a little nervous about seeing Luke Wednesday morning after the way Alyssa had reacted to being questioned by Ryan. I needn't have worried, however, as Luke was as cocky as ever.

"Hey, Teach," he said as I strolled into the classroom several minutes before nine o'clock. Luke and his buddy Griffin were the only ones there so early. "That sure was interesting meeting Ryan Martin. Is he your brother or your husband?"

Griffin snickered and muttered something under his breath that sounded suspiciously like, "Or both?"

I looked steadily at Griffin. "I'm sorry. I couldn't make out what you said. Could you repeat that, please?"

He snapped his mouth shut.

I turned back to Luke. "My family is none of your concern, Mr. Bacalli. Thank you for cooperating with the investigation, however. You too, Mr. Jin." I put my stuff down on the front table and turned around. "I must admit, I'm glad to see you both here in class." I was shocked they'd shown up, if truth be told. Why would they come to class if they were starting a new career in breaking and entering and stealing stuff? To my mind, it indicated they were innocent.

"Yeah, well, why wouldn't we be here? We're not criminals. We didn't steal anything," Griffin blurted out.

Okay, that was a tad suspicious.

Luke shot him a glare for a split second. "That goes without saying," he said with a very even tone. Too even.

During this exchange, the rest of the students had been trickling in. I addressed them. "Please take your seats, everyone. It's time to start class."

Andro was scarce after my class and didn't even appear in our office at lunchtime. I was surprisingly disappointed not to see him.

To avoid thinking about him, I started obsessing about Alyssa. She still wasn't answering her phone or email, so I went to her classroom right before her recitation. Where I found her.

"Hi, Alyssa," I said, perfectly reasonably. "How's it going?"

"What are you doing here?" she demanded. "It's going horrible. Luke dumped me–not that it's any of your business."

"I'm sorry to hear that." Not. "Breaking up with someone is always difficult." That was all too true. My brain skittered toward Ted and Jessica, and I forced it away. At some point I'd probably have to deal with that, but not now.

Alyssa's students started arriving.

"I see you're busy," I said. "Please stop by my office when you're feeling better. I'd really like to talk with you. It's very important."

At about five o'clock, I was actually doing some neutrino research when the elevator pinged and a herd of elephants burst into the hall. At least it sounded like a herd of elephants. I was curious, so I had to get up and peek into the hall to see what it was. It turned out Andro and his nieces can make a heck of a lot of noise.

"Andro," I said, "there you are. I thought you might be sick or something."

Theresa and Maria were galumphing up and down the hall every which way.

I giggled. They were really cute.

He frowned at them. "Come on, girls. What did we talk about? When we're inside, we don't run around." His words didn't seem to have much effect.

"Hi, Madison," he said to me. "I'm fine. Yasmin's the one who's a bit under the weather. So I got to spend the afternoon with the girls. I had to stop by and get some papers for my class tomorrow." He stepped closer to me and lowered his voice. "To tell the truth, they're running me ragged. I don't know how Yasmin does it every day."

I could certainly watch the girls while he rummaged around in his office for a few minutes. "Would you like some help? I can keep an eye on them."

"That sounds great. Thanks." He popped into his office.

I walked down the hall a bit to Maria and Theresa. "What are you guys doing?"

They froze and peered at me.

"I'm Madison. Remember, we met at my house the other day? You brought tamales. They were really yummy. Thank you for bringing them."

They looked at me like I was an alien from outer space.

Andro rushed out of his office with his briefcase. "Wow. I haven't heard a peep out of them. You have a way with kids."

For some reason, this made me feel really good. "Yeah. I guess I do."

"So?" he said.

"So what?" I asked.

"Do you need to get some stuff?" he asked.

"For what?" I asked.

"I don't know. You always seem to lug a bunch of books and papers around with you."

I narrowed my eyes and cocked my head. "What are you talking about?"

"What are you talking about?" he said.

We looked at each other as Maria and Theresa bounded around the corner.

He smiled. "Didn't you say you'd come over and help me with Maria and Theresa tonight?" Then louder, he said, "Girls, come back here, please."

They appeared behind us, out-of-breath, having run all the way around the tower.

I did not recall saying I would help him baby-sit tonight. Clearly, he had more of an effect on me than I realized. "Right. I do need to get my stuff. Just a sec."

In no time the four of us were walking in the front door of Andro's brick ranch house. Correction: Andro and I walked, Maria and Theresa skipped. I was amazed to find out he lived in the same neighborhood as me, albeit several blocks away. Of course, maybe it wasn't quite so amazing when one considered it was the only neighborhood in Boulder with houses under half a million dollars.

"Mama, we're home," Maria called out.

"Mommy, Uncle Andro brought some lady," Theresa said.

Yasmin stumbled, barefoot, into the living room wearing an orange and brown dress. "What? We have company?" She didn't look sick. She looked like she'd been crying.

He put down his stuff. "It's just Madison."

Just? I didn't know what to make of that comment, so I ignored it. "Hi, Yasmin."

"Hi, Madison." She forced her lips into a smile. "Andro, I thought we were supposed to tell one another in advance if we were inviting someone over?"

"Oh? Does Andro invite a lot of people over?" I asked.

He raised his eyebrows at me.

Theresa flipped on the television set, and she and Maria settled on the floor in front of it.

"Relax, Yasmin," he said. "Madison volunteered to watch the girls while I make dinner. I figured you'd still be in your room."

"Oh." Yasmin's fake smile faded. "Okay. Good. Thanks, Madison." She glanced at her daughters entranced by the flickering screen. "Actually, I'm feeling a bit better. I think I'd like to spend some time with the girls."

"Fine. By all means." He smiled. "Madison, how do you feel about helping me with dinner?"

"I'm game." I followed him into the kitchen as Yasmin reached over and turned off the television.

He opened the fridge. "Do you want a beer?"

I grinned. "What do you think?"

He grinned back at me, took two bottles of Negra Modelo out, opened them and handed me one.

I took a frosty swig. "So, what are we making?"

"Let's see. We need something quick and easy that the girls will eat." He opened the fridge again and stuck his head in.

I tried not to stare at his butt as he leaned over.

"Cheese enchiladas, I think." He started taking stuff out and putting it on the counter.

I had no idea how to make enchiladas. "Uh, what would you like me to do?"

He opened the cupboard and took out some more stuff. "You are the sous chef."

"Okay," I said. "What does a sous chef do? And what does that make you?"

He finished putting his ingredients on the counter and got out a frying pan, bowl, grater, and casserole dish. "I'm the chef. As the sous chef, you do whatever the chef de cuisine says."

That sounded intriguing. I blushed. "And what would you like me to do?"

I must have had a strange expression on my face, because when Andro looked over at me, he started laughing. "Well, I was going to have you grate the cheese, but now I'm thinking your idea might be better." His blue eyes twinkled.

I grabbed the bowl. "No, grating sounds good. I know how to grate." I settled on a stool at the counter, and started grating.

Still chuckling, he heated up the frying pan with a little oil in the bottom, and then started a complicated dance of tortillas. He cooked one for a couple seconds and then lifted it up and put another one underneath, lifted both tortillas and put another one underneath and so on.

"What are you doing?" I finally asked.

"I'm softening the tortillas to bring out their flavor." He glanced over at me, bemused. "What do you think I'm doing?"

"I have no idea, but it looks neat." In point of fact, he looked amazing whisking the tortillas here and there like an old pro. "And it smells good."

He started sliding the tortillas onto paper towels. "Less looking, more grating," he said with the hint of a grin.

The kitchen was getting warmer and warmer what with the stove on and the oven preheating. Yeah, that was why it was warm. I took another swig of beer and tried to focus on my task.

Out of the corner of my eye, I spied Andro sautéing chopped onion and garlic, and then he added some salsa and canned tomatoes to the pan. He looked good standing there in front of the stove. Maybe it was just the novelty of actually seeing a man cook. Ted literally refused to set foot in the kitchen. Huh. In hindsight, that was probably not a good sign.

"How's it going, grater?" he asked. "I'm almost ready for the cheese."

I redoubled my efforts, not wanting to disappoint him. "Almost done."

He put a little oil on the bottom of the casserole dish. "Time's up. I need you," he grinned, "to finish."

Wow, that was one hot kitchen. I pushed the bowl of grated cheese over to him.

He put some cheese inside a warmed tortilla, rolled it up and placed it in the casserole dish, and continued until all the tortillas were finished. Then he poured the sauce over the top, put the rest of the cheese on top of that and placed the pan in the oven. "It needs to cook for about ten minutes."

"It's a little warm in here." I chugged my beer.

"It's not that warm." He sipped his beer. "Do you want another beer?"

"Yes, please." He got me one and then I gazed in fascination as he got out the plates, some cilantro, sour cream, and lettuce. A man that knew his way around the kitchen was rarer than a unicorn.

"Five minutes," he called out to the family room.

Yasmin called back, "Thanks."

Andro sighed. "If you're done ogling me, maybe you'd like to set the table, Madison?" He pointed at the plates on the counter.

I jumped up. "Of course. And I wasn't ogling." Not much, anyway. I grabbed the plates and took them over to the table as he got out some cups.

"You're acting like you've never seen a man cook before." He put together a quick fruit salad with cantaloupe, grapes, and sliced bananas.

"I haven't," I said. My dad certainly never cooked.

"Really?" he asked. "That's hard to believe in this day and age." He put the fruit salad on the table.

Yasmin appeared with Theresa and Maria in tow. "Sit down, girls." She smiled fleetingly as she pointed at the chairs.

I finished setting the table as Yasmin got out the milk and Andro took the casserole out of the oven.

And then dinner was ready. As I sat down at the table across from Andro and he smiled at me, I had a horrible realization. I was totally smitten. I should have gotten travel insurance for that man-cation. It had been cruelly cancelled and no refund was

going to be forthcoming.
Yasmin said, "Let's say grace."
We bowed our heads. I lifted my eyes and snuck a peek at Andro as they all thanked God.
Andro, with bowed head, caught me looking at him. Darn it.
Quickly I looked down again as they finished saying grace.
Yasmin served Theresa before serving herself. "Thanks for helping out, Madison."
"You're welcome," I said.
Andro helped Maria get some food.
"I hope you're feeling better, Yasmin," I said.
She sighed. "Did Andro say I was sick?"
I glanced at him. "Not exactly. I think his term was under the weather."
"He's kind. Actually, once in a while being a widow gets to me more than usual, and I miss Armando even more than ever. On those days it's hard to get out of bed."
"That's rough. I'm so sorry." I couldn't even imagine losing the love of my life so horribly and suddenly.
I tasted the enchiladas. They were delicious with warm gooey cheddar cheese, garlic, spicy salsa, and yes, flavorful tortillas.
"You're doing better and better all the time, Yas," Andro said.
"It still makes me so angry that someone could do this and not be punished," Yasmin said.
"It's understandable you're mad," I said. "It's all very unfair." I wished Ryan had had some good news on that front.
"They should not get away with it," Andro said, his face a frozen mask.
I looked around the table at Andro and Yasmin and little Maria and Theresa, and wholeheartedly agreed.
After dinner, Yasmin took the girls to get ready for bed.
Andro and I did the dishes with me washing and him rinsing and drying. Every time I handed him a dish, our hands brushed against each other–accidentally, of course.
"Thanks again for dinner," I said. "It was really good. If your science career doesn't work out, you could be a chef." As I stood next to him at the sink, prominences arced like we were the ends of a magnetic loop on the surface of the sun.
"Thanks." He took another plate, his dry thumb touching

my soapy one. “Yasmin was much worse earlier. I think having company maybe helped her come out of it.”

“You know, I asked Ryan to ask his friend in Boulder PD about the case,” I said.

“You did?” He stared at me. “What’d he say?”

“They hardly have any evidence.”

“Oh.” He frowned.

“But, I was thinking, why don’t we get some?”

He put down the dish. “What do you mean?”

“You know all the guys that were there, or at least you could find out who they were. We could interview them and find out what happened.”

“We could, at that.” Andro was silent as we finished up the dishes.

“So, do you want to stay a little while, or do you want a ride home?” he asked.

I was a little nervous about what might happen if I hung around. But I was also so hyped up from standing next to him for the past half hour, I felt like there was no chance I was going to get to sleep that night. “I think I better go, and I’d like to walk.”

“Do you want some company?” he asked, partially blocking my path.

I didn’t think I could stop myself from amorously attacking him if I spent any more time with him. Especially since the earlier kiss between us had been so amazing. “No, thanks. You probably have to do some work for tomorrow? Something to do with the stuff in your briefcase?”

“Oh, right. I forgot. Well, let me walk you to the door.”

He did so and opened the door for me. Was he leaning toward me?

I had to brush up against him to get out the door, and it felt like bolts of lightning were running across my skin. I paused right in front of him, leaning his way for a few seconds but nothing happened. “Good night,” I finally mumbled. I’d never wanted to kiss someone goodnight so badly before, but I’d be damned if I made the first move.

“Good night,” he said and closed the door.

Was it me, or was he sending mixed signals?

There was nothing left to do but start walking. Unfortunately.

As I walked in the front door at home, Ryan jumped up off the couch. “Where have you been? There’s been another quantum robbery!”

Chapter Thirteen

"Quantum robbery?" I asked. "What the heck is that?"

Ryan pulled the belt of his robe tight. "It's what I'm calling a weird robbery in which part of a wall's disappeared."

I dropped my book bag on the floor. "There was another one? At the UMC again?"

"No. It was down at a bank in Denver." He paused for dramatic effect. "They got at least half a million dollars and a guard was injured."

"Shit." I sank down on the couch. "That sounds way worse than the UMC robbery. Is the guard okay?"

He plopped down next to me on the sofa. "They don't know what happened to him or if he'll be okay. He's still in the hospital."

"That's awful." I frowned. A bank robbery in Denver was outside Ryan's jurisdiction. "How'd you find out about all this?"

"The FBI called me," he said. "They want me to come down to the crime scene tomorrow to consult."

"Wow. Good for you." I punched him on the arm. Minus the injured guard, being consulted by the FBI sounded like a dream come true for Ryan.

"Do you want to come?" he asked.

"Me?" I asked. "Why?"

"In case I have to explain that quantum stuff to the agents. Please?"

I couldn't very well turn down a please from the guy who was letting me stay at his house. "Sure," I said. "Count me in."

First thing Thursday morning Ryan and I loaded up on coffee and took off for Denver. As we sipped and snailed through rush-hour traffic, he glanced at me. "So where were you last night? I called your office and there was no answer. You didn't answer your cell either."

"My cell's on its way back here from Missouri. You haven't seen it have you?"

He shook his head. "Not unless it looked like a tofu and egg-white omelet."

That sounded awful.

"Well?" he asked. "Where were you?"

"I was at Andro's."

He chuckled. "I knew it. Man-cation, my ass. That was the stupidest thing I ever heard of. A date with Andro. Good for you, putting that asshole Ted behind you."

"For your information, I went over there to help him baby-sit. There was no dating involved," I said. And then I added, "Unfortunately."

"Unfortunately?" He guffawed. "So why didn't you make a move?"

"Me? Why didn't he make a move?" Yeah, why didn't he? He must not like me after all. Ugh. Why did I feel like I was in junior high all of a sudden? "Ryan, you've seen us together. Do you think he likes me?"

He guffawed again. "How old are you? Twelve? He didn't make a move because you told him you didn't want to date."

"Well, crap. Andro would be the one man in the world who actually listens to what I say."

"It was bound to happen eventually," Ryan said with a smile.

"What do you think I should do?"

"If you want to date him, you're going to have to ask him out."

"I don't know," I said. That sounds like a lot of pressure."

"Welcome to what men have to put up with every day." He grinned.

"Well, crap."

Ryan laughed.

When we got to the bank, two agents were outside waiting for us. I knew they were FBI agents because they had on jackets that said FBI in ten-inch-high letters on their backs. They walked up to us as we approached the front of the bank.

"Ryan," the man said. "How's it going, dawg?" He slapped Ryan on the back. He could have been Ryan's twin, tall and sandy-haired.

"Hey, Nate. How's it going?" Ryan beamed. "I haven't seen you in what, six months?"

"More like nine."

"Do you guys know each other?" I asked, always a brilliant observationalist.

"Yeah," Ryan said. "We were in grad school together at UC Irvine."

Suddenly, Ryan being asked to assist an FBI investigation made a lot more sense.

The female agent, petite with graying blonde hair pulled back into a ponytail, said, "You must be Professor Martin?" She stuck her hand out.

"Yes." I shook her hand. "Nice to meet you. What are your names?"

Her lips formed a straight line. Was that supposed to be a smile? "I'm Agent Baker and this is Agent Sawyer. Thanks for coming down." She gestured toward the front door of the bank.

Ryan and his buddy seemed oblivious to us two women.

"Of course I'm happy to help," I said. "But I'm not sure how much help I can be."

She shot a look at her partner, but he was still focused on Ryan.

We didn't hear what the guys said, but apparently it was very funny, judging from their laughter.

I entered the bank with Agent Baker following. She turned and yelled out the door, "Agent Sawyer, Officer Martin, maybe you could join us?"

"Yeah, sure," they mumbled, looking sheepish.

There were a few polyester-clad bank employees at their stations. They seemed very interested in us, craning their necks, as we walked by.

"Isn't this a crime scene? Why are the workers here?" I asked.

"The crime scene is back by the vault. Don't worry, it's been secured," Agent Baker said. I didn't know enough about crime to know I should be worried about that.

In the back of the bank two more agents, both twenty-something men, lounged against the wall behind some yellow crime scene tape. They were not introduced.

"Try not to touch anything," Agent Baker said.

Agent Sawyer cleared his throat. "Yes. Come this way, please." He ducked under the tape, and the rest of us followed.

Down the hall was a huge ragged opening in the sheetrock wall and in the metal-reinforced wall behind it.

"Weird." I stepped closer, peering at the breach. The edges did seem to have the same curious spongy quality as the holes in my office wall and the UMC wall. I straightened. "I know you said no-touching, but can I touch it with gloves or something?" Ha. I was learning crime scene techniques.

"All right, with gloves." Agent Sawyer handed me latex gloves.

Gingerly, I brushed the border with my gloved fingertip. It was spongy. "I hate to say it, but this does seem like the result of quantum mechanics. Come look, Ryan." I stepped back as he tread closer.

He studied it with Agent Sawyer looking over his shoulder.

Agent Baker frowned.

"So, how's the guard doing?" I asked.

Agent Baker shook her head. "Not well. He hasn't regained consciousness."

"What happened to him?" I asked.

"No idea," Agent Baker said. "A security guard found him unconscious on routine a security sweep. He didn't have any obvious injuries."

Ryan moved away from the hole and contemplated me over the head of Agent Baker. "Yeah, we've seen this kind of break-in before. At the university there was a robbery at the student union with the same M.O." He pointed at the security camera mounted near the ceiling. "What do the security tapes show?"

Agent Sawyer shook his head. "Nothing. Static. Did you get anything on record in the university robbery?"

"No," Ryan said. "We don't have any cameras in that area of the student union. We didn't think there was any reason for them there. It's all student offices."

"Too bad," Agent Sawyer said.

"I don't understand what's going on," Agent Baker said. "Can you explain what some obscure physics theory has to do with robbery?"

The two unnamed agents took a step towards us like they were interested.

"Quantum mechanics isn't an obscure theory," I said. "It's the foundation of all modern physics. One of its main ideas is physical objects, such as particles, are also waves." I took a breath. Agent Baker was frowning and Agent Sawyer just looked confused.

Gamely, I trudged on. "The mathematical representation of this is something called a wavefunction. Wavefunctions are characterized by probabilities."

Now Ryan looked unhappy too.

"Can you put it in English?" Agent Baker asked.

"What it means is we live in a world in which almost anything is possible," I said.

The two younger agents had gone back to lounging against the wall, albeit closer to us.

"Obviously, not everything that could happen does happen." I paused. "You might ask why?"

After ascertaining no one else was going to say it, Ryan said, "Why?"

I flashed him a smile. Thanks, Ry. "Because a conscious mind, a person, collapses the wavefunction and instantiates a particular reality."

Agent Baker snorted.

One of the agents pointed at the base of the damaged wall. "Hey, what's that fog?"

I scrutinized the area in question. It did seem foggy. That couldn't be good. It reminded me of that bizarro limbo I'd been in. "Move away from the fog. Get away from it." All we needed was to have some federal agents sucked away somewhere.

At my dire tone, the agents drew their weapons.

"I'm not kidding. Get away from there!" I ran about ten feet down the hall as Ryan and the agents backed slowly away.

"What is it?" Agent Baker asked.

"I don't know," I said. "But I know it's not regular fog. It could be dangerous."

The misty area slowly increased in size until it was almost six feet tall and two feet across. Gradually it became more opaque and took on the shape of a person.

I was getting a very bad feeling.

The mist coalesced until an extremely blurry person stood in the hall.

The mouths of the two younger agents fell open.

"What the hell is that?" one of them asked.

The person-shaped mist gradually came into focus until a normal-looking man stood in front of us. It was a chubby Asian-American twenty-two-year-old man to be precise. A man I knew. "Griffin, are you okay?" I said.

"My head," he yelled, squinting. "Help me."

"What's wrong?" I asked.

The two younger agents cautiously approached him, guns still drawn. "Did you see what I saw?" one asked the other.

Agent Baker walked to me. "Do you know this man?"

Griffin collapsed on the gray industrial-grade hallway carpet.

Ryan ran over to Griffin and knelt down next to him, checking for a pulse.

When I tried to join him Agent Baker stopped me. "I asked you a question."

"Yes," I said. "He's one of my quantum mechanics students. Griffin Jin."

"Make it stop," Griffin whimpered, clutching his head.

"Griffin," Ryan said. "What's wrong? Talk to me."

Griffin didn't answer. He just kept clutching his head and grimacing.

Ryan turned to look at us. "I think he needs an ambulance."

Agent Sawyer got out his radio and called in the cavalry.

The ambulance came and took Griffin away. One of the agents rode with him to the hospital. I wanted to think they were concerned for his health rather than making sure he didn't escape, but that didn't seem likely. At least I was concerned for his health.

Ryan and I were strongly requested to join Agents Baker and Sawyer at the Denver field office, so we followed them over there. It was very quiet in Ryan's car as we drove and worried about Griffin.

"I hope he's going to be okay," I said.

Ryan glanced at me. "I hope we're going to be okay."

"What are you talking about?"

"It's one thing to be assisting an investigation. It's another thing entirely to be questioned in an investigation."

"Shit." Now I had something else to worry about.

Once we arrived, a frowning Agent Sawyer sat us down in a small conference room but I managed to cadge some FBI coffee from him. I took that as a good sign. Not surprisingly, FBI coffee wasn't great.

Agent Baker appeared, sans jacket, and sat down next to us. "Well, that was interesting."

"How's Griffin?" I asked.

"Not good," she said. "The docs think he had a brain aneurysm."

"Oh no! That's horrible," I said. "Will he survive?"

"No way of telling," Agent Sawyer said. "At least there's no way for us to tell. How about you? Can you tell?"

Ryan and I glanced at each other. What were they getting at?

"We're not medical doctors," I said.

"I don't have any more information than I told you already," Ryan said. "We had a robbery in the UMC in which the perpetrators dissolved the wall somehow. Madison, here, thought quantum mechanics might be involved."

Agent Baker said, "Why did Madison think quantum mechanics was involved?"

Ryan looked at me but firmly kept his mouth closed. I guess he didn't want to implicate me. Yay, Ryan. He really was my favorite cousin.

I took a deep breath. Hopefully I wouldn't implicate myself. Or Andro. "Using quantum mechanics I accidentally made a hole in my office wall that was similar to the hole found at the UMC crime scene."

"Accidentally?" Agent Baker scowled. She must have been playing bad-cop.

"I had been studying this quantum mechanics stuff and I really wished there was a door into the office next door, and I was very agitated." This sounded stupid, even to me. "The next thing I knew, the wall got all misty and then disappeared. Pretty much the opposite of what just happened with Griffin when he appeared out of nowhere."

"What can you tell us about this Griffin?" she asked.

"I don't know anything about him except what I learned when I interviewed him after the UMC robbery," Ryan said. "I'd be happy to share my notes with you."

Agent Sawyer nodded. "Good, thanks."

"All I know is he's a student in my quantum mechanics class and he's a senior computer science major," I said.

"What's your relationship with him?" Agent Baker asked.

"What do you mean, what's my relationship?" I said, struggling not to raise my voice. "I'm his teacher. He comes to class and I lecture the class. He turns in homework and I grade it and give it back to him."

"Have you ever seen Griffin outside of class?" Agent Sawyer asked.

"No," I said, my voice as cold as the ozone hole above Antarctica. I did not like what he was implying.

"We did see him that time at the coffee shop," Ryan blurted.

I didn't recall that. I shot Ryan a very annoyed glance. "Was it the first week of school, with Luke?"

Ryan nodded.

"I barely knew who they were then."

Agent Baker said, "Is there anything else you'd like to tell us about Griffin Jin?"

I wanted to tell her I really hoped he would be okay, but I could tell that wasn't what she wanted to hear.

I started shaking my head as Ryan said, "What about Luke? Isn't Luke Griffin's roommate and best buddy?"

Agent Sawyer piped up, "Luke who?"

"Luke Bacalli," I said. "I think he's Griffin's roommate, but I'm not sure. They definitely hang out a lot."

"What's their address?" Agent Sawyer asked.

"I have no idea, but you can probably get it from the university," I said, glancing at Ryan. How did he know anything about Griffin or Luke? And was he going to volunteer anything else? He was making me look like I was hiding stuff.

Both of the agents looked at me. No doubt they were

suspicious of me because Ryan kept volunteering info and I didn't.

The silence in the room grew to uncomfortable levels.

"Professor Martin, where were you last night at midnight?" Agent Baker asked.

I gulped. "I was at home with Ryan and his family. At midnight I think I was asleep."

"Can anyone verify that?" Agent Baker asked.

"I guess not. No." Shit. Maybe if I'd made a move on Andro...

"She was home," Ryan said. "I would have heard if she left."

The agents didn't look too convinced.

"Let's go over this quantum mechanics thing again," Agent Baker said.

I did not sigh although I really wanted to, as I started to explain again.

Ryan and I were stuck with the agents for another forty-five minutes before they finally let us go, warning me not to leave town.

The drive home was long and quiet. I was drained. Being grilled by federal agents really takes it out of you. What would come of all this? How much trouble had I gotten Ryan into? Would the FBI take us into custody? Were Luke and Griffin involved in the bank robbery?

And most of all would Griffin be okay?

Chapter Fourteen

As I entered the lobby of the physics building, I ran into that woman who works in the main office. What was her name?

"Professor Martin," she said. "There you are. Professor Chen's been trying to get a hold of you."

Her name started with an N. "I'm sorry. I had a personal emergency this morning."

"Nothing serious, I hope," she said.

Well, I wasn't in jail yet. "No. Is Professor Chen available now?"

She glanced at her phone. "He's about to go to lunch. But you might be able to catch him."

I followed her into the main physics office.

Chen was exiting his office. "Madison. Finally."

I had my excuses ready, but he didn't give me a chance.

"I wanted to tell you that Alyssa came to talk to me again," he said. "She was full of complaints about you: you wouldn't let her do the research she wanted, you were interfering in her love life, and other outrageous claims. I've had enough of her. I told her we were letting her go after this semester."

Poor Alyssa. "I think that decision is a bit hasty, sir. I wish you would reconsider."

"No. My decision's final." He shook his head. "Now, if you'll excuse me, I have lunch plans." He strode out of the office.

I dragged myself up to my own office. This day was not going well.

I knew it probably wouldn't do any good, but I called Alyssa.

She actually answered. "Alyssa? This is Madison."

"What do you want?" She sounded like she'd been crying.

"I just wanted to check and see if you're okay. Professor Chen mentioned your conversation."

"No, I'm not okay. My life is ruined."

"Don't give up. There might be a chance you could stay in school. We need more female physicists."

"It's not only that. Luke has a girlfriend, some slut that works at the health center. Courtney something."

Ugh. That sounded bad. I thought of Alyssa showing up at school the other morning in Luke's t-shirt. That sounded really bad. "I'm sorry."

"At least now I know why he wouldn't sleep with me."

Ugh, more information that I needed. "Maybe I'm not the best person to talk to about this. But, please stop by my office when you're feeling better and we can talk about your future."

"Who cares about school at a time like this?" She ended the call.

As soon as I hung up, Andro popped into my office. His crisp burgundy- and navy-striped shirt fit perfectly, drawing attention to his chest. At least it drew my attention. "I know you're not a morning person, but this is a bit ridiculous." He flashed his even white teeth. "Did you oversleep?"

He looked good. Maybe this day wasn't going quite so badly. I flashed him a grin. "Ha, ha. Even I can't sleep in until after noon." At least not without company. Should I do it? Ask him out? Was I really ready to date so soon after the Ted fiasco? And thinking of the conversation I'd just had, could any man be trusted? Then I had a disturbing thought: was I rushing things because I might need another alibi? Reluctantly, I decided I was too confused and there was too much other stuff going on right now to start something up with him.

"Madison?" he said.

"Sorry," I said. "What were you saying?"

"I asked if you were free tomorrow after work," he said.

A smile exploded onto my face like a nuclear bomb. Had he asked me out? "Why?"

"I said, I decided to take your advice and investigate Armando's accident. I invited all his coworkers over for beer and I thought you could come over and help me and Yasmin interview them."

Suddenly I didn't feel quite so much like smiling. He didn't want to date me. He just wanted help with an investigation.

But I was in favor of catching bad guys. "Sure. I'd be happy to help."

"Do you want to go to Burritos and Beers for lunch today to strategize?"

"Thanks, but I better not," I said. "I have a lot of work to catch up on." I did have a ton of work and it wasn't going to get done if I was full of beer or spent the afternoon flirting with Andro.

"Are you all right?" he asked.

"Yep. Thanks for asking. I just have to get ready for class tomorrow and I haven't gotten much research done this week. I'm swamped." I forced a smile.

"If you say so." He didn't look convinced. "Okay. I guess I'll see you later?"

"Yep. Bye." Darn it.

He shuffled into his office.

Friday morning in class I waited in vain a few extra minutes for Luke or Griffin to show up. They didn't. "Today we're going to review chapter three," I said at the beginning of class. On the bright side, without Luke and Griffin there, class went surprisingly well.

I was nervous as I stood on Andro's front porch after work with a case of beer. I'd been avoiding him all day. Could I remain platonic? Was that even what I wanted? Confused, I rang the doorbell.

He opened the door and his face lit up when he saw me. "Madison. Great. Welcome." He stepped out of the doorway, but not far enough.

I had to brush against him to get in the house. And there were those lightning bolts arcing between us. Darn it. Danger. Danger, Dr. Martin.

He smiled. "I wasn't sure you'd make it you've been so busy the last couple days."

I tried not to smile back at him. "I said I would come so I did."

I stepped into the family room which was filled with Chicanos standing around sipping *cervezas*.

Yasmin approached wearing cute black cropped pants and a white lacy blouse. She looked much more cheerful and prettier than she had the other night. "Hi, Madison. Nice to see you again. Let me take that beer to the kitchen."

"Hi, Yasmin," I said. "You look nice."

She flushed as she took the beer. "Thanks." She went off to the kitchen.

"Why did Yasmin blush?" I whispered to Andro. "Do you think she might like one of these guys?"

"I have no idea," he said. "Do you think so?"

I shrugged.

"She did get all gussied up. That would be wonderful. Armando's been gone over a year. She needs to move on with her life."

I shushed him as the woman in question approached us with frosty beverages.

"Here." She shoved a bottle of beer at Andro. "This was your idea, get investigating." She turned to me, smiling. "I assume you'd like one, too?"

Me? Why would she assume that? But I grabbed the proffered beverage. I couldn't be rude, after all. "Thanks."

I smiled at her. "So, do any of these fine young men strike your fancy?"

She flushed again. That meant yes.

"Come on, Madison," Andro said. "Give the poor girl a break."

He led me over to two guys drinking beers in front of the fireplace. They were both wearing worn jeans and t-shirts. "Santiago, Hector, I'd like you to meet one of my colleagues from the university: Madison. Madison, these were Armando's best friends."

I waved. "*Hola*. Nice to meet you."

"*Hola*," Santiago said. He was slightly shorter than Hector and Andro.

"Hi," Hector said. His plaid shirt was neatly tucked in.

"We wanted to ask you what you remembered about Armando's accident," Andro said.

Santiago looked at the floor and shook his head.

Hector muttered something under his breath.

"Sorry," I said. "I didn't catch that."

"Poor Armando," Hector said. "Good guy. Great guy. Didn't deserve to be run down like a dog in the street."

"The cops didn't do shit," Santiago added.

Andro's face froze. "We know."

It hit me that Andro looked like that when he was feeling particularly emotional. I was starting to understand him. For some reason that made me feel good. Focus, Madison.

"That's why Andro and Yasmin asked you here," I said. "If it's all right, can you tell us what you remember?"

"Guess so." Santiago took a swig of his beer.

I held up the micro-cassette recorder I'd brought (since my cell was still MIA). "Can we tape you?" I asked.

Hector shrugged. "If it'll help Armando and his family." He glanced over at Yasmin.

"Yeah," Santiago said.

I flipped on the recorder.

"So, what happened?" Andro asked carefully.

"We were driving on 36 from Louisville," Santiago said. "It was about six a.m."

"Why from Louisville?" I asked.

"The office was there. We'd meet up before a job, load the truck, and ride to the job site together." Hector shifted on his feet.

"So, anyway, one of the power saws fell out of the back," Santiago said. "I don't know what those jokers were doing back there."

Hector interrupted. "I saw it fall. I was sitting inside with Santiago and Armando, so I told Armando. He cursed and pulled off onto the shoulder."

"Yeah, that Armando could curse," Santiago said. "Remember?"

The two men chuckled softly and Andro joined in.

"Where along 36 was it?" Andro asked.

"At the bottom of the hill close to town," Hector said.

Santiago frowned. "There was hardly any traffic, we didn't think there was danger."

"If only that were true," Andro said.

They all looked so sad. A wave of sadness washed over me.

Santiago held his hands up. "I didn't tell him to get out. He was the boss. He got out on his own."

"Can you tell us what happened next?" Andro asked.

The two men took sips of beer at the same time.

"Armando walked back to the saw," Santiago said. "A SUV came down the hill."

"Yeah, out of nowhere," Hector said. "It was moving, maybe doing eighty or ninety."

"And then you know what happened," Santiago said, looking down at the floor.

Another wave washed over me. Poor Armando.

I glanced at Andro. His face was a frozen mask. He knew what happened, all right.

"Thanks, guys," I said. "I know this is tough. Do you remember anything about the SUV? Did you see the license plate?"

"It was black, four door," Santiago said. "Didn't see the plate, or at least I don't remember."

"Me neither. But I think it was an Expedition," Hector said.

"What?" Andro said. "You knew the make and model?" He turned to me. "Was that in the police report?"

I shook my head. "I don't think so." I wracked my brain. "I think all Ryan said they had was black SUV."

A clue. This was an excellent development. I felt a tiny ripple of optimism.

"Was it new?" Andro asked. "What year do you think it was?"

Hector said, "I'm not sure what year."

"It was beat up," Santiago said. "Not new."

"What else do you remember?" Andro asked. "Did it slow down? Swerve? Stop? How many people were inside?"

"It slowed down," Santiago said. "I think there were two white guys inside."

"Anything else?" Andro asked.

They thought for a few moments, sipping their beers.

"There were a bunch of stickers on the bumper," Hector added.

Andro shook his head and I knew he was thinking: the cops really dropped the ball on this one.

"Do you remember what any of the stickers said?" I asked

eagerly.

Hector squinted.

Santiago took a swig of beer.

I did too. I'd gotten so caught up in their story I'd forgotten to drink mine.

Finally, Hector shook his head. "Sorry, man. It was a long time ago."

"I didn't even remember there were stickers until Hector mentioned it," Santiago said.

"Please try and remember, *amigos*," Andro said, "for Armando's sake. And for Yasmin and their girls. They deserve justice."

Hector gulped and nodded. "I'll try." His eyes drifted to Yasmin across the room.

Santiago and Hector's comments were the only helpful information we uncovered. We asked the other guys what they remembered and they didn't remember much. I couldn't follow most of their conversations because my Spanish wasn't too good.

They all hung around for another hour or so chatting and drinking beers, and then most of them departed. Only Santiago and Hector stayed behind.

Yasmin let Maria and Theresa join the group and they starting running around like cute little hooligans. Hector and Santiago seemed delighted by the girls' antics.

I joined Andro on the couch.

"I still can't believe Hector knew the make and model of the car and the cops didn't listen," Andro said, shaking his head. He was very attractive when he was incredulous.

I nodded. "It's a fripping shame."

"You and your made-up word." He turned to me and grinned. He was very attractive when he was playful.

"But," he said, "seriously, thanks for coming up with the idea to investigate." His eyes bored into mine. He was very attractive when he was mesmerizing.

Danger, Madison. I looked away from him.

Santiago was talking to the girls. I noticed Yasmin and Hector sitting at the kitchen counter. She laughed at what he said and touched his arm.

"Bingo," I whispered and pointed at them. "Check it out. I think Yasmin likes Hector." Touching was a dead giveaway.

Andro touched my arm, causing a river of heat to run up my arm and back down toward my nether regions. Was it hot in here?

"You were right," he whispered, grinning.

Had someone sucked all the oxygen out of the room? I'd been about to say that touching was a good sign, but now I couldn't string the words together.

Andro liked me. I felt an overwhelming urge to go for it. Frip my man-cation! "So, uh, Andro."

He looked like he was on the verge of chuckling. "What's wrong with you?"

"I, uh, just wanted to ask you, if..."

"I've never known you to have any trouble speaking your mind." He smiled. "Spit it out, girl."

I forced myself to finish the sentence. "So, do you want to go out tomorrow night?"

"Saturday night?" he asked. "What, like a date?"

"Yeah." I nodded, suddenly terrified.

A slow grin spread across his face. "Ya, baby. Definitely."

Wow.

Chapter Fifteen

I floated in the stratosphere all the way home. Andro and I had a date tomorrow night.

When I stepped into the kitchen, Ryan, Sydney, and Cathy were finishing dinner, tofu-something by the looks of it. Sydney jumped up from the table. "Madison. Hi. You got a package. We left it in your room. We weren't expecting you for dinner. Can I fix you something?"

I smiled at her. "Thank you very much, but I can rustle something up. I'm not a guest."

Cathy snorted. "In that case, why don't you do the dishes?"

"Sure." I glided over to the table and started scooping up plates and silverware.

"Are you feeling all right, Madison?" Sydney asked.

"What's wrong with you?" Ryan asked.

"Maybe she's high," Cathy said.

"Mom," Sydney said. "Madison doesn't get high." She peered into my face. "Do you?"

"I bet she heard about Griffin," Ryan said, protecting his not-quite-empty plate from me. He scooped up the last of its contents with his fork.

I paused. "What about Griffin?" Please let him be okay.

"My buddy Nate from the FBI called. The docs said Griffin's going to be all right. They might even release him from the hospital tomorrow. And the Bureau isn't going to hold him right now in the bank robbery. Not enough evidence."

Phew. He was okay. "That's great news."

And if the FBI was letting him go, he must be innocent. By implication, that meant Luke was in the clear too. Awesome. I ascended into the mesosphere.

Sydney fixed some herbal tea for herself and Cathy and they went to admire Emily.

I finished clearing the table and filled one side of the sink with water, dish soap, and dirty dishes.

Ryan got himself a beer. “Do you want one?”

“Sure.” I nodded.

He handed me a Fat Tire. “Okay, what’s up with you? Did you discover a new particle or something?”

“I took your advice and asked Andro out on a date.” I took a swig of beer.

His eyes bugged out. “You did? And he said yes?”

I started washing dishes. “Why do you look so surprised? Why wouldn’t he say yes?” I was on the verge of spraying him with water.

“Sorry. Of course he would say yes.” He grinned. “I’m just surprised you took my advice. You never take other people’s advice. A date with Andro. You go, girl.” He stuck his fist out for a bump.

My clenched fingers met his. “Thanks.”

He leaned back against the counter and took a pull from his beer bottle. “Why didn’t you just go out tonight?”

Good question. “Because.” I didn’t know what else to say to that, so I sprayed him with the sink’s hose sprayer.

Saturday night I had a whole big audience consisting of Ryan, Sydney, Emily and Cathy as I stepped into the kitchen, modeling my third possible outfit for the big date. Personally, I wanted to go with outfit number one, jeans and t-shirt, but Sydney and Cathy nixed that one.

Emily didn’t explicitly say so, but I thought she was on my side. She had gurgled positively at outfit one, anyway.

Outfit number two had been my suit which got laughed out of the room.

Outfit three was a turquoise and brown skirt I’d picked up on clearance for about six bucks, a matching turquoise short-sleeved blouse, and my leather sandals.

“That’s not bad,” Sydney said. “For you.”

“Don’t you have some nicer shoes?” Cathy asked.

"Guys don't care about shoes," Ryan said. "What about a shorter skirt? Or a tighter shirt?"

I glared at him. "Not helping. I'm trying to look pretty, not slutty."

He cracked up. "Slutty might work better. You're no spring chicken."

Sydney laughed. "Ignore him. You look nice. Wear that."

"I'm kidding, of course," Ryan said. "You do look nice. Are you nervous?"

Suddenly, a flock of pterodactyls started flying around in my stomach. "Uh, no. What do I have to be nervous about?" Only my first first-date in over three years. "No worries." So, I was trying to convince myself, what of it?

There was a thunderous knock on the front door.

When I opened it, Andro stood on the other side. "Hi." He wore black dress pants and a dramatic cerulean-blue dress shirt that matched his beautiful eyes.

"Hi," I said.

"Sorry if my knock was too loud. I was trying to be firm, but not too firm. You know, strong but not too aggressive. You know?" He fidgeted back and forth on the balls of his feet.

At the sight of his obvious nervousness, my pterodactyls flew away or maybe they became extinct. "Relax, Andro." I touched his arm. "This is supposed to be fun."

I stepped out onto the front stoop and yelled, "Bye" back into the house.

"Curfew is at ten p.m. sharp, young lady," Ryan said.

"Yeah, right." He started to say something else, but I shut the door mid-sentence.

"You look nice," I said to Andro. "The shirt brings out the color of your eyes."

"You look nice too," he said.

"I think you wore that outfit the day we met."

He smiled, his shoulders relaxing. "I think so, too. I'm surprised you remembered."

"I'm surprised you remembered." I smiled. "Admit it, you thought I was a kook when we met."

"Well..." We got in his car. "Maybe a little kooky. But kooky in an attractive way."

It was sort of a compliment. I'd take it.

We quickly found ourselves at Twenty Ninth Street, the open-air mall, where we'd agreed to go to dinner and a movie. We parked on the East side, near the movie theatre, and walked toward the mall section. The buildings were all faced with red sandstone, and the pedestrian area was filled with exuberant flower-filled planters and science displays. I loved this mall.

"So, what are you in the mood for? Mexican? Italian? Asian? What?"

The Italian place would probably be the most romantic, but I didn't think I could handle Andro in a romantic atmosphere. It would be too intense. "What do you think?"

"I don't know," he said.

I asked him out so I should probably decide. "What about the Asian place?"

"Sounds good," he said. "I think it's called Pee Wee."

I laughed. "As in Pee-Wee Herman or as in I just had an accident in the kiddy pool?"

"Remind me not to go swimming with you," he said, shaking his head in mock consternation.

We started off with edamame and crab wontons. The edamame was yummy, but it was hard to look glamorous when the soybeans kept shooting around the table as I tried to suck them out of the pods. It was bad enough when one landed in my glass of Sapporo, but it was downright embarrassing when one smacked him in the cheek.

Luckily he didn't get upset. He guffawed. "You're horrible at eating that. Use your fingers or a fork or something."

He had a point. I opened the next pod with my fingers, glancing up at him. His longish brown hair was tousled, his cheeks were a little flushed, his blue eyes twinkled, and there was a hint of a smile on his lips. He looked happy. Wow, he was very attractive when he was happy.

"So," I said, "I'm guessing you got over your nerves?"

"You guessed right." He grinned. "Having your date shoot her food at your face pretty much takes the pressure off."

"Glad I could help." Having your date be calm when you hit him in the face with a soybean also took the pressure off.

He started telling me a funny story about Maria and Theresa

and then our entrées arrived.

"Wow. That was quick," I said. "Didn't we order like a minute ago?"

"It was really fast," Andro said. "They have good service here."

I checked my phone. We'd been there forty minutes. How could that be? I felt giddy. I concluded that I must have had too much beer. But when I looked at my glass, it was full--complete with the soybean still sitting on the bottom.

"Aren't you going to eat?" He said, digging into his sweet and sour chicken.

"Do you even have to ask?" I stabbed some chicken in my Asian coconut curry with one chopstick.

He started laughing.

I looked up at him. "What?"

The rest of the dinner flew by as quickly as the beginning had. All too soon, the meal was over, the waitress brought the bill, and I gave her my credit card.

"Hey," he said, "I was going to pay."

"But I asked you out. It was my idea." And what an excellent idea it was, if I did say so myself.

"But, the guy…"

I looked at him sideways. "You better not be about to say the guy is supposed to pay. That's archaic."

"But." He regrouped. "You have to at least let me pay for the movie."

"That sounds like a plan. Besides, nowadays movie tickets are about fifty bucks a pop, so I should come out ahead." I grinned.

I lobbied for the new science fiction flick, but he didn't go for it.

He picked the new romantic comedy, and the tickets weren't fifty bucks apiece. Quite.

We got settled into the stadium seating and as the lights went down he reached for my hand. Warmth snaked from my hand to the rest my body. I could barely focus on the commercials. That wasn't good. Where was I going to get a giant M & M chocolate sports car when I needed it? And how was I going to follow the movie?

When the movie started, I became concerned for the people

sitting near us. How could they concentrate on the film when Andro and I were saturating the air with so many bolts of romantic energy?

And then he leaned over in the dark and kissed me.

I melted. It's a wonder they didn't find me in a pool under the seats. It was even better than our other kiss, and I'd thought that was awesome. He pressed his lips against mine with just the right blend of strength and gentleness, pouring his feelings into me until they intermingled seamlessly with mine.

And then we were rudely interrupted.

"Turn it off."

"Answer your phone, loser."

The girl sitting next to me poked me on the arm. "Your purse is ringing, lady." She glared at me.

Oh right. I'd gotten my purse and my phone back from Missouri. I dug through my purse until I found the offensive device.

"Just turn it off," Andro said, his eyes liquid desire.

The little window said it was Ryan. He knew I was on my big date and I didn't think he would call unless it was important.

"Turn it off, lady."

"Just a sec." I scooted past Andro, brushing his knees, ran down the steps to the hallway behind the theater and answered. "This better be good, Ryan."

"Madison. Good. All hell's breaking loose. I'm at a fraternity party on The Hill and they're doing quantum stuff. Crimes. You have to get over here. I just hope you can stop them."

Andro and I drove over to The Hill, where we followed the bass beat. In front of one of the fraternities we found a swarm of college kids on the lawn and a Boulder PD car with two uniformed officers standing on the sidewalk with Ryan.

Ryan sprinted over to us in the car. "Thanks for coming."

"I don't see anything quantum-y or even weird," I yelled over the music, looking out the car window.

Then, one of the officers got blurry. "Uh, oh. That can't be good." I pointed. But the only thing that happened was all his clothes disappeared. And he was a good-looking fit guy.

"Ouch." Andro said. "It's gotta be difficult to arrest people if you're naked."

I was still checking out the officer.

"Madison, come on," Ryan said. "Get out. We need you. Do you think you can collapse the wavefunction?"

I glanced at Andro.

"Do you need some adrenaline?" He wiggled his eyebrows. "I guess I could kiss you if it was in the interests of national security."

Our lips met and I felt like I could do anything. Quickly, I scampered out of the car.

"I'll park and meet you back here," Andro said.

"Hurry back," I said as he started driving away.

When I turned my attention back to the hapless, shirtless, pantless policeman, he was standing on the sidewalk staring down at his nakedness.

The other officer's mouth was hanging open. "What the hell? Ben, what happened to your uniform?"

I almost hated to cover Ben up he was so fine, but I concentrated on q-lapsing and he appeared clothed in blurriness. It coalesced into a police uniform.

"What else?" I asked Ryan.

"The police car," he said, pointing.

"What about it?" It looked like a regular police car to me.

"The lights and siren are gone. Bizarre." Ryan shook his head.

"Say no more." I q-lapsed and rematerialized them. Immediately, they flashed and screamed. The siren was very loud. The partiers on the lawn looked our way.

"What else?" I asked Ryan.

"What?" he said, I think.

"What?" I said.

Oh good grief. I concentrated on q-lapsing to quiet the siren and the thumping music. Mission accomplished on the siren. Stopping the music was more of a struggle but it eventually sputtered and stopped.

"Hey," one of the kids yelled.

"What the hell?"

"Pigs!"

The crowd was not happy. I now noticed several of the young

women were missing their tops. "Those girls aren't wearing any shirts." They didn't seem overly concerned about it either.

"I told you it was crazy here," Ryan said. "Somehow I don't think that's how they arrived at the party. Check out the magically-refilling cups of beer, too." He pointed at some guys lounging on the front patio.

First things, first. I concentrated on q-lapsing to give the topless women some tops but I couldn't manage it. I was worn out and I was getting a headache. But I kept trying.

In the meantime, the cops had called for backup.

Soon, several more police cars zoomed up, sirens blaring.

And then my own personal backup, Andro, arrived, panting. "You wouldn't believe how far away I had to park."

"I'm glad you're here," I said. "I'm not feeling so well."

"Gee, college parties have changed a lot since I was in school," Andro said. "Or else I studied way too much. Those women are topless."

"Help me q-lapse to give them shirts," I said.

"Wait. Stop," Ryan said.

Andro blinked at him. "What? Don't give them shirts? You're not saying you want to ogle some young, probably drunk, co-eds, are you? You're a married man, Ryan."

"No. That's not it." Ryan stepped right in front of me and looked me in the eyes. "What do you mean you don't feel well?"

Andro frowned.

"I'm getting a huge headache," I said. "And I feel a little nauseous."

The cops were finally managing to disperse the crowd, and the students trickled away in small wobbly groups. But a couple of the guys on the patio didn't get up. They were moaning and clutching their heads.

I stumbled and Andro caught me.

"You're acting sort of like Griffin. I think I figured something out," Ryan said. "Collapsing the wavefunction screws up your head, somehow. That's why Griffin got that brain aneurysm."

Ah ha. My head was killing me.

"Stop, Madison," Andro said. "Don't try to q-lapse any more."

"Okay." I tried not to grimace. "You talked me into it."

"I want you to take her straight home and put her to bed,"

Ryan said to Andro.

"Yes, sir," Andro said.

That sounded great. Too bad I wouldn't be able to enjoy it. With my pounding head, just walking to the car took all my concentration.

Chapter Sixteen

Most of Sunday I spent in bed, but Monday morning I was as good as new. I was even sort of pleasantly surprised to see Luke and Griffin before class Monday morning--until they started talking. They sat down in the front row as the rest of the students trickled in.

"Hey, Teach," Luke said, in his usual cocky drawl. "How was your weekend?"

"My name is Professor Martin and my weekend was fine. Thanks for asking, Luke. Griffin, I'm glad to see you are doing better than the last time I saw you." The last time I'd seen him he'd been in a heap on the floor of the bank.

In his *Byte Me* t-shirt Griffin smirked. "Why? Did you hear something from that security guard relative of yours?"

Was he asking me for information about the bank robbery investigation? "I heard you were in the hospital. I'm glad to see you're out. You must be feeling better."

He didn't have a response for that.

"So, did you do anything exciting over the weekend?" Luke asked. "Maybe go to a fraternity party?" He flashed his pearly whites at me.

I hadn't seen Luke at the party Saturday night but apparently he'd seen me. Very interesting. Now the whole thing including all the topless women made much more sense.

"Madison?" someone said from the doorway. It was Andro from his shiny leather shoes to his wavy brown hair.

I felt an impulse to smile goofily but suppressed it. "Andro. Hi. What brings you here? It's almost time for my class to start."

He walked over to me and said softly, "You didn't stop by our office and I just wanted to make sure you were feeling all right, you know, after the other night."

Unfortunately, he didn't talk softly enough because my students started chuckling.

But Andro was concerned about me. A grin may have slipped out. "I'm fine. Thanks for your concern." I glanced at the students, who were thoroughly enjoying themselves. "But let's talk later." I inclined my head at the young men.

He seemed surprised to see them sitting there watching us. "Oh, yeah, right. We'll talk later." He hustled out the door.

"Professor Martin and Professor Rivas sitting in a tree..." a coward in the back of the room sang out. Most of the other guys giggled. Who knew grown men giggled?

I put my hands on my hips, sticking my elbows out. "You have got to be kidding," I said in a very stern tone.

The students sobered up.

I turned back to Griffin and Luke. "Anyway, you guys missed class Friday. You're responsible for the material we covered that day."

Pankaj, also sitting in the front row, said, "Professor Martin, it is time to be starting class, now. Past time."

I forced myself to smile at him. "You are correct, Pankaj. Settle down everyone, and pass your homework to the front."

Sheets of paper rustled like aspen leaves in the wind.

"Today we're going to start by reviewing what a vector is," I said.

"Why we doin' that?" one of the students said.

I collected the papers.

Griffin interrupted. "Even I know what a vector is."

"Yeah?" Luke said looking at Griffin, with a smirk on his face. "What is it, then, G?"

"Ah," Griffin stammered.

"I'm sure you have all used vectors before," I said. "But in quantum mechanics we have to be very specific. So, let's review. A vector is a quantity that has both a magnitude and a direction." I started writing on the board.

As soon as I got back to my office I called Ryan. "Guess what?" I asked him.

"Okay. What?" Ryan said.

"Luke and Griffin came to class this morning and asked me about the fraternity party."

"They came to class just to ask you about a party?" he asked.

"No. They came to class to learn some physics." I paused. "Or, wait, I guess they could have come to ask me about the party. Do you think so?" I shook my head. "Anyway, the point is they knew about the party and were probably there."

My eye was drawn to movement in the big hole in my wall. Andro stood there, waving at me.

I waved back.

"I already thought they had something to do with the party since it was so weird," Ryan said. "Have you seen the paper today?"

"No," I said. "I rushed to class and then called you right after."

"You should check it out. I guess there were a bunch of quantum events around town over the weekend. I've had some phone calls about it already this morning. This afternoon we're having a pow-wow. Oops, there's someone on the other line. It's Nate. I have to take this. Talk to you later." He hung up on me.

I didn't have time to be irritated with Ryan because Andro was striding toward me. He stopped right in front of me. Energy bolts zapped between us. "How are you this morning?" he asked.

Much better now. "Good," I managed to eke out between grins.

He looked down at me with longing in his eyes.

"How are you?" I asked.

He closed the distance between us.

Was he going to kiss me right in my office? Hopefully.

He leaned down.

His hand caressed my cheek. "You were so out of it after the frat party I never got my goodnight kiss on our date."

"Me neither," I said, the ends of my mouth quirking up.

"What can we do about that?" His blue eyes bored into mine.

I lifted my chin and closed my eyes slightly.

The space-time continuum froze as he gently held my chin and his lips explored mine. Slowly, my mouth parted and his tongue darted in.

I leaned in and pressed my body against his. Mmm.

He took a step back. “Whoa.” His face was flushed. “You have no idea what you’re doing to me.”

My skin felt like it was on fire and my pulse zinged. “I have a pretty good idea.”

He pointed behind my desk. “You go back there and sit down and I’ll sit way over here.”

After a couple seconds of thinking, I said, “You’re probably right. We shouldn’t be making out at work. We are professionals.” I walked back behind my desk.

He settled into a chair and smiled at me like he was thinking about making out at work.

I grinned. He was adorable and I was in big trouble. Strike that. I was in universe-sized trouble. “Speaking of trouble, Ryan said something about the paper. Did you see it?”

“Yes. Online,” he said slowly. “I didn’t see anything troublesome though.”

I frowned and opened my browser. “What’s Ryan talking about then?” I scanned the headlines. There was an article about the fraternity party but it was just-the-facts-ma’am boring. In fact, it omitted all the really interesting facts, like toplessness and actual nakedness.

When I turned, I was surprised to see Andro so close. He’d gotten up and was leaning over my desk to see the computer. Certain parts of me felt like they were heating up. Out of the corner of my eye I saw something blurry. “What’s that?” I pointed at the couch.

Andro turned around. Was he blurry around the edges? “*Mi Dios*.”

There were two fuzzy figures lying on top of one another on the couch. Human-shaped fuzzy figures that moved closer and then farther, and then closer…

Realization dawned. “Oh, my. What is that?”

Andro just turned back around and gave me a look that said, *Don’t be naïve*.

“Never mind,” I said. “I know what that is. Quick, think something sad.”

“Armando,” he muttered.

“Yes, Armando,” I said. Definitely sad. Very sad.

The figures faded away.

He collapsed back in the chair. “That was weird.”

“Yeah. I feel like I should apologize since I’m a better q-lapser than you,” I said. “I’m sorry if I was responsible for that.” I waved my hand in the general direction of the couch.

Andro smiled. “I’m sure it was a group effort.”

My pulse was still zinging. “I think I’m going to go see Ryan and see if he needs me to q-lapse something.”

“Good idea,” he said. “I think I’m gonna go over to the rec center and work out.” He started walking back to his office, pausing near the wall. “And we need to have another date. Soon.”

“Yeah.” I smiled. “I’ll check my schedule.” Ha. I knew my schedule was wide open.

Ryan’s office was surprisingly similar to mine: small and filled with run-down furniture. Unlike mine, there was a guy in uniform sitting in there with him. He was about Ryan’s age, but much more muscular, and he had that sexy shaved head some guys sported these days. And he looked familiar.

I knocked on the open door. “Hi. I’m not interrupting something, am I?”

Ryan jumped up. “Madison. No, I’m glad you stopped by. This is my friend Ben Willis. He works at the Boulder PD.” That explained the uniform and the patches that said Boulder PD. “You guys sort of met before.”

How does one sort of meet?

Ben stood up and held out his hand for a shake. “Madison, it’s nice to meet you officially. Ryan’s told me a lot about you. Thanks for your help the other night.”

“The other night?” I asked, mystified.

He blushed. “You know, at the frat party, I was naked. You helped me out. At least Ryan said it was you. I’m still not entirely sure what happened.”

“That was you?” He looked different with his clothes on. “You’re welcome. It’s nice to officially meet you, too.” It’s not every day you meet someone you’ve already seen naked.

But, no biggie. I struggled to change the conversation. “Are you, by chance, the fellow Ryan was going to ask about the death of Armando Rivera?”

Ben nodded as he sat back down. “Yes. Were you the one who found out the make and model of the car?” He indicated the empty chair next to him.

I sat. “Yes. Well, actually, it was Andro Rivas, Armando’s brother-in-law. Did it help? Do you have any leads?”

Ben sighed. “It did help. The problem is there are too many black Expedition SUVs registered in Boulder. We need to narrow it down. Did you get any other info? A partial plate or anything?”

“Just that it was an older, probably late nineties model.”

“Yeah, I got that. I don’t have any news, in that case. Sorry.” He frowned. “Unfortunately, we’ve been unusually busy lately.”

“Did you see the paper?” Ryan asked me.

“Yes. I looked at the paper,” I said, “but I didn’t see anything weird.”

“Interesting choice of words,” Ryan said, picking up his tablet from the desk. “Check it out.” He handed it to me.

It showed *News of the Weird* so I scanned that. The first article was titled *Are We Safe?* and gave an account of a nude police officer that tried to break up a party. I glanced at Ben.

“Ryan says you can use physics to control reality,” Ben said, meeting my eyes.

“Sort of,” I said, back to scanning the paper.

The next article was entitled *Police Blotter* and described one man who complained to police that his car had been turned into whipped cream. Several women in Boulder also reported their shirts just disappeared.

The next article was *Least Competent People* in which a man claimed the front window of a convenience store had disappeared so there was nothing wrong with taking stuff, and asked the police officers walking by to help him carry the loot. There were several other articles. I put the tablet down. “Yes. There’s definitely something weird going on.”

“That’s not the half of it,” Ryan said. “I have some friends on the force in Longmont and Louisville and in Denver that said weird stuff has started happening there, too.”

“All those places? That is worrisome,” I said. Very worrisome. Were all these people q-lapsing? How? It’s not like they were all physicists or even physics students.

Ryan sighed. “Madison, please tell Ben about your abilities.”

"Okay. I could probably q-lapse right now." I still felt zingy from my latest encounter with Andro.

"Q-lapse?" Ben asked. "What's that?"

"It's physics," I said. "Quantum mechanics more specifically. Some people might consider it controlling reality."

Ryan indicated his computer. "I was just telling Ben our theory about the website."

"What theory was that?" I asked.

"You know, that Luke and/or his buddy Griffin made the website to teach people how to control reality."

"Oh, right," I said. "But I got rid of that webpage."

"It's back." Ryan pointed at his desktop computer screen showing the webpage in question.

"Ugh." I stood up. Suddenly, all this weird news made much more sense. The three of us studied the webpage.

"I didn't tell you what Nate, my FBI contact, told me this morning," Ryan said. "The security guard from the bank robbery finally regained consciousness and he told the FBI quite a story: two young men appeared out of thin air inside the bank, dissolved the vault wall, grabbed a bunch of loot, and disappeared again. The descriptions he gave of the men match Luke and Griffin."

"Freaky." Ben shook his head. Unfortunately, it was sounding less and less freaky to me. "The guard's medical condition must have affected his mind. Did he have a stroke or something?"

"No," Ryan said. "It turns out he had a heart attack."

"You don't think Luke and Griffin gave him a heart attack somehow, do you?" I asked.

Ryan shrugged. "Who knows?"

Ben shook his head again.

"Ben, I'm sensing you're a little skeptical about quantum mechanics despite what you experienced Saturday night," I said.

"To tell the truth, I don't know what happened Saturday night." He crossed his arms. "I was dressed and then I wasn't. Maybe I was roofied?"

He was starting to aggravate me. "You don't have to believe in the theory, you just have to believe in the consequences." I turned to Ryan. "Do you want me to get rid of the webpage?"

Ryan nodded. "If you can." He must have been thinking of the

other night when I couldn't do it.
Ben stood up. "I'd like to see that."
"I've had just about enough of your attitude," I said pointing at him. "How can you not believe something you saw with your own eyes?"
I noticed my hand was fuzzy, and then a small bolt of lightning peeled off my index finger and zapped Ben in the chest.
"Ow." He stepped back. "What the hell was that?"
It must be some kind of static electricity.
"Yeah," Ryan said. "What just happened?"
"A consequence of quantum mechanics." I turned to the computer screen. "And here comes another one." I stared at the screen, focusing on collapsing the wavefunction. The webpage got blurry, the words and pictures ran together, and then it morphed into a blank gray page.
Ben stood rubbing his chest. "Can I check it?"
"By all means." I stepped aside.
He retyped the URL in the browser and the blank page reloaded. "Wow. There's nothing there." He looked at me in surprise. "I sort of thought Ryan was pulling my chain. You did do something to that webpage."
"I don't get it," Ryan said. "Why was it so easy this time? I thought you needed adrenaline or something."
"My system is revved up," I said. "I'd rather not get into the particulars of why."
"Why not? Are you on something?" Ben asked. "Something illegal?"
"No. Of course not," I said. "I was studying, interacting with a certain specimen of *homo sapiens* and noting the effects on levels of adrenaline when..." I deliberately didn't look at Ryan.
He snorted. "You mean you were making out with Andro, right?"
"In very crude layman's terms one might say..."
"So, that's a yes," Ryan said.
I shut up before I implicated myself further.
"I don't get all this," Ben said. "The webpage tells people about collapsing the wavefunction–or at least it used to–but that's only part of the story. People still need to be on adrenaline," he glanced at me, "or super-horny, or something. So

how come we're having incidents all over the area?"

Super-horny? Where'd he get that?

"They must be on some drug that acts like adrenaline," Ryan said. "Oh, no. I can't believe I didn't put this together until now."

Ben and I looked at him.

"What?" I asked finally.

"There were a bunch of drugs stolen from the campus health center last week," Ryan said.

"That reminds me of something." It was on the tip of my brain, but I couldn't quite get at it. "Sorry. It escaped me."

"It looks like you're right about her, Ryan," Ben said.

He better not make another comment about me and horniness. "What about me?" Was that a burst of lightning building up in my hand again?

"You're the closest thing we've got to a quantum cop," Ryan said.

Quantum cop. I liked the sound of that.

Chapter Seventeen

Alyssa stood waiting outside my office.

"Hi, Professor Martin," she said. "I was wondering if I could talk to you." She looked properly sheepish.

"Sure." I unlocked the door and we went in. She sat down and promptly knocked a huge pile of papers off my desk. "Oh, sorry." She leaned down to pick them up and hit her head. "Ouch."

I sat down. "Don't worry about it. I knock stuff off my desk all the time."

As I pondered if it would be rude to check my email while a student was in my office, I couldn't help noticing someone had stuck a sticky-note on my computer: 'Date tonight? I'll pick you up at home at seven. Be there or be a parallelepiped. –A'

I picked it up and grinned like the cat that caught the canary. No. I grinned like the cat that caught a whole flock of canaries. I forced myself to put down the note.

"What's that?" Alyssa craned over my desk to look at the tiny piece of paper. "Who's A? And what's a parallelepiped?"

"It's a three-dimensional solid whose faces are all parallelograms."

"Huh?" she said.

"It could be a cube, also known as a three-dimensional square. It's a reference to the old saying, *Be there or be square."*

"That must be from before my time. How old are you, anyway?" She narrowed her eyes. "Well, whoever A is, he's as big a geek as you are. Wait," she glanced behind her at the hole in the wall and leaned forward. "It's not Professor Rivas, is it?"

I raised my eyebrows at her. Surely, she knew I wasn't going to get into a discussion with her about my personal life. And how could she say Andro was geeky? Or me? "Why are you here?" Surely not to insult me.

"I wanted to apologize for losing my temper with you. I'm sorry," she said, her eyes shining. "I may have said some things I regret and didn't mean. I was upset. I'm not too good in the romance department. But I am good at physics. I hope you'll let me prove it to you."

I finally figured out why I felt so protective of Alyssa: she was me, albeit a decade younger and klutzier. And I sure knew what it was like to break up with someone.

But I wasn't going to think about Ted. Stupid cheater Ted. Oops.

"I was hoping you'd help me out with Professor Chen." She sniffled. "I'm really sorry for the things I said. It's always been my dream to be a physicist. I just got a little side-tracked there for a few days." She looked at me with dewy eyes. "Can you forgive me and take me back as your student?"

It wasn't bad as apologies went.

"Do you forgive me?" she asked again.

I leaned back in my chair. "I forgive you if you promise to be more polite and to focus on your studies," I said. "You need to quit being so distracted by men." Ugh. Just how much did we have in common?

"It's all that stupid Courtney's fault. Everything was going great until she came along," she said.

Courtney. That's what I'd been trying to recall this morning. "Did you say she worked at the health center?"

"Yeah, and she's a total b–"

"Okay, I get the picture," I said quickly. Could she be the one that stole the drugs? For Luke? I scribbled 'Courtney Health Center' on a piece of paper in case I forgot again.

"Anyway, back to you," I said. "Will you try to focus more on school?"

"I guess." She looked down. "Will you help me with Chen?"

"I'll try." I nodded. "I think the best way to win over Chen would be for you to do some really good physics that we could show him. Did you come up with any dissertation ideas yet?"

She scrunched up her nose. "I want to do something related

to particle accelerators so I can use what I've learned so far."

"Good idea," I said. "What about focusing on something that might be detected at the Large Hadron Collider in Europe?"

"That sounds good, but I don't know what that would have to do with neutrinos."

"What about the fourth family?" I suggested.

"What's that? I'm not familiar with that," she said.

"It's the idea that there's a fourth set of matter particles."

"Another set of quarks and leptons?" Alyssa asked.

"Yes. They call the quarks top-prime and bottom-prime and the leptons are tau-prime and tau-neutrino-prime. You could calculate the constraints the Large Hadron Collider places on their existence. Can the LHC detect them?" I leaned forward. "Now, that would be interesting."

"That does sound neat," she said. "We'd have to do a literature search first, though."

I beamed at her. "Good girl. Go to it."

She beamed back at me and headed for the door. "Okay. Thanks Professor Martin, I mean, Madison."

She was going to be a physicist yet.

I'd learned my lesson after Saturday night and did not solicit input on my outfit for my second date with Andro. That didn't stop Ryan and company from trying to give me advice, but I ignored them and stayed in my room until seven o'clock.

Just as I emerged, there was a confident knock on the door. I strolled over and opened it. It was Andro and he took my breath away with his friendly smile.

"Hello?" he said.

"Hi, there." I filled with a warm glow as I realized he was genuinely glad to see me.

"You were expecting me, weren't you?" he asked.

"Oh, yeah," Ryan said, nodding, coming up behind me. "She's been expecting you."

I took a step away from Ryan, which put me a step closer to Andro and tiny lightning bolts started collecting on my skin as if in preparation for a miniature multicell convective storm.

Andro smiled. "I have a request, Ryan."

"Shoot," Ryan said.

"Please don't call us with any quantum emergencies," Andro said.

"All right," Ryan said. He agreed easily--too easily. I didn't trust it.

Andro faced me. "I have a request for you, too, Madison. How about if you don't bring your phone? I left mine at home."

I glanced from Andro to Ryan. "What a fabulous idea." I dug my phone out of my purse and handed it to Ryan.

"In that case don't do anything I wouldn't do, young lady," Ryan said.

I pointed at Sydney feeding Emily on the couch. "Okay, but what exactly would that entail?"

Ryan could only come up with, "Hmm," in response.

Andro laughed. "Good point, Madison. Shall we go?"

"Definitely." I followed him out to his car.

We sat on the patio at Carelli's, an intimate little Italian place in our neighborhood. The weather was gorgeous, about seventy-five degrees with a slight breeze and the sun setting behind the mountains.

I concentrated on eating my dinner salad, because with the golden rays of the sun shining on him, Andro was dazzling. I wasn't going to think about that kiss this morning. Oops, that probably counted as thinking about it.

"You're definitely more proficient with a fork than you are with chopsticks."

I glanced up at him. "Am I eating too fast?"

"You're fine," he said. "What about some conversation?"

"My salad is good," I said.

"Obviously," he said. "You look very pretty tonight."

"You, too," I said.

He chuckled. "Thanks."

I groaned. "You know what I mean. I guess it's my turn to be nervous. Last time you were so obviously on pins-and-needles, it was cute."

"Cute. Just what every guy longs to hear," he said with amusement evident in his voice.

"Well, maybe guys that use the word *longs* do." I grinned, feeling like I'd known him forever.

"If you're feeling good enough to tease me, maybe you feel

good enough to answer a question," he said.

"Okay."

"Back at your house when you pointed at Emily you implied that you were up for anything."

Oh, wow. I did imply that.

"But I know you just broke up with that Ted guy and you had been saying you weren't ready to date yet," he said.

He better not bring up my stupid man-cation idea.

He smiled and I knew he was thinking about it.

"Uh, what was the question?" I asked, heading him off at the pass.

"I feel like we have a chance for something real here." He cleared his throat. "Do you?" He was nervous, after all. How cute.

"I would have to say yes," I said. And then I flashed back to my discussion about men with Alyssa earlier today.

He smiled at me and I tried not to melt.

"But I'm not ready to be totally intimate yet." Ack. What was I saying? "I'd rather take it kind of slow."

He raised his eyebrows. "I'll have you know I'm a good Catholic boy." He grinned.

Darn it. "Well, of course you're good. Why wouldn't you be?" I grinned back. "I deeply apologize if I implied you possessed any type or quality of non-goodness." And what would said non-goodness entail, I wondered for a second before squashing the thought.

"I should hope so," he said.

The waiter brought our entrées and the rest of the meal flew by.

After we paid, splitting the bill, we sauntered back out to the parking lot.

"What next?" he asked.

I drew a blank. "Home?" Tonight was turning out a tad anticlimactic after our date Saturday night complete with a near-riot and our steamy kiss this morning.

"Great," he said. "My home or yours?"

"I don't want to go to my house. Ryan, Sydney, Emily, and Cathy are there."

"And we can't go to my house. Maria and Theresa and

Yasmin are there," Andro said.

"I guess we just call it a night?" I said. "It is a school night."

"No," he said. "That's boring. Wait. I've got it." He hurried to unlock his car.

"Where are we going?" I asked, getting in.

"Wait and see." We drove west on Baseline Road, past the business district, past the residential area, past some park, past more houses and then started driving up. We followed the switchbacks up to a park on the top of the foothill. He parked amongst a few other cars.

The view was awesome. All of Boulder was laid out before us like a sparkling jewel, lights shining, as night settled over it. "What a view. This is beautiful," I said.

"I knew you'd like it." He slid across the front seat.

I was distracted by the car across the parking lot as it started to rock up and down. I looked back at Andro and he slid a little closer yet. "Hey. This is a make-out place."

"It is?" he asked, trying to look innocent. "I came for the view."

I tried really hard not to laugh. It didn't work.

Once I could breathe regularly again, I said, "As long as we're here, we might as well try a little kiss."

"Good idea. What could it hurt?" His right leg pressed against my left leg as we sat side-by-side on the seat. He took me in his arms and his mouth eagerly sought mine. As my lips touched his, I pressed my body against his. He slowly lowered his back onto the front seat and I followed, never losing contact with his lips.

My lips filled with molten lava that slowly oozed down my neck and enflamed my breasts. I rubbed them against Andro's chest and he moaned. A river of heat flowed down between my legs. I mashed my body against his.

He pulled away. "I need a break for a second." He sat up and scooted away. "This is taking it slow?"

I sat up too. "Well, it was your idea to come up here. And we're still dressed." I felt as if sparks were flying off me like a Van de Graff Generator. And the car wasn't as dark as it had been a moment ago. I glanced around and then looked outside. "Is there some kind of light on in here?"

Out of the corner of my eye, four patches of fog materialized next to our car. "Hey, did you see that fog? Where'd that come from?" I asked him.

"No. I'm looking at you. You're getting fuzzy and sort of glowy." He stared at me.

I stared back. "You, too."

"Oh, no," he said.

A blurry little lightning bolt literally boiled off him, followed quickly by one off me. They hit the dashboard and sizzled out. Wow.

"Huh. Some kind of imbalance of electric charges?" he said. "Like static electricity?"

I said, "Static electricity," at the same time.

And then the car door next to me opened.

Luke stood outside with three other people--one of which was Griffin. "What do we have here?" Luke said. "Two professors hooking up."

"Hey. We're not hooking up," I said. Not quite.

"Yeah, right," Luke said.

The two women, a curvaceous Chicana and a tall blonde, laughed.

"It worked, man," Griffin said. "You were right. We focused on them and here we are."

They just showed up? Wait. Were they the fog I'd seen earlier? I craned my neck looking around and the mysterious fog was gone.

Andro slid over and put his arm around me. "Mr. Bacalli, Mr. Jin, I suggest you and your friends leave us alone."

I was embarrassed to have been caught almost in the act so I scooted out of the open car door.

Luke and Griffin and their dates, I guessed, stepped back.

Andro followed me out.

"Yeah," I said. "What he said." Another blurry spark left my torso to dissipate in the cooling evening air. It kind of tickled.

Griffin pressed down on the hood of the car and let go, making it dip and bounce back up.

"Leave my car alone," Andro said, a bolt of lightning coming out of his fingertip.

Griffin ducked just in time. "What the fuck?"

Luke whooped. "How'd you do that? I want to do that."

I didn't know the women standing in the background, but I

was betting one of them was Courtney. "Let's calm down. No one wants to get hurt or to hurt anyone else."

Griffin took a step toward me. "The U.S. Attorney is investigating us for bank robbery."

"And we think you're why we were questioned." Luke took a step toward us.

"Could it be you were questioned about robbing a bank because you robbed a bank?" I asked.

Under my breath I said to Andro, "Should we call for help? Oh, damn, we can't."

"Do you really want to get into something with us?" Andro said voice steely, as another spark arced off him.

Griffin dodged the spark by disappearing and then reappearing a couple feet to the right. That couldn't be good for him after his aneurysm.

"You guys shouldn't q-lapse," I said. "It's dangerous."

"Like hell." The smaller woman flipped her glossy brown hair. Then she disappeared and reappeared.

"I'm serious," I said. "This stuff is dangerous. Please don't do it. You might get hurt. Griffin, remember how you felt when they found you at the bank?"

He scowled.

"She's just trying to psych you out, man," Luke said. "She's scared."

Scared? Why would I be scared? They probably weren't here to talk. Okay, I was a smidge scared.

The blonde woman stepped forward. "There's four of us. It's four against two."

"If you attack us we will defend ourselves," Andro said.

"We don't want to hurt you," I said.

The taller blonde woman said, "Bring it on, bitch."

How rude.

"Do it like we planned," Luke said.

All four of them held up their hands and scrunched up their faces.

I felt a little tingling in my chest and glanced at Andro. I could tell from his expression he felt something too. "Andro, did I tell you that bank guard had a heart attack?"

"No. You did not mention that," he said, frowning. "But maybe you should have." Maybe so.

The tingling was starting to feel like a pressure. Definitely so.

"Last chance," I said. "Give up, now."

They ignored me.

Andro held his blurry hands out in front of him and reluctantly I followed suit. I focused all my weird sexual energy into my fuzzy fingertips and tried to q-lapse.

Thin bolts of energy streamed from our fingers smashing into the students and they stumbled back.

"Ouch," the smaller woman said.

"That hurt," the taller woman said.

The pressure in my chest went away. "Are you okay, Andro?"

"Yes," he said. "No thanks to these brats."

"Shit," Luke said, shaking. "How'd you do that?"

"Do you want more?" Andro asked.

"Shit," Griffin said. "Let's get out of here."

"I don't feel so well," the small brunette said.

"Yeah, let's go," the blonde said.

"Fine." Luke sighed.

They got blurry and disappeared.

Andro and I leaned back against the car.

"That was bizarre," he said. "What was with that lightning?"

"I don't know, but I'm glad we could do it and they couldn't."

My sexual buzz had worn off. I was drained and my head hurt. "Can you take me home?"

"Yeah." He nodded. "I have a headache now anyway." He squeezed my hand. "Sorry, babe."

Chapter Eighteen

Tuesday morning when I emerged from my bedroom and plodded into the kitchen, the family sat around the table in their pj's and robes. Emily and Cathy were eating breakfast. Ryan's plate was empty.

"So?" Sydney asked, cradling Emily in her lap.

"Yeah, how was it?" Ryan asked.

Cathy focused on her bowl of whole-grain cereal.

I sat down at the table after loading up the coffeemaker with real coffee. "Dinner was awesome. I was a little nervous at first, but got over it. Andro actually said he thought we had a chance for something real."

Sydney squeaked. "He said that? Wow. That's big."

"Guys don't usually talk like that," Ryan said. "Are you sure he didn't say something veal? Was this before or after you ordered? You were at an Italian place, right?"

I ignored him. "And, then, after dinner we went up to the end of Baseline Road and parked."

Cathy muttered something that sounded suspiciously like 'slut.'

"Mom," Sydney said, the hint of a laugh in her voice.

"Whatever," Cathy said and took another spoonful of cereal.

I was definitely starting to detect a negative vibe from Cathy. "Anyway, we were, uh, just talking in this parking lot with a great view of Boulder."

Ryan snorted. "Yeah, right."

"What he said," Sydney said. "Yeah, right, you were just talking." She had a lewd glint in her eye. "I've met Andro."

I flashed back to how perfectly my lips fit together with his, and how firm and warm his chest was.

"Earth calling Madison," Ryan said.

I blushed. "Sorry. So where was I? We were talking and stuff and then Luke and Griffin and two girls attacked us and we had a quantum duel."

Cathy choked on her cereal, poor thing.

"What?" Sydney said, and started hitting her mom on the back.

Ryan just shook his head slowly.

"And Andro and I won and ran them off and they disappeared into thin air," I said. "And that's how my date went." I got up to pour myself some coffee as it gurgled to the finish line.

"What the heck is a quantum duel?" Sydney asked.

I took a sip of coffee and looked at her over the rim of the mug. "They attacked us using quantum mechanics and we defended ourselves using quantum mechanics."

"How did they attack you?" Ryan asked.

"I think they tried to give us heart attacks." I grimaced.

He sucked in a breath.

Cathy shook her head.

"Why would they do that?" Sydney asked. "How would they do that?"

"By collapsing the wavefunction," I said. "Q-lapsing."

"The security guard at that bank down in Denver had a heart attack during the robbery." Ryan pressed his mouth into a thin line. "They thought it was a normal heart attack."

"It may have been an abnormal heart attack," I said.

"Are you all seriously claiming some kids can give people heart attacks?" Cathy asked.

I shrugged. "If not, it was a mighty big coincidence that both Andro and I started feeling pressure in our chests at the exact same time they confronted us."

"I'm almost afraid to ask," said Sydney, "but how did you defend yourselves?"

"Actually," I said, "we shot lightning bolts out of our fingertips."

Cathy fell out of her chair. I tried really hard not to laugh and succeeded. Mostly.

"Lightning? How?" Sydney asked. She looked down at her

mom sympathetically. "Are you okay, Mom?"
Cathy scowled. "Yes," she grunted, getting up.
"Lightning bolts?" Ryan asked. "Was that what you did the other day with Ben?"
"Yeah." I'd been pondering what'd happened most of last night so I'd come up a hypothesis about it. "Have you ever seen static electricity in a dark room? It looks like little blue-ish lightning bolts."
Ryan and Sydney nodded. Emily gurgled.
"It was like that but bigger. And Andro and I were very agitated," I glanced at Cathy, "for some reason."
Sydney smiled. "I bet."
"So when we were attacked, we managed to q-lapse," I said, "and shoot these bolts of electromagnetic energy at the kids."
Cathy stood up abruptly. "I've had enough of this nonsense."
"What exactly is the problem, Cathy?" Ryan asked, frowning.
"This quantum stuff is all a bunch of B.S., pardon my French." She stabbed her finger in my direction. "Why are you two encouraging her?"
As I took in her frown, somehow, I didn't think it was quantum mechanics that had Cathy's panties in a bunch. I forced myself to smile at her. "If you tell me what's really bothering you maybe I can do something about it."
"Do you really want to know?" She put her hands on her hips.
"Sure," I said.
"What are you doing here?" she asked. "Why are you staying here? You're hardly helping with Emily and you're hogging the guestroom."
I should have guessed. "That's what you're mad about?" I turned to Sydney. "I thought I've been helping with Emily. I'm sorry if I haven't been doing enough. I'd be happy to do more. Just tell me what you need."
I couldn't move out because I didn't have any money. My last job, a post-doc, didn't pay much more than being a student research assistant. Professor Chen said I'd start getting paid any week now by the university.
"No. We aren't going back on a promise," Sydney said. "Besides, you've helped plenty with Emily, Madison."
Ryan interrupted. "We promised Madison she could stay with

us as long as she liked if she got a job at the university, even before we knew we were pregnant."

Cathy's face started getting red and blotchy. "If you're all going to gang up on me, I can leave. I know when I'm not wanted."

Yikes. Sydney would fall apart without her mom to help her. "Wait a minute." I held up my hands. "No one said you weren't wanted, Cathy."

"Yeah. That's crazy-talk, Mom," Sydney said. "I couldn't do this without you." She pointed her chin at Emily in her lap.

I noticed Ryan didn't say anything.

"What I'm hearing is you want to get off the cot in the nursery and stay in the guestroom," I said. "That's reasonable." I had a light bulb-over-the-head moment. "Maybe we could turn the garage into a little bedroom for me. There's too much junk, er, stuff to fit a car in, but a bed would fit."

"No," Ryan said. "You don't have to do that, Madison."

"It might be neat," I said. "There's a nice big window in there. I could put a carpet down and hang some tapestries to block off the rest of the garage." And best of all it would give me my own entrance/exit in case I wanted to have an overnight guest.

"That sounds great, Madison," Sydney said, relieved.

"It should work until it starts to get really cold out," I said. "What do you think, Cathy?"

Cathy looked at the floor. "I guess that sounds nice," she said so softly she was almost inaudible.

"What?" Ryan asked.

"That sounds good," Cathy said with a tiny smile.

"It's settled then," I said. "I'll move into the garage tonight." I was happy with myself. If only all my problems were so easy to solve. I started back to my bedroom with a big mug of coffee but Ryan headed me off at the pass.

"You don't have to move into the garage if you don't want to," he said quietly just outside the kitchen.

"No. It's fine," I said. "It may have certain advantages."

He stood there blocking my way.

"What?" I asked. "Do you want me to kick up a hullabaloo, so Cathy leaves?"

I could see the gears and wheels turning in his head. Finally, he said, “No. Of course not. That wouldn’t be right. Would it?”

I grinned. “Are you asking me, or telling me?”

“It’s fine.” He stepped closer, fiddling with the belt of his robe. “Madison, I’m worried about you. What if Luke and Griffin attack again? You’re in no state to fight them off right now. You seem tired.”

I shrugged. “I don’t see what I can do about it. Do you?”

He scratched his head. “Go over to Andro’s and make out with him for a while?”

“Oh?” Just what was he implying? “Why do you say that?”

“I can read between the lines.” He grinned. “I know what kind of discussion you were having at lookout point to make those bolts of lightning.”

Ryan’s idea was tempting. I missed Andro. I remembered how our bodies fit together. My skin began to flush. I remembered how it felt to kiss him. My lips tingled.

He peered at me. “Or maybe you could just think about him for a while.”

The pocket of his ratty bathrobe started ringing. He took out his cell and answered it. “Martin, here.” He listened for a few moments and then said, “Sure. Madison, too? Just let me know where and when.” He listened a while longer and then said, “Thanks, Nate.” He hung up, repocketing his cell.

He shook his head. “The U.S. Attorney is trying to build a case against Luke and Griffin for the bank robbery. His assistant wants to meet with us down in Denver in an hour. Can you make it?”

Ah ha. “Luke and Griffin did say something about this last night, just before they attacked us.” At least that part of the evening was starting to make sense. “My schedule is free. But can we make it to Denver in an hour?”

“If we hurry,” he said.

We made it down to the Alfred A. Arraj Courthouse in time thanks to the carpool lanes and Ryan’s autobahn-worthy driving. After we got through security we ran through the building to the conference room and slipped into the meeting a couple seconds under the wire.

Agents Sawyer and Baker looked pleased to see us. Nate

even went so far as to wave enthusiastically.

"It's about time," the man presumably-in-charge said. He had dark bags under his eyes. "I'm Mr. Khalilzad, Assistant U.S. Attorney. Thank you for coming. Have a seat."

"Yeah. Thanks for coming, guys," Nate said.

"I'm Madison Martin," I said as I sat down.

"I'm Ryan Martin," Ryan said. "We both work at the university up in Boulder."

"I know who you are." Mr. Khalilzad sighed. "I met with the bank security guard and Agents Sawyer and Baker the other day and took their statements about the bank robbery. I must admit their story was hard to believe. It's unfortunate the security cameras malfunctioned during the robbery and so were down for repair during the incident when the young man appeared the other day. The agents claim you can back up their story."

Ryan said, "Yes, sir. We can."

I nodded. It probably wasn't a good sign that Ryan used the word sir. I couldn't recall him ever using it before. "Perhaps you could summarize what you've got so far, and we could fill in the blanks," I said.

Agent Baker suppressed a smile while Agent Sawyer covered his mouth with his hand.

Ryan snickered.

Mr. Khalilzad smiled and said, "That's not usually how it works, Miss Martin."

Ugh. He called me Miss. "It's Doctor Martin or Professor Martin."

Ryan gave me a dirty look that said, *don't antagonize him,* as clear as day.

"Sorry," I said. "So, what? I should just tell you what happened?"

"That would be nice," Mr. Khalilzad said. "But, first, Mr. Martin, please wait outside."

Ryan was already on his feet.

When he closed the door behind him I started talking. "Nate, Nathan, er, Agent Sawyer, called Ryan and asked him–"

"Please just tell me what you personally did or observed concerning the bank robbery," Mr. Khalilzad said.

I forced down a yawn. "Right. Sorry." I glanced around the

generic meeting room. "Is there any chance I could get some coffee?"

"Maybe later," Mr. Khalilzad said. "You were saying?"

"I arrived at the bank with Ryan last Thursday. These two agents escorted us to the back of the bank where there was a weird, spongy hole in the wall that went all the way into the vault." I caught Nate's eye and he nodded slightly.

"I got some latex gloves from Agent Sawyer and touched the wall," I said. "It was like the hole in my office. I told the four FBI agents about my experiences with quantum mechanics. A fog appeared at the base of the wall. This fog resolved itself into Griffin Jin. Then Griffin screamed and collapsed on the floor."

Mr. Khalilzad's face was totally motionless, which I took to mean he didn't believe me at all. Surprise, surprise.

"An ambulance came and took Griffin away," I said. "Agents Sawyer and Baker made us go back to their office where they questioned us about quantum mechanics." I paused.

The corners of Khalilzad's mouth turned down. "And then?"

"And then we went home," I said.

Khalilzad made me wait in the hall while Ryan went in.

Straight arrow that he is, I'm sure Ryan told him the same story.

When Ryan was done and they let me back in the room, Mr. Khalilzad blew out some air. "Well, this is unfortunate."

Agent Sawyer looked down at the table and his empty yellow legal pad.

"We told you what happened, sir," Agent Baker said.

Agent Sawyer said, "Yes, sir. We did."

The Assistant U.S. Attorney pounded the conference table with his palms. "This is very frustrating. We have an eyewitness. He's still in the hospital but we have his sworn statements. We have the sworn statements of four FBI agents, and now you two corroborate their crazy story. I wish the security cameras hadn't malfunctioned. Even the ones outside were screwed up during the robbery."

That didn't sound like a coincidence to me. "Isn't that evidence in itself?"

He was still for a moment before shaking his head. "I can't go to my boss with this. He'd get laughed out of court. Magic fog and some kind of physics mumbo-jumbo."

"Maybe we could leave out the mumbo-jumbo?" I asked, thinking of Luke and Griffin causing that pressure in my chest.

The four other people in the room froze and stared at me.

"Or, not," I quickly added.

"Not cool, Mad," Ryan said, shaking his head. "Ever hear of the whole truth and nothing but the truth?"

"Of course," I said. "I was kidding."

"Thanks for coming in," Mr. Khalilzad said. "I don't think this case will be going to trial." He gathered his papers and left the room.

Crap. We just watched him leave.

Agent Baker shook her head. "We should have seen that coming. The story sounds crazy."

"Hey, maybe you could do that collapsing stuff for Khalilzad and prove it to him?" Agent Sawyer said. "I'd like to see it myself."

While I'd been waiting in the hall a few minutes ago I'd tried to q-lapse to get some coffee but nothing happened. "Uh, it can be a little unreliable." Ironically, if I'd drunk enough coffee already I'd probably be able to q-lapse to get more. But then I wouldn't need it. Who was I kidding? You can never have too much coffee.

"Plus, then she'd probably have to do it in court," Ryan said. "And what would happen if it didn't work there?"

There were nods all around.

Ryan said, "Madison, if Luke and Griffin aren't prosecuted, are you worried about interacting with them?"

I gulped. "Yes. Surely, there's some way to get them? Maybe when the security cameras are fixed they'll have some data?"

The agents just looked at me.

"What about the witness, the guard?" I said. "Maybe if he talked to the prosecutor again he could convince him?"

Agent Baker said, "They already have the witness statement. And our statements." She pointed at herself and Agent Sawyer. "And now yours."

"Maybe we could put Luke and Griffin in the position where they're forced to q-lapse," I said.

"I did not hear you suggest some kind of entrapment," Agent Sawyer said with a grimace.

"I guess I'd be willing to try taking adrenaline in a demonstration for Khalilzad," I said.

Agent Baker perked up for a moment. "Do you think that would work?"

"I'm not sure," I admitted.

Ryan shook his head. "So that's it? Those kids just have carte blanche to do whatever quantum crimes they want?"

Agent Sawyer scowled. "That's the way it looks right now."

Chapter Nineteen

When I got back to my office around noon, Andro wasn't around.

At one o'clock when I heard his door open, I jumped, nervous as an astronaut with a leaky spacesuit. We hadn't talked since our date. Had it only been last night? A lot had happened since then. But at least Luke and company hadn't attacked again. Maybe they got the good news that they wouldn't be prosecuted after all.

I waited a few minutes but Andro didn't come over and say hi. I'd decided to pop over to his office when my phone rang.

"Thanks for coming to the meeting this morning, Professor Martin," Agent Baker said.

"I'm sorry it ended so badly," I said.

"Yeah. We've got our work cut out for us," she said grimly. "I don't know if you've heard, but there have been a rash of quantum crimes all along the Front Range in the last few days."

I gasped. "How many is a rash?"

Andro appeared in the opening between our offices. My gasp must have caught his attention.

Agent Baker sighed into the phone. "It's hard to say. Law enforcement has been very slow to report the incidents because they're so weird. The officers don't want to be accused of being drunk or high or crazy. Actually," she paused, "there've been rumors of quantum crimes beyond the Front Range, possibly across the country."

"Oh, no." That was the last thing we needed.

Andro, frowning, took a step into my office through the hole in the wall.

"We're trying to contact all our FBI field offices and determine how widespread the problem is," she said.

"Please let me know if there's anything I can do," I said.

"I'm glad you said that," she said. "We're going to have a task force meeting tomorrow morning in Denver. We need you to attend and explain how collapsing-the-wavefunction works. And, if possible, we'd like to see a demonstration."

No pressure. I bit back my agreement. Tomorrow was Wednesday morning and I had to teach my class. "I'd like to attend, but I'm supposed to work."

I put my hand over the phone. "Andro, is there any chance you'd be available to go to an FBI task force meeting about quantum crimes tomorrow morning?"

He pointed at himself. "Me? Why me? You're the expert. If they need an expert, you should go."

"But I have class." Not that I wanted to go to class and teach two notorious quantum criminals more about quantum mechanics−especially when they might attack me.

Andro shook his head.

"Professor Martin?" Agent Baker said.

I expelled a breath of air. "Fine. I'll be there. I'm not one hundred percent sure I can q-lapse on command, however." Note to self: find some adrenaline, or at least lots and lots of coffee. Or? I eyed Andro, still standing in my office and still looking mighty fine. If Andro went with me I'd probably have no problem getting excited.

"If you can't do a demo, we'll deal with it," she said. "Isn't there another scientist there at the university who has experienced collapsing the wavefunction?"

I put my hand over the phone again, and said to Andro, "Are you a scientist who's experienced collapsing the wavefunction?"

He shook his head while drawing his hand across his neck.

"Professor Martin, are you there?" the agent asked.

I looked at Andro with raised eyebrows.

"No," he whispered.

"I have no information on that topic," I finally said into the phone.

"Are you sure about that?" I could hear the skepticism in her voice.

"Yes," I said. "I'm sure."

She gave me the meeting info and we hung up.

"What was that about?" Andro asked.

I leaned back in my chair. "Good morning, er, afternoon, Andro. How are you? Are you feeling okay after last night?"

"Yes." He walked over to the chair near my desk and sat down. "The experience rattled me, but I'm all right. Are you?"

"I'm not great." I told him what happened at the Assistant U.S. Attorney meeting that morning.

"Frip." He crossed his arms. "Those kids just get away with a bank robbery? And probably attacking that poor guard?"

"It looks that way."

"What about us?" he asked. "What if they attack us again?"

"I don't know. We could press charges about last night but it's so weird."

"Yeah. No one would believe us," he said, frowning.

"I guess if we're attacked, we'll just have to defend ourselves again. We did it before."

"True," he said.

"And on the bright side, since they got away with the robbery there's no reason for them to be mad at us any more," I said.

"I guess," he said slowly. "You didn't answer my earlier question. What was that phone call about?"

"FBI Agent Baker asked me to help them fight quantum crime. It seems to be spreading. Are you sure you don't want to go to the task force meeting with me?" I asked.

"How much quantum crime are we talking about?" he asked.

"She said a rash but I don't know what that is. Apparently, people are reluctant to report it." Talk about news of the weird.

He sighed. "I'll have to think about it. Yasmin was really upset last night when I told her what happened, the quantum attack and the lightning bolts and the other stuff."

I couldn't blame her. Quantum attacks and lightning bolts did sound bad. "What other stuff?"

"You know, the hooking-up stuff." Andro stood up and started pacing around my tiny office. "She read me the riot act and said the attack was God punishing me for my evil ways."

"What evil ways? You're not evil. You're the opposite of evil. You're great." Action item: don't gush like a schoolgirl. I stopped myself from saying more.

"She's Catholic," he said. "I'm supposed to be Catholic. Premarital sex is forbidden."

How could something that felt so good be bad, especially at our age? "But we didn't have sex."

He stopped pacing and turned and looked me in the eyes. "Can you honestly say we weren't headed that way? What do you think would have happened if we hadn't been interrupted?"

I blushed. "I, uh, we wouldn't, er, I wouldn't. I mean, not in the car." I took a deep breath. "I don't know what would have happened. But I'm not some temptress leading you down the path of the devil." He was responsible for his own non-Catholic actions.

He stepped around the desk and grabbed my small hands with his big ones. "You're right. I'm sorry. I'm not blaming you. I know it's not your fault. It's no one's fault. I'm just feeling guilty. Did I mention I'm Catholic?" He flashed me a split-second smile.

I grinned weakly and withdrew my hands. "Yeah. You might have mentioned that." I paused. "So, where does that leave us?"

He went back to the empty chair and sat down. "You were right before. We have to slow down."

"Slow?" I smiled. "I can do slow. Slow is my middle name." Wait. That didn't come out right.

He laughed.

Wednesday morning found Ryan and me, too early, driving autobahn-style down to Denver again.

"Did you have any trouble getting out of work?" he asked.

"Nope," I said. "I told that woman in the physics office I was sick."

"That woman?" he glanced at me. "Surely she has a name?"

"The department secretary. I don't recall her name. It's N-something." I sighed. I knew he was thinking I was lame for forgetting her name. "I'm under a lot of pressure, give me a break." Okay, maybe I thought I was lame for forgetting her name.

"Aren't we all," he said under his breath. Poor Ryan. Being a new dad had to be stressful as well as wonderful. And these quantum crimes couldn't be helping.

"Thanks for fixing up the garage for me," I said. "I sort

of forgot to do anything." Luckily, when I'd gotten home I'd remembered Cathy was in the guest room and didn't disturb her. I was pleasantly surprised when a note directed me to a bed and all my stuff in the garage. I would have guessed they would be too busy to do anything.

"I figured when you weren't home by ten o'clock," he said. "It was just stuff we had lying around the house. Sydney did most of it. And Cathy."

"So, how's it going with Cathy? Moving her into the guest room must have helped. Are you guys getting along any better?"

"It's going. If I just knew how much longer she was staying that would help."

"Just say the word if you want me to start acting up and chase her away." I smiled. "I could talk about quantum mechanics a bunch and maybe zap her with a mini-lightning bolt."

"Thanks." He chuckled, glancing at me. "Hopefully, it won't come to that."

After another dozen miles he said, "It's too bad Andro couldn't come. He would have come in handy to help you collapse the wavefunction, right? Do you think you can do it?"

"Crap," I said. "I forgot to get adrenaline. Our hypothesis is adrenaline makes it easier." I really needed to investigate that hypothesis scientifically. "I think Luke and his friends must be taking some."

"Why do you say that?" Ryan asked.

I looked at him. "Did I not mention that Luke's girlfriend, Courtney, works at the health center?"

"No. You did not mention that. There was some adrenaline stolen from the health center."

"That's what I'm saying. I think they're behind it," I said. "Is there any place we can get some adrenaline right now?"

"Not that I know of," he said.

"Then, I guess we'll see if I can do it soon enough." I yawned.

"Why couldn't Andro come?" he asked. "It seems like making out with him helps you collapse the wavefunction. Did he have trouble getting out of work?"

I pursed my lips. "No. His class is on Tuesdays and Thursdays. I'm not really sure what's going on with him."

"So, the honeymoon's over already?"

I sighed. "We never got to the honeymoon."

"You must be losing your touch, Mad."

"It's not me," I said. "He's got issues."

He nodded. "Maybe so. You don't end up single in your thirties for no reason."

"Hey. I'm single and almost thirty."

"You must be the exception that proves the rule," he said, gently.

Damn straight.

When we arrived at the field office, there were about twenty law-enforcement types sitting in orderly rows in a large meeting room. I only recognized Agents Sawyer and Baker and Ryan's cop friend, Ben. Sawyer and Baker looked worn out. Ben looked hot. I sat next to him, and Ryan sat next to me.

Ryan noticed me checking Ben out and leaned over to whisper in my ear. "You could always kiss him if it was an emergency. You know, to collapse the wavefunction."

"Shh. He might hear you," I said, trying not to blush.

"Hey there, quantum cop," Ben said to me, smiling. "Hey, Ryan."

Ryan waved back at Ben. "Hey."

"Hello, Officer Willis," I said, all business. No, I wasn't overcompensating.

"Somebody got up on the wrong side of the bed," he murmured.

Agent Baker quieted the room. "We are here this morning to discuss an emerging problem which I am going to call quantum crime."

The other folks in the room shifted uneasily in their seats.

"The quantum crime we have the most information about is the bank robbery that occurred here in Denver last week. Agent Sawyer will brief you on that."

Sawyer stood up and summarized the bank robbery including the control reality webpage, the guard's account of the robbery including his heart attack, Griffin appearing out of thin air, and the Assistant U.S. Attorney's decision not to pursue the case. He sat.

Then Agent Baker stood and said, "We have some additional

information about Jin." She pointed at a crew-cutted man on her right.

"The suspect, Griffin Jin, had amphetamine and traces of phenylpropanolamine in his system when he was admitted to the hospital," he said. I wondered how the agent knew so much about Griffin's medical condition. I thought that stuff was supposed to be confidential. And who taught him how to pronounce phenylpropanolamine?

"Officer Martin also has some information which may be relevant," Agent Baker said. "Ryan?"

Ryan stood up, buttoned his suit coat and said, "Hi, I'm Ryan Martin. I'm Chief of Police up at the university. Two weeks ago the Student Health Center had a bunch of drugs stolen," he consulted his phone, "such as phenylephrine, pseudoephedrine, ephedrine, and phenylpropanolamine." Ryan's pronunciation wasn't as good as that other guy. "Recent, very preliminary, evidence," he paused to glare at me, "may indicate Griffin Yin procured and ingested these drugs to help him carry out the quantum bank robbery."

I slunk down in my chair.

"This case is on-going, but we do have some leads," Ryan finished.

"So, that's what we know, so far," Agent Baker said.

The crowd grumbled.

"What about the freaky robberies down in Colorado Springs?" someone yelled.

"And Denver?"

"And Kansas City?"

"And New York City?"

I gulped. This had spread all the way to New York?

Still standing, Ryan cleared his throat. "As Nate mentioned there does appear to be a webpage that gives instructions on how to collapse the wavefunction." He sat down heavily.

"What the hell does that mean?" someone asked.

"Shut it down," someone else said.

Uh oh. The natives were getting restless.

Agent Baker held up her hands. "So far, most of the quantum crimes have been of the mischief or nuisance variety." That was consistent with the *News of the Weird* I'd seen earlier. She continued. "We'll compile a list of suspected quantum crimes and map them out later. Before we do that I'd like Professor Martin to explain what's going on. She works up in Boulder in the university's physics department and is an expert in quantum mechanics." Agent Baker extended her hand to me. "Madison? And please comment on the webpage, too."

I stood up. "I'm not sure what you want from me here." I was so nervous I was in danger of losing last night's dinner.

"To start just give us your theory about how this works," she said.

I cleared my throat. Nothing like being put on the spot. "There's a branch of physics called quantum mechanics which uses complicated math to describe tiny things like subatomic particles. To make a long story short quantum mechanics says things are represented as probabilities. To make them realities a human mind is necessary to collapse the wavefunction."

Somebody said, "Huh?"

"Good question." I tried to smile. "Quantum mechanics says everything is a probability. Things are uncertain until a conscious mind chooses among the probabilities to make something certain. We call that collapsing the wavefunction, because it's the wavefunction that represents the probabilities."

Twenty law-enforcement types grumbled and shifted in their chairs.

Agent Baker nodded her head. "We'll take your word for the physics. But as I understand it quantum mechanics is only part of the quantum crime story, right?"

"Yes," I said. "My hypothesis is that it takes three things to consciously collapse the wavefunction and control reality." I took a breath. "Three things are required."

The rest of the room was frowning and shaking their heads.

I tried not to vomit. "One." I held out one finger. "You must know about quantum mechanics and collapsing the wavefunction. Two." I held out two fingers. "You must believe you can collapse the wavefunction. Three." I held out three fingers. "You must have adrenaline or something similar in your system."

"So what about the webpage?" Agent Baker said.

"The webpage would be how people know about this quantum stuff," I said. "But, don't worry about the webpage. I got rid of it."

"Thanks, Madison," Agent Baker said. "You can sit down."

That was it? Awesome. Gratefully, I sank back onto the chair.

The crew-cut guy with the pronunciation skills stood up again. "Professor Martin's third point about adrenaline is an interesting one. Adrenaline is produced by the human body or it can be injected or ingested in some form. As most of your know, adrenaline is a molecule made of nine carbon atoms, thirteen hydrogen atoms, a nitrogen atom, and three oxygen atoms." I didn't know that. Thankfully now that the pressure was off, my stomach was settling down and I could enjoy atom talk.

"Natural adrenaline, L-Adrenaline, is a hormone and a neurotransmitter and is synthesized by the body in the adrenal medulla," he said. "It has a strong effect on the sympathetic nervous system including the heart, blood vessels, gut, bladder, and genitalia. Natural adrenaline degrades quickly and thus has a short lifetime in the body." He talked some more about adrenaline but I stopped paying attention, zoning out like it was high school biology class.

"Professor Martin? Madison?" Agent Baker said. Everyone was looking at me.

"Sorry. What was that?" I asked.

"Do you think you could do a demonstration of collapsing the wavefunction, now?" she asked.

Shit. Reluctantly, I stood up, and glanced around the room. "Did you have something in mind?"

She pointed at the computer screen next to her. "Can you get rid of the control reality webpage?" The page was also projected on the large screen on the front wall. How could that be? Was it archived?

I gulped. "But I already..." I walked over to the computer as two dozen federal agents and law-enforcement officers stared at me. I refreshed the screen. It was back. Live. Shit.

"I'll try." I'd done it before, after all. But now I was surrounded by dozens of law-enforcement officers who didn't believe I could control reality. Ryan was probably the only one in the audience who believed in me. No big deal, right?

I tried to block the nay-sayers out and focus on the computer screen in front of me. I tried to q-lapse the webpage away. Go away webpage. But I couldn't concentrate. The energy in the room was too negative. Finally I gave up and faced the room.

"I'm sorry. I can't do it now," I said.

The officers muttered to each other.

"Recall, the second requirement is belief," I said. Your negative thoughts are interfering with the process."

I thought I heard snickering.

Agent Baker scanned the crowd, frowning. Then she turned to me. "If I'm not mistaken, you're also missing the third requirement, the adrenaline. We might be able to help you with that."

It felt like a supernova was going off in my stomach. "I'm not so sure about that. I'm pretty nervous. I must already have adrenaline in my system."

"Yeah. I bet she's nervous," someone in the crowd said. "She should be nervous."

"Who said that?" Agent Baker asked.

Ben jumped up from his chair. "I was skeptical like you guys until I saw her collapse the wavefunction with my own eyes. She removed the webpage and she shocked me with a lightning bolt."

"Yeah, right," someone said. "Then why is the webpage still there?"

The crowd laughed.

Ben's eyes widened. "I'm not kidding. It really happened."

"Cyber Investigations can handle a webpage," a man in the front said.

"Yeah," a woman said. "Let the Cyber Action Teams deal with it."

"She's obstructing the investigation. Take her into custody," a voice called out.

"Take the cop into custody," someone else yelled.

Ben sat down abruptly.

The room appeared to be on the verge of erupting into insults and rude suggestions, followed by who-knew-what. I didn't want to find out what.

I cowered behind Agent Baker. They did have guns after all. "Uh, Agent Baker, did you say you guys had some adrenaline? I'd be willing to take it and try again." I hoped the adrenaline hypothesis was correct or I'd soon be looking at a room full of agents with guns–drawn.

She used her cell phone and told someone on the other end to bring the drugs to the conference room. After she hung up, she turned to me. "I was hoping you'd say that."

Within minutes, a young woman marched into the room with a hypodermic. She came right up to me and said, "Lift your sleeve, please."

She looked about twelve years old. "Maybe we should have a doctor do this?" I said.

The needle approached my arm. "I am a doctor," the woman snapped, administering the drug.

Now I definitely felt nauseous and even more jittery, but I stepped back over to the computer. I stared at the screen, focusing on q-lapsing. The webpage got blurry, the words and pictures ran together. Then it morphed into a blank gray page, again. Good. If only it would stay that way.

Agent Baker pointed at the computer. "And there you go. She did it."

The guys in the back stood up trying to see the screen.

A couple of the agents in the front row came up and looked at the computer. One of them pressed the reload button and then grunted when the same gray page reappeared. "It is gone."

"How do we know it isn't some kind of trick?" someone in the crowd yelled out.

"Yeah. Maybe it's her webpage," someone else said.

How could they not believe what was right in front of their eyes? "Check it," I said. "All of you check it if you don't believe me."

There was more grumbling in the back. "Don't believe in quantum physics," someone said.

I put my hands on my hips. "Who said that? Who doesn't believe in physics?" I was starting to get angry.

One of the men in the back stood up. "Me. This is all a load of crap."

"Oh, yeah?" I could feel energy building in my hand and before I knew it, a small bolt of lightning smacked the agent in the middle of his broad chest.

He jolted back, scowled, and drew his weapon. "What the hell was that?"

"That's quantum mechanics," I said. "That's collapsing the

wave function."

"That's assaulting a federal agent," the guy next to him said, drawing his weapon.

Suddenly, I was facing a room full of guns pointing at me.

Damn. I froze.

"Calm down, everyone," Agent Baker said, holding up her hands.

I couldn't breathe and couldn't tear my eyes away from the guns. I had to get out of there.

And then I was.

I was back in the foggy limbo. Shit. That might be just as bad, if not worse, than a room full of guns.

I concentrated and forced myself back to the conference room.

The agents' faces were slack and/or their eyes bugged out.

"What the fuck?"

"Shit."

"How the hell?"

The good news was the guns weren't pointing at me anymore. The bad news was I'd just scared a bunch of FBI agents.

Agent Baker said, "You better get out of here ASAP."

"Ryan's my ride." I didn't want to q-lapse again if I could avoid it. My head was already starting to hurt.

She nodded.

Ryan and I hustled out.

Chapter Twenty

It was almost lunchtime when I trudged, head pounding, to the physics building. How could that meeting have gone so badly? I was lucky they didn't arrest me. I wasn't paying attention and almost smacked into someone coming out the door as I was going in. Unfortunately, that someone was Professor Chen. Very unfortunately.

"Madison, you look horrible," he said. "You should have stayed home if you're so sick."

"I'm not sick," I said without thinking. Too late, what I said and who I said it to, registered. Shit. I'd told him I was sick. "I mean, I was feeling sick, but I got better."

Chen looked like he could spit bullets. "I don't know what kind of shenanigans your previous employers let you get away with, but at this world-renowned university professors do not skip class. That kind of behavior is totally unacceptable here. It's an actionable offense−especially for new faculty. Do you understand me, Madison?" He leaned over me, his straight gray hair flopping forward.

My throat constricted. I was just trying to help the agents. My stomach acted up. "Yes, sir," I whispered. "I'm sorry, sir." That adrenaline shot was not agreeing with me.

"Do we have a problem?" he said, frowning.

"No." Bile rose in my throat headed straight for Professor Chen. I clamped my lips together and clenched my eyes tight, concentrating on q-lapsing and willing the vomit away.

The pressure in my throat and mouth eased.

"What the hell?" Chen's eyes were wide open as he took a

step away from me.

Hell? I couldn't believe my ears. "Excuse me, sir?"

His mouth hung open and he pointed at me. "I thought I saw... You got all blurry." He shook his head.

"Sorry, sir?" I asked.

"I guess you are sick," he finally said. "And I'm not feeling so well myself. I have to go." He hurried away.

That was a close one. Too close.

After lunch I was busy catching up on stuff for my class when the phone rang.

"Hello, Professor Martin? It's Nancy."

I drew a blank. "Hello?"

"You know, from the office."

I still didn't know. "Sure."

She sighed. "I work in the physics department office."

Oh. Right. "What can I do for you, Nancy?"

"Professor Chen wants to see you at two o'clock in his office." She paused. "You may want to bring counsel."

"Counsel? Like a lawyer?" I asked. What in the world was going on?

"I probably shouldn't be telling you this but the university is a little too worried about negative publicity because of all the problems they've had in the past."

"Huh? What negative publicity?" I asked. "What are you talking about?"

"Oh, right, you weren't here," she said. "Never mind. That's history. Let's focus on now. A story was posted about you on several web pages. You perpetrated some kind of mass hypnosis on the FBI?"

"What?" How could there be stories already? The meeting was only a couple hours ago. "That's not what happened."

"Whatever," Nancy said. "So can you make the meeting?"

I looked at my calendar. It was blank. Unfortunately. "Yes, ma'am. I'll be there." We hung up.

I wanted to look for these so-called news stories but I needed to get a lawyer–in forty-five minutes. Crap.

I figured Ryan must have a lawyer friend in his extensive buddy-network, so I reached for the phone.

After several rings he finally answered. “What do you want Madison?”

“I just was wondering if you might know a lawyer,” I said.

“It’s always about you, isn’t it?” he asked. “Did you ever stop to wonder how I was doing?”

“How are you doing?” I asked softly.

He ignored me. “As a matter of fact I do know a lawyer, my friend Tom. Tom happens to be sitting in my office right now because we just met with my boss. I was implicated in a hoax on the FBI!”

“What hoax? There was no hoax.” How did information get around so quickly? I sighed. “I’m sorry.”

“You’re sorry?” Ryan said, volume escalating. “I’m screwed. That’s how I’m doing. The administration has to avoid negative publicity at all cost.”

I cringed. “So what happened with your boss?”

I heard him talk to someone else in the background. Then he said, “My lawyer advises me not to discuss the matter. But if I could discuss it, I’d tell you I’ve been placed on administrative leave.”

Poor Ryan. “I’m sorry,” I said again. I’d just about die if I cost him his job. He had a whole family to support.

“I hate to see what Sydney’s going to say about this,” he said. “Boy, is she going to be mad. And with good reason.”

Should I say I was sorry again?

“And Cathy. I hate to see what she’ll say,” he added.

“She’ll probably blame me,” I said.

“She probably will.” He was quiet for a moment. “Maybe you better stay with Andro for a few days until they cool off.”

I gulped. I was being kicked out of my home? “Whatever you want, Ryan.”

Where was Andro? His office was empty.

“Why do you need a lawyer?” He finally asked.

“My boss wants to meet with me at two o’clock and he suggested I bring one.”

“Oh.” He paused. “That doesn’t sound too good.”

“No, it doesn’t. I’m a little worried he might fire me.”

“I’ll send Tom over there as soon as we’re done. I have to go.” He hung up.

In the meantime, I surfed the web looking for the supposed incriminating articles. I could only find one on a blog that didn't mention me by name but did smear the university. Good grief. Some of these bloggers were idiots.

At one forty-five a small man in a rumpled brown suit knocked on my open office door. "Professor Martin?"

I stood up. "Yes. Tom?"

He nodded. "I'm Tom Clark."

"Nice to meet you. Please, call me Madison. Come on in." I gestured at the chair on the other side of my desk. "Thanks for coming on such short notice."

He sat.

"Is Ryan okay? He sounded upset."

Tom nodded and then caught himself. "I'm not at liberty to discuss other clients."

"I understand," I said. "Do you have much experience with the university?"

"Yes," he said. "I've represented faculty in a number of matters. Why don't you tell me your situation?"

"The secretary asked me to bring counsel to a meeting with my boss at two o'clock," I said. "She said he was concerned about negative publicity for the university."

He wrote something on his yellow legal pad. "Do you know if the university counsel will be attending the meeting?"

I shook my head. "I don't know. Why?"

"If there's a lawyer for the university there it means they're serious about getting rid of you," Tom said.

I suppressed a sigh. "But I signed a contract. I don't think they can just fire me, can they?"

He leaned forward. "Probably not. Do you have a copy of the contract?"

I handed it over. It'd taken me twenty minutes to find it earlier, but I had.

Tom flipped through the pages.

"So?" I glanced at the clock. We were creeping up on two o'clock.

"This looks pretty standard." He put it down on my desk. "You professors get a nice deal. They can't fire you outright unless you're guilty of academic misconduct or moral turpitude."

"Moral turpitude?" I asked. "What is that, anyway?"

He glanced at his watch and stood up. "That's the question. Should we go?"

I followed him downstairs.

Professor Chen was ready for us in his office. Alone. I breathed a sigh of relief. Maybe this wasn't too serious. "Madison." He nodded curtly. "And who's this?"

"Tom Clark," I said. "My attorney."

Chen shot a look at Nancy through his open door. "I see." He sat up straight as he shook Tom's proffered hand.

"So, what's this about, Professor Chen?" I asked.

"I received some very interesting phone calls after lunch today from reporters." Who knew reporters still existed? "They said you'd tricked a bunch of FBI agents and were obstructing an investigation." He grimaced and leaned back in his chair.

"That's crazy," I said. "That's got to be slander or libel or one of those things. I was helping with an investigation. I didn't do anything wrong."

"You skipped your class this morning," Chen said.

"I called beforehand and said I couldn't make it." Granted, I'd said I was sick when I wasn't but that wasn't so serious, was it?

"I had information relevant to a bank robbery," I continued. "They asked me to come to their meeting. Call FBI Agent Baker or Agent Sawyer, they'll confirm. You want me to help law enforcement if they ask, don't you?"

"One of the reporters mentioned that criminals were using physics to commit their crimes," Chen said. "I assured the reporter that was impossible. Now I understand the nonsense Alyssa was spouting was because of you. You're the problem, not her."

"I'm not a problem." I sputtered. "You know physics and quantum mechanics. And you saw me collapse the wavefunction earlier today."

"What are you talking about?" he asked, scowling.

"When I got all blurry," I said, "I collapsed the wavefunction to choose a reality in which I didn't vomit on you." If he was this upset now I'd hate to see how upset he would've been if I had vomited on him earlier.

Professor Chen's chair slipped but he caught himself. "I didn't see anything of the kind." Perspiration beaded his upper lip.

"But..." I said. What happened to seeing is believing? He saw me get blurry. Maybe I should have puked on him.

Tom interrupted. "This discussion doesn't seem to be getting us anywhere. What precisely did you want to tell Professor Martin?"

"In short, I am extremely disappointed in your recent behavior, Madison. The university does not need any more negative publicity. We have to act quickly to nip this in the bud. Committing a felony such as obstruction of justice is considered moral turpitude and is grounds for dismissal."

"My client has not been charged with any crime," Tom said. "Rumor and innuendo are not grounds for dismissal especially if they come from a reporter."

"Yeah," I said, shaking. How could I lose my dream job already?

"Legally you do not have any grounds for dismissing Professor Martin," Tom added. "If you attempt to do so we are prepared to take you to court."

"As Department Chair I have a fair amount of leeway in work assignments," Chen said, frowning. "I'm perfectly within my rights to suspend Madison."

"You can't suspend me. I haven't done anything wrong. What about my students?" I asked. "Most of them need my class to graduate."

"That would have to be a suspension with pay, Professor Chen. Correct?" Tom said.

I didn't care about the stupid money. I cared about my students.

Chen stared at Tom.

Tom stared back.

I looked from one to the other. It was like they were locked in a macho contest of wills with my career caught in the balance.

Finally, Chen said, "Yes. But you can't teach and you can't be on campus."

"Please don't suspend me. I haven't done anything. My students need me. This is wrong. You're making a mistake."

Chen glared at Tom. "Too bad. You're suspended, Madison. Give Nancy your keys. I'll schedule a hearing with the board and let you know when it is."

My first thought as I got up to leave was I should q-lapse and make this all go away. The problem was I couldn't figure out what to do specifically. I couldn't go back in time and not run into Chen this morning. I couldn't control what reporters did. One or more of the agents must have ratted me out. Surely, that wasn't kosher, but again, I couldn't control what had already been done.

In the hall I thanked Tom for his help, although I wasn't sure he'd been too helpful. Had his aggressive attitude pushed Chen into suspending me?

Tom wanted to discuss what would happen next, but I was too upset after turning in my keys so I asked him to call me later.

I knew I should be angry, but I was too worried. Maybe the anger would come later. I managed to make it to my office–where I wasn't allowed to be anymore–before any tears escaped. Luckily I never locked my office.

This whole thing was crazy. I couldn't believe Chen had turned on me so quickly. I cradled my head in my hands and dabbed at my eyes with a tissue. It was like he was scared of me or something. I lifted my head. Note to self: don't scare your boss. That almost prompted a smile.

I heard Andro's office door open. In a moment, he strode through our quantum door. "Hi, Madison. I wanted to ask you if you were available for dinner Saturday night?" He slowed, taking in my expression. "Wait. What's wrong?"

I let out the breath I'd been holding. "Chen just suspended me."

He walked toward my desk. "That doesn't make sense."

"I agree."

He sat down on my desk. "You're really suspended? Why would Chen do that?"

My eyes wouldn't stop leaking. "He was mad that I supposedly hoaxed the FBI. He said some frippin' reporters called him."

"That sounds awful. I'm sorry." He grabbed my hand and cradled it in his own.

Andro held my hand. I felt a little better.

"Chen obviously made a mistake," he said. "They're just gun-shy about negative publicity around here. You know, because of all the scandals." Exactly how many scandals had there been?

He looked at me for another moment and then held out his arms. "Hug?"

I stood and let him wrap his arms around me. I felt much better immediately. He smelled good, like Polo aftershave and man. We stood there hugging for several moments.

He said, "You didn't answer my question. How about dinner Saturday night?"

I moved out of his arms. "That sounds nice. Thanks."

He sat back down on the desk and smiled. "Good. I'll look forward to it."

I smiled back at him. "Good. Me, too." It was nice to have something to look forward to.

"Do you want help moving your office stuff home?" he asked.

I sniffled. "Ryan asked me not to come home."

He peered at me. "Your face is getting blurry. What was that about Ryan?"

"Ryan's mad at me. He asked me to stay away from the house. Can I stay with you for a couple days?"

He slowly shook his head. "What with the girls and Yasmin, I don't think that's a good idea. We wouldn't want to set a bad example. Besides, we're supposed to be taking it slow." He caressed my shoulder. "I'm sorry. I would love to have you stay with me. That's the problem. One thing might lead to another, and, you know." He shrugged. "We agreed this relationship had potential and we shouldn't rush it."

We did agree to that. Damn it. "But if I'm so hard to resist, why are you willing to go out with me this weekend?" I asked.

"Oh, right. We're going on a double-date with Yasmin and Hector." Andro beamed. "I got Yasmin to agree to go on a date. Isn't that awesome? She's finally moving on. And she'll keep me on the straight and narrow."

"That's great about Yasmin moving on." But what exactly did he think I was going to make him do? "Gee, a double-date sounds great." Chaperones. On the bright side, I didn't feel like crying any more. I did, however, feel a little like smacking him.

"Are you mad at me?" he asked, confused.

Yes. But I didn't want to pick a fight. I exhaled slowly. "No. I look forward to our date Saturday. I just have to find a place to stay."

He stood up. "I'm really sorry I can't let you stay with me. Do you want me to call some buddies and see if I can find a couch for you?"

Sleep on some stranger's couch? "No, thanks. I'll figure something out."

"Okay, if you're sure." He clearly caught my bad mood, and went back to his office frowning.

I texted Ryan with my bad news. He texted back some sympathy.

I spent the rest of the day and evening hiding in my office doing physics research and preparing for the Friday class I wasn't going to be able to teach.

I had to be reinstated as a professor. I had to. I'd been working my whole life to get here. So I was going to behave as if that was a sure thing. I couldn't face the alternative.

At ten o'clock I snuck into my garage bedroom at Ryan's house through its private entrance. The irony of my so-called love nest didn't escape me.

Chapter Twenty-One

Thursday morning I snuck out of the house early and went over to the rec center for a shower, after which I snuck into my unlocked office in Gamow Tower. Needless to say, I was not in a good mood.

At nine o'clock I wondered if my students had shown up for class and what they thought when I didn't show up. I was blowing them off?

Ryan called my office at about nine-thirty. "Morning, Madison. Listen, I'm sorry about last night. Where'd you end up staying?"

"Morning, Ryan," I said. "I'd rather not say where I was last night."

"With, Andro, huh? All right. You go, girl." I imagined I could hear him smile over the telephone.

"You seem to be doing better than the last time I talked to you," I said.

"Yeah. I have good news. Nate called first thing this morning. Minor quantum crimes are occurring all over the U.S. I guess there are even more than they mentioned at the task force meeting yesterday."

Had that meeting been only yesterday? It seemed like forever ago. "That's not good news. That's horrible news." I grimaced. "Why isn't it in the paper?" I'd read several online papers already this morning accompanied by mediocre cups of coffee from the coffee cart in the building next door. The coffee in the physics department office was better, but I couldn't exactly waltz in there.

"What? Oh, right. It's horrible. Nate says the news services haven't caught on yet. But, that's not the good news. He thinks his boss will come around and ask us for help."

"How is that good news?" I asked. No good deed went unpunished in my experience, especially when it came to the FBI.

"He can hardly ask for help unless he admits those comments that were leaked to the press yesterday were a mistake, right?" he said.

I wished I could be as optimistic as him. "I hope you're right." After a few more pleasantries, including Ryan promising to email me the latest FBI info, we hung up.

I tried to do some physics research after that, but kept brooding over the info Ryan emailed. According to the FBI's analysis, the first quantum crimes had centered in the Boulder and Denver area but they were quickly spreading. Why were the crooks so good at quantum crimes when my abilities were so intermittent? Finally I gave up working and trudged over to Boulder Brews to get some decent coffee.

At eleven o'clock Alyssa showed up at my office. She sashayed right in and sat down.

"Hello?" I said.

"Did you forget about our appointment?" She rifled through her book bag.

I had, but I wasn't about to admit it. "Of course not. I have some bad news though. I've been suspended. I think that means I can't be your advisor any more." Of course, Alyssa wasn't out the woods with Professor Chen herself.

She gasped. "Why were you suspended?" She leaned over. "Do you have moral turpitude?"

Ugh. That sounded like an STD. "Why's not important."

"But, you're the best advisor I ever had," she said. "You put up with my bad moods and everything. All male-induced, by the way. I'm totally done with men. They're just trouble."

Yeah, good luck with that.

"But you, you're a woman. I never had a female professor before."

I raised my eyebrows. "Never had a female professor? Surely that's not true. You've been at a university for, what, seven years?"

"Did you ever have one?" she asked.

I wracked my brain trying to think of a female professor I'd had. I couldn't come up with a single one. "Not that I recall. But that's not important. As it stands, I can't help you finish your degree. You need to find someone else."

She smiled at me. "What do you take me for? I'm not dumping you when the going gets tough. You didn't do that to me."

In point of fact I seemed to recall she did fire me earlier in the semester. But she apologized and asked me back. That counted for something, right? I was not grasping at straws.

I finished off my umpteenth coffee of the morning. "In that case tell me about your literature search."

She regaled me with tales of her jousts with the Web of Science and showed me a bunch of papers. I was impressed. "Excellent job, Alyssa," I said.

In the glow of my approval, she smiled. "You were the one who said we had to show Chen he was wrong about me by doing really good physics."

I did say that. It was good advice. If I was smart I would follow it. I smiled at her. "I'm glad you stopped by today. You cheered me up a little."

"Good," she said, leaning over the desk. "What's up? Can I help?"

I started to say no, but then I stopped. I didn't have anyone on my side any more. My former boyfriend Ted was long gone. Apparently, I couldn't completely count on Ryan right now and Andro was a mystery.

For that matter, q-lapsing was pretty mysterious. "Well, I'm confused about collapsing the wavefunction. I've been calling it q-lapsing. How come it works for me sometimes and doesn't others?" I paused. How come other people could do it? But maybe I shouldn't mention that. I didn't want to give her any ideas.

She nodded. "What does the data show?"

"I don't know." I tried to take a sip from my now-empty mug. "I guess I don't have enough data."

"Why don't you get more?" she asked.

I remembered the white quantum mist with a shudder. "It's dangerous." Still, if I got really good at it, I could prove it to Chen and all the FBI agents and whoever else I came across.

"Why don't you try it now?" she asked, and managed to knock

over my empty cup. "Sorry." She quickly righted it.

What the hell. I could try to q-lapse my cup full of more coffee–the good stuff from Boulder Brews, not the not-so-good stuff from that cart. I concentrated on filling the cup with steaming deliciousness.

And then it was there.

I pointed at the cup. "Now I'm more confused. I don't have any adrenaline in my system."

She pointed at my extended finger. "Your hands are shaking. How much coffee have you had today? Maybe the caffeine is stimulating your system enough."

Could it be? I took a sip of the new stuff. It was yummy. How many times had I been drinking coffee when it worked? Could coffee play a part? My mind reeled. Was I undergoing a paradigm shift? Or had I just had too much caffeine?

"Madison?" Alyssa asked. "Are you okay?"

"Is it just me, or is the room spinning?" I was experiencing vertigo. My head started to throb.

"Of course not." And then she clutched the arms of her chair and squeaked. "Maybe. Stop whatever you're doing. I'm getting dizzy." Her blood drained from her face.

I exhaled. I concentrated. *Calm. I. Was. Calm. The. Room. Was. Still.*

She let go of the chair arms. "On the plus side, I guess you're getting better at that q-lapsing."

I nodded. Who knew what would happen next? "Do you feel shaking?" I felt shaking.

"Stop it, already," she said, clutching her chair again.

I focused on my breathing. In. Out. In. Out.

"Don't start hyperventilating," she said.

We heard footsteps come down the hallway and then Andro appeared in my open doorway.

Alyssa jumped out of her chair. "Andro, I mean Professor Rivas, you have to help Madison."

"Did anyone else just feel a small earthquake?" he asked.

"That was Madison," she said. "She's freaking out and randomly q-lapsing."

He took a step into my office. "Madison?"

I gave him a little wave. "Hi, there." *Calm. I'm very calm.*

"You do look odd. Blurry?" He walked past Alyssa towards my desk.

She shook her head violently. "Be careful. Don't give her any ideas. Next thing you know she'll get dizzy and then we'll all be dizzy. Calm. Tell her she's calm."

"You're calm?" he said, staring at me over my desk.

I was happy to see him. He looked delicious as usual. Really yummy. I would be happy to see more of him. Was his shirt starting to get transparent? And then his shirt disappeared.

"Madison," Alyssa hissed from behind him.

Yikes. *Calm. I'm calm. Everything's normal.*

"What?" He finally noticed his shirt was gone. "What happened to my shirt? I was wearing a shirt."

Alyssa shrugged.

"There seems to be something wrong with me," I said. "I can't seem to stop q-lapsing."

Andro frowned. "That's a new one. What about the adrenaline thing?"

Speaking of adrenaline, a kiss would be so nice about now.

He stepped around my desk.

"I think she had too much coffee, way too much," Alyssa said.

"I have an urge to kiss you," he said, leaning towards me. Yay.

I stared at his full red lips. One little kiss wouldn't hurt, would it?

Andro's hands reached behind my head, gently pulled me toward him, and pressed his lips to mine.

As our lips connected, I placed my hands on his chest and felt tingly all over. "Mmm."

"Madison," Alyssa said. "You guys look blurry. Are you q-lapsing? Stop. I thought you said it was dangerous."

Andro broke away, grinning. "You are most definitely dangerous."

I grinned too. "Really?"

He sat on my desk, leaning over me. "Really."

Alyssa stomped over to us. "Are you insane?" she said to me. "And you," she said to Andro. "Why do all men think with their pants?"

All traces of amusement drained from his face as he stood up. "I don't know why I did that. I'm sorry. It goes against taking it slow. Plus, it was inappropriate in front of a student."

I knew why he did it. I q-lapsed him into it. "I'm not sorry." I smiled.

He grinned for a split-second. "Okay, I'm not that sorry. But I should get back to work." He backed away and glanced down again, shaking his head a little. "And give me back my shirt."

Aw. I focused and his shirt reappeared. It had all been totally worth it even though I was getting a headache.

"Are you sure you should go back to work?" I asked. "I should do some more collapsing the wavefunction experiments. Don't you want to help?"

Andro walked quickly toward the door. "Get Alyssa to help. She won't tempt you to do anything inappropriate." He spun around to face me. "She won't, will she?"

"Ew." Alyssa said.

"No," I said.

"Good. In that case, I'm out of here." He fled the scene.

I faced her. "I feel a little better. More in control. And more powerful. In fact..."

I turned to the hole in the wall and concentrated on fixing it. Slowly the opening filled with a white mist that solidified into cinder block. Yes. I smiled. "Excellent."

Very faintly from next door I heard, "You fixed the wall! Good job."

"Did you use up some of your quantum energy?" Alyssa asked.

"I don't know," I said. "I really do need to understand this more. Are you up for some experiments?" I figured she'd stay unblurry and danger-free if she just observed.

"Definitely," she said.

Alyssa recorded my q-lapsing experiments with the double-slit apparatus the rest of the day and well into the evening. I did get blurry when I q-lapsed. The more improbable the q-lapse, the more blurry I got.

Another interesting discovery was: headaches followed q-lapsing, and the weirder the instantiated possibility, the bigger the headache.

Luckily, I didn't have any run-ins with the quantum mist. I

knew from before that the mist was accompanied by a really big headache, so I deduced the mist was due to an extremely bizarre q-lapse–such as a q-lapse in which one was transported instantaneously hundreds of miles. I avoided doing that.

Finally, about eleven o'clock that evening, Alyssa pooped out and went home.

I didn't have a home at the moment, so I kept working. I collapsed on my office couch at some point and slept like someone who was really, really tired.

At eight o'clock Friday morning, I snuck down to the department office to see if I was still suspended. I wanted to teach my students–except maybe Luke and Griffin.

The light was on in the physics department office and in Chen's office. I'd always suspected there were people that got up that early but now I had the data to prove it.

When I started to go into the department office however, Nancy shook her head at me and shooed me back into the hall. Once we were outside, she closed the door behind her and said, "He's still mad. Let him cool off some more. I don't think that lawyer of yours did you any favors."

I knew Tom had been too confrontational. "Thanks, Nancy. And thanks for the heads-up about the meeting earlier."

"You remembered my name," she said, looking surprised.

"Of course, I did," I said. "Why wouldn't I?"

She didn't buy that for a second. "If Chen sees you, he's gonna call campus police, so get out of here." Ryan was campus police. What if he had to come to remove me from campus? Ugh. Now that would be embarrassing.

I felt bad about missing my class and wondered if they got a substitute or what. But moping wouldn't get me anywhere so the rest of Friday I practiced q-lapsing, seeking sufficient data to actually run some statistical analyses. I wanted to know how often one could q-lapse and what factors affected the outcome. How did the experimenter's emotional and adrenaline state affect the outcome and how was the experimenter affected by q-lapsing? Additionally, what did probability have to do with it? Were more probable things easier to instantiate or not?

One significant thing I discovered was chocolate-covered coffee beans from Boulder Brews kept a person the right amount of jittery.

Alyssa stopped by after her classes and helped for a couple hours. I was right about her. She was one of the good ones. I hoped Chen would come around about her.

I took time out only for a catnap on my couch Friday night and got back to work early Saturday morning. And I didn't even have to go out for coffee. I just q-lapsed it into my cup.

Alyssa stopped by again Saturday after lunch to help.

Somewhere in there Andro called and we finalized our double-date plans for Saturday night.

At five p.m.-ish I said to Alyssa, "Enough. I don't want to take up your whole weekend. Thank you so much for helping. Having a record of this stuff is invaluable."

She smiled. "You're welcome. I must admit it's exciting."

I held up my forefinger. "You promised you wouldn't experiment with q-lapsing on your own."

She nodded solemnly. "I remember the agreement."

"So, anyway, get out of here. Go have some fun." I smiled.

"Is that an order?" She started to smile.

"Yes," I said.

"You too, then. Don't work too hard." She started walking for the door.

"You don't need to worry about me. I have plans."

She stopped dead, a huge grin on her face. "You have a date with Andro, don't you?"

"Uh." A smile escaped. "Yeah." I did!

"Tell me everything."

"There's not much to tell. We're just having a low-key dinner with Andro's sister and her date at the Rio."

She sighed. "I love The Rio. Their margs are the bomb."

"The what are the who?" I said.

She laughed. "Never mind. Have fun. You might even see me there." She sauntered out.

After she left, I decided I had to call Ryan and beg him to let me come home. It was an emergency. I needed to make myself pretty and my stuff was there. He took pity on me and relented. There may have been a rude comment in there somewhere about how it was a lost cause trying to make me pretty, but he was kidding. I think. Pretty sure.

Thus, at six fifty-nine I was primped and ready, standing in front of the door waiting for Andro to knock.

Chapter Twenty-Two

At seven fifteen Saturday night I was still waiting for my date, still standing stupidly in front of the door. Had I gotten the time or date wrong? Had something happened to Andro?

Ryan walked by, rocking Emily. "You're still here? I would've thought Prince Charming would have whisked you away by now. Where's your pumpkin carriage?" He chuckled at his own joke. He may have been punchy from lack of sleep.

My cell rang. Saved by the ring-tone. It was Andro calling to say they were running late because Yasmin had trouble deciding what to wear.

I smiled into the phone. "I can sympathize with that. How late are we talking? Should I meet you there?"

"That might be best. Hector was already planning to meet us there. I'd rather not keep him waiting too long. Do you think you can recognize him?"

I nodded.

"Madison?"

Oops. "Sorry. Yeah. I nodded. I'll meet you there." We hung up and I went and caught the bus. Boulder had an awesome public transportation system.

A little after seven thirty I tried to insert myself into the lobby of the Rio. It was as jam-packed as a neutron star. I wasn't sure I could fit inside. Nonetheless, I persevered. The din of voices was almost deafening. I thought I saw Hector there near the door.

"Madison?" he asked. I could barely make out what he was saying.

"Hi, Hector." His striped dress shirt was brand new. It still had creases from the packaging. "You look nice."

"Where's everyone else? Where's Yasmin? She didn't back out, did she?" There were little worry lines between his eyes.

I touched his arm. Okay, someone shoved me into his arm. "Don't worry. Yasmin didn't back out. She's just running late. She's excited about tonight." At least that's how I felt when I couldn't figure out what to wear–excited and nervous. I hadn't had the what-to-wear problem tonight because I needed to do laundry, so my choices were limited.

Hector exhaled and dropped his hunched shoulders. "Good."

"Maybe we should put our name in for a table?" I said, girding myself to fight my way through the crowd to the hostess stand.

Hector sighed. "I already did. They said it would be an hour and a half wait."

"An hour and a half? What do they serve here? A cure for cancer?"

Hector smiled. "Actually they're known for their margaritas. The university students love them."

That's what Alyssa had been talking about. "I think I better try one of those, then. Let's go to the bar."

He agreed and we squished our way north through the crowd. Hector seemed to know where he was going, so I followed him. He elbowed his way right up to the bar and ordered.

Within a few minutes, he handed me a margarita. My hero.

"Thanks a lot, Hector," I said. "What do I owe you?"

He shrugged. "Don't worry about it."

"Thanks. I'll get the next one." I took a sip of the cold and limy beverage. I couldn't taste the tequila but the lime puckered my lips. Yum.

"Madison. Over here," a woman yelled. "Professor Martin."

It sounded like Alyssa. I scanned the crowd and spied a waving arm next to a familiar head. "Hector, I see a student. Is it okay if we go over and say hi?"

He took a swig of his Corona and nodded.

We squeezed our way over to Alyssa. She stood at a chest-high round wooden table with a bunch of other twenty-somethings. They were all drinking margaritas and even had an almost-full pitcher of margaritas on the table.

"Hi, Alyssa," I said. "I see you made it. Good for you. This is my friend, Hector."

Hector waved.

"This is my roommate Callie, and her boyfriend Jacob." Alyssa waved her arm toward each person as she mentioned him or her. Callie smiled brightly at me. She was a short bouncy blonde. Jacob, about five nine with chin-length wavy hair, just nodded. Hipster, check.

"And this is Jacob's roommate, Tyler." And then, as Alyssa brought her arm back, she managed to knock the whole pitcher of margaritas on herself.

"Party foul," Tyler said. He was a little taller than Jacob with sandy blond hair and big dimples. He looked like a fraternity guy to me. He also seemed entranced with Alyssa.

"Doh," Jacob said.

Hector forgot about his beer and stared at Alyssa, gaping. Why?

My eyes were drawn to her soaked white blouse, as if to a car accident. I could see her breasts clearly through the wet fabric. She must not have been wearing a bra. "Alyssa. Your blouse!" I crossed my arms in front of my chest.

"What?" she asked me across the table.

In the meantime, Callie had noticed. She stopped trying to sop up the spill on the table with napkins, picked up a bar menu, held it in front of Alyssa's chest, and whispered in her ear.

Alyssa squeaked. "Oh, no." Frantically, she tried to cover herself with her hands.

The crowd jostled Callie and the menu dipped.

I felt someone tap me on the shoulder, and turned around. It was Andro.

"Hi there, gorgeous," he said, smiling.

"Hi there, yourself," I said back.

And then he gave me a hug. Or the crowd pushed him into me. One or the other. But in any case, his body felt great against mine, very firm and warm.

Yasmin was having a little trouble getting Hector's attention. She tapped him on the shoulder more than once.

Hector was still staring at Alyssa, eyes bugged out and mouth hanging open. Good grief, you'd think he'd never seen breasts before. He whispered, "*Mi Dios*," and dropped his beer.

The bottle splashed beer on one of my pant legs before falling over and rolling under the table. I was glad I'd worn jeans tonight.

When I glanced back at Alyssa, she was wearing a *Geekfest 2014* t-shirt. And I had a sneaking suspicion I knew how she'd managed it.

Alyssa's friends were frozen in shock, staring at her.

"Just a sec," I said to Andro and then put my drink down and scooted around the table to Alyssa. "Did you just do what I think you did?"

She nodded. "Sorry. But what else was I going to do? Put on a show for everyone?"

I couldn't blame her. "How'd you do it, though? How'd you get adrenaline-y?"

She opened her purse and showed me a baggie of chocolate-covered coffee beans. "I got my own stash." She shrugged sheepishly.

"Please be careful," I said. "And don't tell anyone else how to do it."

I looked across the table at my group and they were all agitated. Hector was waving his hands around and speaking in Spanish. Yasmin looked like she might cry. Andro had his hands on Hector's shoulders, trying to calm him down.

"Yikes. I have to go. I'll see you Monday?" I said to Alyssa.

She nodded.

By the time I squeezed back through the crowd to where Andro and everyone were standing only Yasmin was still there. "Where'd they go?" I asked.

"What?" Yasmin said.

"What happened to Andro and Hector?" I said in Yasmin's ear.

"They went outside to talk," she said into my ear.

"Let's join them," I said.

"What?" she asked.

I grabbed my drink and her hand and led her through the crowd to the giant-sized front door. It took both of us to push it open.

Andro and Hector stood outside talking, still looking agitated.

"What's up?" I asked them. "Did you see Alyssa do something

bizarre?"

Yasmin shook her head. "No. That's not it. I told Hector all about that quantum stuff. It's about Armando."

"Your husband?" I asked.

Andro interrupted. "Hector says he saw the picture on Alyssa's shirt on the SUV that ran down Armando."

Hector nodded. "Yes."

I gasped. "Oh, my God." I took a big gulp of my marg to help me cope.

Yasmin said, "Are you sure, Hector?"

"Yes. I am sure," he said solemnly.

"Maybe that girl killed him," Yasmin said.

"No," I said quickly. "That's not even her shirt."

"It's not?" Andro asked.

"No. I think it belongs to another kid, Luke," I said.

"Bank robber Luke?" Andro asked.

I nodded and took another sip.

Bright red spots appeared on Yasmin's cheekbones. "Good. We're finally going to get the devil who killed my Armando."

"I hope they fry him," Hector said.

Yasmin nodded vigorously.

"We have to report this to the police right away," Andro said. "I wonder if Ben's on duty?" He pulled out his cell phone. Ben had given us his contact info after we saved him at the frat party.

A guy in a greasy all-white outfit opened the side door. "Hey, you can't take liquor outside the restaurant," he said to me.

I slammed the rest of my drink. "What liquor?" I asked and handed him the glass.

Ben was on duty, so the four of us went over to the police station. I wasn't mopey about my date being ruined, but I was a little drunky. That big margarita and an empty stomach was a lethal combination. I hadn't tasted the liquor but apparently it'd been in there.

Ben scrounged chairs for us all near his desk, and he entered stuff into his computer as he interviewed Hector.

Yasmin kept interrupting, "So you're going to arrest this Luke guy, right? Right?"

I leaned my elbow on the desk and my head on my hand and

may have dozed off.

"I said," Andro nudged me, "are you worried that Luke might attack us?"

"Huh?" I lifted my head.

"Did you fall asleep?" he asked.

"Yeah, I guess so." I smiled sleepily. "I should eat something."

"So not too worried. You are, as they say, a cheap date. One drink and you're falling asleep." He smiled. "I promise I'll buy you dinner as soon as we're finished here."

"Good. Because if anyone did attack now, I couldn't collapse a paper bag," I said.

"We got him," Ben said. "I ran the list of black late-nineties Expeditions and one is registered to this kid Luke Bacalli."

Hector muttered something under his breath.

Yasmin looked like she might tear up.

Andro put his arm around her.

For my part, even with everything that had happened, I was a little surprised Luke was actually a killer.

Ben sported a big smile. "Thanks, you guys. We'll have to take a look at the vehicle and probably question them, but this looks really, really promising." He jumped out of his chair. "I have to go tell my supervisor I found a murder suspect." Before he dashed off, he stopped and asked Hector, "You're willing to testify in court, an official court of law, right?"

Hector nodded and said, "Yeah."

Ben ran off to find his boss.

"Of course Hector would testify," Yasmin said. "What was that Ben getting at?"

Hector sighed. "He was probably checking that I wasn't an illegal."

"No," I said. "I bet he asks everyone that."

Hector looked skeptical. Yasmin shook her head.

Andro merely raised his eyebrows.

Ben's supervisor, a fat balding white guy, came back with Ben. We gave him the information about the *Geekfest 2014* logo and the sticker on the car. He acted impressed. "Good job, Ben," he said, messing with his comb-over. "You're going to make detective yet. We've got Hector's statement and I think we can get a warrant for Luke Bacalli's arrest or at least bring him in for questioning."

"What about Griffin?" I said.

The supervisor looked confused. "Who?"

"We don't have anything on him," Ben said.

"Frip." Griffin would be free to continue his quantum crime spree. On us.

"You guys can go for now. Mr. Bustamante, we have all your contact information?" the supervisor asked Hector. "And you're willing to testify?"

Hector sighed. "Yes, sir."

Yasmin was starting to look irritated.

"Thank you very much for doing your civic duty," Ben's boss said.

"*De nada*," Hector said, already starting for the door. Was the Spanish sarcastic? I glanced at the supervisor. If so, it hadn't connected.

"Thanks," I said to Ben. "But be careful with these guys. I'm serious. Luke and his friends are dangerous."

He nodded. "I'll call you after we get him down here." Ben followed after us to the front. "If this pans out, I'll owe you."

I hoped that happened. But I was too worried about what Luke and Griffin might do when cornered to be optimistic. What if they'd perfected that heart attack thing?

Andro put his hand on my back and led me toward the door. "Should we warn the police more about what they might be getting into?" he said in my ear.

"Probably," I said. "But they wouldn't believe us." Personally, I was glad I'd been practicing q-lapsing this week. I was getting pretty good, so I should be ready for any attacks. Right as soon as I sobered up.

"Ben might believe us after his experience at the frat party," Andro said.

I shrugged. "So, give it a try. Tell him."

Andro took Ben aside and talked to him for a couple minutes.

When Andro and I joined Hector and Yasmin outside, Yasmin was saying, "Thank you so much, Hector. You're my hero." She gave him a peck on the cheek.

He blushed and looked down at the ground. "Thanks. But Armando was my best friend. He deserves justice."

We all nodded.

Andro rubbed his hands together. “Back to the restaurant?”

“I’m not up for another hour-plus wait,” Hector said.

Yasmin showed off her rarely-seen beautiful smile. “Hector, why don’t you just come over to my house?” she said. “I can cook something for you.”

“Hey, what about us?” Andro asked her.

Yasmin nudged his arm with her shoulder. “You know you’d rather be alone with Madison. Go ahead. I won’t give you a hard time about it.”

It sounded good to me, but the way Yasmin was smiling I was guessing she was the one who wanted to be alone with her beau.

“Shall we?” Hector asked Yasmin, and stuck out his arm for her.

She beamed and grabbed his arm and they headed down the sidewalk presumably to his car.

“Shall we?” Andro imitated Hector.

I ignored the proffered arm. “I need to eat something and get a lot of caffeine in my system. Or adrenaline. We both need some caffeine or adrenaline. Or both. ASAP.” I didn’t mention kissing. I was too hungry and worried to think about kissing. Oops. Or at least think about it a lot.

He frowned. “So you think we’re in danger?”

“Yes,” I said. “As soon as Griffin and Luke figure out what’s going on, I really think we’ll be in danger. Don’t you?”

“Yeah.” He nodded. “What about Yasmin and Hector?”

“Luke and Griffin haven’t met them and don’t know who they are,” I said. “I think they’re okay for now. We are not. Come on.” I grabbed Andro and pulled him toward the coffee place down the street.

Chapter Twenty-Three

The downtown Boulder Brews was also neutron-star-packed on Saturday night, wall-to-wall people. Andro and I picked our way through the crowd to the counter where I tried to order a quadruple espresso.

The freckle-faced worker said, “Sorry, ma’am, we don’t have a quadruple espresso.” He shook his head. “Would you like something else?”

He ma’amed me. I hated being ma’amed. It made me feel old.

“Why don’t you get two double espressos?” Andro said with a smile.

I slammed my hand on the counter. “Excellent idea. I’ll have two double espressos.”

“And for you, sir?” the kid asked Andro.

“I’ll just have one regular espresso,” he said.

I turned to face him. Oops. I turned too quickly and felt a little woozy. I grabbed the counter. “Did I tell you that caffeine helps with q-lapsing?”

“Yes. You may have mentioned that,” Andro said.

As soon as we got our drinks, I poured both of mine into one cup and slammed it. “Whoo. That’s a lot of caffeine.” I put my hand on my stomach. “The good news is, I don’t feel so drunk. But now I feel sort of nauseous.”

Andro looked at me over the top of his tiny paper cup. “If that’s the good news, what’s the bad news?”

“That was the bad news, too.” I tried to q-lapse and put some more espresso in my cup. Success. I gulped that down, too. “But more good news: I can q-lapse.” Now I felt really nauseous.

He belted back his espresso and made a sour face. "Let's get some food."

"Good idea." We dropped our cups back on the counter.

"So, can you do it?" I asked him as we stepped out onto the sidewalk.

He just smiled at me. "Do it?" he finally said. "What are you asking? What's *it*?"

"What's that look for?" My pulse ratcheted up. I knew what that look was for. Wow. "Uh." Get a grip, Mad. You're in danger. He's in danger. "You know I mean q-lapse."

He grabbed my hand. "And you know one way we can get revved up to do it."

As a matter of fact I could recall a couple steamy incidents. I blushed and squeezed his hand. "That hasn't been definitively scientifically proven."

He squeezed back. "Sounds like we need to do some experiments."

My heart raced.

We ducked into Boulder Burritos next door where the décor was minimalist, lots of stainless steel and light-colored wood. The customers were minimalist too, packed like a stellar nebula. Everyone must have been next door drinking brews.

I ordered some soft tacos and Andro got one of their everything-but-the-kitchen-sink burritos. The food came right up and we had our choice of tables.

My tacos were almost too spicy, but sour cream put out the flames. They were soon gone. They were just what the doctor ordered. My nausea dissipated.

Andro labored on with his enormous burrito.

I grinned at him. "I'd hate to see how big the everything-including-the-kitchen-sink burrito is."

He put his meal down on the plate and groaned. "I don't think I can finish this."

I held up my hands. "Don't let me stop you. You could digest a while and then try some more. I'm in no hurry to go home." Truth be told, I wasn't sure I could go home. I'd forgotten to ask Ryan. And then there was the imminent quantum attack factor. I debated q-lapsing another taco into existence, but decided against it.

Andro frowned. "Our date didn't go so great, did it?"

I caught the faint sound of music coming from the kitchen, and q-lapsed to make it louder.

"What did you just do?" he asked. "You got a little blurry there around the edges for a second."

I pointed back at the kitchen. "I turned up the music."

He nodded his head in time with the tune. "Oh, yeah. Nice."

"I don't think our date turned out that bad," I said, smiling. "And it's not over yet, is it?"

"It is getting better." He slipped around the table and into the seat next to me. "How come you don't want to go home?" he asked. "Reluctant to leave me?" He put his arm around me and grinned.

"I don't want to put Ryan and his family in danger. When they attacked us the other night, it seemed like Luke and Griffin homed in on us, somehow."

He dropped his arm.

"Of course, I'm reluctant to leave you, too," I added quickly.

"Me, too," he said. "Say, would you like to dance?"

I suppressed a laugh. "In the burrito store?"

"Sure. Why not?" He stood up and held out his hand.

"Okay." I stood up, took his hand, and turned up the music some more.

As we moved to the rhythm of the music, Andro gradually drew my body closer and closer to his until we were pressed firmly against one another.

"I like this dancing stuff," I said. I breathed in his unique scent.

"You are a very good dancer," he said.

"Mmm." As we swayed back and forth, I wrapped my arms tightly around him and rubbed my hands on his warm, firm back.

"What did you say?" he asked.

"You're a really good dancer, too," I said. My right hand started migrating down his back.

He jumped back a centimeter. "Hey, watch the hands, young lady, or you're going to see something else start dancing."

I snickered and moved my hand up. "Sorry."

Andro put his hand behind my neck. "Nothing to be sorry about. I was just warning you." He leaned his face down, and his full lips made contact with mine.

I closed my eyes and moaned as tingles shot from my mouth to all points south. I could feel my face, neck and chest flush. When we came up for air, I said, "Whoo."

He wiped sweat from his forehead. "I agree. Whoo."

"Maybe we better cool it," I said.

"Don't stop on my account," he said and flashed me an X-rated grin. Wow. Ted hadn't had a grin like that.

"You're changing your tune, Catholic-boy," I said, plopping back down in my seat and grabbing my soda.

He joined me at the table.

"Can I ask you a personal question?" I asked.

He smiled and reached for his drink. "You mean besides that one?"

"Yeah." I couldn't believe I was about to ask him this.

"Shoot," he said.

"So, uh, are you a virgin?" I asked.

A burst of laughter exploded out of Andro's mouth. "I'm in my thirties, Madison. That would be a bit extreme."

"I don't get it. You're Catholic and you're not married."

"What can I say?" There was that grin again. "I'm not a very good Catholic."

"But..." I was not going to ask him why he didn't want to have sex with me. I took a drink of my soda, slurping it noisily, and looked down at the table.

"But, you want to know why I stopped when we were parked the other night?" he said gently.

I shrugged. "Well, yeah." Was he attracted to me or not? He was sending mixed signals.

"I respect you. I didn't want our first time to be in some car. You deserve better than that."

I looked him in the eyes. "Good answer," I whispered.

He smiled and I swear his blue eyes twinkled.

I was so falling for him. In fact, I was falling so hard you'd think the force of gravity had increased.

"Hey, we're getting ready to close up," one of the workers yelled at us, and the moment was over.

As we walked out, I said, "I really appreciate your respectful attitude, but are you sure you're a guy?"

Andro laughed and put his arm around me. "Yes, I'm sure. Are you asking me to prove it to you?" He looked down at me, a hint of a smile playing around his lips.

"Uh." Yes.

He laughed again. "C'mon, I'm parked over here." He pointed back toward the Rio.

In the car, he said, "Back home, Madison?"

"No, better not. What about my office? It has that nice couch." I screwed up my courage. "You could join me if you like."

"Thanks for the offer, but your office?" he asked. "That's not romantic."

"I don't want to go home," I said. "Where else can we go? We can't go to your place. We can't put Yasmin and her daughters in danger."

"No. We are not going to do that." Andro put the car in gear. "I've got a better idea. Have you heard about this new-fangled invention called a hotel?"

"Wow, you're smart," I said. "You must've gone to college or something."

"Why, thank you." He chuckled. "As a matter of fact, I did go to college or something. And don't worry, I know just the place."

Ten minutes later found us at the Boulder Bed and Breakfast. The college-age kid at the desk didn't bat an eyelash at us checking in near midnight with no luggage. He just yawned, gave us a key, and said breakfast was served from seven to ten o'clock.

When we got to our room, it looked like a flower explosion. The wallpaper, bedspread, and carpeting were all covered with pink roses and tiny, blue flowers.

"Wow," I said, walking inside, trailing fingertips on the puffy bedspread. "This is flowery. I thought I'd seen flowery before, but I was wrong."

Andro smiled. "Well, some occasions just call for a plethora of posies."

I chuckled and sat down on the bed. "Perhaps occasions such as de-flowerings?"

He groaned.

I patted the bed next to me. "What are you waiting for?"

"Nothing." He joined me on the four-poster bed.

My lips were drawn to his as if I was an electron and he was a proton. My heart raced as his tongue slid into my mouth, and we dipped back onto the bed. This was really going to happen.

And then Andro stopped.

"What's wrong?" I asked.

"We may be missing some vital supplies," he said, frowning. "I can't believe this."

"What? You don't have any condoms?" I asked.

He shook his head. "No. I don't. I thought Yasmin would be chaperoning us. Do you have any?"

"No. I thought Yasmin would be chaperoning us." I sat up straight. "Actually, this is a good time to talk STDs. I'm HIV negative, are you?"

He nodded. "Clean bill of health. No STDs. You?"

"Me, too." I sighed. There was absolutely no reason we couldn't enjoy ourselves–except one. "This might be a good time for you to practice q-lapsing."

"Good idea." He smiled. "But I better get my adrenaline pumping some more." He touched my cheek with his hand, tilted his head, and touched his lips to mine.

I put my arms around him and pulled him to me, smoldering, as his chest rubbed against my breasts. Our tongues explored each other's mouths.

Andro broke away. "Whoo. That should do it." He held out his hand, got fuzzy, and suddenly held a box of condoms.

A whole box? That seemed like kind of a lot. "You think you got enough there?" I asked, smiling.

"We'll see, won't we?" He grinned wickedly as he put the box on the nightstand. "Now where were we?"

I had a thought. "What if you can't q-lapse after we, uh, consummate our..."

"Relationship?" He smiled.

I felt all tingly and he wasn't even touching me. "Okay, relationship." I smiled back. "What if you lose your ability? Luke and Griffin might be hunting us."

"That's a risk I'm willing to take," he said. "What about you? What if you lose your ability?"

"That's a risk I'm willing to take." That was a risk I really wanted to take at this point.

As we kissed, I gently pushed him back onto the bed, and

started unbuttoning his shirt. Soon, I rubbed my hands on his smooth chest and kissed it, working my way down to his navel and the runway of dark hairs disappearing into his pants.

I unbuckled his belt buckle and he grabbed my hands. "Not so fast, *mi amor*," he said gently.

"Come here." He pulled me down onto the bed next to him and started unbuttoning my blouse. His fingers brushed my skin, feeling red-hot.

I leaned up and shrugged out of my shirt.

He covered my collarbone in soft kisses, and blood flowed to my chest. Slowly his kisses moved down and he ran his hand up my stomach and squeezed my breast. Heat rushed to my breasts as his fingers slipped under my bra and caressed my nipple.

It felt like there was a biomass-burning event running from my breasts to my pelvis. I leaned up and unhooked my bra.

He intently peeled it off. He cupped my breasts with his hands, rubbing the tips of his fingers over my erect nipples.

"Mmm." I arched my back.

He lowered his head, and kissed my nipple before engulfing it with his mouth. It felt fantastic.

I ran my fingers though his glossy hair, as his tongue ran back and forth over my nipple. I arched my back again.

"Mmm, that feels good." My voice was so husky I almost didn't recognize it.

He lifted his head up and looked me in the eyes. Our lips sought each other eagerly.

His hands brushed down my stomach to my pants and unfastened the top button. Ever so slowly he urged the zipper down.

I already felt like I was going to explode. "Hurry up." I reached for his zipper and quickly started tugging his pants down.

He chuckled, disengaged himself and stood, shucking his pants and underwear in a few seconds.

In the meantime, I wriggled around trying to get mine off without getting off the bed.

Andro stood in all his nakedness and smiled at me.

Wow. I had to stop what I was doing and appreciate him. From the top of his head, to the tips of his toes, he was awesome. Whoever said men weren't beautiful had never seen Andro naked. And just when I'd gotten an eyeful he turned out the light.

"Hey! Turn the light back on. I was looking at you."

I felt the bed move as he climbed on. "Would you like some help?"

Looking at him? "Huh?"

"With your pants?"

"Please." I lifted up my hips and my pants disappeared into thin air.

"Hey, I'm gonna need those back, eventually."

Before I had a chance to say anything else, his fingers caressed my panties, and then, poof, they were gone, too.

In the dim light, I could just make out he was smiling like a physicist who'd won the Nobel Prize.

"What are you waiting for?" I held out a hand. It didn't seem possible, but feeling his eyes on me made me hotter than ever. It was as if little bolts of lightning ran across my skin as he looked at me.

And then a real burst of lightning erupted from my hand and hit the lamp on the nightstand, knocking it over. "Oops."

A grin spread slowly over his face. "I guess it's dangerous to keep you waiting."

"Yes, it is." I sent an energy bolt over his head.

He laughed.

It turned out Andro was a bad Catholic.

Very, very bad.

Very, very good for me.

Chapter Twenty-Four

I was awakened with a kiss and the scent of coffee. I opened my eyes.

"*Buenos días, mi amor*," Andro said. He held two steaming paper cups.

"*Buenos dias*," I said, grinning like a fool. "Is that coffee? Can I have some?"

Andro nodded.

I grabbed one of the cups, and gulped some down. "Ah. You're my hero. Thanks."

"I hope you're not saying I'm your hero because of the coffee," he said with a crinkle on his forehead.

Oops. I gulped some more coffee and set the cup on the nightstand. "Of course not." I pressed my lips against his lips. "Last night was incredible. I can't believe I could have thought you were a virgin."

"That's better." He kissed me and I kissed back and we lost track of time for a while.

And then as Andro reached for the much-depleted box of condoms, my cell phone rang. Grudgingly, I answered it.

It was Agent Baker. "Professor Martin, we need you. We're helping Boulder PD arrest Luke Bacalli for vehicular manslaughter." Boulder PD assembled that evidence quickly. Good for them. "We think his lawyer may have gotten wind of the warrant so we need to move ASAP. We're afraid he's a flight risk." They should be afraid–he was a flight risk.

And what twentyish-year-old man even had a lawyer?

I covered the phone. "They must have found physical

evidence implicating Luke in Armando's death. They're going to arrest him."

Andro scowled. "Good."

"They want my help," I said to him. "Are you in?"

"Professor Martin?" Agent Baker asked.

Andro nodded.

"Agent Baker, Professor Rivas and I would be happy to help. Just tell us where and when." I got the details and we hung up.

"I'm sorry we didn't get to the finish line now," I said as I got up and looked under the bed for my clothes. I scooped up my shirt and bra but my pants and underpants were nowhere to be found.

"It's just as well," he said. "We'll probably have an easier time q-lapsing if we're all riled up."

"Please get my pants and underwear back from wherever you sent them."

"Hmm." He grinned, but after a moment he relented and nodded. "Here, you go, babe."

And there they were.

We met Boulder PD and the FBI agents at their staging area in the liquor store across the street from Luke and Griffin's apartment. There were, like, fifty people swarming around inside and behind it, under the *LI OR* sign. It was a little odd seeing all the law enforcement officers standing between the liquor displays and cases. I picked Agent Baker out of the crowd and Andro and I approached her.

"Professor Martin, there you are," she said. "And this is Professor Rivas? You know how to do the quantum stuff, too?"

Andro nodded. "Yes."

A frown flickered momentarily over Agent Baker's face before she smiled thinly and held out her hand for a shake.

I knew she was wondering why he hadn't come forward to help before now. Or maybe she was wondering why I hadn't mentioned him before.

"Nice to meet you," she said.

"Likewise," Andro said.

"So what's the plan?" I asked. "You guys have an awful lot of people here."

"Yeah. I'm not clear on why the FBI is even involved," Andro said.

"I told Madison at the task force meeting there had been some bizarre crimes around the country," Agent Baker said. "We have reason to believe Griffin and Luke are involved." Considering Griffin appeared out of thin air at the bank right in front of us, I was guessing they had strong reason.

"I'm confused," I said. "I thought we were here about the hit-and-run that killed Armando."

She nodded. "That's why Boulder PD is here." She paused as if gathering her thoughts. "The quantum crimes are escalating in number and in seriousness. There have been three more attempted bank robberies in the last week. They fit the quantum M.O."

"Oh, no," I said. And what did attempted mean? Had people gotten hurt?

"Our boss has finally agreed quantum crimes are a real problem and we formalized the Quantum Crime Task Force," she said. "But none of us know how to collapse the wavefunction. We need you to teach us how to do it, Madison. This Luke kid might do it now, right?"

"You want me to teach you now?" I squeaked. "I don't think that's practical."

"How about some time later, then? After all this is over?" she asked.

I nodded. Hopefully, I could teach them. I'd taught Andro and Alyssa, right? I deliberately didn't think of Luke and Griffin. Oops. Make that tried not to think of them.

Ben approached the three of us. "Hey, there, quantum cop. Andro." He smiled at me before turning to the agent. "Agent Baker, we're ready to go." He pointed back at the group of Boulder PD officers in SWAT gear.

I had a very bad feeling. "Whoa. Hold it. You all can't just storm in there. People will get hurt."

"What do you suggest then?" Agent Baker said.

I looked at Andro and he nodded slightly. "It would be better if Andro and I went in alone. We can counter whatever quantum stuff they throw at us." Hopefully.

"I'm not sure the two of you going in alone is a good idea,"

Agent Baker said. “But if you’re sure, we brought some adrenaline for you to take.”

I nodded. “We may need it to follow him if he q-lapses to escape. Are you prepared to try that if we have to, Andro?” I turned to him.

He looked at me steadily. “We focus on q-lapsing to be in the same location he is, right? Yes. I’m prepared. It’s for Armando and his family.”

Agent Baker said, “I wish we had more time to plan this, but the longer we wait, the more likely it is he’ll flee.”

Despite the tension of the situation, I yawned. “Sorry,” I said. “Late night.” I blushed a little as I glanced at Andro.

He smiled at me.

Agent Baker didn’t deign to comment.

“I really need some coffee,” I said. “Can someone pop across the street to Boulder Brews and get me one? It helps with collapsing the wavefunction.”

Ben held up his hand. “I can go.”

“Thanks,” I said. “Get one for Andro, too, please.”

Ben nodded, jogged over and said something to the cop at the door, and jogged out.

When I looked at Andro, he was staring at me.

“What?”

“You yawned,” he said.

“So? I think you know why I’m so tired.”

Agent Baker pretended to ignore us.

“If we could sedate Luke somehow, he’d be easy to take into custody,” he said.

“That is an awesome idea,” I said.

“I agree,” Agent Baker said. “Let’s do it.” She was already waving one of the other agents over to her. They conferred for a few minutes.

“Are you sure you’re up for this?” I asked Andro.

“I’m sure I’m up for it,” he said. “I’m not sure I’m up for you to do it. I don’t want you in danger.” He frowned. “I wish there was a way to do this without you.”

“Well, there’s not,” I said. “And I’ve been practicing q-lapsing a lot lately.”

“Why didn’t you do it to get some coffee?” he asked.

Good question. "I'm sorry to say I didn't think of it. I guess I'm too tired." Through the window, I could see Ben already approaching with two enorme paper cups. "Well, I can't do it now. We made Ben run across the street." I pointed.

Agent Baker stepped back to us. "All right. Here's the plan: we're going to position agents and SWAT around the apartment, with backups in staggered positions farther away. We're going fill the apartment with a sort of sleeping gas. Then you two go in and assess the situation. Hopefully, the target will be asleep, and then you'll just call the officers in." The plan was making me uneasy. Didn't it violate Luke's rights? And what if other people were in the apartment? Like Griffin. It hit me that they might be trying to take Griffin in as well.

"Sounds good," Andro said.

"And if he's not asleep, we'll deal," I said. We'd have to deal.

We all nodded solemnly.

Ben gave us the coffees, and we snuck in thank-yous before Agent Baker sent him on another errand.

I started drinking.

Another agent, wearing one of the black jackets with giant FBI lettering on the back, brought us tiny radio transmitters and receivers, as well as ampules of adrenaline and showed us how to use them. Yet another agent gave us flak vests with lots of pockets, which we sorely needed by that point.

Ben came back with respirators that went on over our nose and mouth and had two big round chemical cartridges sticking out the sides.

Then we just had to wait around until everyone got into place.

I drank my coffee and surreptitiously q-lapsed to refill the cup when no one was looking. That worked well. "Do you want to practice q-lapsing a little?" I said quietly to Andro.

He held out his forefinger and a tiny spark boiled off it.

"Excellent," I said.

"You know what might make me even better at it?" he asked.

"I do know." I stepped right next to him and leaned my face up. Our lips met, and I got that buzzy feeling as tendrils of heat darted around my body. "Mmm," I said, my body pressing against his.

"If you two are ready?" Agent Baker said impatiently.

Andro and I separated.

"It helps with q-lapsing," I said, regarding her.

She appeared skeptical. "We have confirmation that the suspect is in the apartment. As soon as you're in position, we'll release the gas."

"Yes, ma'am," I said.

Ben and some other black-clad officers led us across the street, into the building, and up the stairs to a door on top floor of the apartment building.

Through our tiny radios, we heard, "Gas release now."

Another voice said immediately, "Martin, Rivas, get ready." It was Agent Baker.

I was startled each time I heard a voice through the ear bud.

We waited for what seemed centuries outside that door. The air through my respirator smelled faintly of a men's locker room, at least I was guessing it's what a men's locker room smelled like. Musty. Blech.

Andro grabbed my hand and squeezed it.

I squeezed his back.

Someone on the radio said, "Suspects asleep. Go, go, go."

Ben opened the door.

Andro and I ran through the doorway into a typical college-guys-apartment complete with a giant TV, elaborate stereo, fancy computer system, crappy hand-me-down furniture and an empty-beer-can pyramid.

Immediately to the right of the door was an archway leading to the kitchen. To the left was the door to the bathroom, which left two partially open doors in front of us.

I said, "I'll take the right one," quietly into my mic.

Andro nodded and started jogging left as I jogged right.

I carefully pushed open the door in question. The bedroom was dominated by a queen-sized bed, and there were clothes everywhere, including apparently on the bed. It was so messy it was hard to determine if there was a person in the bed. Part of me, the wimpy part, hoped we were too late and they'd fled already.

I heard, "Griffin is asleep," through the earpiece and jumped, knocking the door against a poorly placed dresser.

Something in the bed in front of me stirred.

I froze, my heart threatening to burst out of my chest like some kind of extraterrestrial parasite.

Slowly, a tousled head raised itself out of the jumble, opened its eyes and looked at me.

So much for plan A. "Andro, get over here," I whispered fiercely into the mic.

"Huh?" Luke said, struggling to sit up. "Who's there? Professor Martin?" He slurred. "Why are you wearing that mask?"

Andro ran in and skidded to a stop next to me.

"Professor Rivas?" Luke said. "Is that you? What are you guys doing here?" He shook his head. "What's wrong with me?" He sat up and rubbed his head.

Over the earpiece, I heard, "What's going on in there?"

"Luke's awake, but groggy," I said into my mic.

Luke's eyes narrowed, and then he bellowed, "Griffin, wake up. We're being attacked." Luke got sort of fuzzy, grimaced, and then jolted out bed, wearing wrinkled boxers.

We heard some loud thumping from the bedroom next door.

"Frip," I muttered.

"What?" my earpiece said.

"They're both awake," I said into the mic.

Andro turned to face the door just as Griffin lumbered into view, wearing only tighty-whities.

"What ta' fuck you doing here?" Griffin slurred from the living room.

"Use your powers to put them back to sleep," said the voice in my ear.

Andro and I glanced at each other. He looked weird in his mask. I must have looked weird as well. Then, I stared at Luke, thinking, *Go back to sleep. Go to sleep.*

Still shaking his head, Luke got blurry.

And then everything in the room got blurry, the walls, floor, ceiling, furniture. The edges of everything became indistinct and the ceiling, in particular, started to become transparent.

I glanced at Andro but he was fuzzy and staring through the doorway at Griffin in the living room.

Luke was fuzzy and staring at the ceiling. The ceiling seemed to be disappearing. I could dimly see blue sky and white fluffy clouds.

That wasn't good. "Stop it, Luke."

He said, "What?" Possibly I was hard to understand through the mask.

I aimed a bolt of electricity and zapped him. "You need to turn yourself in."

He flinched and glared at me, but quickly resumed staring at the ceiling. "Fuck you, Madison. This is none of your business."

It was my business. I was responsible for teaching him quantum mechanics. "Yes, it is." I zapped him again. "Surrender."

He jerked. "What?"

Behind me, I could hear a sizzling sound and a slurred "Ouch."

The ceiling disappeared completely and Luke took a deep breath. "Griffin," he yelled, "breathe the fresh air. They're wearing some kind of gas masks, so they must've sprayed something in here. They tried to drug us."

I heard "Shit," clearly in Griffin's voice, from the living room behind me, but didn't spare a glance.

Luke disappeared but almost before it registered, he was standing in front of his dresser, running his hands along the surface, searching for something. "Where are they?" he said.

There was some kind of scuffle in the living room.

I stepped toward Luke and zapped him with several bolts of lightning.

He flinched as they hit. "Shit." Then he paused to q-lapse some books at me like missiles.

"Stop it." I tried to yell, but it was hard to breath with the stupid respirator. I tore it off, but not before one of the books caught the top of my left arm. When I finally caught a breath, I tried to zap everything on the dresser with lightning. I was not successful.

Luke scrambled for something. "Ah ha." He held up two ampules like the ones the agents had given Andro and I. He jammed one into himself and disappeared.

"Luke's in here," Andro yelled, voice clear, from the living room.

I turned and ran in there.

Andro had also lost his respirator at some point. He was glaring at Luke.

Griffin looked the worse for wear, lying on the carpet.

Luke leaned over him.

I started to q-lapse to hit Luke with more lightning.

But Luke finished giving Griffin adrenaline, and they disappeared.

“Shit,” I yelled. “They disappeared.”

“Copy that,” the voice in the earpiece said.

“Should we try the adrenaline?” Andro asked.

“I guess we have to,” I said, reaching into my vest.

The voice in my ear said, “Affirmative.”

“I hope this works,” I said.

“Me, too,” Andro said.

Andro and I administered adrenaline to ourselves.

Chapter Twenty-Five

I felt all jittery. Gee, maybe it was because I just injected myself with adrenaline. I held out my hand to Andro and he grabbed it. "Do you feel okay?" I asked.

He nodded. "Yes. Let's get this over with."

"Focus on being where Luke and Griffin are," I said.

"Right." He squinted in concentration.

"Here we go," I said into the mic.

"Affirmative," Agent Baker said in my ear. "Be careful."

We are where Luke and Griffin are. We are where Luke and Griffin are.

The crappy apartment disappeared in a white mist.

The first thing I noticed after that was the sound of waves breaking on a beach. I also smelled the salty fishy odor of the ocean. I was still holding a hand, presumably Andro's, and the ground under our feet was gritty and unstable. "Andro are you there? Where are we?" I asked. "Can you see anything?" All I could see was mist.

"No", he said in a high squeaky voice. "Don't let go of my hand."

"Don't worry, I have no intention of letting you go. How do you feel?" I had a mild headache.

"I do have a headache," he said, "but I can handle it."

"Me, too." I stared in the direction of where my hand should be clutching his. Gradually, our hands came into focus, and then our arms. I focused on him as his shoulder, torso, neck and his lovely head appeared out of the mist.

He smiled shakily at me. "There you are."

"There you are," I echoed with a goofy grin.

The white mist cleared and we were on a strip of pristine white sand beach. The light was fading as the sun set behind us. Also behind us was a tropical forest complete with palm trees and hooting birds. The breeze off the ocean ruffled our hair. "Where are Luke and Griffin?" I asked, looking around.

Andro pointed at two tracks in the sand that led into the forest. "I'm guessing they went that way."

We remained standing together on the beach for a moment. Into my mic, I said, "Agent Baker, we're on some beach. Agent Baker? Do you copy?"

There was no answer.

"We must be out of range," he said.

"I guess that means we're on our own," I said. We could do this. We had to do this, or who knew when the quantum crimes would end? If they would end?

We slowly walked across the beach to the opening in the forest where the footprints in the sand ended. We followed a dirt path through the plants about hundred yards to a clearing. Carefully, we peeked out from the trees and spied a huge glass and concrete mansion on another beach, complete with a wall of windows looking out on a pool and beyond that the ocean. The setting sun illuminated the clouds over the water with orange and pink light.

"This must be some tiny uncharted island," he whispered.

"With a mansion on it?" I asked.

"Okay, a tiny charted island," he amended.

We crept toward the pool deck, using scattered palm trees for cover.

Luke, wearing only long, blue board-shorts, strolled out of the house onto the pool deck. "That was a close one."

Griffin, wearing red board-shorts and a t-shirt and clutching his head, lumbered out behind him. "I don't feel so good."

"So, make yourself feel better," Luke said.

Instead, Griffin collapsed on one of the chaise lounge chairs by the spa. "Don't know if I'm up to it," he grunted.

Luke sighed loudly. "Come on, fix yourself. Why do I have to do everything? I'm sick of fixing the webpage. As of now, you're delegated to fix it when it disappears. And the money from the last job is almost gone. We need another one." He paused. "No doubt I'll have to plan it."

"Okay, dude," Griffin said. "Geez, chill." He shifted in the chair and rubbed his forehead. "Why don't we just make money? You know, zap it into our wallets."

Luke's mouth fell open. "I knew I kept you around for a reason, G."

"We should attack now," I whispered, "before Griffin's back to one hundred percent."

"I agree," Andro said quietly. "What's the plan?"

"Let's try to put them to sleep," I said. We concentrated on q-lapsing and putting them to sleep. *Fall asleep*.

Griffin stopped clutching his head and started yawning.

Luke yawned and then looked around. "Something's going on. Griffin, pay attention."

You are very tired, Luke. You are very tired, Griffin. Fall asleep.

"Why am I so sleepy, dude?" Griffin shook his head and sat up on the chair.

"It's got to be Martin and Rivas again." Luke finally spied us on the edge of the patio. "There they are." He pointed. "How did you find us?"

Andro and I glanced at each other and stepped onto the pool deck together.

"The same way you've found us before," I said. "Do you want to come back with us quietly? Or is this going to get ugly?"

"Mad," Andro said under his breath. "Don't provoke them."

"You want ugly?" Luke flashed us a humorless grin. "We can give you ugly." He poked Griffin. "C'mon, Griff. Help me out here, dude."

Griffin lumbered up from his chair.

The edges of Luke started to get blurry as he peered first at the pool and then at us.

And then a river of water leapt out of the pool, heading straight toward us.

We concentrated and deflected it. My headache wasn't getting much worse.

The pool continued to empty, but now harmlessly to our left.

"That's it?" I asked. What was I so worried about? I touched my chest. Why didn't they try their heart attack trick?

"Maybe it would be better not to challenge them," Andro said to me.

Luke yelled in frustration and patio furniture started throwing itself in our direction.

Andro and I ducked for a minute before I gathered my wits enough to stop the furniture in mid-air and send it back to the young men. Soon Andro caught on and looked fuzzy around the edges as he threw furniture, too.

The first couple of chairs caught Luke and Griffin by surprise. They had to duck, but after that they just sent the chairs up over their heads.

Eventually all the furniture was out on the beach.

"Well, this could be going better," I said. My nerves were congealing into anger.

"I agree," Andro said. "The gloves come off." He stepped toward the young men, holding his hands out in front of himself. "Take that, punks." Streams of lightning erupted from his fingertips.

One hit slow-moving Griffin. "Ouch."

"Yeah! All right, Andro." I stepped next to him and joined in hurling bolts of electricity at Luke and Griffin.

"Ow," Luke said as he failed to weave away from one. Then, two chairs from the beach flew back to the pool deck, landing in front of them. Luke quickly picked one up and held it in front of him to absorb the electricity bolts. Griffin soon copied him.

We stepped closer and closer to them, getting in more and more hits−on the chairs, unfortunately. How frustrating.

Luke stared at our hands with beady eyes, getting fuzzy, but nothing seemed to happen.

"We can keep this up all day," I said. Unfortunately, it looked like Luke and Griffin could, too. We were pretty evenly matched.

"Not so good without your girlfriends to back you up, huh?" Andro said.

Luke straightened up and smiled genuinely. "Good idea." He grabbed Griffin's hand. "C'mon, G." They disappeared.

I sighed. "Here we go again." I grabbed Andro's hand and we q-lapsed to be where Luke and Griffin were.

The white mist quickly resolved itself to be the hallway of a very-familiar-looking apartment building. Namely, it looked just like the building hallway we just vacated–except this one had a ceiling.

Now my head was splitting, but quickly I spoke into my mic. "This is Madison. I think we're back in Boulder. Do you copy?"

The familiar, startling voice was back in my ear. "Madison? This is Agent Baker. We copy. Are you back in the apartment complex? Where were you?"

"Forget where we were," I said. "Now, I think we're outside the apartment of Luke's or Griffin's girlfriend."

"We already took the girls into custody," Agent Baker said.

Andro, listening in, frowned.

"You did?" I asked. "But, how?" The girlfriends must not be too proficient at q-lapsing after all.

"It's not important right now," she said. "We're around the corner. Surveillance shows you outside Courtney's apartment. Are Luke and Griffin near you?"

"We believe so," I said.

A yell exploded from inside the apartment in front of us, easily heard through the closed door. "Where is she? Where's Courtney?"

"That's an affirmative," Andro said into his mic.

The door crashed open.

"You two," yelled Luke, eyes blazing. "I might have known. What did you do to them?"

"Calm down, Luke," I said. "They've just been taken into custody. They're safe."

"Fuck that," Luke said. "We'll see how you like having people you love in danger." He got all blurry and disappeared.

My head hurt so badly, it was difficult to think. It took a moment for me to compute what he said. Danger?

In the living room, Griffin appeared to be stumbling around, tears running down his cheeks. "It hurts so much. Make it stop."

Then I got it. "Oh, my God," I said. "I think Luke just threatened my family."

"That's not good." Andro quickly took a step into the room. "We can make it stop hurting, Griffin." Andro spoke into his mic, "Griffin appears to be incapacitated. Move in, move in."

I heard "Affirmative," in my ear.

"I have to go after Luke," I said. "He's met Ryan. Ryan and his family could be in danger."

Andro shot me a worried look. "Be careful."

"Join me as soon as you can," I said.

"I'll be there as soon as Griffin's taken care of," he said.

Thundering footsteps were already approaching from down the hall.

I tried to q-lapse and follow Luke but it was hard to concentrate with the pounding in my temples. I had to get to Ryan and his family.

Reluctantly, I reached into my vest pocket for another dose of adrenaline and administered it. The pain receded a bit. This time, I heard a lawn mower when I was enveloped in mist. When it cleared, my worst fears were realized as I appeared on Ryan's front lawn next to Luke and Ryan.

I had a moment of disorientation as I realized it was still just midmorning.

Ryan's mouth hung open and he stood frozen behind the roaring lawnmower.

I said, "Luke's at Ryan's house," into my mic. "We need backup."

My ear bud said, "Affirmative." The liquor store was only about two blocks away so they might get here in time. I prayed to God they would.

Luke smiled broadly and then turned to look exaggeratedly at the lawnmower.

"Stop," I said. "Whatever you're thinking of doing, don't do it."

"Mr. Bacalli, I presume," Ryan finally eked out. "To what do I owe this pleasure?"

Luke just grunted and started to get blurry around the edges.

"Take cover, Ryan," I yelled, narrowing my eyes and concentrating on zapping Luke. But my head hurt.

Then the lawnmower got fuzzy and raised up off the ground and started moving slowly toward Ryan.

I immediately focused attention on the mower, willing it to stop. I spared a glance from the mower for a couple seconds, looking for Ryan. Had he gotten out of the way?

He'd backed up toward the house.

In the meantime, Luke had gotten control of the mower and it was moving through the air, whirling blade-first, toward Ryan. It was almost too surreal to be scary. Almost.

"Look out, Ryan." I stared at the mower, trying to q-lapse and make it disappear or at least drop to the ground. It got blurry.

Then a fuzzy Andro appeared in front of me, clutching his head. He collapsed on the grass.

"Andro!" I rushed over to him, passing right by Luke and shoving him hard.

Luke stumbled and the noise from the lawnmower stopped. There was a crash as it hit the ground. "Shit," Luke said.

I leaned over Andro and said, "Stay with me, Andro." I brushed my fingers lightly over his face. "We need an ambulance at Ryan's house ASAP," I said into my mic, voice shaking.

"Affirmative."

The roar of the lawnmower started up again.

"Save Ryan," Andro grunted.

I heard the front door open and then Sydney's voice said, "What's going on out here?"

A few feet from the front stoop, Ryan gulped. "Sydney. Emily. No."

Sydney stood in the open door with Emily nestled in her arms.

"No. Get inside, you guys," I yelled.

Ryan stepped in front of them as the roaring lawn mower flew at them, blade first. He seemed to be having a little trouble fully grasping the situation of a killer lawnmower floating through the air and just stood there, frozen.

It was almost close enough to slice him. "Oh, no." I was having trouble concentrating I was shaking so much. But I stared at the mower, walking towards it, willing it to stop. *Stop. Stop. Stop.*

It approached Ryan.

Ryan, hair blowing, eyes glued to the bizarre apparition, groped for something in the small of his back as he backed away.

"Ryan?" Sydney said from inside the house, staring at the mower.

Stop. Stop. Stop.

"Get inside, Sydney." Ryan tripped over the edge of the front stoop, and a gun thumped onto the grass near him.

Stop. Stop. Stop. Without thinking, I grabbed the gun, pointed at Luke and pulled the trigger.

There was a loud bang, my arm jerked and then the mower, blades still, fell to the ground. The sudden silence was deafening.

When I looked around, a white-faced Ryan was getting to his feet in front of the closed front door and Luke was lying on the grass oozing blood from his gut. He appeared to be unconscious. "I shot him," I said to Ryan. I couldn't believe it. I looked at the gun in my hand. How did that get there?

My ear bud said, "Who was shot?"

My head felt like it was being squeezed in a vice.

Ryan took the gun from my shaking hand and said into my mic "Luke. It was self-defense. He was attacking us with a lawnmower."

I stepped to Andro and leaned over him. "Andro, are you still with us?" Please, God.

Andro nodded slightly, eyes squinted shut. "Yeah," he whispered.

"Where are those stupid agents?" I said. "Where's that stupid ambulance?" My head was pounding. I considered lying down on the grass next to Andro.

In my ear, Agent Baker said, "We're almost there. I can see you."

Sure enough, a convoy of nondescript black SUVs approached from up the street.

I closed my eyes, trying to will the pain away. It didn't seem to be working.

I heard a bunch of car doors slam. When I looked toward the street, black clad agents were running toward us.

I needed to lie down, so I did.

Everything went dark.

Chapter Twenty-Six

I came to in the back of an ambulance sitting in Ryan's driveway. The white-haired male EMT standing over me said, "That's more like it, young lady. You feel much better, don't you?"

The vise was gone. I didn't know what they'd given me, but whatever it was, it worked. I nodded. "Where's Andro?"

The man pointed at Ryan and Andro standing outside, peering in at me. They looked great. Totally safe.

Behind them stood Agents Sawyer and Baker, and also Sydney.

"Andro, are you okay?" I said. "Is everyone okay?"

He smiled and reached into the rig for my hand. "*Si, mi amor.* And so are you."

Something was wrong with this picture. Where was Luke? "Wait. You guys need to take care of Luke. He was shot." By me. Ugh. I felt sick to my stomach. There was no sign of him. "Where is he?"

The EMT said, "Another unit already took him to the hospital. They got to him in time."

I breathed a sigh of relief. "Thank God." I didn't want to add 'killer' to my resume.

I looked at the EMT. "So can I get out of here?"

He nodded. "Yes. If you sign this form."

"Thank you for your help, sir." I scribbled on the form and then scrambled out of the vehicle.

Outside I couldn't resist giving Andro a quick hug. He smelled wonderful. I could have stayed there in his arms forever but Ryan cleared his throat.

I transferred my hug to Ryan. He smelled like sweat and grass. "I'm really glad you and Sydney and Emily didn't get chopped up by a lawnmower," I said.

"Me too," he said.

"Me, too," Sydney chimed in from the back of the group.

"Where's Emily?" I asked.

"She's safe. Inside." Sydney gestured toward the house. "With my mom."

"That lawnmower thing was pretty bizarre," Ryan added.

We separated and I examined him. "That was mighty lucky you happened to have your gun. Since when do you mow the lawn packing heat?"

Ryan put on his unflappable cop-mask as he shot a glance at the agents. "Ben called and gave me the heads up. I just figured if anything went wrong, I'd better be ready."

"Hurray for Ben," I said from the bottom of my heart.

"I heard that." Ben grinned as he appeared from behind Agents Baker and Sawyer. "Hey there, Quantum Cop. Looks like you got the bad guy after all."

Andro slipped his hand into mine and our fingers intertwined. I glanced from him to Ryan standing on the other side of me. "With a lot of help."

"All right, thanks all around," Agent Baker said. "Now we need to take your statements, if you're up to it."

After Ryan, Andro, and I finished with our FBI statements, we withdrew to Ryan and Sydney's kitchen.

Andro made a quick phone call and checked in with Yasmin. Yasmin and the girls were safe and sound. And Yasmin was thrilled to hear Armando's killers were behind bars.

Sydney got out her griddle. "Pancakes, anyone?"

My stomach rumbled. "I can't believe it's only lunchtime."

"Yeah, so much has happened," Andro said.

"Definitely pancakes, woman," Ryan said. "Bring 'em on. Get cracking."

Sydney smirked as she got out the supplies. "Since you just saved our lives, I'll let you get away with that comment."

The rest of us settled onto stools next to the counter.

Cathy appeared in the kitchen doorway and slammed her

suitcase down. "That's it. She put us all in danger. Either she goes," she pointed her bony finger at me, "or I go."

Technically, wasn't I still banned from the house? So, I was gone, wasn't I?

"Gosh, Cathy," Ryan said. "I'm sorry to hear that. We've really appreciated your help. But if you've gotta' go, we understand."

Sydney put down the spatula. "Mom, don't be like that. We love you. We want you to say."

I noticed Ryan didn't chime in that time.

I was going to stay out of it and apparently Andro concurred.

"I mean it. Her or me," Cathy said, scowling and pointing at me.

"You can't blame Madison for something a criminal did," Ryan said.

Sydney glanced at Ryan and then looked sadly at her mom. "This is not what I want, but if you insist, would you like a ride to the airport?"

Cathy's eyebrows shot up. "No." She fumbled in her purse and pulled her cell phone out. "I can get my own ride." She stormed out of the kitchen and out the front door, lugging her rollerboard and trying to dial her phone at the same time.

As she slammed the front door, I said, "I'm sorry if I caused trouble between you and your mom, Sydney."

Sydney shrugged as she flipped a batch of golden pancakes. "Don't worry. It's not your fault. Mom gets upset easily but she gets over it easily, too. I'll let her cool off a bit and give her a call."

Ryan started. "But you won't invite her back right away, will you?"

Sydney gave him an evil grin before she softened. "No."

"So, am I officially allowed to sleep here again?" I asked.

Sydney looked at Ryan. "What's she talking about?"

"I'm sure this morning's events will have a positive impact on my boss," Ryan said.

"I don't know why you wouldn't think you're welcome here," Sydney said. "But you are. You're welcome here any time. I, at least, don't go back on my word."

That was a relief.

We all stuffed ourselves with pancakes, fruit and coffee, and rehashed the events of the morning.

At about two o'clock I received a call from Professor Chen. He said, "I guess I was wrong about you, Professor Martin. A Special Agent from the FBI called and said you were a big help in a bust this morning. Your suspension is over. You're reinstated to teach."

"Yes!" My fist shot into the air.

"Will you be ready to teach your class tomorrow morning?" Chen asked.

"Of course, sir," I said. "Thank you, sir."

"And Madison, I apologize," he said softly.

"I appreciate you saying that, sir. What about Alyssa? Can I have her back as my grad student?"

He sighed. "If you think you can handle her."

"Yes," I said as we hung up.

"Guess what?" I said to Andro, Ryan, and Sydney.

All three said variations of you're reinstated. At the same time.

"Yes," I said. "I have to go into the office now and get ready."

Ryan snickered. "Of course you do."

Andro said, "Really? I thought we could spend the rest of the day together."

I grinned goofily. "What about meeting for dinner? And dessert?" I couldn't wait to see what was for dessert...

"I guess that will have to do," he said with a smile.

At my office there was a voice mail from Agent Baker. "Professor Martin, or maybe I should say Quantum Cop?" She chuckled. "Please call me back and arrange a time when you can teach me and other agents how to collapse the wavefunction. We need to shut down these quantum crimes once and for all."

I called her back.

She answered on the first ring. "Agent Baker, here."

"Any time on Tuesdays and Thursdays would work for me to teach you guys," I said. "Maybe we could do it here at the university? We have some equipment here that might help."

"Fine," she said shortly.

"Is something wrong?" I asked. She should be more upbeat having caught the presumed quantum crime masterminds. Personally, I was pretty sure they were the quantum masterminds. Proving it might be another story.

She sighed. “I just hope we can learn how to q-lapse. Frankly, it seems a little like magic.”

“It may seem like magic,” I said, “but it is not magic. It’s physics.”

“What was it that author said? A sufficiently advanced technology is indistinguishable from magic?”

“Arthur C. Clarke. I’m impressed you know about him.”

“I know a lot,” she said with steel in her voice.

I was suddenly reminded she carried a gun. “Yep. Yes. I’m sure you do. You know loads.” Quit babbling, Mad.

“Changing the subject, how’s Griffin?” I asked.

“Whatever was wrong with him when we picked him up, the docs took care of it. We’re keeping him sedated so he can’t escape.”

That didn’t sound fair. Did they have any hard evidence against him? But considering everything that had happened, I couldn’t blame them.

“Okay,” she said. “You don’t sound happy, Madison. You should. This was a win today.”

Today did not feel like a win. I felt uneasy for some reason. “I hope you’re right that the worst is over. And to make sure the worst doesn’t start up again, I’ll make sure the control reality webpage stays down.”

“Good idea,” she said. “I’ll keep in touch, Madison.” We hung up.

I immediately got on the internet. The webpage was still gone when I checked.

I kept my eye on the clock as I prepared for Monday’s class so I wouldn’t be late for my dinner with Andro. Promptly at five-forty-five, I walked over to The Hill to meet him at The Sink.

He was standing outside, smiling, as I walked up. “Wow, you’re on time. I thought I’d have to call and remind you when you didn’t show up.”

“Impossible. How could I forget you?” I smiled back at him. “You’re practically a superhero.”

He chuckled. “Well if I am, you are too, Quantum Cop.”

I chuckled as we went inside. The restaurant was filled with students drinking beer and eating pizza and burgers. Sunday night, go figure. The Sink’s ceiling was low, making it seem cozy, and the walls and sturdy wooden tables were covered with graffiti.

"Interesting décor," I said.

"Oh, you haven't been here before? I keep forgetting you've only been in town a couple months," he said. "It seems like we've known each other forever."

Yep. It was definitely cozy in here, and it wasn't just the décor.

We both ordered Famous Sink Burgers and, considering our killer-headaches this morning, passed on the beers. Our consensus on the Luke situation was to wait and see. And be careful.

As was typical when I ate with him, the meal flew by and soon it was time to go.

When we stepped back out onto the sidewalk into the night air, he rubbed his hands together. "So, where to? Maybe we should go back to Boulder Bed and Breakfast?"

"I've got a better idea." I grinned. "Why don't you just come home with me?"

He smiled. "Intriguing idea. But are you sure Ryan and Sydney won't mind?"

"Did I tell you I have my own private entrance now?"

"No. Well, then, by all means," he said. "Let's go."

Finally my garage apartment would live up to its potential.

Monday morning after another great night, Andro and I procured coffee and cinnamon rolls from Boulder Brews. Ryan and Sydney were still eating tofu when we left the house. Emily was gurgling adorably. None of them seemed surprised to see him.

As the two of us stood on the corner of Baseline Road waiting for the light to change, I said, "I'm excited to be going back to class. I'm a physics professor."

Andro chuckled. "You're so cute. Technically, you've been a physics professor this whole time."

"I know, but it was pretty iffy there for a while." I took a bite of cinnamon roll. It was still warm. Mmm.

"This is where it all began, isn't it?" He pointed at the crosswalk.

The sun was exceptionally bright, and I was glad I'd worn

sunglasses. "What? Oh, yeah." I glanced at his handsome face. He looked happy, his blue eyes sparkling and his cheeks slightly flushed.

I was sure I looked the same: happy. "Despite everything's that's happened, I'm glad it happened. If it hadn't we might not have gotten together."

He chuckled. "You did make quite a first impression with your crazy story."

"Crazy, but true," I interrupted.

"Okay." He nodded. "But, I think we would have met and gotten together in any case."

"Maybe we were fated to meet." I grinned goofily and took a sip of coffee.

"No doubt, *mi amor*," Andro said gently.

"What exactly does *mi amor* mean, anyway?" The crosswalk sign lit up. I carefully looked both ways and started to step in the street. "My something?"

Andro said, "My love."

I froze on the sidewalk. Did he just say what I think he said?

Chapter Twenty-Seven

Andro and I may have spent a few too many minutes publicly kissing there on the corner. But some occasions call for public displays of affection, don't they? I was a few minutes late for my class. As I entered the classroom, something felt off. I walked up to the front table and put my bag down.

"Hey, Teach," Luke said, grinning his cocky grin from a seat in the front row.

Oh. My. God. I couldn't process what I was seeing and hearing.

"Professor Martin, are you all right?" Pankaj asked.

I gulped. "Hey, Luke. You're looking surprisingly well." He didn't even look injured. Why wasn't he in the hospital? Why wasn't he in custody? Would he take offense if I took out my cell phone and called the cops on him? Or screamed?

Pankaj smoothed his already-smooth dress shirt and said, "Are you planning on starting class any time soon? It is past time."

Luke smirked.

Then the room sort-of melted. The ceiling, walls and floors became fluid and slow-moving waves undulated up and down. The table, desks and chairs flickered, alternating between transparency and solidity. The students all jumped up from their seats as their desks winked in and out and the floor roiled.

I struggled to keep my balance in the front of the room. It was like being on a ship in the middle of a hurricane.

"What is happening?" Pankaj asked, panic in his eyes.

I glanced at Luke and he had his eyes closed, concentrating

on wreaking havoc, apparently.

A chorus of *What the fuck?*'s had erupted from my less-polite students.

I couldn't panic. My students were depending on me. "Students, please exit the room if you can," I said. Would Luke hurt his fellow students? I guess it was time to admit I didn't know what the hell he was capable of.

The students tried to make their ways through the room to the door.

I turned my attention to Luke. "Whatever you think you're doing, stop it," I said in my sternest teacher voice. "This doesn't solve anything."

"Maybe it will convince people to leave me alone," he said.

I concentrated on q-lapsing to put the room back together. "Or, maybe it'll make us come after you harder than ever."

He didn't answer.

In my peripheral vision I saw the students, minus Luke, shuffling or crawling out of the room, holding their arms in front of them to keep from walking into anything.

The room slowly took on a more solid form. I glanced around to see Jose kneeling in the corner, praying, tears streaming down his face.

Luke noticed him right after I did and flicked his hand toward him.

Jose began floating up toward the again-solid ceiling.

"Stop it, Luke," I said.

"*El Diablo*," Jose screamed as he flailed his arms and legs around trying to make contact with something. He seemed terrified.

I ran over to him, my feet leaving the ground as I reached the corner. Luke must have modified gravity.

I grabbed Jose and q-lapsed to restore gravity to normal. "It's okay, Jose. Don't worry."

He floated back down to the floor.

When I turned around, Luke was gone. Shit.

I put my arm around the shaking Jose and led him out of our classroom. In the hall the walls, floors, and ceiling were fuzzy and fluid, moving like ocean waves. Shit, shit, shit.

I looked around for the fire alarm, saw a blurry red thing on the wall, concentrated to solidify it and pulled. The alarm rang for a few moments and then stopped. I concentrated on q-lapsing and bringing it back. It began ringing again.

People streamed out of classrooms, muttering to one another.

I quickly led Jose and the others toward an exit. I had to concentrate on solidifying the floor in front of us as we took each step, but we finally made it out the east side of the building.

Outside, people were milling around white-faced and slack-jawed because everything was blurry out there, too. Unfortunately, some people had lost contact with the ground, yelping and grabbing at other people, trees, signs and whatever else they could reach.

I couldn't see Luke anywhere. But he had to be here somewhere to cause this chaos.

I stabilized where I was standing by q-lapsing.

Then I yelled "Andro!" at the top of my lungs. He must have come out from his office. "Andro, please come here."

He appeared at my side out of white mist. "What the hell is going on?" He glanced around. "You're not doing this, are you?"

"No. It's Luke. We have to stop him. He's screwing with reality."

"Luke? I thought he was hurt." Andro said.

I grimaced. "Apparently not."

"Where is he?" he asked.

Before I could answer, Nancy half-jumped, half-walked to our little island of normalcy. "What's going on? Did some experiment go wrong?"

Andro and I looked at each other. That was as good an explanation as any.

"Yes," I said. "We need to evacuate the area. Do you know who to contact?"

She nodded. "But I forgot my phone inside."

So did I, but I q-lapsed my phone into my hand and handed it to her. "Here. Professor Rivas and I will try to fix things." She started calling someone.

"We have to find Luke," I said to Andro. "He's got to be around here somewhere."

"I don't understand how he's become so powerful," Andro said.

"Me neither," I said.

More people exited the fuzzy buildings and collected on the fuzzy street. They were not happy people. They were confused, verging on panicking, people

Nancy held out my phone. "It's the FBI, for you."

"Madison, what the hell is going on over there?" Agent Baker asked. "The local cops got some bizarre reports and they're freaking out. Ben called us and said the world was going crazy."

Briefly, I considered pleading ignorance, but that wouldn't get us anywhere. "It's Luke. He's recovered from his injury and he's messing up reality somehow."

"How?" she asked. "Forget that. Can you fix it?"

"I don't know," I said over the screams and whimpers of panicking, verging on terrified, students.

Agent Baker interrupted me. "Just a minute."

I gazed across campus at insubstantial fuzzy buildings, floating people, bicycles and cars.

Turning to Andro, I grabbed his hand. We had to fix it.

He squeezed my hand and forced a smile for me.

Agent Baker came back to the phone. "It's spreading. It's heading straight for Denver. We're getting reports from law enforcement. Everything's going crazy. Do something." Her voice got kind of shrill there at the end.

I saw Ryan hop-gliding across the street from his office.

"Fine. We'll fix it," I said to Agent Baker and hung up. If we didn't, who would?

I handed Nancy back the phone.

As Ryan approached our gravity-normal location, his steps settled down. "Whew. That must be what it's like to walk on the moon. Am I glad to see you two." He pushed his glasses up his nose. "Luke?"

Andro and I nodded. My brain was racing. Why was our little patch of land normal when I wasn't concentrating on it anymore?

"I guess his injuries weren't as severe as we thought," Andro said.

"How are we going to stop him?" Ryan asked.

"Just a minute." I turned to Andro. "How hard are you concentrating on keeping this area sane?"

He shrugged. "I'm not really concentrating on it."

After my initial efforts, neither was I. "So, the two of us working together don't have any trouble counteracting whatever it is Luke's doing."

"It makes sense," Andro said. "Normalcy is much more probable. Let's try to increase the area of sanity."

I was just about to suggest that. "Okay," I said. "Which way?"

Nancy stopped talking on the phone and piped up, "Save the physics building. There might be dangerous stuff in there which could become unstable."

Good point.

"You two," I pointed at Ryan and Nancy, "concentrate on normalcy. I want you to stay put and think everything is normal. You can q-lapse." According to my hypothesis, everyone had the potential to q-lapse. And adrenaline was definitely flowing freely around here.

"Okay," Ryan said. "I trust you, Mad."

Nancy said, "I'll give it a try."

"Andro, let's get closer to the physics building. That's the last place I saw Luke."

He nodded. "Let's do it."

Still holding hands, we took a step toward the physics building, concentrating on q-lapsing to bring things back to normal. As we took a first and then a second step it seemed to work. The sidewalk quit looking hazy, and dirt and debris settled onto the ground. When we got closer to the blurry bike rack, where two female students were hanging on for dear life, we ran into a snag.

"Help us," one yelled.

"What's happening?" the other yelled.

"Help." The first one reached out to grab us. "Save us."

"We are," I said. "We're trying to fix things." We tried to keep concentrating on q-lapsing, but it didn't work. The sidewalk started blurring out again. We took a step away and renewed our concentrating. It didn't work.

"What's going on?" Andro asked.

"I don't know." I seemed to be saying that a lot lately. "It's like these students are canceling out our efforts or something."

"I don't see how," he said. "They're not concentrating. They don't know how to q-lapse. They're just panicking."

"They are consciousnesses," I said. "Maybe their conscious minds have accepted this bizarre new reality on some level. But, whatever they're doing, let's get away from them. It can only help."

I called out to the young women, "Sorry. Hold on. We're trying to fix this."

"But..." They sputtered.

We raced away from them, trying to q-lapse to solidify the ground in front of us. It started working again, until we approached another group of panicking students.

Andro muttered, "Damn," under his breath.

"I'm sensing a pattern." I examined our path, where normalcy was holding. "Let's go back to the others and regroup."

At our original location several police officers had converged around Ryan, and Nancy was arguing with someone on the phone.

"What happened?" Ryan asked.

"I don't know." I grimaced. There it was again. "It worked part of the time, but not when we were near other people."

Andro said, "It was like the other people were working against us."

Ryan nodded. "So, if we could get them out of the equation, you could do it?"

"What are you thinking?" I asked. "That sleeping gas?"

One of the police officers snorted and said something like *not legal* under his breath.

Ryan glanced at him before he said, "We're outside. It would disperse too quickly to be effective. Besides we don't have enough." He paused. "Could you think them asleep?"

I slowly shook my head. "I don't see how. We'd have to overcome their conscious minds. If we could do that we probably wouldn't be having so much trouble putting things back to normal."

Nancy grunted on hung up the phone. "Well, no one's coming. Everyone said they had their own problems to deal with. We're on our own."

Everyone? "Who did you contact?" I asked.

"I called Boulder PD," she said. "I called the Colorado National Guard and Homeland Security. I even called the on-campus R.O.T.C. office." Her eyes widened as she noticed the crowd of officers around us. "No one answered at the campus police–now I see why."

"All those people are having quantum problems?" I asked. That was not good. Where the hell was Luke now?

"On the bright side," Andro said, "the phones still work."

What would have to happen for the cell phone system to go down? I shuddered.

"So, what's the plan?" Nancy asked.

I resisted the urge to say *I don't know*. "Uh, we have to convince all these people that there's nothing wrong."

"You convinced me," Nancy said.

I was really starting to like her. "Suggestions on how to do that, anyone?"

"This may sound crazy," Roberto said. "I'm no scientist but what about talking to them?"

Doh. Hadn't we already tried that? Actually, I guess we didn't. I almost slapped my forehead. "Good idea. Who's in? We go up to people and explain to them that everything's okay."

Ryan nodded. "My guys are all in, right?" He glanced at the other police officers as they all nodded.

"I'm totally in," said Nancy.

"Okay. Let's give it a try," I said. "As you walk around, concentrate on thinking everything is normal, and when you approach people tell them everything is fine."

"Works for me," Andro said.

Ryan directed his men to various groups of people clutching fuzzy trees and the like.

Andro and I went back to the two girls at the bike rack.

"Hi there, young ladies," I said, well out of grabbing range.

"What's happening?" one asked.

"How come you're okay?" the other asked.

"We're fine, because everything is fine," Andro said. "Your troubles are all in your mind."

I nodded. "Your conscious minds have succumbed to unusual input. You need to concentrate on normalcy."

"Huh?"

"What the hell are you talking about?"

"It's not in my mind that I'm floating."

"I'm here to tell you it is all in your mind," I said.

"She's right," Andro said. "Listen to us and you'll be all right."

They just glared at us, still clutching the bike rack.

Well, crap. It wasn't working. What was next? Hypnosis?

Nancy sidled up to me. "How's it going over here?"

Andro gestured at the young women. Clearly, it wasn't going great over here.

"Brittani? Kimberli?" Nancy bent over so she could look at the young women right side up.

"Ms. Hernandez?" one of them answered. "What's happening?"

Andro tapped me on the shoulder and pointed behind us. The other groups were having much more luck than we were. People were standing on solid ground and the street looked ordinary, not fuzzy at all.

"I don't get it," I whispered to him.

He shrugged.

"Some physics experiment went wrong," Nancy was saying. "But they turned it off so things should go back to normal. Most stuff is better already. See?" She pointed at the groups of people standing on the ground outside the fuzzy physics building.

One of the girl's bodies started going down. "Oh. I do feel better."

The other managed to get her feet back under her. "Figures. Frakking crazy scientists."

Nancy looked at me and grinned. "Yep."

The girls now stood on the ground, on their own two feet, smoothing out their t-shirts. The bike rack looked solid again, too.

Two other girls ran over to us. One said, "You guys, was that totally freaky or what?"

"Totally."

They all nodded with exaggerated motions.

"We should post it."

They all pulled out their phones.

"Do you think we have to go to class this afternoon?"

"We better not."

"Yeah, I need time to recover."

"I think things are under control here," Nancy said.

"Thanks, Nancy," I said.

The physics building itself was also starting to look less hazy. I grabbed Andro's hand. "We still have to fix the building. C'mon. Concentrate." *Everything is normal. The physics building is normal.*

Slowly the building finished solidifying, and my head only hurt a little. Hurray, for high probabilities.

"All right," I said. "Good job, Andro."

I spied Ryan across the street in front of the campus police office–all of which looked normal. I gestured for him to come join us.

Andro willed his phone into his hand. "I have to call Yasmin."

Ryan walked up. "I'm glad that's settled."

Hanging up, Andro said, "At least Yasmin and the girls are okay. But remember what Agent Baker said? The disturbance's spreading. Just because it's okay here doesn't mean it's okay everywhere. In fact, it's probably not. We don't know how far the disturbance has gotten. We should do something–we may be the only ones who can."

"You're right. We have to find Luke. But we need some kind of plan." I was still pondering why Andro and I were so unsuccessful at changing reality back while the campus police officers and Nancy were so much more successful.

Ryan said, "I need to call Sydney and check on her and Emily." Andro handed him his phone.

While Ryan was talking on the phone, I asked Roberto "What did you tell people to convince them things should go back to normal?"

"Ryan said to say it was a kooky science experiment that was over now," Roberto said.

"I'm sensing a pattern," I said to Andro.

"How do we stop this?" he asked.

"Clearly, we have to tell everyone about the ending of the kooky science experiment," I said.

"How are we going to do that?" Ryan asked, hanging up. "My girls are okay. Now."

I didn't like the sound of that now. Little Emily must have been terrified. "I don't know how to tell everyone." I said.

"Calm down, Mad," Andro said, putting an arm around me.

"Agent Baker probably knows how."

"Agent Baker, right." I grabbed the phone and called her.

She answered before the first ring-tone ended. "Madison, what do you have? I hope something. It's fucking freaky around here at the Denver Field Office. Everything's fuzzy. I feel really light and stuff keeps floating up and hitting the ceiling."

I was still processing the staid middle-aged agent saying fucking freaky. "At least you have a ceiling."

"What?" she shrieked.

"Never mind. We need a way to tell everyone a scientific experiment had unexpected side effects but they're over now."

"What experiment?" she asked.

"There wasn't really an experiment," I said. "But people can't seem to understand the whole conscious-mind-collapsing-the-wavefunction thing. You can't and you know all about it."

"What do you mean, I can't?" she asked.

"You could use your mind right now to collapse the wavefunction and make everything normal," I said. "But you're not."

"Oh. Wait a minute," she said quietly and paused. "You're right. That worked. Okay. We need to get the message out to everyone. No problem. We've got reverse-911 and The Emergency Broadcast Network. I'll get right on it."

I sighed in relief. "Good. Thanks."

"No, thank you, Madison." She paused again. "But if we take care of this, you know what you have to take care of."

I sighed. "Yeah. Luke." Where was he?

Chapter Twenty-Eight

I convinced Andro we needed to go over to Boulder Brews and get some coffee, preferably with whipped cream and chocolate sprinkles, before dueling Luke for control of the planet. He bought the refreshments. He totally knew how to cheer me up.

I took a big sip of caffeinated goodness. "Well, that was an interesting morning." Boulder Brews looked the same as ever.

"I'll say." He looked at me over the top of his enorme cup. His eyes approached twinkle-dom. "You were awesome."

"Thanks. You were awesome, too."

He slapped his hand down on the tiny tabletop. "It's official. We were both awesome."

I smiled.

"What was with modifying gravity?" he asked. "Why'd Luke do that?"

"I don't know. But, it could've been much worse. I'm glad he didn't try modifying the other fundamental forces."

"I agree." He nodded. "If he modified the Electromagnetic Force, atoms would fly apart. That might make it hard to be alive."

"Or worse, if he reduced the Strong Force, neutrons and protons would fly apart," I said. "That would make things dicey."

"Are you saying he went easy on us?" he asked.

"No. I'm not saying that. He's not going easy on anyone or anything." I couldn't believe I'd actually felt kind of bad about shooting him. I gulped the rest of my drink and stood up. "Are you ready then?" My smallish headache had receded.

Andro put down his cup and stood up. "I guess so. To the

island mansion?"

I nodded. We were on the same page. Luke had probably returned to his lair. "With a brief stop at the FBI Field Office for supplies." We popped into the field office where things seemed to be back to normal. After the day they'd had, they didn't even seem surprised to see us.

Outfitted in our FBI vests and flak jackets, pockets laden with adrenaline, we held hands and concentrated on q-lapsing.

A little later found us in the dark creeping up on a beachfront glass and concrete mansion. There was no sign of anyone. The house was totally dark. We crept closer, finally stepping onto the pool deck.

"What the heck time zone are we in, anyway?" Andro whispered.

"I don't know. It's got to be on the opposite side of the world from Colorado."

We stole toward the house. Luckily, the moon was bright enough that we could avoid stepping into the pool or spa by accident. We got to the wall of sliding glass doors and found they were all locked.

"Not very hospitable of them," he said, reaching for my hand. We quantum tunneled through the glass door. Inside, we froze.

I cocked my head. "Do you hear anything?"

"Not a peep," he said. "I don't think he's here."

"We won't know until we check. Should we split up? It'll go faster."

"No," he whispered. "I think we should stick together."

I got a warm fuzzy feeling and it had nothing to do with q-lapsing.

Later, after we'd searched the whole house, finding nothing, I smacked my forehead with my palm. "Why'd we just assume he was here? We should have tried focusing on Luke himself."

"Hindsight's twenty-twenty," he said.

I looked at him in the moonlight. "I'm sorry I got you involved in all this. I'd never forgive myself if anything happened to you. You know that, right?"

"Yes. And I'd never forgive myself if anything happened to you." He held out his arms and we embraced.

I smelled his Andro-smell as my cheek warmed. I tipped my

head back and lifted my chin.
He leaned his head down and pressing his lips to mine. My heart did somersaults worthy of a gymnast on the moon.
"Mmm," I said, as we separated. "Now, I'm really ready for action."
A bark of laughter escaped from him. "I'm beginning to think you're always ready for action, Madison."
I flushed. "I meant I was ready to go after Luke."
"I know what you meant, *mi amor*," he said, his voice low, his eyes liquid in the moonlight.
Wow. A spark arced off my hand and hit the floor. "So anyway, are you ready?"
He lifted his hand, pointed at a lamp and a bolt of energy shattered it. "Looks like it."
We held hands and concentrated on being where Luke was. *We are where Luke is. We are where Luke is.*
I don't know how it happened, but after a moments I couldn't feel Andro's hand anymore. "Andro!" I yelled.
There was no answer.
"Andro, answer me." It dawned on me that I couldn't feel my own hand anymore. Nor could I feel my other hand, or my arms or legs or torso or head, or anything. I was in that damned misty limbo again. Oh no. "Andro, where are you?" He didn't answer. Where was he? "Shit."
And then I heard a chuckle, followed by "Tsk, tsk. Language, Teach."
I recognized that voice. My blood chilled–or it would have if I'd had any. "Luke? Is that you?" I hoped Andro was okay because he was going to have to wait until I'd dealt with Luke.
"Bingo, Teach. I knew you weren't as dumb as you looked."
I could just imagine Luke's stupid, cocky grin. "That's rather rude." From where my hand should have been, I focused on q-lapsing and sending a beam of energy his way. Then, I heard a sizzle and a muffled *shit*. He wasn't going to get away this time.
"How'd you do that?" he asked.
Instead of answering I concentrated on sending many more energy bolts his way. Unfortunately, this resulted in me starting to get a headache. I didn't have time to wonder how I could have a headache without a head. I sent off some more energy bolts

instead.

I heard several sizzles, yelps and then silence. This either meant Luke had figured out how to neutralize the energy, or, my ears had stopped working. I did smell the sharp tang of ozone. At least some part of me still worked.

"Luke?" I asked and heard myself. Good, I could still hear.

"Madison?" he asked. I could hear the sarcasm in his voice.

"What are you doing here?" I asked. "And why don't you attack me or something?" He must be disabled somehow.

"Maybe you are as stupid as you look."

I zapped him again, but the yelps were fewer and the ozone smell increased. Wait. Why was I smelling ozone?

"Quit that," he yelled as I sent more energy bolts his way.

Unfortunately, my latest energy bolts seemed to just dissipate. Oh no. Could he be decreasing the Electromagnetic Force? Was that the source of the ozone smell? If so, I could expect my atoms to fly apart any second. Shit. We were too evenly matched.

To avoid being disassembled, I tried to distract him. "What's the matter, Luke? Not feeling so well? Can't get out of here? I could take you to a hospital, if you give yourself up."

Could I? Could I even get out of here? Shit. My headache was getting worse.

And I couldn't even try to find Andro until I'd neutralized Luke. I hoped Andro could hold out wherever he was.

Then I felt sort of floaty. A floaty feeling couldn't be good, right?

I had a strong sense of déjà vu.

"What are you doing, Luke? Stop it." If I'd had a body and there was a ground here, I'd be floating up into the air. Was he messing with gravity again?

"I don't have to stop doing anything–and no one can stop me," he said. "Certainly not you. Not even if you had your cousin's gun. Thanks for shooting me, by the way. I learned a lot."

Wow, he was annoying. I tuned out my headache and his bragging. The déjà vu was important. When had I felt it before?

I did a mental forehead smack. It had been the first day of class this semester–when there were two of me.

I concentrated with every fiber of my being to will a second Madison into being. *Another Madison is here.* Was the white mist in front of me getting more solid?

"I'm here," my voice whispered in my ear.

"Good," I whispered back.

"Did you say something?" Luke asked.

I had the sensation of someone putting a hand on my arm. Yeah, arm!

"Nope," other-Madison said loudly.

I pulled my arm toward where my body should be until I felt other-Madison's hand and then held onto it.

"We have to hit him with everything we've got," I whispered to her.

I nodded in agreement.

"Strong Force?" I whispered back to the first Madison.

It was odd. I felt exactly the same as ever and yet I knew I was the second Madison.

"You are talking over there. To who?" Luke said. "And I think I can see something."

The mist was definitely parting. I was starting to see the fuzzy first-Madison–which meant Luke would too. And I didn't want to give him any ideas.

I turned to first-Madison. "Now?"

She nodded and took a step forward, holding out her hands in front of her as the fog cleared.

I did the same. We both knew the plan because I'd/we'd been thinking about it right before we split.

Luke stood there for a moment with his mouth hanging open as he looked from me to other-Madison and back again. "What the fuck?"

But me and other-Madison were already q-lapsing to attack Luke. We concentrated on decreasing the Strong Force coupling in him, straining against more probable scenarios. *The Strong Force is weak. The Strong Force is weak.* My head throbbed.

Luke got a very strange look on his face for a second. And then he disintegrated into a swirl of invisible quarks, gluons and electrons.

"Well, that's done," other-Madison said.

"Now all we have to do is find Andro–"

"And get out of here," other-Madison finished my sentence.

"Andro," we both shouted. We tried focusing on where Andro was–but it didn't work. Oh, God. Did that mean he wasn't anywhere?

"Andro," we shouted again.

I felt a little tickle in my brain, which led to a tingle in my lips. Then, I felt my face, neck and chest flush.

First-Madison and I looked at each other, red-faced, and didn't have to say we were onto something. It was like we could read each other's minds. This tingling must have something to do with Andro.

"Andro!"

A patch of fog appeared in front of us.

The misty area slowly increased in size until it was about six feet tall. Gradually it became more opaque and it took on the shape of a person.

I was getting a very good feeling as the tingles moved to points south.

The mist coalesced until Andro stood in front of us, looking very confused.

"Uh," he said, pointing from one to the other of us. "Uh."

First-Madison looked at me and I looked at her. We nodded and q-lapsed to merge back together–all part of the plan.

The splitting and merging thing had definitely felt weird. I could remember both points of view. But that wasn't important now.

I threw myself into Andro's arms before he could say *uh* again. "Thank God, you're all right."

"Thank God, you're all right, Madison." He leaned down.

I was caught in his blue eyes and couldn't escape.

He pressed his lips against mine and the laws of physics were suspended, spacetime turned itself inside out. Wow. I'd never had a kiss like that before.

We separated.

"There were two of you just now?" His cheeks were flushed.

"Yep," I answered, everything flushed.

"Did the other one have to go?" he asked plaintively.

I snorted with laughter. When I could breathe again, I said, "I can't believe I ever asked you if you were sure you were a guy."

"Uh," Andro glanced around at our extremely nondescript white misty surroundings. "Where are we? And what about Luke?"

"You're just asking these things now?" I grinned. "Minor details, huh?"

"Yeah, well, I was a little distracted there for a moment–being a guy and all."

"That's been well established." I leaned into him and he put his arm around me.

"I think I destroyed Luke," I said. "Literally. His atoms flew apart."

"That sounds bizarre," he said.

"As for where we are," I said, "I don't know. It's some kind of quantum limbo. I was in it, or something like it, before." I moved to face him. "Are you saying you weren't just in the same kind of place?'"

He rubbed his slightly stubbly chin. "I'm not really sure where I was. I may not have been anywhere." He looked down at me. "I think you might have just saved me from nowhere. Thank you."

"You're welcome." My headache started to demand attention, but I pushed it back. "How do you feel?"

"Not so good, to be honest," he said. "My head is aching."

"Mine, too. Let's try to get out of here. Let's focus on q-lapsing to be back in my office."

We are in my office. We concentrated, and just as I was beginning to give up hope, my office came into focus. I'd never been so glad to see a battered desk, an ancient couch, and all the rest.

We collapsed on the couch.

"Shouldn't we call someone to tell them you saved the world?" Andro asked.

"I'll call in a minute," I asked. "Are we sure the world's okay?"

He glanced out the window. "Looks okay to me. Good job." Then he looked at me. "So did Luke explain how he did all that stuff like change gravity?"

"It didn't come up, no pun intended." And it probably should have.

"Oh." He leaned back. "My head hurts."

"Mine, too. Let me see if I have any aspirin or anything." I stood and rooted around in my desk.

"Can't you just will some aspirin into our hands, or make our headaches go away?

"I'm tired of q-lapsing. I'm just plain tired. Saving the world really takes it out of you."

"Aw," he said with a small smile. "I was hoping we could get that other Madison back."

I smiled too. I found some aspirin in the drawer and some water from the mini-fridge and hooked us both up.

Back on the couch, I relaxed. "Now, two Andros, that would be interesting."

"You couldn't handle two Andros," he said, leaning close and planting a kiss on me.

"Mmm," I purred. "I don't know. I think we'd need a lot of experimental data to prove that hypothesis."

"I concur," he said, and started experimenting.

After a minute I had to come up for air. "Wow. Okay. Stop," I said. "I should call Agent Baker."

"I should call Yasmin and check on her, too," he said.

I dialed Agent Baker.

"Madison?" she asked. "Where are you?"

"I'm in my office in the physics building," I said. "Where are you?"

"We're at the university in the physics department office," she said. "Come down. Did you get him?"

"We got him," I said. "See you in a bit." We hung up.

Andro was still talking to Yasmin. "Bye, Yas." He hung up. "Yasmin and the girls are fine. Now, where were we?" He leaned my way.

"I like the way you think," I said. "But Agent Baker and some others are downstairs in the physics office. I told them we'd come down."

He looked disappointed. "Do we have to?"

"Yes," I said. "It will just take a minute."

Down in the physics office there was a large crowd. When I

walked in the door, Agent Baker said, "She got him."

Everyone started cheering.

"Yeah!"

"All right!"

"Hurray!" I couldn't tell who was saying what.

Ben saluted me. "Hey, Madison."

Agent Baker asked, "What happened?"

"I basically dissolved him."

"She dissolved him," she yelled to her cohorts.

"Yeah!" the crowd said.

They started chanting, "Quan-tum Cop! Quan-tum Cop!"

I let it wash over me for a minute. It was over. We were safe.

"Quan-tum Cop! Quan-tum Cop!" It felt good.

I spied Ryan and some of the other university officers in the crowd. Keeping hold of Andro's hand, I elbowed my way over to Ryan.

"Madison, are you okay?" he asked. "Andro?"

"Yeah, Ryan," I said. "I'm fine. We're fine."

"Quan-tum Cop! Quan-tum Cop!"

Andro nodded. "Yeah."

"Are you okay?" I asked. "And your family?"

"Quan-tum Cop! Quan-tum Cop!"

"Yeah," Ryan said. "We're all okay. You got him?"

"We got him."

"Good," Ryan said. "And Griffin's in custody. I think it's over."

"Me too," I said. Somewhere in there, Andro started caressing my arm. Whoo.

"Quan-tum Cop! Quan-tum Cop!"

"Thank you for saving everyone." Ryan's voice sounded thick with emotion.

He was so sweet. I started to get choked up, myself. "Thank you for your support–"

Agent Baker said, "So, we need to debrief you guys."

"Can't it wait?" Andro asked. "We're tired." He didn't look that tired.

"Quan-tum Cop! Quan-tum Cop!"

"Yes," she said. "I guess you've earned it."

Andro took another tack, leaning over and kissed my neck. Whoo. Yes. We needed to go.

Agent Baker gave us a wry smile.

"Thanks so much, everyone," I yelled.

The group quieted.

I clambered onto a chair. "I appreciate all your help. Thanks. I was a group effort. Good job everyone."

They cheered.

"Go home to your families." I jumped down. "Gotta go."

Agent Baker nodded as Andro and I headed for the door. "We'll start the debrief–"

"Another day," I said.

As we walked out the door he smiled his X-rated smile.

Wow. I was in big trouble. I could fall hard for this guy. "Back to my office?"

"Definitely," he said.

A few minutes later I patted the couch next to me. "Come here."

"Where were we?" he said in a low, husky voice.

"Right about here." I pointed at my lips. We kissed for a while and it was heavenly. My headache faded away.

He reached for the top button of my shirt. "You're sexy when you save the world."

"Whoa, there, partner. It's the middle of the day on a..." What day was it?

His kisses traveled down my neck. "Monday, *mi amor.*"

"We don't want to get too carried away in my office in the middle of a school day," I said. "A student might come in. I might have office hours now." In fact, I probably did have office hours now. What time was it?

"Campus was evacuated," he said, kissing.

"That doesn't sound right," I said.

"I thought you were always ready for action?"

"Did I say that?" I grinned.

And then we were lying on the couch. Mmm.

I started getting a feeling of déjà vu...

Quantum Mechanics

Quantum mechanics (QM) is the branch of physics focused on very small things. Atoms are made of electrons, neutrons and protons. Neutrons and protons are made of quarks. Electrons and quarks are believed to be indivisible and so are called elementary particles. Thus, the behavior of elementary particles is described by quantum mechanics.

QM has been extensively proven via experiments. For example, it explains the periodic table of the elements in chemistry and how atoms bond together to form molecules. Fun fact: the origin of the term 'quantum leap' comes from an electron in an atom jumping from one discrete energy level to another. Such a transition involves the electron emitting or absorbing a particle of energy called a photon.

In QM the quantum state of a particle is described by a wave function. Wave functions are considered the set of all probability amplitudes. These probability amplitudes provide a relationship between the wave function of a system and the results of observations of that system. More specifically, the probability of obtaining any possible measurement outcome is equal to the square of the corresponding amplitude.

Significant ideas of quantum mechanics include wave-particle duality and the uncertainty principle. These ideas seem to conflict with our every day experiences but have been proven in experiments. Even Albert Einstein said about QM, "God doesn't play dice with the world."

Every elementary particle exhibits wave-particle duality, which means it has the properties of a wave as well as a particle. This idea really goes against our intuition. Think about how the waves on the surface of a lake can interfere with each other to get bigger or smaller. If a baseball was like a particle, wave-particle duality means a baseball could get bigger or smaller as its wave interferes with the wave of another baseball. Clearly, baseballs don't behave like particles and vice versa.

The uncertainty principle states we cannot know exactly two different qualities of a particle, such as position and momentum. This doesn't mean we don't have the technology yet to measure this. It means it is impossible. The uncertainty principle actually follows from the wave nature of particles.

For more information and details about these and other topics, check out the Physics Is Fun website: www.physicsisfun.net

Thank you for reading *The Quantum Cop*. I hope you enjoyed it!

* If you would like to know when my next book is available, you can sign up for my new release e-mail list at www.lesleylsmith.com.
* If you'd like to give me feedback on this or any of my books, please consider emailing me at feedback@lesleylsmith.com. I enjoy suggestions for upcoming adventures. What do you think Madison will get up to in the future?
* Please check out the Physics Is Fun website www.physicsisfun.net for lots of information about fun physics topics.
* Reviews help other readers find books. I appreciate any and all reviews.
* A sneak peek of my new book *Reality Alternatives* follows.

–Lesley L. Smith

Reality Alternatives

Chapter One

You wonder what this book's about. You examine the front cover. You open it up and look at the page or screen. You start reading.

* * *

"Come on, Professor Carsen. Go ahead and try it," my research assistant Emily said as she handed me the Virtual Reality Immersion gear. It consisted of a big black helmet with a lot of wires coming out of it. We'd connected to a special quantum computer which Emily had created under my direction. We sat in my lab surrounded by computers and other equipment at the university. Yes, it was a little messy with all the gear piled up but I'd worked for years to accumulate it via research grants. I wasn't about to part with any of it.

For some reason, now I was getting cold feet. We'd been working on this new quantum experiment for months and now we were finally ready to go. The experiment needed a human's consciousness so I needed to put on the helmet and connect to it.

I took the helmet but didn't put it on.

"What's wrong, Chloe?" she asked, not looking nervous at all. Of course, she'd done VR before, loads of times. Her roommate was a VR expert and worked for a VR company.

Oh, yeah, and her experiment and her research grant weren't on the line.

"I guess I'm nervous." I turned the helmet upside down and peered inside. It looked a lot like a motorcycle helmet. I wasn't nervous about VR. I was nervous that I'd find out all my hard work had been for nothing. What if my hypothesis was wrong? What if I put on the helmet and didn't see anything?

"I thought you had to get your brain waves into the program so you could look for parallel universes?"

"I do." According quantum mechanics, human consciousness plays a special role in the universes. I hypothesized I could use this specialness along with quantum entanglement to hone in on consciousnesses in parallel universes. I knew it was kind of a freaky idea, but I had some elegant and well-received mathematics that backed me up.

It was time to walk the walk instead of just talking the talk.

She reached for the helmet. "Well, I'll do it if you want. I want to find another world. It sounds fun."

"No. I'll do it." I paused.

"Sometime soon?" She smiled.

"I'm doing it. Here I go." I carefully placed the Immersion helmet over my head. It felt like a motorcycle helmet, but smelled mildly of plastic and chemicals. Disoriented, I swayed a little.

"Maybe you should sit down." Emily took my hand and led me to a lab stool. "There. Are you okay?"

It was very dark. All I could see were a bunch of pinprick LED lights in shades of red, green, yellow, and white. "Yeah. I guess."

"Can you get to the menu?"

I wasn't familiar with the VR technology even though it wasn't new. "Remind me about the VR menu." Even to me my voice sounded muffled.

"You blink to control access."

"Right." I knew that. I blinked deliberately and the access menu floated in front of my face. I blinked some more and, poof, the menu disappeared. "Ack."

"What happened?" she asked. "I couldn't hear what you said."

"Nothing." I blinked again slowly and the menu reappeared. I blinked more quickly to scroll down the left column. When I got to *VR Immersion* I blinked deliberately again.

Suddenly, I was falling. I groped around for something to steady me. My hands hit the edge of a lab table and I grabbed on.

"Professor Carsen?" Emily's voice seemed to come from a

great distance. "Chloe?"

I saw something blurry in front of me. As I tried to focus in on it, my sense of the lab with its stool and table and special computer faded away.

The blurry something was bluish. I saw a blue-gray something. What was it? I leaned forward, staring. It moved. It sort of waved, like the surface of the earth during an earthquake–or like the ocean. That's what it was: water.

I jerked back. Why was I seeing water? What did it mean? Could it be another world?

"Chloe?"

But there was no ocean around here. According to the theory, my mind should entangle with the mind of another version of me. I should see, or maybe even experience, what she saw or experienced. It was hard to fathom why I'd be seeing an ocean.

"Are you all right?" Emily's voice seemed louder.

Something was wrong. I blinked deliberately and the menu popped back up. I blinked my way out and tore off the helmet. I breathed in the fresh air greedily.

"What happened?" Emily leaned over me, looking concerned.

"I don't know." I shook my head. "On the bright side, I saw something." That was bright. It was incandescent.

"Yeah!" she said. I agreed.

"On the dark side, I think I saw the ocean."

"The ocean?" she said. "That's weird. I thought you said you'd probably see Montana in another universe. There's no ocean in Montana."

"I know that."

"Could there maybe be an ocean in Montana in some other universe?" she asked slowly.

"No." I paused. Could there be? "No. I don't see how."

"Are you sure?"

"The elevation alone would make it impossible."

"But Montana wasn't always at this elevation..."

"It has been for, like, the last eighty million years."

"Could the time be off somehow?"

"Not eighty million years off. And the brain waves over there have to be similar enough to entangle with mine. I don't see how that could happen millions of years ago." Damn. It must not have worked. I must not have seen another world. What did I see then?

She backed away. “Okay. I’m just asking.” Her phone pinged and she glanced at it. “Shoot. I have to go. I’m supposed to meet some friends to study.”

“Go ahead. I need to ponder things.” I forced a smile. “Thanks for your help. I appreciate it.”

“You’re welcome.” She grabbed her backpack. “I don’t think you should try the helmet again without me. You seemed pretty dizzy or something.”

“Thanks for the advice.”

“If not me, someone else,” she said, reading in my tone that I wasn’t going to take her advice. “What about your brother, Dr. Carsen? He seems to stop by the lab a lot.”

When he wasn’t away working for the National Guard, Colton worked here on campus at the health center as a physician. He didn’t stop by a lot. He stopped by once in a while when we went to lunch.

I stood. “Okay. Thanks a lot, Emily.” I led her to the door. “You don’t want to be late for your study session. And I have a lot of work to do. I need to double-check everything.”

She left and I went over to the computer.

I doubled-checked everything, but I couldn’t find anything wrong with our physical equipment setup or our special computer. And several other physicists had checked my math so my hypothesis was sound.

I decided to try the VR helmet again. I dragged a more comfortable chair into the lab from my office first though, and sat in it before I put on the helmet.

I blinked slowly and the menu appeared. I blinked more quickly to scroll down the left column. When I got to *VR Immersion* I blinked deliberately again. I was getting the hang of this.

I saw something blurry in front of me. I saw blue-gray waves. I focused. As I scrutinized it, my sense of the lab went away.

I saw waves. I smelled something chemical. I sniffed. Chlorine, maybe. And then I saw concrete. A pool. I was looking at a pool. That made much more sense. There were several pools in town.

I focused and got a sense of someone by a pool...

* * *

The Harry Potters started arriving at two p.m. It was amazing how similar they all looked with drawn-on scars, round plastic glasses, and capes.

My oldest son, Zach, rolled his eyes as each one passed him at the neighborhood clubhouse entrance. Rolling your eyes was apparently a big brother requirement–at least at birthday parties for little brothers.

Several of the parents greeted me as they dropped off their sons.

Chris's father, Nick, stopped near the door. "Hi, Chloe." I got a whiff of his lavender-scented aftershave.

I nodded. "Hi, Nick." I grinned back at him. If memory served, this guy was also our state representative, so it didn't hurt to be friendly.

"What time should I pick Chris up?" he asked. Chris had long since scampered off to join the rest of the boys.

"Six-ish," I said.

"Hey, Nick." My husband Aidan touched the small of my back.

Nick waved back at him.

"So, we'll see you at six," I said.

Nick nodded and departed.

"I'm going to go pay the manager the rental fee," Aidan said. We'd rented out the house-sized empty building for the afternoon. "Can you hold down the fort?"

I smiled. I loved having a househusband. He was so good at taking care of details. "Considering only a few kids are here so far, and I have Zach to help, I think we'll be fine."

He nodded and headed for the manager with the checkbook.

I walked over to Zach. "Thanks for your help with the party," I said. He'd helped set up the various folding tables and chairs, put up the *Happy Birthday* banner and placed latex helium balloons around this main room. "I know your brother appreciates it."

"Whatever, Mom." He smirked. It seemed like that was his go-to expression these days.

We both looked at Trevor who, as birthday boy, was already lording it over the other boys, telling them where to put their gifts, and showing them where the snacks were.

I saw the ghost of a grin flit over Zach's face before he noticed me noticing. "I guess the little squirt only turns double-digits once." Zach couldn't fool me. I knew he had a soft spot for the little squirt. I suppressed my own grin.

Once all the Harrys arrived, they ate. Trevor had requested hot dogs, string cheese, grapes and pretzels. After that we did N.E.W.T. exams in Divination where they studied tea leaves and made stuff up, Care of Magical Creatures where they identified imaginary creatures on cards and explained how to take care of them, Defense Against the Dark Arts which involved goofing around with fake light sabers, and Astronomy.

I couldn't resist teaching them some real Astronomy during the Astronomy N.E.W.T. So sue me, I'm a physics professor. I'm sure if it hadn't been dark in the clubhouse I would have seen Zach rolling his eyes the whole time. I'd brought my true-to-life star map painted in glow-in-the-dark paint and put it up on one of the walls.

I was pointing out constellations with the laser pointer. "So, here's Cassiopeia, which looks like a chair, see?" I said. "She's supposed to be Andromeda's Mother, or some people say she's the Queen of Ethiopia. And here's Ursa Major which contains the most famous constellation, the Big Dipper. Has anyone ever seen the Big Dipper before?" I asked.

A chorus of *me*'s and *I have*'s erupted from the crowd.

"Excellent," I said. "I'm glad to hear it. The name Ursa Major means the Great Bear, and it points at the North Star, Polaris. What's your favorite constellation, Trevor?"

Trevor said, "Orion. With the belt."

"Can you show it to us?" I asked.

Trevor jumped out of his chair and lunged for the map.

In the meantime, Aidan was getting the cake ready with Zach's help in the kitchenette. Zach manned the flashlight as Aidan lit the birthday candles.

I was keeping an eye out for the lit candles, so as soon as they appeared I said, "And now I think it's time for what we've all been waiting for, birthday cake. Come on." The little flames on the cake lit up the whole room.

Everyone ran over to the table, and we sang *Happy Birthday*.

Trevor looked at his friends and family and beamed in the candlelight.

"Come on, buddy," Aidan said. "Make a wish and blow out the candles."

Trevor paused a moment and then blew the candles out. The boys cheered and at the same time, wind blew the doors of the clubhouse open. I went and closed them.

Zach flipped on the lights and said, "What'd you wish?"

Trevor just smiled mysteriously. He knew you weren't supposed to reveal your wish if you wanted it to come true.

Aidan started cutting the cake. He'd made it from scratch. It was dark chocolate cake with fudge chocolate frosting and milk- and semi-sweet chocolate chips throughout–basically death by chocolate. I could only eat about a cubic centimeter of the stuff. It smelled heavenly, however. Probably just breathing it in was fattening.

We handed out small pieces of cake to everyone. With the party excitement the last thing we needed was an upset stomach–or worse.

By the time everyone had their piece, the birthday boy was already asking for more. "Come on, Mom," Trevor said. "Give me another piece. It's my birthday. I'm double-digits, now."

"Nope," I said. "Sorry, buddy. Not going to happen. You'll get sick. You can have a piece tomorrow."

He gave me a stony look that I knew meant he wasn't happy with me.

I crossed my arms and gave him my *I'm not backing down* look. I was as firm as Corundum.

He scowled and grabbed his magic wand, mumbling and waving it at his plate. Then, as if by magic, another piece of cake appeared on his formerly empty plate.

"What the f–?" Zach started to say.

He was saying what I was thinking. What just happened?

I interrupted him, "Zach, don't say that. Aidan. Come over here, please. Did you see this?" I pointed at Trevor's plate.

Aidan had been rolling up the star map, but put it down and walked our way.

Trevor smiled widely and said, "It worked. I made cake. My magic wand works!"

The other boys crowded around him. “Cool!” “Awesome!” “Neat!”

My mind was reeling. There was no such thing as magic–at least that’s what I thought.

Immediately, the boys started waving their wands around but no more pieces of cake magically appeared.

Zach grabbed Trevor’s wand out of his hand and rotated it, staring.

“You better give that back,” Trevor said.

“I will, in a minute, squirt,” Zach said.

Maybe I’d imagined the extra piece of cake on Trevor’s plate?

Aidan approached the table and asked, “What’s going on?”

“I’m not sure,” I said.

Trevor wasted no time in shoving the extra piece of cake into his mouth.

The other boys were still eating their first pieces of cake.

Aidan whispered into my ear, “What might have happened?”

I whispered back to him, “It almost seemed like Trevor did magic to get another piece of cake.”

“Wow. That would be great,” he said, grinning. “I’d love to have a magic son.” Aidan was definitely a native son of Missoula Montana. There wasn’t a yoga position he couldn’t do, granola he wouldn’t eat, or a weird idea he wouldn’t consider.

I didn’t know what to think.

The rest of the party occurred without any further mysterious incidents.

After the guests (exhausted) had gone and we were packing up, Trevor asked, “When can I get my wand back? I want to do magic.”

I’d taken it from Zach and put it in my back pocket.

“I like magic,” Aidan said. “If Trevor can do tricks, I’d like to see them.”

Zach was shaking his head and scowling.

“Can I?” Trevor asked. “Can I, Mom?”

I had to admit I was very curious about what’d happened. I handed the wand over. “Sure, little dude. Knock yourself out.”

Trevor eagerly took the wand back from me.

“Wait,” Zach said. “What are you going to do?”

“I’m going to get another piece of cake.” He stared down at an empty paper plate.

While they were all looking at Trevor's plate, I stared at the remnants of the birthday cake still on the table. The seemingly-magic piece of cake earlier couldn't have materialized out of thin air.

"Abra Cadabra!" Trevor said. "Make-uh the cake-uh!" He waved his wand around.

"No way," Zach said.

"Wow." Aidan sounded surprised.

A piece of the birthday cake had disappeared from the serving platter. Wow, was right. I glanced at Trevor's plate. There it was.

"Hey, let me try," Zach said, reaching for the wand.

"No. It's my party." Trevor clutched the wand to himself. "I get to do magic. Not you."

"I'm trying anyway." Zach picked up a paper plate and waved his hand around. "Abra Cadabra! Make-uh the cake-uh!" A piece of cake appeared. He paused for a second and then said, "No effing way! It worked even without the wand."

"Wow," Aidan said. "And language, young man."

I glanced at the larger cake still on the platter. I thought another piece was missing. I didn't want to believe it, but the evidence was right in front of my eyes. Somehow my boys moved pieces of cake from the platter to their plates without touching them. "Huh."

"No fair," Zach said. "It was supposed to be my magic."

"Can anyone do it?" Aidan asked. He grabbed his own plate. "Abra Cadabra. Make-uh the cake-uh." He waved his hands.

The cake on the table looked the same. I glanced at Aidan's plate. It was empty.

"Darn," Aidan said. "Didn't work."

"You can use my wand if you want, Dad," Trevor said.

"Thanks, buddy." Aidan took the wand from Trevor and tried again, but nothing happened. "I guess it's not the wand."

"You try, Mom," Zach said.

I was in favor of empirical data. I grabbed an empty paper plate. "Abra Cadabra. Make-uh the cake-uh." Bam. There was a piece of cake on the plate. I almost dropped the plate in my surprise.

"Wow," Aidan said.

"Awesome!" Zach said.

Trevor frowned. "Why can you guys do it?"

"What do you mean, Trev?" Aidan asked.

"It was my wish," Trevor said. "I wished I could do magic when I blew the candles out."

We all digested that for a moment. It was impossible for his birthday wish to come true, right?

"It must not be your wish, buddy," Zach said. "It must be something else."

"Can you guys do any non-cake related tricks?" Aidan asked.

I was still staring at the piece of cake on my plate. It looked like a regular piece of delicious chocolate cake. It was impossible, wasn't it?

"Abra Cadabra!" Trevor said. "I want an X-box!" Nothing happened. "Darn."

"Abra Cadabra!" Zach said. "Make-uh the sports car!" Nothing happened. The boys continued trying to do magic, but nothing seemed to be working.

Aidan sidled up to me. "Are you okay, Chloe?" he asked softly.

I held out the plate. "There's a piece of cake here."

He smiled and nodded. "Yes."

"There didn't use to be."

"Yes, that's true."

"Wow." I felt weird. Was this what a paradigm shift felt like?

"I agree," Aidan said. "Wow."

"Ahem." Someone cleared his or her throat from the direction of the door. We all turned and saw Chris and Nick standing there. "We just wanted to come in and say thanks," Nick said. How long had they been standing there? What did they see?

Aidan rushed over to them. "Yes, thanks for coming." He ushered them out through the open door.

We eventually got everything rounded up and we headed out.

After we got home from the party and put everything away and convinced the boys that yes, double-digit young men did still have bedtimes, Aidan and I collapsed in the master suite.

"What happened at the party? How did you guys get extra cake?" Aidan asked, getting into bed.

I shook my head as I slipped between the cool sheets; they

felt smooth and relaxing against my skin. "I don't know. Were we in some kind of sugar coma? Or could Zach have pranked us?"

"He's good at practical jokes, but he's not that good," he said.

"I don't claim to know everything," I said. "But I didn't think magic was real." It went against everything I knew, all the physics I'd studied for the last fifteen years.

"Well, I've always said you've put a spell on me." He nuzzled my neck. "Maybe magic is real."

I shivered.

* * *

I was yanked out of my life.

Somehow I was lying in a plush chair in a lab. My neck hurt.

Emily and Colton were leaning over me, glaring.

"Are you all right?" Emily asked.

I was just with my family, my husband Aidan and sons Zach and Trevor. It was lovely.

"I'm concerned," Colton said. "Should I call 911?"

But I didn't have a family. Aidan and Zach and Trevor didn't exist. What just happened?

"Chloe!" Colton put his face right in my face. "Answer me."

I was so confused. I looked at Colton. He held a black helmet in his hand. I looked at Emily. They both seemed upset.

I glanced around the room, my lab. I did know this lab. I did know these people. Oh, yeah, this was my life. So, where had I just been?

"Chloe," Colton said.

"I'm okay," I said. "Just disoriented."

"I'll say," he said.

"How long were you in there?" Emily asked.

"In where?" Oh, right, I was doing an experiment. "I don't know," I said. "What time is it?"

"It's late, almost eleven," Colton said.

"At night?" I asked.

"Yes, at night," he said. "What's wrong with you?"

"Chloe, have you been here all day?" Emily turned to Colton. "Maybe you should call 911."

"No, I'm fine." I sat up. My back creaked. "I just lost track of time."

"Were you in the experiment this whole time?" she asked.

"I guess so," I said. My fuzzy brain was clearing. I jumped up. "I think it works!"

"What?" they both asked.

"I think I accessed a parallel world. Oh, wow. It works." This was the greatest moment of my life. "This is huge!" I wanted to get right back into the experiment, it was so exciting.

"It works?" Emily beamed and hopped in excitement. "Wow. What's it like?"

"What works?" Colton asked, his nose wrinkled.

"My," I glanced at Emily, "our, experiment works. I accessed another world. I explained this to you before, Colton."

"Yeah," he said. "I never understood what you were talking about."

"Well, the point is, it works. It didn't feel the way I thought it would though. It seemed real." I touched Colton's arm. He was real. This was real. Here. Now. I had to check.

That other place wasn't real like this was real. But it seemed so real. At the time, it seemed as real as this.

I wanted to go back there. I rubbed my neck.

"What did you see?" Emily asked.

"It wasn't like seeing," I said. "It was like being. It was like I was there, me, Chloe. I had a whole other life."

"What the hell, Sis?" Colton said.

"I don't know how to explain it." I stretched my back.

"Cool!" Emily said. "Can I try it?"

I didn't want to surrender the equipment to her.

"It sounds dangerous," Colton said. "I don't think you should do it again."

I just looked at him, not answering.

They didn't understand.

I had to do it again.

CPSIA information can be obtained
at www.ICGtesting.com
Printed in the USA
LVOW10s1122260617
539398LV00006B/1027/P

9 780986 135026